Brava, Valentine

Also by Adriana Trigiani

FICTION
Very Valentine
Home to Big Stone Gap
Rococo
The Queen of the Big Time
Lucia, Lucia
Milk Glass Moon
Big Cherry Holler
Big Stone Gap

YOUNG ADULT FICTION
Viola in Reel Life

NONFICTION
Cooking with My Sisters (co-author)

Brava, Valentine

— *A Novel* —

A D R I A N A   T R I G I A N I

HARPER

An Imprint of HarperCollins*Publishers*
www.harpercollins.com

HarperCollins books may be purchased for educational, business, or sales promo-tional use. For information, please write: Special Markets Department, Harper-Collins Publishers, 10 East 53rd Street, New York, NY 10022.

FIRST EDITION

Library of Congress Cataloging-in-Publication Data is available upon request.

ISBN (Hardcover): 978-0-06-125707-0
ISBN (International): 978-0-06-197066-5

10   11   12   13   14   ID/RRD   10   9   8   7   6   5   4   3   2   1

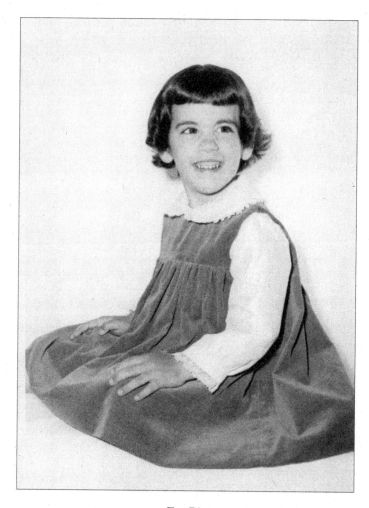

For Pia

Contents

Brava, Valentine

Shake Down the Stars

THE MOST MAGICAL THING HAPPENED on the morning of my grandmother's wedding in Tuscany. It snowed.

This is definitely Italian snow, not the New York City variety of midwinter precipitation. It doesn't fall in big, chunky flakes, nor is it heavy February hail that stings faces and turns sidewalks into solid sheets of ice. Rather, this is a flurry of white glitter that sifts through the air and melts instantly when it lands on the stone streets.

From my window at the Spolti Inn, it seems the entire village of Arezzo is swathed in a lace bridal veil. I sip hot milk and espresso from a warm mug as I watch an old horse-drawn carriage pull up in front of the inn to take us to the church. It doesn't feel like 2010. It could easily be a hundred years ago, not a modern touch in sight. Time stands still when people are happy. The ticking of real time resumes as soon as the rings are exchanged—for all of us.

Gram and Dominic's wedding plans were made quickly and effortlessly (the beauty of an eighty-year-old bride is that she really knows what she does and *doesn't* want). The airline tickets were bought online after a series of negotiations that eventually led to the splendid group rate that brought the Angelini and Roncalli families to this Italian village, into this moment, this morning.

We've all got roles in this romantic tale. The great-granddaughters are flower girls and the great-grandsons miniature groomsmen. My sisters Tess and Jaclyn and I are bridesmaids, as is our sister-in-law Pamela, while my mother is matron of honor. Dominic's granddaughter Orsola will represent his side of the family in the bridal party. My father will walk his mother-in-law down the aisle and into the arms of Dominic Vechiarelli.

"It snowed that day," I imagine I'll tell my children. I'll explain that after ten years as a widow, my grandmother found love again. Teodora Angelini's story relies on fate, timing, and the best of luck. It's also a story filled with hope—reminding all of us who haven't found love that, regardless of age, experience, or locale, it's a bad idea to close the book before "The End." You just never know. Not one of us, not even the bride, saw this day coming.

"Somebody shoot me!" my mother shouts from the hallway. "My hair is a wet mop!"

"Jesus, Mary, and Joseph, Mike. We're in a freakin' hotel. Pipe down," I hear my father bark back.

"Do you have to yell?" Tess hollers from her room. "Why does this family always have to yell?" she yells.

"Shh. You'll wake the bay-bee!" Jaclyn whisper-shouts from her doorway.

My door bursts open. My mother stands in her full black slip with her hands on her hips. "I blew out my flatiron," she announces. A flatiron blowout in my family is worse than finding a lump. And we have found our share of lumps.

Mom's face is made up, alabaster-perfect and powdered down,

ready for photographs from all angles. Her fake eyelashes give her enough oomph to pass as one of Beyoncé's backup singers. Her cheeks have a peachy Bobbi Brown glow, but that's all that's sparkling about my mother. She's beyond frazzled and close to tears.

"What's the matter, Ma? You're not yourself."

"You noticed?"

"What can I do to help?"

"I don't know. I'm just a-a-a . . . mess." She plops down on my bed. Half of her head is done, straight, glossy strands of freshly dyed chestnut brown, and the other half is still damp and crimped. Mom has naturally curly hair, but you would never know it from her left profile. From the front, however, she looks like a split-screen hair model on the Home Shopping Network: before and after the anti-frizz cream has been applied. She smoothes the front panels of her black slip over her thighs and pulls the hem over her knees.

I sit down next to her. "What's the problem?"

"Where do I begin?" Her eyes fill with tears. She pulls a tissue from under her slip strap and dabs the inner corners of her eyes so as not to irrigate the eyelash glue and cause the mink spikes to float away in her tears like paper canoes down the Nile.

"You look great."

"Do I?" The tears insta-dry in my mother's eyes, and she sits up straight. All it takes is a compliment to pull my mother back to her emotional center.

"Like a million bucks," I promise her.

"I brought my Clarisonic. So at least I'm exfoliated. *That* didn't blow in the outlet, thank God."

"Thank God."

"I don't know, Valentine. I just don't know. I'm completely off my game. I'm shaking. Look." Mom holds up her hand. It flutters partly from nerves, and partly because she's making it flutter. "This is so strange to me. To be a maid of honor at my own mother's wedding."

"Matron," I correct her. "The last over-sixty maid of anything was Mother Teresa."

Mom ignores the comment. She continues, "There's something so out of kilter about this whole thing."

"Gram is happy."

"Yes, yes, and I've adjusted to all of it! It began with the news that my mother, eighty years young, fell in love. Then once I swallowed that, she decided to marry. I accepted her decision. Then she announces that not only will she become Dominic's bride, she has decided to move to Italy. For good. It's been a series of whammies, I'll admit it. One beaut after another, I'll tell ya. But I survived the shock of each little bomb she dropped and put aside my doubts and misgivings and went with it. Don't I always go with the flow?"

"Always. So what's the problem?"

"I feel disloyal to my father." Tears fill her eyes once more.

"Mom. He'd be happy for Gram."

"You think? He didn't much worry about her happiness when he was on earth."

I look at my mother. She never says anything unkind about her father.

"See what I mean?" Mom throws her hands in the air. "This wedding is bringing out the worst in me. I'm even judging my dead father. What the hell is wrong with me?"

"I wish I knew," my father says. He stands in the doorway wearing his pressed blue-and-white-striped boxer shorts (yes, my mom irons his underwear) and starched formal dress shirt, which is so long it mimics one of Ann-Margret's mini-dresses from *Viva Las Vegas*. His thin, hairless, sixty-nine-year-old legs are covered to the knee in black stockings held up by elastic braces.

My mother has placed two half-moon-shaped Frownies under each of Dad's eyes. When he makes an expression, the sharp corners of the anti-wrinkle patches poke his eyeballs, so Dad keeps his eyes open wide without blinking, which gives him the look of a threatened gorilla. "Get these goddamn patches off my face."

Mom checks her watch. "Five more minutes, Dutch, and you won't have lines or bags."

"Remove them. I want to be able to see *now*. I can't look down. Or sideways. Believe me, it won't be pretty if I fall down and break a hip. Can you imagine the medical care around here? They probably tie you to a plank with rope and make you lie there until the bones fuse." Dad tries to yank the Frownie patches off his face.

"Don't try and remove them on your own!" my mother yells.

"What is this adhesion?" Dad pats the patches.

"Adhesive. It's a natural glue of some sort. I'll get the rosewater spray to dissolve them. Dutch, I mean it. Don't pull at them. You'll make scabs."

"Get the spray," Dad says clapping his hands together in a tick-tock beat. "Get the spray. We got a schedule to keep here. You don't want to be late for a wedding that features two eighty-year-olds. Anything could happen."

Mom rushes out.

"What is wrong with her?" my father asks. He looks out the window, his eyes bulging out of his head like a pug's. "Snow. I thought it was balmy in Italy. What the hell is going on?"

"It's good luck."

"Is it?"

"I don't know. I'm just saying." I shrug.

"Have you ever noticed that whatever clime blows through on a wedding day, somehow it's interpolated as good luck?"

"Interpreted."

"A mushroom cloud of poison gas could linger over Tuscany and by God, that would be a good sign." My father shakes his head.

"The triumph of love over nuclear annihilation."

"As if that could be true. It rained when your mother and I got married. But we were twenty-one and twenty-two, and what the hell did we know? Rain, shine, we just wanted to get to the Inn at Oldwick."

"Thanks, Dad. I like to imagine you and Mom on your honeymoon. Especially right after breakfast."

"When you're young, it's all in front of you, when you're old, well, you got your memories and the occasional stirring of your adrenals to remind you of what you once were. Between you and me, your grandmother and Dom are a ticking time bomb. If they get a year out of this deal, they'll be lucky."

"Don't say that, Dad. Don't even *think* it."

"Excuse me for being a naturalist."

"Realist," I correct him.

My father places his index fingers on the Frownies and holds them down to blink. "Whatever. I'm happy for Teodora, I think it's all great and well and good. But lest we forget, they are a coupla old people. I mean *old*. They're merging when most people are done. So I guess, good for them. Right? What the hell." Dad sits down in the rocking chair by the window. "Big changes."

"Yep." I sigh.

"For you the most."

"For me the most." If only my father knew how much I dreaded this day for selfish reasons. I am losing the most important person in my life. Gram is my master craftsman, my confidante, and my friend. I don't even want to think about going home without her, much less back to work.

"Has it sunk in yet?"

"Not really, Dad. But it's happening. It's done, so I have to do what I have to do."

"That's all you can do."

Mom comes in with the rosewater spray. "Dutch, lean back. Close your eyes." Mom hovers over Dad as he tilts his head back.

"I feel my carotid artery pulsing." He places his hand on his neck. "Is it normal to hear your heart beat in your ear?"

"This will only take a second." Mom spritzes the wrinkle patches.

"In my eye! In my eye!" Dad covers his eyes with his hand. "I'm burning! I'm burning!"

"Get a towel!" Mom barks at me. "Soak it!"

I bolt into the bathroom, turn on the water, saturate the towel (or try to—it's one of those thin Italian towels that are more mop-peen than bath towel), and run back to my father. I place it on his face.

"Cold! Cold!" he screams.

"Flush. Flush them, Dutch!" my mother tells him.

Tess rushes in wearing black tap pants and a hoodie that says JUICY FOREVER across the chest. "We are not the only patrons in this hotel!" Then she sees our father swabbing his eyes like he's been evacuated after a gas explosion on his favorite TV drama, *24*. "What's wrong, Dad?"

Dad hangs his head and dabs his eyes with the towel until the Frownies are damp enough to peel off. He holds up the half-moons and hands them to Mom. "Don't ever make me glue this crap on again. I like my wrinkles. I'm going to be seventy—everything on me is shriveled. Especially after the cancer. My balls are like prunes—"

"Dad!" Tess and I stop him before he describes them in further detail.

"Dutch, I've seen them before and I've seen them after, and there's not that much difference in the general circumference," Mom reasons.

"Mom!" Tess and I are disgusted.

"It doesn't matter. My point is: I look old in pictures because I am, in actuality, old. It is what it is, and what it is, is *not* going to get better."

"All right, all right," Mom says impatiently. "As if self-improvement is a crime." .

"That's it!" I wave them out. "Everybody out. I have to get ready. The carriage awaits."

"Is it here?" Mom asks.

"Come and see." I pull back the curtain. My mother, father, and sister stand in the window with me. We look out over the village and take in the enchanted scene. The horse pulling our carriage shakes his head, making the bells he wears jingle sweetly. The sheer beauty of the moment soothes us as we look on in awe and silence.

"Okay. Enough with the view," Dad barks. "We gotta get a move on. That old nag is gonna be looking for a bucket of oats. And frankly, so will I."

"What about my hair?" Mom looks in the mirror.

"Pull it off your face and use some Bed Head gel. Tess packed, like, three kinds. Right?" I look at my sister.

"In my room. In the red duffel. There's a pack of bobby pins too. And a HairDini if you want some extra volume."

"An upsweep. Good idea." Mom goes, followed by Dad, who fluffs the ample seat of his boxer shorts like a skirt.

"Mom is losing it," Tess says as she sorts through my makeup kit.

"It's an emotional time."

"Why? Why can't it just be fun? Do you ever notice our family can't be happy for anybody that's happy?" Tess takes a tube of mascara out of my case, unscrews it, and pumps the brush. She leans into the mirror and tries my long-lasting dark brown Rimmel. "We have to inflict negativity on every event."

"That's a little harsh."

"Really? Don't you notice? We appear completely nuts to outsiders. How about last night at the rehearsal dinner? Mom got up to give a toast and started sobbing and made it all about her childhood. 1–800-therapy, anybody?" Tess throws the mascara back into the makeup case. "Thank God most of the people who attended didn't speak English."

"It was pretty uncomfortable," I admit.

"Thank God Gianluca saved the night with his funny story about never having a sister and now he has one with Mom. You know Mom loved that because she's old enough to be his aunt. But now she can shave off a dozen years because Gianluca's, like, what . . . fifty?"

"Fifty-three," I correct her.

"No way. He looks good. You know, for a guy his age." Tess snaps open a compact of concealer and dabs it under her eyes. "He was really chatting you up."

"I'm not interested," I lie. I don't have to tell my sister that when I saw Gianluca for the first time again last night, my heart pounded like a blowout on a flat tire hitting the rim at eighty miles an hour. *Whomp. Whomp. Whomp.* I'm surprised the guests couldn't hear it. I won't tell her that Gianluca's grasp of my hand as I turned away to talk to someone sent an electric shock through my entire body. I wasn't expecting *that* either. Tess doesn't need to know that I came back to this room and dreamed of Gianluca all night, woke up at 3:00 A.M., and had to open the windows for air because the mental pictures were so steamy, they drove the temperature in the room up to boil.

I take the concealer from Tess and dab it under my eyes. The dark circles we inherited are a nice complement to the dark secrets we carry. Gram's love affair with Dominic was the last big reveal. She had been seeing him for ten years, since my grandfather died, and nobody knew it. Only after I saw them together at the tannery last summer did I realize that Gram had a lover. And even when I found out, I kept the secret, as only a good Angelini/Roncalli girl can. I lean into the mirror. Eight layers of this yellow putty will cover generations of intrigue.

"If I were single, I'd be all over Gianluca. He is one hot Italian," Tess continues.

"I'm all the hot Italian you can handle." My brother-in-law Charlie stands in the doorway.

"You see? I could never cheat. I even get caught talking about it." Tess sighs.

Thankfully, Charlie is dressed. The sight of another pair of boxers on yet another male relative might put me over the edge. Furthermore, Charlie's legs are so hairy that in shorts, he looks like he's wearing felt pants.

"How do I look?" Charlie opens the front panels of his jacket to reveal a lavender silk vest under the jacket of his morning coat.

The minute Gram announced her nuptials three months ago, Tess put Charlie on a diet. She also sent him to the gym. It doesn't appear that he's lost a pound, but he's gained a few inches in his neck from lifting weights. Now his head cradles directly into his shoulders, giving him the look of a Sicilian Humpty Dumpty.

"You look buff," Tess purrs.

"You gonna wear clothes to this thing?" Charlie asks her.

"No, I thought I'd wear tap pants."

"I never know with you," he says.

"Help!" Mom calls from down the hall. "Call 911!"

"They don't have 911 here," my brother-in-law Tom shouts back.

I follow Charlie and Tess down the hallway. Their daughters Charisma and Chiara, dressed in pale blue organza gowns, stand in Aunt Feen's doorway with Mom. We blow past them and into the room.

My great-aunt Feen, who declined her sister's invitation to be in the wedding party and had to be dragged overseas like my mother's XL shoe duffel/body bag, sits on the edge of the bed with a blood pressure cuff hanging off her arm. She is dressed in a black wool suit that I've seen at every wedding and funeral since I can remember. Her Papagallo flats lie next to her stocking feet, which sport double toe corn pads and elastic bunion slings. I kneel down next to her.

"What happened, Aunt Feen?"

"I got dizzy. The room was spinning."

"Were you trying to take your own blood pressure?" Charlie asks.

"Who is he?" Aunt Feen looks up at Charlie, whom she has known for twenty years, as though he's a stranger.

"It's me. Charlie."

"I know *who* you are, but you're an in-law. Get out."

Charlie leaves the room.

"That wasn't very nice," Tess says diplomatically.

"I don't need a crowd in here." Aunt Feen lets the blood pressure cuff fall to the floor. "I thought I was having a stroke."

"Then we have to take you to the doctor."

"In Italy? Are you crazy? They'd kill me over here."

"It's a modern country with modern medicine," I say.

"Really? It takes an hour to get hot water in the tub. How modern can it be?"

"If you're faint, you need to see a doctor," my mother insists.

"I'm seventy-eight, I'm faint most of the time. I wish God would take me."

"Did you eat breakfast?"

"Two rolls with butter, two poached eggs, a little gabagool, and a Snickers bar I had in my purse."

"Could be sugar and fat shock," I reason.

"It's not lack of nourishment!" Aunt Feen bellows. "I'm an eater!"

"Then what is it, Aunt Feen?" I rub her bony shoulder.

"This wedding. I have a bad feeling."

"See? I'm not the only one." My mother squeezes onto the bed between Tess and Aunt Feen.

"I just think it's crazy." Aunt Feen shakes her head. "What for?"

"What do you mean, what for? They love each other," Tess says defensively, still chapped that Aunt Feen banished her Charlie.

"Love. Love? What good is love?"

Mom and I look at one another. We look at Tess, who rolls her eyes.

"Well . . . ," I begin, "love is . . . a start."

"Oh, big deal. There is no happiness in this world, in this life. It's a vale of tears that leaves you lonely and bereft. I know it firsthand—the cheat of this world. The big cheat of this life. I loved Norman Mawby, and he was sent over to France in World War II, none of youse would remember that, but he was a bright, shiny boy from Grand Street, very neat and clean, and I loved him bad. And we wanted to get married, but he died on the fields of France, a country I will always hate. He died, and I was robbed."

"But you married Uncle Tony—"

"I never loved that hack."

"Aunt Feen!" Mom cries.

"I didn't. He was sloppy seconds. When I cried at his funeral, I was crying for all the years I wasted with the bum."

We are stunned into silence. I look at the clock. "Well, Aunt Feen, the good news: I don't think you've suffered a stroke. You appear to be completely normal. We need to get to the church."

"All right, all right," she says. "Let's get this nonsense over with already."

"Girls, I'll get Aunt Feen down the stairs. You need to get dressed." Dad comes in, filling the room with the layered scents of Aramis cologne, Brylcreem, and Bengay. With his thick hair brushed back without a part, he is a dead ringer for Frankie Valli on the reunion tour, except for two squares of red under his eyes where the Frownies were ripped from his skin. They resemble odd patches of sunburn, but will hopefully fade as the day goes on.

Tess and I go out into the hallway. Jaclyn, looking like a sprig of mint in a strapless pale green cocktail dress with a hem of tulle, comes out of her room. Her black hair is piled high on her head, as if she's a duchess from the court of Louis XIV. "What is going on?" she asks.

"Old issues," I tell her.

Jaclyn pulls us into her room.

"Where's the baby?"

"Tom took her for a walk."

"In the snow?" Tess looks at me. My sister and I are very critical of our brother-in-law, who takes the baby everywhere, including places like Giants Stadium for a football game. We should not be surprised that he's rolling around the streets of Arezzo with her. This is nothing.

"He put the plastic hood on the stroller," she says defensively before she leans in. "Pamela and Alfred had a helluva fight. I heard it through the wall."

"What about?" Tess asks.

"Money."

Our brother, Alfred, is one of the few bankers in the New York/New Jersey area that haven't lost their jobs in the worst economic collapse of our lifetimes. That's how good Alfred is at whatever it is that he does. I can't imagine that they have money problems. My brother pastes his paycheck stubs in a scrapbook.

"She's a spender," Tess whispers, as though it's a disease.

"Yeah, but he's a saver," I remind them.

I leave my sisters to their gossip and go to my room. Closing the door behind me, I throw off my robe, relieved to be alone. My dress is hanging in its linen bag on the back of the door. I slip it off its hanger and step into it.

The silver lamé sheath glides over me. I slide on a pair of matching metallic pumps. I open my jewelry case and pull ropes of faux pearls out of its pockets, layering the strands until Coco Chanel might stick her head out of her grave in approval and say, "Très élégante!"

I grab my purse and meet my sisters in the hallway.

Tess wears a forest green velvet gown with a matching bolero. Her thick black hair falls in loose curls. She whistles when she sees me.

"Thanks," I say.

"You're going to knock Gianluca out with that number."

I blush.

"I knew it," Tess says smugly. "A sister always knows."

The idea of a horse-drawn carriage is a lovely one, unless you're cramming nearly every member of my immediate family and their children into one vehicle. Which is what we did. The wet streets made the wheels slide to and fro like a rusty Tilt-A-Whirl carnival ride, and even Aunt Feen, who hasn't broken a smile since 1989, had to laugh when it skidded around a sharp corner and we all wound up on top of her.

The Basilica of San Domenico is tucked into the village like an antique book in a cupboard. Built of sandstone with a simple facade, its only hint of color comes from the mosaic of midnight blue and ruby red in the stained-glass rose window over the entrance. A tower with dual church bells on metal beams hovers above the entrance. Those same bells rang on the wedding day of my great-grandfather and his beloved Giuseppina Cavalline, over one hundred years ago.

There are more of us in the wedding party than in the pews (another sign that the bride and groom aren't twenty). Aunt Feen has taken a seat in the front. Her head is bowed in nap, not in prayer. Dad, Charlie, Tom, and Alfred are outside, getting air, which is what men in my family do whenever they are dressed up.

Charisma and Chiara play hide-and-seek behind the Gothic pillars with my brother's sons, Rocco and Alfred Jr., who seem to be, for the first time since their births, on a long leash. There is definitely something going on between Alfred and Pamela, and the kids are getting a free pass on discipline in the meantime.

"Pamela, looking good," I say.

Pamela wears Indian chic in Italy. Her gown, panels of magenta and silver silk, has an empire bodice with geometric cutouts. The spaghetti straps show off her sculpted shoulders and thin arms. Her blond hair hangs long and straight without a single flyaway. Clearly, she remembered to bring an adapter for her blow dryer.

"Thanks." She smiles, but it's forced. Pamela, my sisters, and I have made up since our rift last Christmas, but the current aloof demeanor is just as bad as the cold front used to be.

"How do you like the hotel?"

"It's rustic," she says.

"It's good to be together."

"Oh, yeah." She looks off. Her eyes follow Rocco and Alfred, who dart among the pews. "I'd better wrangle the boys before they tip over a saint or something."

The entrance doors of the church open behind us, and Gram stands in the light, tall and lean, in a beige silk suit with staggered white sequins along the cuffs of the jacket and the hem on the skirt. I look down at the shoes I built especially for this day, an elegant eggshell pump with a kitten heel and pearl beading around the vamp. She extends her hand to me, and I take it.

"Thank you, Valentine," she says.

"For what?"

"For everything. For helping me plan this day. For your support. You've been there for me every step of the way."

"You deserve every moment of happiness, Gram. And you should never thank me. I thank you."

Gram's eyes fill with tears. Mom comes over with a tissue and dabs Gram's eyes.

Tess pokes me to get in line to process up to the altar. I take my bouquet of violets in one hand and smooth my multi-strands of pearls with the other. I look straight ahead to the altar.

The priest, a scruffy Capuchin in chocolate brown robes, takes his place in front of the altar.

Dominic, in a morning coat, and his son Gianluca, emerge from the sacristy and take their places.

My heart flutters when my eyes meet Gianluca's. It seems like a thousand miles from the back pew to the communion rail. I like the distance right now. Maybe it will take the edge off the sudden and crazy mad desire I have for him, who, when the wedding license is signed, will be *family* to me. Dear God.

"Valentine!" Orsola whispers in my ear.

I turn. Orsola, Gianluca's daughter, gives me a quick hug.

"We're late. Always late." Orsola's husband walks up the side aisle and slips into the front pew next to Aunt Feen.

"No worries. You're right on time, cousin. To the second."

Orsola wears a bronze silk wrap dress with a matching picture hat. Tess hands her a bouquet of violets. She blends into the processional line so seamlessly you'd never know she was Dominic's grandchild instead of one of Gram's.

Chiara and Charisma sprint up the aisle, scattering rose petals as though they're in a three-legged race.

Mom fusses with the whimsy attached to Gram's hat. I know it's 2010, but when it comes to weddings and hats in my family, it will always be 1962—we love a pillbox. "It finishes a look," my mother says.

Dad pulls his cell phone out of his pocket and takes a quick snap of Gram and Mom before they begin their walk down the aisle. I don't know why he bothers, since anyone he'd send the photo to is right here in the church.

A violinist plays Frank Sinatra's "All the Way." My sisters precede me single-file as we process down the aisle. I feel like a shiny dime following two fifty-dollar bills and a bronze Manzù sculpture, but I insisted on the silver lamé, and it's too late now for a costume change.

My mother sniffles behind me.

I look straight ahead to the priest, but then, without moving my neck in his direction, I take in Gianluca.

Why does he have to look so good? I repeat *why, why, why,* to myself with every step/pause that I take behind my sisters. This would be so easy had there been a decline in his appearance over the Christmas holidays. Why couldn't he be one of those guys who ages overnight? No, he looks better than he did a year ago. Better than he did on our roof in the leather jacket last fall. The gray silk morning coat is the exact shade of his hair. He stands out in the dark church like a light feather against a cloudy morning sky. I almost miss a step, the stone floor gives, as though I'm walking on clouds.

"Watch it," Mom whispers from behind.

I regain what's left of my composure.

Gianluca looks out over the pews, his eyes as blue as the boots of Saint Michael in the statuary behind him. He is truly handsome, in that distinguished Cary Grant–in–the–later–years sort of way. Like Cary, Gianluca's profile is strong, his nose and jaw chiseled by God with a straight edge. Okay, maybe Gianluca resembles Saint Thomas More by way of Bay Ridge slightly more than Cary, but in the morning coat, in this color scheme, in this place, he's pure movie star in the golden age of Hollywood. The right suit makes a man royal.

I remember when Gianluca kissed me on the balcony in Capri last summer, and how I didn't want him, and after he kissed me, he was all I wanted. Maybe I broke up with Roman after that because I wanted more of Gianluca's kisses. Stolen kisses are one thing, but relationships are legit, at least, that's how my mother raised me. Gianluca was clear with me then; he wanted more than a little romance. But this morning, I wonder if he still wants me. Probably not. He was very friendly at the rehearsal dinner, but not in pursuit. Why would he be? When he came to New York and wanted something more, I told him plainly that I didn't want him or any man, and he believed me. I meant it.

Then why do I stare intently at him, as one would at a price-less painting under a pinlight on a museum wall? As each step in the wedding caravan brings me closer to him, I'd like to stop and sit down in an empty pew and catch my breath. Gianluca feels my stare. He smiles at me. I'd like to die right about now.

The priest rattles off the vows in Italian so quickly Gram could be agreeing to anything, including upgrading the plumbing in the church rectory. But she looks up at the priest with rever-ence and a full understanding of what she is promising to do. (In general, Italians move slowly, unless they're in church, where Mass is on fast-forward.)

The service becomes a blur to me as I'm overcome with my own emotions. I'm not alone. My sisters are weepy, my mother is blotting tears, while my brother stands off to the side surveying the ceremony in his disaffected, remote way, as if he's watching a report about a mini-merger on Maria Bartiromo's show.

Gianluca gives his father the ring and kisses him on the cheek. My father looks to the floor as Gianluca expresses his affection for his father. Dad and Alfred have never had that kind of bond.

As Dominic places the ring on Gram's hand, it's a wake-up call for their children. Mom won't be able to jump on the E train to see Gram whenever she wants. Gianluca will have to move out of the home he shares with his father to make room for his step-mother. I'm not the only person in this room whose life will change, but somehow I can't help feeling that I have it the worst.

I've been in full-tilt denial about losing my grandmother to her new husband and her new country. I will be all alone at the Angelini Shoe Company, upstairs in the living quarters and downstairs in the shop. As Gram and Dominic's marriage begins, our old life together ends. The years I've spent as Gram's appren-tice have been the best years of my life. Now, I'm going to have to take all I've learned from her and build upon it.

My eyes mist with good memories and deep regrets. I mourn

the conversations that we won't have over coffee in the morning, the afternoons when we sat on the roof, roasted chestnuts on the old grill, and laughed. I'm sad that she won't be there when I launch the *Bella Rosa*, which I pray will build the business to a new level and give us revenue to survive. The problem is all mine. I don't like change, and enough is never enough. A hundred years with my grandmother would not have been enough. But Gram's happiness is more important than all of that.

The priest holds his hands over Gram and Dominic as he blesses them. The flames in the candles, once clear and bright, become murky white puddles through my tears. I hold my small bouquet of violets tightly. I promised myself I wouldn't cry, but I can't help it.

I feel a hand on my wrist. Gianluca smiles gently and gives me his handkerchief. Before I can thank him, he is back by his father's side. I wipe away my tears. Tess nudges me. Gianluca's chivalry is not lost on my sister.

Gram and Dominic kiss. The priest makes the sign of the cross over them.

Aunt Feen stands, balancing on her pearl-handled cane for support. "Hallelujah," she says. "Let's eat!"

2

From the Bottom of My Heart

GRAM AND DOMINIC CHOSE THEIR favorite restaurant in Arezzo for their wedding reception. Tucked into a narrow side street off the plaza, Antica Osteria l'Agania is a quaint, local spot that has been in operation since Dominic was a boy. We are welcomed through a rustic oak door by the maître d'. The large wrought iron scrollwork handle is decorated with a small cluster of bridal greenery and white ribbons.

We enter a large main room with wooden beams on the ceiling, surrounded by stucco walls painted a dull gold. The large picture windows are dressed with gold chiffon Roman shades. One long farm table, situated at the center of the room, is covered in a white lace tablecloth with small silk tassels in the shape of bells draped over the sides. Orsola works her way around the table, placing small net bags of confetti (pink and white candied almonds) at each place setting. Small bouquets of violets are placed down the center of the table, surrounded by clusters of twinkling votive candles.

Whenever I see a garden of flickering cut-crystal votive candles, I think of my ex-boyfriend Roman Falconi and our first date at his restaurant, Ca'Doro. For a moment, I miss that long, tall chef from Chicago.

"What's the matter?" Tess asks. "Don't tell me—"

"No, I've moved on. I've definitely moved on."

"If you want Roman back—"

"No, I don't want him back."

"Are you sure?"

"I'm sure." Here's the thing. I could use an escort today. Whenever there's a family function, I'm reminded I'm single, so I shuffle through the Old Boyfriend File, my version of *People* magazine's "Where Are They Now?" to see if there's anyone I could have scrounged up to accompany me, instead of suffering through solo. It's not healthy to walk through the boneyard of my romantic past because the results are always the same, but I do it anyway. If self-improvement is a theme in my family, so is self-punishment.

On ordinary days I love being single, and I consider it a choice, not a curse, but I've learned that a woman needs a date at family funerals and weddings, if only for diversion from the drama. It's comforting to have a date to dump all the extra emotions upon, like gravy on macaroni. That's why in-laws were invented—if only to point out that your family is crazier than mine, as Charlie reminds Tess, and Tom reminds Jaclyn. Even Clickety-Click—Pamela—can be seen supporting my brother in her firm Germanic fashion. The spouses quell the histrionics—or at least, they try to.

Wedding receptions in Italy are not like our extravaganzas back home, and tonight, I wish they were. I would prefer to hide in a big crowd in a cavernous, noisy hall. It's easy to slip away when the disco ball descends and the guests are covered in white polka-dots in the dark. I like to have the option of slipping out early, before the Beach Boys medley and the chicken dance, without anyone missing me. Loud music that drowns out any unpleasant comments or intrusive conversation is also a plus. This intimate wedding reception (intimate for Italians is a head count under fifty)—twenty of us gathered around one table, most of us blood relatives—will be a lot of work.

Gram and Dom make the rounds, greeting the guests. The bride is so openly happy and optimistic, I can't help but be. I had no way of knowing how I would feel once Gram was actually married. Her happiness is as important to me as my own, so I never wavered in wanting her to be with the man she loved, even if it meant giving up her life on Perry Street and starting over in Italy. But now that the ceremony is over, and she's officially Mrs. Vechiarelli, it's another feeling entirely to be on the other side of it. Now it's back to reality.

We take our seats around the table. I look for Gianluca, who hasn't arrived yet. He disappeared after the ceremony as soon as we were done taking pictures. I was curious, wondering where he went, but quickly reasoned that there are Italian customs I know nothing about—and who knows, maybe he had to go to city hall and sign papers or meet with the priest. It could be anything.

"I left the seat next to you wide open," Tess whispers. "Where is Gianluca?"

"I don't know." I check the door again.

"He's the only single man at this wedding."

"Besides Gepetto over there." I point to a robust eighty-year-old with a thick swatch of white hair and a matching mustache who hammers loose tobacco down into his pipe like he's pounding rocks at the state prison. "He's starting to look good to me."

"You can date twenty years above your decade, and not one year more," Tess says.

I guess Gianluca, eighteen years my senior, qualifies in the under-twenty category.

Dominic and Gram make a stop and talk to Gepetto. The blood relatives are clumped in the center, with the children staggered in and out of the adult seating, in the hope that separation will keep them out of trouble. My brother-in-law Tom pours champagne into our glasses; evidently the waiters don't dispense the booze fast enough for him. He fills Aunt Feen's glass.

My brother, Alfred, takes his seat across the table from me. "What do you think?"

"It seems like a nice restaurant," Alfred says as he taps the table absentmindedly with his soup spoon. My brother usually appears spit polished and fresh, but today he seems tired. He has dark circles under his eyes, and more than a bit of gray shows through his shiny black hair, parted neatly to the side. He loosens his tie.

"No, I mean about Gram getting married."

"I'm going to miss her," he says. "I don't see her every day like you do, but I like knowing she's there."

"Me too." I reach into my purse for Gianluca's handkerchief. My brother's sweet comment, coming from a guy who isn't known for those, moves me.

"Why are you crying?" Alfred says.

"Oh, I don't know, about a million things." I rarely cry, so when I have a good sob, it's about *everything*. I'm sad about my relationship with my brother, who I will never be close to after a lifetime of trying. I cry about the changes ahead back home, and how much I will miss Gram. I weep because I don't have a date to this shindig and because world peace has not been achieved in my lifetime. I just let it flow.

The door to the restaurant opens, and a woman enters. She's a knockout, a tall blonde in a jet-black mink coat. My mother looks up—she has a sixth sense whenever a sable enters a room.

Every head in the room turns to drink in the sight of this mysterious goddess, and the men's heads stay turned. It's as if invisible LoJacks have been attached to their necks and rotated in her direction. Yes, she is *that* beautiful. "Maybe she is here to pick up take-out," I say to Tess.

"Don't think so," she says softly.

The bombshell is followed by Gianluca, who guides her by the arm to the table. He helps her out of her coat. The men exhale like they've found middle C on the pitch pipe as they drink her body in. Her shape is lushly proportioned: tiny waist, ripe bust and hips—like a bow tie on its side. Her *bella figura* lives up to her *bella faccia*.

"You got to be kidding me," Tess says under her breath. "Gianluca brought a *date?*" Tess yanks her purse from the chair she was saving for him and shoves it under the table. "He's on his own."

I'm stunned. Maybe I'll switch seats. There's an empty next to the bachelor Gepetto.

Gram, unaware of the goddess, leans over me and takes my hand. "Valentine, what did you think of the ceremony?"

"It was perfect."

"I think so." Gram smiles. "How was the carriage ride?"

"Like a hayride to the pumpkin patch," Aunt Feen complains loudly. "Bumpy, rickety and annoying . . . like old age." Then she picks up her glass of champagne and drains it like she's dousing a parched houseplant upon returning from a two-week vacation at the shore. Tom quickly refills her glass.

"It was quaint," I correct her.

"Too much hoopla." Aunt Feen dabs her lips with the napkin. "Simplicity should be a goal in life."

Gianluca brushes past us to greet the guests at the far end of the table.

Tess scoots her seat back.

"Where are you going?" I don't want her to leave me.

"I'm going to say hello to the blonde," she says.

"Why?"

"It's a fact-finding expedition," she says, then whispers, "make friends with the enemy."

"I'm going with you." I take a swig of champagne and follow my sister. When I stand, my pearls rattle like Marley's chains in *A Christmas Carol.*

"Hello!" Tess says to the lady.

"Ciao." The mink lady's blond hair cascades over her bare shoulders, accentuated by a portraiture sweetheart neckline on a black velvet strapless (of course) cocktail dress. Her green eyes are framed by thick black eyelashes. She's downright hypnotic. She wears a luscious perfume that has the scent of lavender and honey. I can't tell how old she is, and it doesn't matter. She's one of those women who can't be placed in a particular decade.

"*Parla inglese?*" Tess chirps.

She replies, "*Un po.*"

"*Che nomme?*" I ask.

"*Mi chiamo Carlotta,*" she says. Then she points to Tess and me. "*Sorelle?*"

"*Si, si, siamo sorelle.*"

Tess says, "*Teodora é la nostra nonnina.*"

"Boy, that Rosetta Stone program paid off," I compliment my sister.

"*Si,*" Tess nods proudly.

My father, brother, and the men from the village gather around behind us, squeezing us closer to Carlotta. We encircle her like contestants in a cakewalk, and guess who's the coveted grand prize, the Lady Baltimore layer cake?

Tess and I step back, our personal space violated by this intruding pack. This room is not large to begin with, and it's best if everyone stays seated, but Carlotta is a lure, and her beauty and whatever else she's got have created a tight stag circle around her. Tess and I turn to go back to our seats, and we have to actually push hard to break the seawall of men to return to our places.

Carlotta throws her head back and laughs as she chats with the adoring men. She *is* captivating. If I were Gianluca and had to choose between her and me in this moment, I'd go with Carlotta.

I look down at the garlands of pearls around my neck. This morning, they were chic, and now they seem more plastic than fashionable faux, more childish than sophisticated, and about twelve strands too many. I'm the overdecorated lower branches of a Christmas tree where the kids have free rein to hang ornaments. Cluttered. In contrast, Carlotta wears a simple gold chain around her long neck, 24K for sure. It nestles in her ample cleavage like two tributaries feeding into the Mighty Miss-i-ssip. The rope of gold glitters against her tawny skin.

"I know what you're thinking," Jaclyn says.

"I'll bet you don't."

"You're younger," Jaclyn reasons.

"I don't think that matters."

"Well . . . you're every bit as attractive as she is." Tess's brow furrows as she observes her husband pour Carlotta a glass of champagne. Even Charlie Fazzani is smitten.

"Let's face it—she could do the Anita Ekberg turn in the Trevi fountain in *La Dolce Vita* better than Anita Ekberg. I could do the same scene, and all I'd be is . . . wet."

Gianluca has joined the boys as they vie to dazzle Carlotta. I put my champagne flute down and head for the kitchen.

The kitchen is twice the size of the dining room. A chef, a tense man in his forties, and two cooks prepare the meal.

"*Avrebbe bisogno di un po' d'aiuto?*" I ask.

The chef breaks a smile and shakes his head that he doesn't.

"*Le dispiace se rimango a guardare mentre lavora?*"

He nods that I may. Better to be in this hot hell than the one in the dining room.

The cook pulls a large strainer out of a boiling vat of pasta. The steam sends clouds of mist over the worktable. The chef reaches up and grabs a copper pot shaped like a wok with a handle and puts it on a low flame. Then he spoons butter into the pan, followed by cream and a handful of sugar. Then he opens a small bottle of liqueur. He leans across the worktable for me to sniff. It's a sweet brandy of some sort.

"*Questo l'ho fatto io. E' un liquore fatto di pesche e more,*" he explains.

He drops a bit of the liquor into the butter and cream, then swishes the mixture around. The sweetest scent of a summer garden loaded with thickets of ripe berries rises from the pot.

The cook takes the pasta shaped like delicate rosettes and spills them into the pan of sauce without losing one to the floor or leaving one in the strainer. The chef lifts the pot to the worktable and flips the mixture, without using a spoon, until the rosettes are coated in the buttery cream sauce.

The second cook takes small plates and ladles the pasta onto the plates. The chef takes sprigs of sugared violets and places them in the center. The waiters gather the plates on their arms and exit to the dining room.

"*Mangia!*" the chef says, clapping his hands, shooing me out of his kitchen. But I want to stay. I want to watch him create our meal. I want to learn and retain his techniques. I want to wash dishes, scrub pots, anything, just so I won't ever have to go back into the dining room and have to face this long meal of many courses with my family and Carlotta and Gianluca and the mess of it all. I've hit the wall. I want to go home. To the United States of America. To sleep in my own bed. Alone.

Mom peeks into the kitchen. "It's time, Val."

I'm a middle child, who only stands up for what she wants when absolutely forced to in a life-and-death situation. At all other times, I suck it up and defer to the will of the group. Gianluca showing up with a hot date isn't exactly life or death, unless you consider humiliation terminal, so I give up and follow my mother into the dining room, where the guests are seated and already fawning over the pasta.

Gianluca has his seat turned toward Carlotta and away from the guests. Lovely. Aunt Feen is munching off a flat of bread, while the children amuse themselves with the cutlery. My father entertains Gepetto with a story, in English, which he pretends to understand while Gram and Dom take their places at the head of the table. Dominic stands.

"*Benvenuti tutti al nostro matrimonio. Teodora ed io ci consideriamo davvero fortunati d'esserci trovati e siamo lieti di avere le nostre famiglie unite in amore.*

"*Vi ringraziamo d'essere qui presenti a celebrare con noi questo bellissimo giorno, e tutti i bei giorni del nostro avvenire. Auguriamo che il nostro matrimonio porterà tanta fortuna alle nostre famiglie. SALUTE!*" He raises his glass.

The glasses touch, clinking together softly like piano keys.

The pasta course is followed by succulent roasted capon on polenta. Next is a small purse of filet mignon in pastry, then a fresh salad of greens and pignoli nuts with sliced oranges. I forget my troubles and slights, and do what I do best no matter what else is happening in the universe: eat. I enjoy every single bite. Every once in a while I look down to the end of the table where Carlotta and Gianluca are engrossed in conversation, and shovel in another bite in their honor.

Finally, after a meal with more courses than a Berlusconi bacchanal, the wedding cake is brought from the kitchen. It's a traditional white layer cake, but on the top tier, instead of a miniature bride and groom, there is a pair of tiny pink marzipan pumps next to a pair of men's wing tips made of chocolate. The guests applaud as the cake topped with candy shoes is placed in the center of the table.

The waiters quickly fill the center of the table with platters of pastries iced in pink, dusted with sugar, or drizzled in honey. I'm going to sample every cookie, and I'd like to see somebody try and stop me. I motion to the waiter to bring espresso so I might stay awake through my binge.

Aunt Feen rises from her seat and holds up her glass. "I'd like to make a toast."

The guests are silent as all eyes go to Aunt Feen. "My sister

Tessie—that's right, Tessie—I know you fancy-pants Italians called her Teodora, but that's your choice. I'm gonna call my sister what I called her all my life. Tessie . . . Now, where was I? . . . Tessie is my sister . . . and she happens to be a good egg. Dominic, I don't know you from a hole in the wall, but you seem okay. It's a little kook-a-luke for two eighty-year-olds to get married—that's just me. But you did it and it's done and that's where we are . . ."

It's more than fine that half the people in this room don't speak English, because if they did, they would know to be insulted. I look down the table at my mother, who is mouthing words with no sound coming out, like a carp marooned on dry land. As Aunt Feen drones on, Jaclyn and Tess exchange worried looks. My sister-in-law Pamela has her eyes squeezed shut as if she's witnessing the massacre finale in the *Texas Chainsaw* movie.

Aunt Feen continues, "So raise your glasses to the seminarians—"

"Octogenarians," my father corrects her softly. This is a first—he's correcting someone else's misuse of the English language. My immediate family exchanges looks of utter surprise. What could be next? Sophia Loren actually looks her chronological age?

Feen waves her hand dismissively at my father and turns to Dominic and Gram. "Octopuses. Whatever the hell you are. *Cent'Anni.*"

The glasses clink with a ferocity, as if to drown out any further commentary by Aunt Feen. I hear Charlie say, "Whoa," under his breath, while Jaclyn freezes her gaze, like Bambi seeing flames, upon Aunt Feen.

My family's insanity can only be kept under wraps before the general public for four hours max. We're on hour five, and it's dire. I chew on my pearls.

Gram and Dominic share a kiss at the end of the table, but cut it short when Aunt Feen bellows, "Cut the cake!" Evidently, the newlyweds are not moving fast enough for Aunt Feen. She stands up, picks up the silver knife decorated with white ribbons, and wields it over the cake like a sword. A collective gasp goes up in the room.

"Auntie," my mother says, and then laughs gaily as though we have knife play at all our family gatherings.

Aunt Feen stands firmly gripping the knife with two hands poised over the cake like a chef preparing to hack an eel in half in a Benihana commercial.

"Oh, Auntie, put the knife down," Mom says casually, then glares at my father to do something.

I look around to my father and brothers-in-law, who evidently, when they gawked at Carlotta's assets, inhaled her perfume loaded with kryptonite and have lost their ability to wrangle knives out of the hands of old ladies. They look away. Even Gepetto looks off in the distance, exhaling smoke in gray puffs like a leaky exhaust pipe. Clearly, the men don't believe this is their problem. So I stand up and place my hand out. "Aunt Feen, give me the knife."

"I'm gonna cut the cake," she yells. "Cut the cake!"

"No, you're not. The bride cuts the cake," I say firmly.

"And the mouse takes the cheese!" Aunt Feen bellows as she circles the knife above her head. The guests shriek. Aunt Feen yells, "And the cheese stands alone!"

"Give me the knife, Aunt Feen," I repeat. "Now."

Gram rises and scoots behind the seated guests until she's behind her sister. "Feen . . . ," she whispers, "give it to me." Gram gets a grip on the knife handle and Aunt Feen relinquishes it.

"Ah, what the hell." Aunt Feen drops down into her seat. "Cut your cake. Cut your cake."

Dominic joins Gram, and together they place their hands on the knife handle and evenly slice it into the lowest layer. The gentle cut of true love triumphs over the potential hack job of hate. The guests resume their revelry as the cell phones come out and we commence snapping happy photos from all angles. Gram and Dominic hold for pictures as the waiter takes the cake to the kitchen.

"That was close," Tess whispers.

"We have to get her out of here," I whisper back.

Aunt Feen drains her wine and slams the empty glass onto the table. Every head turns toward the thud. Aunt Feen lifts herself out of her chair, gripping the table edge for balance. She stands. She straightens her shoulders. She surveys the room. Even Gepetto, who doesn't understand a word of English, looks frightened as Aunt Feen looms over the table.

"And one more thing . . . ," she announces, raising one hand with a pointed finger to the ceiling. And then, like the drop delivery of a box spring from 1-800-MATTRESS, Aunt Feen falls full-body backward.

To the sound of twenty chairs scraping the wood floor, accompanied by cries of "Dear God" and gasps of "O Dio," Aunt Feen hits the floor on cue, and at the drop of her Second Act curtain.

The Hospital of Santo Pietro looks less like a haven of healing, and more like a perfunctory credit union back home. The sparse waiting area has a plain desk and lamp, and simple wooden benches along the wall. There is a suite of small rooms tucked behind the waiting area, according to my mother, who peeked. I don't have a good feeling about this place, and from the looks on the faces of my family, they don't either. This place makes Queens General Hospital (the insignia in Latin is translated to: *Don't Go There*) seem like the Mayo Clinic.

Aunt Feen is inside with the doctor. For whatever reason, when she came to she glommed on to Charlie, who carried her out of the restaurant in his arms and into the carriage, which brought us here. Aunt Feen, forgetting she'd rebuffed him earlier, or maybe guilty because she had, insisted Charlie go with her to be examined.

Tom took the baby and the kids back to the hotel. A quick call to Signora Guarasci, the proprietor at the inn, and she was on hand to help with my nieces and nephews. This is going to be a long night, and my sisters need the backup so they can be here for Aunt Feen.

Mom paces the floor. Her aqua chiffon cocktail dress looks like something the alto section might wear during a "Harvest Moon" number on *The Lawrence Welk Show*. A panel of fabric studded with pale blue seed pearls flows behind her as she paces the floor. Whenever my mother dresses formally, she resembles a bird, going for color, movement, and flight. Her upsweep, which stayed up at the restaurant, has begun its downward spiral.

My father sits between Jaclyn and me on a small bench under a framed movie poster in Italian of the Marx Brothers' *Animal Crackers*.

"Feen went down like a brick." Dad loosens his tie. "Ka-boom."

"I hope there's not permanent damage." Jaclyn's eyes fill with tears.

"Who knows? It's a wait-and-see situation. When it comes to a head injury, I know it's better if you see blood. Then you know she's not bleeding on the interior. P.S. I didn't see a drop of blood," Dad says.

It's times like these that I wish someone in my family had gone into the field of medicine. We could use an expert right now. "You can bleed inside *and* out," I correct my father. "It's not an either/or."

"Okay. Then her fall could be a killer of the silent type caused by a stroke." My father folds his arms across his chest. "A stroke and a sub-see-quent blow to the head . . . she's finished."

"Dad." Jaclyn mops up her tears with a scrap of brown paper towel from the restroom.

When Aunt Feen toppled, the reception officially ended. She came to fairly quickly while lying on the floor, after the thud, but she was woozy. The cake went uneaten, the net bags of confetti remained on the tables, the cookie trays were untouched. We grabbed our purses and followed Aunt Feen to the hospital quickly. I'm worried about my great-aunt, but I'm sad for Gram that her wedding day has been ruined. I get up and go to Gram. "I'm sorry about all of this." I put my arms around her.

"It's okay. I just want Feen to be all right."

The doctor pushes through the door. Dominic rushes over to him. They converse in Italian.

"Does Dr. Kildare over there speak English?" Dad says.

"I do." The doctor looks at my father. He's around forty, slim build, balding, and wears glasses.

"No wedding ring," Tess whispers.

I glare at her.

"Is it serious?" I ask the doctor.

"We did a scan of her brain and neck—there appears to be no trauma to the head."

We actually applaud the good news.

"I'd like to see that scan," Dad says under his breath. "What did they do it with? Pliers and a mirror?"

"*Allora, dottore,*" my mother purrs, "*mi dica la prognosi per mia zia?*" My sisters and I look at one another. My mother flirts whenever a situation requires immediate service. This rule applies to mechanics and doctors as well as Pierre, who dyes Mom's roots at the Jean Louis Hair Salon on Queens Boulevard.

"The scan showed nothing." The doctor shrugs. "She is very lucky."

"So what caused the fall?" Dad wants to know.

"Her blood alcohol level is extremely high," the doctor says. "She's inebriated."

"Drunk?" My father throws his hands up. "Feen is drunk!" My father turns away in disgust.

"We gave her an espresso and two aspirins," the doctor says. "She's sobering up."

"I don't believe this," Jaclyn says.

I'm beginning to miss the cake and the platter of cookies we left back at the restaurant. I could use a cannoli or two right about now.

"So, what do we do?" Mom asks the doctor.

"Take her home and let her sleep it off," the doctor says.

My family goes from a grief-stricken pre-funeral-planning state to annoyance, then anger, in ten seconds flat. Only Gram breaks a smile. She's relieved, and now her new life can begin. We gather our belongings to go.

"I knew no good would come of this trip. You can't take senior citizens abroad and hope they survive out of their comfort zone. I don't think anybody should venture into areas where they don't speak the language," Dad says.

"Really. They don't speak English in Bayside, Dutch, and that's a quarter of a mile from our house."

"You know what I mean. *Foreign* countries. Aunt Feen is too old and too American to be cavorting around the world. She can't handle the stress, so she hit the bottle."

"What stress?" Tess wonders. "She had to get dressed up and sit in a church and then go to a restaurant to eat. How hard is that?"

"It's not. But something is troubling her. Why would Aunt Feen get drunk?" My mother addresses our group. "She's not a drinker."

"She's jealous," I tell them.

"Of what?" Mom asks.

"Of *whom*. She's jealous of Gram."

"Oh come on. They're eighty and seventy-eight—jealous of what?"

"They've been competitive all their lives. Feen has always felt second-class, the baby who could never surpass the older sister. And Feen remembers who got the roller skates for Christmas and who got the socks."

"Valentine, that's ridiculous."

"Really? If you had caught Aunt Feen on her second cocktail, three before she hit cement, she would tell you all about how Gram was the favorite, and how her sister always got everything she wanted. And now, Gram even has a husband. Aunt Feen faked being sick this morning for attention. She fell asleep at the ceremony like it wasn't important enough for her to stay awake at her own sister's wedding, and then, when neither of those things worked to her advantage, when her mere disdain of the whole wedding didn't get it canceled, she did what she had to do to refocus the limelight off Gram and onto herself by getting stewed at the reception."

"Dear God." My mother shakes her head in disbelief. "Is this who we *are*?"

"And look. Aunt Feen won. We left the reception and came to the hospital and sat vigil for her. Now, instead of the bride being the center of attention on her wedding day, it's Feen. Mission accomplished! And now, get ready. When she sobers up, expect complete contrition. She'll be so sorry that she turned this day that belonged to her sister into one that she stole with an *accidental* fall. But don't believe a word of it. This has been an act all along."

"Charlie overheard her playing it up in there to the doctor. She pulled a full Meryl Streep, with tears and everything," Tess says. "Told the doctor she had a nervous condition."

"Aunt Feen ruined this wedding, and that was her intention from the moment she set foot on the flight," I assure them.

"That's sick," Jaclyn says.

It's hard for Jaclyn to imagine that one sister could ever turn on another. Tess, Jaclyn, and I have had our fights, but we get over our disagreements quickly. We root for one another's happiness and do everything we can to support one another. We are not like Great-aunt Feen and Gram. Tess shakes her head sadly at the realization that what I am saying is true.

"It's just awful. That's all," Mom says.

Gianluca and Lady Zing–Zang–Zoom push through the door. Carlotta's perfume fills the air like a breeze after a sweet, summer shower. I hate her.

Gianluca looks around the room. When his eyes find his father, Dominic, he goes directly to him. They speak rapidly in Italian as Dominic explains the diagnosis. I can't catch everything he says, but it sounds like Dominic is telling Gianluca that everything is okay and he is free to go.

Gianluca kisses Gram on the cheek, and then embraces his father. He then goes to my parents and says good night. Then he turns to the group, the rest of us, and sort of does a wave on his way out. I got a wave for you, I want to shout after him, and it's four fingers short of a hand. Now, I hate *him* too. I can't believe I was longing to kiss him only twelve hours ago. Now I'd like to sock him. Take your lips and go, I'd like to tell him. Too late. He took his lips and he's gone. He's out the door with Carlotta—*lotta* everything I ain't got.

A cold winter wind kicks up, sending a chill through us as we walk back to the inn. It took Aunt Feen an hour to sober up, and when she did, Mom, Dad, Dominic, and Charlie loaded her into the carriage to take her back to the Inn. My sisters, Gram, Alfred, and I volunteered to follow on foot.

Arezzo is serene; it closes down early like most quiet Italian villages when night falls. The lights from the houses throw streaks of gold light onto the dark streets as we pass.

Alfred, Gram, and I walk together, not saying much. The only sound we hear is the soft click of our heels hitting the stone streets and the muted chatter of Tess and Jaclyn, who walk ahead of us, no doubt discussing whether to put Aunt Feen in rehab. We revel in a crisis that results in putting one of our own in a short-term residential facility. We enjoy nothing more than packing a picnic basket and visiting our infirm on the weekends.

Gram takes Alfred's arm on one side, and mine on the other. "This is nice, just the three of us," she says.

When it comes to Alfred and me, Gram is on a peacekeeping mission at all times. Even though I'm her longtime partner at the Angelini Shoe Company, and she confides in me, Gram had a lot of decisions to make, big and small, personal and professional, when she accepted Dominic's proposal to marry. Alfred has become a sounding board for all the arrangements, and has helped her shape her life plan moving forward.

Alfred holds the place of authority in our family universe. He is our grandmother's only grandson. He is also the eldest and only son in our family, which gives him the advantage thanks to the ancient Roman law of primogeniture. Alfred is "the prince," and our de facto leader. A decision is never final until my brother gives it his stamp of approval.

"What a day." Gram sighs.

"We'll remember the good parts, Gram," I tell her.

"I hope so." Gram smiles. "I'm relieved my sister is going to be all right."

"She'll be fine," I assure her.

"You know, I count on both of you." Gram tightens her grip on my arm.

Gram had planned to meet with Alfred and me after the reception. One last attempt to encourage us to be nice to one another, I'm sure. I haven't trusted my brother's motives since he tried to sell Gram's building out from under us last year, and close the shoe company that has been in operation since 1903.

I was four years into my apprenticeship when he attempted his takeover. The economic collapse of the American banking system last fall helped me throw him off his plan. As real estate values plummeted, he became less eager to sell Gram's building, but I can tell from his demeanor that he's still up to something. My brother always has a plan B.

In the world of Manhattan real estate, Gram's building is still prime, with its West Village location and spectacular Hudson River views. But Gram could never sell it now for the price she would have gotten only one year ago. This has only made Alfred more resentful toward me. Now that Gram has a new life in Italy, it's clear I'm on my own again. I'm the only thing that stands between Alfred and a hefty sale on Perry Street. I accept that I will be in the fight of my life when the plane lands at JFK tomorrow night.

"I hope you'll look out for Aunt Feen," she begins.

"I will," Alfred promises.

"We all will," I amend. I'm always amending my brother. Plus, I know the truth of the situation. It won't be Pamela and Alfred running over to Feen's apartment with meals. My brother won't do her laundry and take her to her doctor's appointments. He won't be the one to sit with her at the senior center on bingo night. It will be the women, my mother, sisters, and me.

"I didn't mean you wouldn't—I was just assuring Gram that she can count on me."

Alfred's tone is insulting.

"Great," I snark.

"That's enough. Listen to me. I have given a lot of thought to what's to become of the Angelini Shoe Company. And I've come up with a plan. I'm going to make you partners."

"Alfred and me? You can't be serious. We'd have to call the company Chalk and Cheese, because we couldn't be more different."

Alfred puts his hands in his pockets and looks away.

"It's the Angelini Shoe Company now and forever," Gram says firmly.

"All of sudden you're nostalgic? How could this work?" I point to my brother. "Ever?"

"It *has* to work. I trained you, Valentine, and you've proven you're at the start of a great career as a shoemaker—a designer—an artist, which, really, I never was. But you need help."

"I don't need his help. I don't want his help. I'm doing fine without him."

"You need help on the financial end of things."

"The financials are easier than the design," I say defensively.

"That statement alone shows that you don't know what you're talking about," Alfred jabs.

"What don't I know, Alfred?"

Alfred faces me. "We should have sold that building last year, when we could have gotten a fantastic price. We could have been proactive and moved the company to a cheaper site, like Jersey. Now, because we waited, because *you* made us wait, we have to ride this bad economy out until it turns!"

"I'm not riding out my design career! I'm in it for life!"

"No, he means the value of the building versus the debt," Gram says calmly. "Valentine, I wouldn't be comfortable saddling you with everything involving the business. But you've been right on two counts." Gram looks at Alfred to make certain he is listening. She turns back to me. "The custom bridal shoe business should not move from Perry Street—it's been there nearly a hundred years and it should stay there. It's important to keep the original shoe business going as you develop your new line. There is power in the name, and in our tradition, so exploit it. I think you're brilliant to have come up with a design for an everyday shoe. It never dawned on me to expand the company in this way. But you thought of the *Bella Rosa*, and you're doing it, and good for you—good for all of us."

"Thanks," I mumble.

Gram continues, "Now, I've worked everything out with my attorney, Ray Rinaldi. Alfred, I've made my decision, and I expect you to honor my wishes. The workshop and the business will remain in the building. Valentine, you may also continue to live in the building. You will be the chief executive officer of Angelini Shoes. You will be in charge of everything creative, and of the day-to-day operation of the shop. And Alfred, you will be the chief financial officer."

"Don't do this to me, please!" I beg her.

"Valentine, you have to trust me," she says.

"But this is a huge mistake!" I stop and throw up my hands. Jaclyn is right. My family is always yelling—inside the hotel, on the quiet streets of Arezzo—it doesn't matter, anywhere you look, no matter what time of day or night, we are ready for a fight.

"It's what Gram wants." Alfred turns to face me. "It's *her* decision."

My mind reels. I don't want this, but it seems if I don't agree to it, Gram will be forced to devise another strategy—and it won't be in my favor. On the other hand, Alfred has a full-time job—so really, how much would he be around? Not much. I take a deep breath. "Okay, Gram, if this is what you want . . . "

"It's what's best," Gram says.

"But there have to be conditions to this deal."

"Oh, now you have *terms*." Alfred folds his arms across his chest.

"I work there, I've been working there for over five years, and I intend to stay."

"Fair enough," Alfred concedes.

"I run the shop. On the custom side, I buy the materials, make the deals with the vendors, and maintain the stock. I meet with the customer, design the shoe to her liking, and then put it through the construction process on a schedule. I oversee the pattern cutting, and I build the shoe. I've developed the secondary line, and I don't intend to share the copyright of the *Bella Rosa* with anyone. Anything that I design belongs to me. At the moment, I also keep the books, pay the bills, and juggle the loans. If you want to take over the books, handle the loans, and structure the debt and the taxes, great. The time I save with you doing all of that will free me up to do more design work. I'm not interested in being your boss, and I won't have you be mine."

"Fair enough," he says quietly.

"And . . . I'm not going to agree to any of this unless you agree that you will not be directly involved in the creative side—"

"Fine." Alfred cuts me off, not because he doesn't want to argue, but the truth is, he could not care less about the shoes. He could as easily be CFO of a company that makes bricks—Angelini shoes are just a product to him, numbers on a ledger. Legacy is a cross to my brother, not a crown.

"I don't want you underfoot," I tell him.

"Then we have a problem," he says.

"Alfred will be a full partner in every way," Gram says. "He's going to devote himself to modernizing the company, on a day-to-day basis."

"How? He already has a job."

"I'm no longer at the bank," Alfred says quietly.

"What?" Maybe this is what Pamela and Alfred were fighting about—exactly what Jaclyn heard through the walls at the inn. "You quit the bank?"

"I was let go," he admits.

"But you've been there eighteen years!" In an instant, I'm defensive for my brother. He is, after all, a brilliant businessman and the biggest success story in our family. The fact that he didn't respect my work never meant that I didn't respect his. I'm angry for him. "Those banks!"

"I saw it coming," Alfred says. "But that doesn't make it any easier. Believe me, I wouldn't take this job if I didn't have to."

"Gram, it's not right that you went behind my back and made a deal with Alfred without consulting me."

"We needed a plan, Valentine. I didn't want to dump the whole company on you and leave you to struggle in this economy without a plan."

"Fair enough. But Alfred?"

"Valentine," Gram warns. "We're lucky we have someone in the family with Alfred's knowledge and level of experience."

"Of all people! He hates my guts."

"I don't hate you at all," my brother says impatiently. "I don't approve of the way you do things, and I question your choices—"

"Who are you to question my choices? I know how you feel—you think I'm a screw-up, in life and work. How would you like to feel judged all the time?"

"You have good qualities," he says quietly.

"There's a ringing endorsement."

"Look, Gram is right. You need help. Someone to take the reins."

"You're not *taking* the reins, Alfred. We're sharing them. Right, Gram?"

I remember the ride to the church this morning, and how when the horse went off course, and the wheels slid on the wet pavement, the driver held both reins and guided the carriage back to safety. It would never work to have two drivers, each holding one of the reins, each with a different idea about how to direct the carriage back on course. It takes one driver to steer a carriage— and a singular vision to run a company.

I have no idea how a partnership with my brother could possibly work. I can't picture myself side by side with Alfred, making important decisions or haggling about inventory. But this is the deal Gram has made, and it's her company, and her building. She could have given them both to me outright, but she didn't. I have to accept her terms. I have no choice. And she knows it.

"When you return home, I've set up a meeting with Ray at the shop. He'll go over the details, but I've already signed off on my end. I'm no longer sole proprietor of the Angelini Shoe Company. I will maintain an emeritus position on the board of directors, which now includes each of you. When the time comes for me to sell the business outright, that will be a decision that we will make together. In the meantime, can I trust you two to take care of our family business?"

Alfred says yes aloud, and I nod in agreement. I'm afraid if I speak, I'll cry, and I can't give Alfred that satisfaction.

"Your grandfather would be so happy, and so proud that his grandchildren joined forces to run his company." Gram's voice breaks. Grandpop has loomed over this day like a heavy storm cloud threatening rain. In the glow of her present happiness with Dominic, Gram has been thinking about her first husband. She and Grandpop's long and difficult marriage has fallen into shadow, but not so far into the dark as to not be seen. Gram spent more than fifty years of her life with my grandfather, and even in death, his wishes matter to her.

"You took good care of the family brand," I reassure her.

"You can do better," she assures me. "And with Alfred, you will."

The things I will remember about Gram's wedding won't be poignant (the recitation of the vows) or sad (Aunt Feen hitting the floor), they won't be joyous, or romantic, they will be *practical*. With one hand she signed her wedding license, and with the other she cut the Angelini Shoe Company in half, like a sheet of leather.

As we climb the steps of the inn, the night sky changes from midnight blue to steel gray. A small sliver of a powder blue moon pushes through the dark clouds. The moon doesn't throw much light, but it doesn't have to. I can see everything plainly: the road is dark, it's winding, and I have no idea where it leads.

3

Ain'tcha Ever Coming Back

I TURN THE KEY IN the door of my room at the Spolti Inn, careful not to make a sound. I don't want to trigger any late-night powwows with my sisters. I've seen enough of the Angelinis, Roncallis, Fazzanis, McAdoos, and Vechiarellis for a lifetime, not to mention Gepetto, the wedding guest who, in our darkest hour, became one of us as he witnessed Aunt Feen's swan dive into public drunkenness. The way this evening has gone, I should have joined her. Better to be drunk to take the blow of Gram's decision than stone-cold sober.

I don't know what Gram was thinking, sticking me with Alfred as my partner, but she hasn't done me any favors since she fell in love with Dominic. It's almost as if True Love has rotted her brain. And here I am—her defender and champion—left with partial when I deserved the whole. She split the Angelini Shoe Company in two, like a pair of shoes, handing one to my brother and the other to me, rendering one completely useless without the other.

I drop my shawl and my purse on the bed. Then I kick off my shoes.

I look around the room for something, anything, to eat. I'm starving. Well, there's always the welcome platter that Signora Guarasci left in each of our rooms. A bottle of pink liquor, some breadsticks, and a bowl of fresh figs call my name.

I grab the bottle and the corkscrew off the platter and, placing it on the nightstand, stab the point into the cork. I'm so over this day, I could bite off the neck of the bottle with my teeth. I need a drink, and I need it now. How ironic. I spent most of the day at the hospital waiting for my drunken great-aunt to sober up—and the first thing I do in the hotel room is grab the booze. At least this particular weakness is in the DNA, it's not my fault.

I fill the crystal tumbler from the dressing table with pink whatever-it-is to the brim. I rip open the breadsticks, anchor one in my mouth like a cigar, and chew. Then I sit down in the rocker, pull the footstool over, and put my feet up. I hold up the glass and toast myself. Congratulations! You didn't get kissed! You didn't eat cake! You were upstaged by Bella Boobs, and you're in business with your brother, who has never liked you! We've got a winner! I swig.

Then, I look down at the scads of faux pearls that lie on my chest in a tangled clump. What was I thinking? They are ticky-tacky. On top of all the indignities of the day, I didn't even look good.

After twelve hours, the pearls feel like pennyweights around my neck. I lift the mass of them over my head and drop them on the floor. That's the beauty of plastic; it travels well and takes abuse. I could drop them out the window and they wouldn't shatter on the streets below—no, they'd just tuck and roll, like my ego has done all day long. I won't wear multiple strands of Coco Chanel–inspired pearls ever again—unless I'm in France. This look did *not* work in Italy. Or maybe it just didn't work on Gianluca Vechiarelli, and that's what's troubling me. I take another swig.

I text Gabriel Biondi, who would be the love of my life if he weren't gay. We've been best friends since college, and he's the desperate call I can make at 3:00 A.M.—or the transatlantic text I can make at any other hour of the day. Right now, he's devising the seating chart for the sold-out Saturday night show at the Carlyle. He'll be happy to hear from me, if only to procrastinate at work.

      Me: Disaster in Italy.
  Gabe: What?
      Me: Aunt Feen hammered at the reception. Was
           hospitalized.
  Gabe: OMG.
      Me: Gets worse.
  Gabe: How?
      Me: Alfred fired at the bank—Gram put him in
           business with me.
  Gabe: The Apocalypse!
      Me: It's here. I'm sucking flames.
  Gabe: How's John Lukka?
      Me: Learn to spell. You're Italian. GIANLUCA
           brought a date to the wedding.
  Gabe: Expletive.
      Me: Uh huh.
  Gabe: Thought at least you'd get lucky.
      Me: No such lukka.
  Gabe: They cut my hours at the Carlyle.
      Me: No!
  Gabe: It's gonna be a Hard Candy Christmas
           around here.
      Me: It's only February.
  Gabe: OK. Hard Candy Saint Patrick's Day.
      Me: I'm sorry.
  Gabe: Come home.
      Me: In a hurry.

There's a knock at the door. I ignore it.

The knock becomes a series of small, persistent taps. Guilt washes over me. What if Aunt Feen has stopped breathing? What if my dad or mom is sick? I take a big gulp of the wine and throw my phone on the bed. I give up.

"Coming." I open the door.

"Valentina." Gianluca leans against the sash of the door and folds his arms. The fine gray wool of his morning suit appears pressed, as if he just put it on. The only indication that he's been through the same long day I just endured is the loosened tie, a black-and-white-striped foulard whose undone knot gives him the sexy air of formal/casual sprezzatura—even at this hour.

"Hi." I close my eyes and inhale the familiar scent of his skin, a combination of clean lemon and spicy leather, before I take a step back into my room. I wasn't expecting him. *Ever.* I am in postevent decline: my mascara is smudged like raccoon tar pits underneath my eyes, my dress is half unzipped, and I smell like cheap dessert wine. What a confluence of lovely to lure this man into my lair. "Just a moment," I say to him. I go to the bed, snap open my evening bag, and remove his handkerchief. "Here." I hold it out for him. "Thank you."

"I'm not here for the handkerchief."

"Oh." I fold the handkerchief in half, and then, after a few moments of silence, I turn it into an origami accordion in my hand. The hallway behind Gianluca is quiet and still. The only light comes from the security lamp at the far end of the corridor.

"I hoped that I might choose the right room," he says.

"Aunt Feen is down the hall," I tell him, waving in the general direction of her room. What a responsible guy. He came to check on his new aunt, the one with a drinking problem.

"How is she?" he asks.

"She's sleeping it off."

A few moments pass. I refold the handkerchief.

"Are you going to ask me in?"

I pause. Actually, I freeze. Ask him *in*? For *what*, exactly? Maybe Carlotta rebuffed him. Just like the paste version of real pearls, I'm her substitute. Or maybe that's not it at all. Maybe it's a business thing, and he wants to sell me some rare calfskin for the shop. Or maybe it's an old debt. It's possible that I owe him for the horse and carriage. All I know is that he's standing there waiting . . . for *something*.

Oh, if only it were me. My secret hopes for a wedding-trip tryst with Gianluca hit the ground and burst into flames the moment he showed up with Carlotta at the reception. I didn't see that coming; a woman with a love plan never does. My instincts did not serve me well, but to be fair, when I'm with my family, they never do. My instincts focus elsewhere—usually churning around some drama they've created. The pursuit of potential romance and family obligations do not mix.

When Gianluca left the hospital with Carlotta, I felt rejected. Ridiculous, I know. (You cannot be rejected by someone that you do not actually have a date with.) Gianluca and I were hardly a sure thing, but if our past encounters were any indication, there was heat, a mutual attraction, and a certain sympathy that I imagined might lead to something more. It's been a few months since I saw him in New York, and while I've been busy, my thoughts have gone to him from time to time. Okay. More than a few times. What woman doesn't like a man that makes his desires known? He told me he had feelings for me. And I already know that I like kissing him.

And then there's the digestif element, the concept of a treat at the end of an arduous night. I deserve a little romance and male attention after all I've been through on this trip. Payback for being a good sport and unpaid majordomo for my mother and sisters and their families. I have been an undesignated but completely used Extra Pair of Hands (my mother's term) since we gathered at the airport. I lug, I tip, I assist, and I corral—and I do it with a smile.

I hauled my mother's extra suitcases, counting them as my own so she wouldn't have to pay extra. I administered my father's glaucoma eye drops on schedule in Italian time. I helped my sisters with their kids, the patient maiden auntie who diverted their attention in the terminal when a fight was brewing, bought them candy to shut them up, and once on board played rounds and rounds of Tic-Tac-Toe on cocktail napkins until I thought my eyeballs would blow from their sockets and roll down the center aisle and into first class.

I also served as an unpaid assistant nurse for the geriatric travelers in our party. I fetched Aunt Feen's meds, unwrapped her crackers from the cellophane, smeared them with cheese, and upon landing, became her two-legged cane/wheelchair stand-in, which has left me with a stiff shoulder and a sore lower back.

I've been *perfect*. And all I wanted in exchange for my suffering was a little comfort from a Tuscan tanner. *He* kissed *me* on the balcony of the Quisisana last year when Roman Falconi stood me up on our Capri vacation. *He* asked *me* to consider his affections on my roof overlooking the Hudson River. But that was then. Today, all of Gianluca's previous declarations seemed to dry up and blow away like Italian snow when he brought Carlotta to the wedding.

And now, who can imagine why, my self-confidence has . . . waned. I'm back at Holy Agony when I turned thirteen and was caught in the coat closet by Sister Imelda in the arms of Bret Fitzpatrick after our confirmation dinner. She didn't say a word, that prying postulant; she just slammed the door shut and left us in the dark with our shame. There *is* such a thing as the ruined moment, the missed opportunity, love derailed. I should know. I've lived it more than once.

"May I come in?" he asks again.

"Okay," I answer, with a sense of defeat. "Careful of the pearls." I gingerly kick the puddle of faux under the bed as he closes the door behind him. "There's only one chair," I apologize. I'm downright awkward, offering a tour of the two pieces of furniture in my room.

"I make you nervous?"

"No, no, not at all." Only in the land of Valentine Maria Alfreda Roncalli would pent-up sexual energy translate into a case of dyspepsia.

He sits down in the rocker. He stretches his long legs out in front of him. He wears a size 13 shoe. He fills up this hotel room with a lot of man.

"Would you like a glass of . . . I think it's wine?" I offer.

"*Grazie*," he says.

I go to the table. There's only one glass. Of course there's only one glass—this is the spinster suite. I'm lucky Signora left me a bowl of free figs. "Uh, we'll have to share," I tell him as I pour the wine.

"Good," he says.

I bring him the glass. He takes a sip and leans back in the rocker and looks at me.

I sit as far forward on the edge of the bed as I possibly can be without actually standing up. I sort of . . . perch. Let's get the bad news out of the way first. "So, where's Carlotta?"

"I drove her to Deruta, where she lives."

"Oh, great." I don't know what's so great about it, but too late now, I said it. "I always liked Deruta. Pretty pottery."

"And what did you think of Carlotta?"

"That was some mink."

Gianluca laughs. "She's very elegant."

"That would be one word for it."

Gianluca looks confused.

"If the men in my family took a vote, I think they'd come up with a word to describe her, and it wouldn't be *elegant*. How long have you been seeing her?"

"Seeing her?"

"Yeah."

"Since I was nine years old."

"Nine?" Boy. No wonder they are considered the world's best lovers. They practice. These Italians start early.

"Her father makes the equipment we use in the shop."

"Oh, that's interesting." I don't find it one bit interesting. I could not care less. I lean forward and take the glass from Gianluca and sip the wine. I hand the glass back to him. "Childhood romances are wonderful."

"She told you?"

"No, I just assumed."

"Why?"

"The way you were together, I guess. I'm like that with Bret."

"Bret?" he asks quietly.

"Yeah, Bret Fitzpatrick and I finish each other's sentences—still. We broke up years ago, but we're still close. There's a history. It's comfortable." I hope he's jealous of Bret; it would serve him right for sandbagging me by bringing Carlotta to the wedding. So I pile on. "There's a shorthand with an ex who knows you well. You know, like you have with Carlotta. I'm sure you know everything about one another."

He nods.

I continue, "So, how did you like the wedding?"

"I'm happy for my father. And for Teodora."

"Orsola tells me that you're going to take over the shop and let Dominic retire."

Gianluca's expression changes at the mention of his daughter's name. He smiles. "Papa would like that. He wants to spend all of his time with your grandmother. I would like that, too."

"They want to enjoy every moment," I agree. But I was surprised how quickly Gram was able to let go of making shoes. It's almost as if a key turned, leading her into Dominic's house and out of our workroom.

Gianluca rocks in the chair. "It's a good lesson for everyone."

"Absolutely. Seize the moment." I gulp the wine while sharing the wisdom stitched on my mother's pot holders.

"Maybe you will come to Arezzo more often?"

"I don't need an excuse. I love it here."

"*Va bene.*"

Once the *va bene*s start rolling, we're on common ground. At least, that was true in Capri—in the past. I get up and refill the glass with the pink potion.

"And you?" Gianluca asks. "How do you feel about today?"

My eyes fill with tears. I *hate* this wine! It's filling me with false emotions. No one should drink when they're sad. "I'm going to miss Gram."

Gianluca gets up and goes to the nightstand. He picks up his handkerchief, then he sits down on the bed beside me. He dries my tears.

"I'm sorry. I don't want to cry. But I think I've almost drunk that entire bottle of . . . what is this, anyway?"

"Vin Santo. Dessert wine. Isole e Olena."

"I should at least know the name of what I'm killing the pain with."

"What pain?"

"Oh, I don't know. Let me pick from the bouquet of despair. Let's start with the A's: abandonment." The tears flow freely again. I grab the handkerchief out of his hand and dab them.

"Your grandmother has a life to lead—on her own, without you."

"I know!"

"So what is the problem?" he says softly.

"I'm going to end up old and alone and stabbing wedding cakes like Aunt Feen." I sob. The thought of this terrible fate makes me feel worse. I can't stop crying.

"I don't believe it," he says.

"Why would you? You won't end up alone. You've got

Madame Mink." I might as well take a political stand for PETA if I'm never going to kiss Gianluca. "You know, I don't even believe in wearing fur."

"You don't?" He smiles.

"I don't know. It's not the mink. It's *her.* She's . . . spectacular."

"She is very beautiful."

I cry into the handkerchief. "Yes, she is."

"I'm sorry," he says.

"You didn't do anything wrong."

"Yes, I did. I've made you sad."

His admission shuts down my waterworks like a lever. At times, Gianluca speaks English better than me, and other times, he has a difficult time expressing himself in anything but Italian, but occasionally he's as sharp as a needle no matter the language, so pointed he goes right to the center of things. "You want the truth? Yes, you *did* make me sad."

He smiles.

"You think that's funny?"

"No, it's not funny."

"Then why are you smiling?"

"Because I knew." He smiles again. "You care about me."

I get up and move to the window. I throw it open for air.

"Come here," he says softly.

"No, thanks." I turn away from the night air and stand behind the rocker and hold the back of it with two hands like a medieval shield separating me, the lowly single handmaiden, from the Duke of Delish.

"Why not?" He seems surprised.

"I feel played. You know, misled. You had a shot with me last night. I thought you were sending me signals at the rehearsal dinner, which now, in retrospect, were real. But then you blew it today. You brought Carlotta to the reception. I had a whole thing in my head, a perfect little fantasy percolating, about how things were going to go between us at the reception. I thought we'd talk, have a cocktail or two, maybe a little pasta followed by a slice of cake after the knife throwing, we'd share a cup of espresso, a little dancing—you know, typical wedding rituals that lead the single people to partake of wedding-night rituals without any of the paperwork."

Gianluca is stumped.

I continue, "Why do I drink? I talk too fast."

"You don't talk *enough*." He gets up and hands me the glass.

I feel slightly cornered. The fresh air that pours through the window emboldens me like the oxygen they pump into the casinos in late night Las Vegas to keep the grannies at the slot machines until dawn. I can breathe, I can think, and therefore, I am going to be direct with him. "I'm free, you're free . . . get it? I wasn't free in Capri—and now I am, but you're not. You have Minky."

"Carlotta."

"Yeah. Carlotta."

"But I don't *have* Carlotta."

"What do you mean?"

"She's my *friend*. That's all. Her family and mine have been close all these years—in business together. She came to the reception out of respect for my father."

"Oh."

"How do you say . . ." He looks off and out the window, past the shield, beyond me. " . . . that you have it all wrong?"

"You say, I have it all wrong."

Gianluca moves the rocker, the barrier between us. He takes me in his arms. The night air whistles through the window like a breath, sending a chill through me. I place my hands on his face, and through his hair. Then I rest my head on his shoulder. The scent of the citrus and leather on his skin reminds me of the tins of beeswax I keep in the shop. It's the scent of everything I treasure, my childhood in the workroom on Perry Street, the cloth when I buff a pair of shoes I've made, and now, him.

I remember what his arms felt like last year, but he was forbidden then, so I dared not take in the details. I had a boyfriend, and I didn't want to take advantage of this Tuscan tanner who I thought might be trying to take advantage of me. Or was he? It doesn't matter. This is so much better than going back in my mind's eye to the balcony at the Quisisana—because tonight, it's *my* idea. "Kiss me," I whisper.

His lips graze my cheek until he finds my mouth. He kisses me. I am on my tiptoes for a very long time as we connect, our lips moving in full expression, without words. Who needs them now? I am done explaining my feelings. I want to *have* my feelings instead. Better yet, I'm going to have *him*. Gianluca kisses my eyes, my nose, my cheeks—I don't know how many kisses he gives me—ten, a thousand, a million?

"I'm sorry I made you sad," he whispers in my ear. "I'm sorry we wasted so much time."

"I don't care," I tell him. "I got buckets of time. Boatloads . . . all I have is time." He interrupts me with kisses down my neck. He finds the half-undone back of my dress and I hear the soft whir of the zipper as he undoes it. His hands on the small of my waist feel warm as he eases them up to my shoulders. If I wasn't tipsy, I'd stop him, as my parents are down the hall, and Aunt Feen is sleeping off her reception bender with a snore they can hear in Florence. But I don't care about any of that now. I just want *him*.

He spins me gently through the room, like the flutter of snowflakes that made dizzy patterns outside my window this morning. It's as if I'm moving through the air without a destination in sight, not quite flying, but definitely off the ground. This must be how ballerinas feel when they sail through the air during a jump. I am weightless as he carries me to the bed.

This is not a good idea, I'm thinking, as he lays me on the bed, and yet it also feels like the best idea *ever*. I don't hear church bells, or brass blaring, or see satin ribbons unfurling; this isn't going to be triumphant sex, there isn't going to be a parade, but I don't need one. I need *him*. Gianluca wants me—and he's wanted me a very long time. Is there any harm in pursuing something that cannot last? Isn't it time I made up my own rules?

We both know that I'm leaving in the morning. Figuring out the continental divide, doing the math: I'm there, he's here—so what? It's a challenge—what element in my life isn't a challenge? What else might stop me? He's my grandmother's stepson? What difference does *that* make? When the international divorce rate hits 50 percent, the truth is, everybody's related anyhow.

What's the worst that could happen here? So, we make love, it's divine—and then, we *never* do again? I promise I will be very happy with the four hours I will have with him before the sun comes up. I'll treasure the memory like a rope of dazzling diamonds and not be upset at all if I find out the stones aren't real. I swear: whatever I get, whatever we have tonight, will be *exactly* enough. Here's a bold concept for a Catholic girl from Queens: stay in the moment.

"I'm so happy you came back to me." I cover him with kisses.

He smiles as his hands travel from my hips to my waist. My dress falls away as he pulls me closer still. "I wanted you from the first moment I saw you."

"And I thought you didn't like me at all."

"Now do you understand that I do?"

"I understand."

"There was a problem," he whispers.

My heart races. Here it comes. I always expect to get bad news, but usually not this soon, and never after I've already stepped out of my dress. I ask, "What problem?"

"You're so young."

I don't know if it's the crappy sherry, or that I can't get the sound of Aunt Feen hitting the floor out of my head, but when a thirty-four-year-old woman hears she's too *young*, all inhibitions and obstacles disappear. *Young.* The word itself is an aphrodisiac—not that I need one. A great lover knows exactly what to say, which is even more important than a great lover knowing what to do. I needed to hear that I'm still young after a day of feeling like that warped wheel on the old horse carriage. "I'm not too young," I assure him. "I remember eight-track tapes."

"It doesn't matter, because I can't help the way I feel about you."

Even with my smeared black kohl eyeliner giving me the look of silent movie star Theda Bara, and my disheveled silver lamé dress thrown across the bed like a mermaid's fin, I get it. He wants me, and I want him. Beginning of story? End of story? Who needs words? Who's even talking?

Gianluca glides on top of me gently, pulling me close. He reaches around me and lifts me so I'm on the pillows. He shifts, pulling my BlackBerry out from under me. "Lose the phone." I kiss him. He drops the BlackBerry to the floor as the cool night air blows through the curtains and washes over us.

There's a banging at the door.

"Oh, God," I whisper.

"Don't answer it," he whispers back.

Neither of us moves.

We hold our breath.

Bang. Bang. Bang.

"Auntie Val?" my niece Chiara calls out to me.

Bang. Bang. Bang.

Gianluca rolls off me. I point to the bathroom. He goes into the bathroom and closes the door behind him. I grab my robe from the hook on the back of the door and pull it on. I yank the belt of the robe in a knot like I'm rigging a boat to the dock.

I open the door. "What's the matter?"

My niece stands before me in her Hannah Montana pajamas, her black eyes wide open. "Can I sleep with you?"

"Um, I think it would be better if you slept in your own bed."

"Charisma is crowding me."

"Give her a little shove."

My tone causes Chiara to raise her eyebrows. She counters, "She'll wake up. It's too hot in our room."

"I'll open the window."

"Nah." She folds her arms across her chest.

"I think you should go to your room," I say with an urgency she hasn't heard since I yanked her away from the closing doors on the E train exiting the Queens Boulevard stop when she was five. Chiara looks at me suspiciously. I turn perfectly nice, hoping to ditch this kid back into her room, so I can return to Gianluca's arms. "Really, honey. Auntie is exhausted."

"Do you have any candy?" She tries to peer through the partially opened door and into my room.

"No, honey, I don't." I look down the hallway. Where in the hell is this kid's mother? Why doesn't Tess wake up and deal with her? I smile at Chiara. "It will soon be breakfast—and I'll buy you a big jar of Nutella for the plane ride."

"You will?"

"Yep, and a spoon. And you can eat for seven hours on the plane on the way home."

"Do I have to share?"

"No, no sharing." I give Chiara a hug, and then, closing my door behind me, walk her down the hallway and back to her room.

"Mom won't let me eat it out of the jar."

"Yes, she will. I will buy her a jumbo bottle of Coco cologne off of the duty-free cart."

"Good." Chiara pushes the door of her room open.

A woman's loud scream, coming from my bathroom, peals through the quiet.

"What was that?" Chiara grabs me, afraid.

"Go in your room."

I turn and run down the hallway and into my room. Gianluca is standing in front of the bathroom door.

"I frightened your sister," he says as he points to the bathroom. "It connects."

"I forgot to tell you."

The hallway light flickers on. "Is everything all right?" my mother calls out from her room at the end of the long hall.

"I saw a mouse," Jaclyn calls from her door, next to mine, covering for the shock of finding Gianluca in her/our bathroom.

"I'll send Daddy," Mom calls out reassuringly.

"What the hell can I do? Club it with a shoe?" Dad bellows.

"I don't know, Dutch. Think of something," my mother says.

"I'm not chasing mice," he barks. "Hasn't this day been bad enough?"

"I'm afraid!" Chiara comes out of her room and into the hallway and begins to cry. "Maaa-maaa!" Her voice echoes through the hotel like an Alpine yodel.

Tess opens her door, comes out of her room, and joins her daughter in the hall, groggy from sleep. "What's the matter?" I hear her say.

"Aunt Jaclyn was screaming," Chiara explains.

"You shouldn't listen at people's doors," I hear Tess tell Chiara; clearly she thinks it was a pleasant scream that her daughter misunderstood. Tess then closes Chiara's door softly behind her.

"I'll go." Gianluca kisses my hand.

"No, you're staying."

"I can't, now. The children. Your family . . ."

"Right, right. A bloodcurdling scream knocks the starch right out of romance. How about . . ." I'm thinking we could go to his house—and so is he.

He shakes his head no. "Papa and Teodora."

"Right, right." I think again. "Is there a hotel?"

"This one."

We look at one another.

"We're doomed," I whisper.

"No."

"How do you figure? I'm leaving in the morning." I throw myself against his chest.

"You might be going home," he says softly, " . . . but you will never leave me."

Gianluca's lips find my own with such tenderness, then he kisses my cheek, and into my ear he whispers, "Never."

4

Just as Though You Were Here

THE FOLDERS LIE NEATLY ON Gram's long dining room table, just as she left them, plainly marked in her own hand: House/Maintenance, City/Codes and Taxes, Angelini Shoe Company, and Personal. On top of the house folder are sets of keys, marked for every door and window of 166 Perry Street.

I open the file marked Personal first. Gram has written down her international cell phone number, the shop numbers at Vechiarelli & Son, her new address, and a current bank statement from Banca Popolare that lists me jointly with her on the account. It has $5,000 in the plus column and in her handwriting, a Post-it that says: For Emergencies.

I can't imagine what emergencies she could be referring to—until I open up the House/Maintenance folder. Here are a few potential disasters: boiler breakdown, roof leaks, plumbing fiascos, and wiring/electrical issues. I put my face in my hands.

Now that I officially live here alone, the decor and placement of Gram's furniture, the couch, the curtains, the old television set, all seem dated. I need to make the place my own. But where to start? I do revere and want to preserve the memories, the history, of this apartment, but every time I walk through, I miss Gram— and it's because it's still *her* house.

Before she left, she was uninterested in the fate of the contents. "Do whatever you want," she said. But what I really want is for her to be home, and back in the shop with me, the way it used to be.

I make my way downstairs to the workroom. The hallway has the scent of lemon wax and leather, and a tinge of motor oil, because I greased the gears on the cutting machine before going to bed last night.

I push the glass door etched with a cursive *A* open. My anxieties seem to dissipate once I set foot in this shop. This is a magical place where I feel in total control. We call it a *work*room, and while we put in long hours, it's actually a *play*room—where ideas are born.

The patterns June cut yesterday lie neatly on the table, layers of tissue paper and fabric pinned together without a bump or a gather. She propped my sketch of the *Osmina* on the shelf to remind herself to cut the pattern for our newest addition to the line of custom shoes first thing this morning.

I unlock the window gates and roll them back. It's a bleak February morning with low winter clouds that hover over the West Side Highway like a sheet of gray-and-white marble.

Delivery trucks sit in a row at the stoplight heading for the Brooklyn Tunnel. It may snow today, and it wouldn't matter. There's plenty of work to be done inside. We were in Italy for five days, and even though June worked through, according to the schedule, we're behind. There is no such thing as vacation in a family-owned business. When we take time off, we pay for it.

I pull on the overhead lights and sit down at the desk. I move the statue of Saint Crispin, who anchors a stack of bills and the paperwork from our payroll company. June left me a heap of mail with a note that reads, "Good luck." I shuffle through the envelopes.

I open the bank statement. The coffers are full—for now. But the prospects for 2010 are bleak. Our custom line will suffer as luxury goods take a hit in the marketplace. Therefore, I am going to have to move very quickly to establish *Angel Shoes*, our new, economical line of flats. I designed the *Bella Rosa*, a durable yet elegant shoe with hip signature embellishments that I hope will be coveted by women sixteen to ninety. I also hope to get the inaugural shoe, the *Bella Rosa* of the *Angel Shoes* line, into mass production by the fall.

But there is much to do! I need financing to go into production on a large scale, so I can sell the *Bella Rosa* to as many vendors as possible. My ex-fiancé, Bret Fitzpatrick, survived the Wall Street meltdown and now works to finance new business. He took me on because of our lifelong friendship, but also because he believes in the vision I have for growing our brand.

We have to find a manufacturer to make the *Bella Rosa*. Research and leads, subsequent meetings, and conversations point to China, where most American-designed goods are made these days. My grandfather would be horrified at Angelini shoes being made anywhere but Perry Street, and anywhere but the United States, but I have to stay open to all possibilities.

There's a knock on the window. Bret waves to me through the glass, motioning that he'll meet me at the entrance. We've made a habit of these early-morning meetings. He takes an early train from his home in New Jersey and swings by before he makes his way to Wall Street. As he turns the corner, his navy topcoat flutters behind him in the wind, like the wings of a bluebird in a barren tree.

"I bet you wish you were still in Italy." He kisses me on the cheek and pushes past me into the shop.

"You have no idea."

"I got your text. I can't believe Gram hired Alfred."

"He starts today. Mr. CFO."

"Where?"

"Right there." I point to the desk, which I have cleared to make room for Alfred. It's the first time since I was a kid that the desk has not been cluttered with stacks of paper. "This new partnership might kill me."

"It won't kill you. In fact, if you work it and stay cool, Alfred can actually make your life easier."

"Do you think so?"

"Absolutely. You're going to put him to work for you, and he won't even realize it. First of all, I will deal with your brother on the manufacturing plan. He will do the research, draw up the budgets, make the projections, and reach out to factories that can make your shoes. In the meantime, I'm out raising the money to launch the *Angel Shoes* brand. With that money, we will put the *Bella Rosa* into production. Once we have the shoes in production, I will help you place them in the market. Don't worry. I got your back."

"You always have."

"I'm all over it." Bret opens his briefcase.

His light brown hair is ruffled by the wind. I resist the urge to smooth it, as I did for the ten years we dated, one of them— the last year—actually betrothed before we broke up. There might be a million reasons why it didn't work out with us, but it only took one to end it. I wanted to be a shoemaker, and he needed a stay-at-home wife. Neither of us wanted to deprive the other of our dreams, so we decided not to marry. No one was more surprised than I. My childhood friendship with Bret had blossomed into a romance, and when it came time to make the difficult decision to move on, the foundation of mutual respect and love carried us through. We have always had a natural, easy relationship—which is why we could be honest with one another when our lives went in different directions.

He looks at me. "What the heck are you thinking about?"

"I was remembering when we went into business selling industrial cleaner door-to-door in the seventh grade."

"You needed a lot of breaks." Bret laughs.

"I still do. You were such a natural salesman. You talked those housewives into buying that cleaner like nobody else could."

"I believed in the product. Just like I believe in you."

"I'm just a struggling cobbler."

"Not for long, Val. This is so much fun for me. It's going to be something to watch this company grow. And you're different from most of the companies out there. This economic collapse might actually work in your favor."

"I'd like to know how."

"The federal government has really stepped up. There's an incentive program for small business in New York State—they're taking applications for loans right now." Bret hands me a folder filled with forms. "The city will reassess your property taxes and adjust them according to deflation in the real estate market, and they'll give you some breaks on utilities, as long as you keep a minimum of four employees on the payroll. Right now, you've got three—you, Alfred, and June. You need a fourth to qualify—but you have time to hire that person. And then, there's the new development fund. I think you might be able to swing a very low-interest loan to launch the *Bella Rosa*."

"I haven't been able to get any traction with the banks," I admit.

"No one can at this point. The small business rep in New York is a woman named Kathleen Sweeney. I hear she's tough."

"Nice Irish girl."

"Exactly. Here's her information. Call her and schedule an appointment. And it would be smart for you to include Alfred, so he's invested in this."

"Good point. So what can I do for you? How can I ever repay you for all you've done for me?"

"You can come to Maeve's birthday party. She's turning five."

Bret gives me an envelope covered with pink balloons made of felt.

"Already?"

"Already. I can't believe it. Piper is going to be two."

"It seems like yesterday that you told me that Mackenzie was expecting." I can't believe all that Bret has accomplished in the past six years. He's built a family with Mackenzie, broken into the financial world, bought a home, and moved out to the suburbs. When I look back on the same period of time, I think about how I mastered sewing kidskin by hand. We are leading two very different lives. "Are you going to have more children?"

"Mackenzie says the shop is closed. I would love more."

"I think you defer to the lady on those matters."

"Of course. Always."

"I'll definitely be at the party." I give Bret a hug.

"Bring Gabriel."

"The black cloud? No way. He hates kids."

"Yeah, but he gives our suburban New Jersey parties some edge. And when he has a couple glasses of wine, he sings the Rodgers and Hammerstein song book like nobody's business."

"I'll bring him."

I walk Bret to the door. "I don't know how to thank you."

"You don't have to. It's fun for me."

"Yeah, but you're busy, and this is small potatoes. Of course, I say potatoes because you're Irish."

Bret laughs. "I have a feeling when you get these shoes off the ground, it's going to mean some big changes for you."

"Wouldn't that be something? I'd pay off the mortgage and the loans and remove the ax of impending doom that hangs over my head."

"The good news: the ax is imaginary. You'll get Alfred where you want him. And Val, if anybody can do it, it's you." Bret pushes the door open and turns to me. "You're on to something big here."

Sometimes when I look at Bret, I see all the years we've

known each other unspool like a long, endless ribbon without a beginning or an end. We've known each other most of our lives, and there is a trust that is so deep, I wonder if I could ever have it with any other man. "You always come through for me."

"It's easy." He smiles and goes.

I open the invitation to Maeve's birthday party. The invitation has been written in calligraphy and assembled by hand, with glitter and lace. The section with the date, time, and place pops up out of the crease with a bunch of balloons. Maeve's round face appears inside the balloons.

How does Mackenzie do it? Would I ever be the sort of mother who could assemble birthday party invitations with sequins and glue? Would I even be the kind of parent who would *enjoy* doing it?

What a beautiful face Maeve Fitzpatrick has, with her father's serene countenance and her mother's blond hair. I pin the invitation up on the bulletin board. I'll endure anything for Bret— including screaming five-year-olds, a pirate who does magic tricks, and a train ride to New Jersey.

A letter from Gianluca arrives in the mail from Italy, along with a sleeve of leather samples from his shop. Business and pleasure tucked into one envelope.

I open the letter first. His handwriting is artful, that glorious Italian script with the curlicue edges. He wrote it with a fountain pen in midnight blue ink. A fountain pen in 2010! Miraculous!

14 febbraio 2010
Cara Valentina,

Even my name looks prettier when written by an Italian. The letter is dated the night of Gram's wedding, the night we almost spent together. Here's a fundamental difference between us: that night, Gianluca went home and wrote down his thoughts, while I slammed the door of my room at the Spolti Inn and stewed.

> *Please accept my apologies for tonight at the inn. I was carried away with emotions that I have been feeling for quite some time. You could not know of these feelings, for I had not admitted them to myself. But when I saw you at the church, down the long aisle before the altar, I was filled with, and there is no other word to use, a great longing.*
>
> *I have not had the true love I had hoped for in my life, and now, I wonder if it is even possible. Many men, except the poets, seem to search for this particular love, and they find it somehow, in words and intention. But me? I do not know. There was a moment in the church when I thought I saw it, in your eyes, your face, your beautiful face. Later, when I found you in your room at the inn, I wondered if it could be true, that you might reciprocate the feelings I had, and turn my longing to kisses. Now, I hope. Do you feel as I do?*
>
> *My love,*
Gianluca

Oh, for Godsakes. I have to sit down. I'm thirty-four years old, and no one has ever written me a love letter. Full disclosure: there's an old shoe box in my mother's attic with evidence to the contrary. I saved notes I passed in school with Bret (the phrase that sent me swooning then was "You're my girl" written in pencil on lined school paper). And I did put the text messages sent by Roman Falconi ("Love U") in a place called permanent memory on my phone. But I've never received a letter on onion-skin paper stamped "Par Avion," written in indelible ink, that described me as "beautiful" and "longed for," or specifically asked me what I want and what I need, romantically. This is a first.

I imagined that if I was ever presented with a letter describing such ardent feelings, in plush and meaningful sentences, that of course I would *believe* them. I want to believe them. I'd like to think that every now and again, I could render a man *weak*—but this isn't the English countryside, and I'm not Jane Eyre, and he's not Mr. Rochester riding up on his horse to the manor where he hides his mentally unstable wife in the attic. Or is he?

I go to the ironing board and plug in the old equipment, as I have done by rote many mornings. I need something to do, because I don't want to think about what I want to do with Gianluca. When I was a girl, I bought my mother's lines about one man for every woman, referred to it in passing as "a lid for every pot," "a hat for every head," "a glove for every hand"(oddly, no "shoe for every foot," despite the fact that we are in the business). Nevertheless, I thought my life in love would go as my mother's had before me, even though every conscious decision I have ever made regarding my future followed the motto "Whatever Mom did, do the opposite." My mother kept it simple. The old "One God, one man, one life" is the philosophy she built her life upon, but it has not panned out as a realistic path for me.

I lick my finger and test the base of the iron. I leave my finger there a second too long and burn it.

I should never pick up a hot iron when I'm distracted.

"Whoo hoo!" June calls from the doorway. She plows in wearing so much winter gear, I can barely see her face. Her bright blue coat is the only touch of color on this dank morning. She carries a bag with coffee for us from the deli. "Don't yell at me. I got doughnuts. We need to celebrate!"

As June takes off her hat, gloves, and coat, she listens carefully as I tell her the story of Gram's wedding day. When the story turns to night, she sits, peels the plastic lid off the paper coffee cup, and stirs. She leans in as I tell her about Gianluca showing up at my room at the Spolti Inn.

When I'm done, she breaks her doughnut in half, giving me the larger portion. "It's always the man you don't make love to, the one who wanted you and didn't have you, *that's* the man who will never forget you," she says. "The anticipation of sex is often more thrilling than the reality."

"Who are you kidding?" I look at June, who stores the sexual history of Greenwich Village since 1952 in her boudoir drawer like a satin nightie.

"No harm in trying to make you feel better." She laughs. This is what I love about June. Sex is God's greatest gift to the planet, with a sense of humor coming in a close second. Gram taught me how to make shoes, but June has taught me it's important to let go—and have fun.

"Okay, and all right," she says. "I would have liked the story better had you actually made love to the Italian. At my age, we want to hear all about it because we don't get it so much anymore. So now we're both frustrated. Why didn't you and Gianluca leave the hotel and find a quiet spot somewhere to make some noise?"

"I tried! I don't even have kids, and my night was ruined by one. It's like Chiara *knew* her frazzled auntie was going to get lucky and had to do anything she could to stop it. Now I know why they call it getting lucky—because when you don't get it, you feel cursed."

"I don't mean to add to your stress levels." June dunks the last bite of her doughnut in her coffee. "But we need to talk."

June rolls the work stool close to me and places her hands on the table. Her bright red hair is braided in small pigtails that rest on her shoulders. Her rhinestone-studded reading glasses anchor her bangs off of her face. At seventy-one, June is in great shape; her porcelain complexion is flawless from a life of avoiding the sun. Only the creases around her mouth, a legacy of years of smoking, tell her age. She still wears bright blue eye shadow, bohemian East Village style, with leggings and a multicolored voile print smock over a turtleneck. June could be any ex-dancer in New York City. "Honey, I'm old," she says.

"Never."

"Never has arrived. And it's brought varicose veins and memory loss along for the ride. Here's the deal. I'm tired. I don't know how much longer I can cut patterns for you."

"Is something wrong?" I panic. Two hours on the job as boss, and I've already lost my key employee.

"You mean like a disease or something? Oh God, no . . . unless years of smoking weed has finally caught up with me. But I don't think it has. I unwind with God's gift to the garden and so far, so good. No, it's not my health that's forcing this decision. It's the number: seventy-one. Seven. One. My wrists hurt, and my fingers are getting stiff with arthritis. I think I need to retire."

"And do what?"

"Well, I thought I'd sit around and listen to Miles Davis and paint my toenails. And I'd like to catch that show *The View* live— I love that Whoopi."

"You want to watch TV and hang out? May I join you?"

"Absolutely not. You have a name to make for yourself."

"I don't want to do this without you."

"Sure you do. And you can. And you will. Valentine, you know, your Gram's marriage was a wake up call. I'm a little younger than she is, of course, but one year over the age of seventy is equivalent to ten years under seventy. Time is slipping through my hands like cheap satin."

"Anybody can die at any age, June."

"Yeah, but when you're over seventy, you're more *likely* to die. And I want to relax with the time I have left."

"When do you want to leave the company?" Tears sting in my eyes.

"Once you get the *Bella Rosa* going, I think I should go. And we should think about getting someone in here who I can train."

"Okay." But it's not okay. I can't imagine working without June. And I don't want to work with anyone else. We rarely argue, we figure out how to solve a problem without drama, and we even like our coffee the same, light no sugar.

"Look, it's not the end of the world. Things change, Valentine. I'm sure you don't want me keeling over on the pattern table."

"Actually, I would like that."

June laughs. "You've had enough of us old girls around. Teodora understood that. She cleared out so you could have your own life. And with Alfred starting . . ."

"You don't want to work with him either." The idea that June would leave because of Alfred, or even partly because of him, makes me angry about the situation Gram left me in all over again.

"I can handle Alfred." June shrugs. "I just don't want to. And he's not the reason I'm leaving."

The entrance door opens. Alfred, who has not set foot on the island of Manhattan in anything but a Brooks Brothers suit since he graduated from Cornell twenty years ago, wears jeans and a polo shirt with a parka thrown over it for his first day of work at the Angelini Shoe Company.

Gram's attorney, Ray Rinaldi, trudges in behind him, carrying the same briefcase he's had since the Korean War. He wears layers for warmth: a sweater vest under his trench coat and a Cossack hat with flaps over his ears. He's dressed to place a flag on the highest peak in Antarctica.

"First day of school," June says wryly as she picks up her pinking shears to resume her work from yesterday.

"That's exactly what it feels like," Alfred says.

I give Ray a gift bag off the desk. "Confetti from Gram's wedding."

"Thanks. I love Jordan almonds, but I can't have them anymore." Ray points to his mouth. "Too much bridgework."

"Soak them in vodka first. That's my tip," June says.

"Shall we meet upstairs?" Alfred proposes.

Ray and Alfred go up the stairs. June motions for me to have courage as I follow them.

Ray sits down at the end of the table and pulls files from his briefcase. I take a folder of documents that I compiled for Alfred and Ray from Gram's stack on the end of the table. I sit down across from Alfred with a pit of despair in my stomach.

Ray lays out the contracts, I look over them, but the words are a blur to me. I pretend to read them as Alfred pores over them. I look at Ray. He knows I'm making a deal that I never would have agreed to if I didn't feel forced. But I have no choice in the matter. If I want to live and work here, I have to play along.

"Valentine, we're going to establish a rental payment for you in the apartment above the workspace," Ray says.

"That's fine. I told Gram that's okay with me."

"We'll keep it low." Ray smiles.

"I hope so," I tell him.

"It says here that all financial decisions are made jointly." Alfred looks at Ray.

"It does," Ray says.

"But Valentine has full control of the creative also."

"Alfred, your grandmother was very clear. She wants you to serve as chief financial officer, setting budgets and payroll, restructuring debt, and assisting Valentine in whatever she may need to grow the company. This includes research and pursuit of future contracts. Now, Valentine has been engaged in product development with Bret Fitzpatrick . . ." Ray explains.

"He's a fund-raiser," Alfred says. "And he should be compensated for that."

"Yes. And Teodora is comfortable with Bret in the mix, as long as his efforts serve Valentine's vision."

"I get it," Alfred says.

"So any decisions about financing are to be made by you and Valentine—jointly," Ray clarifies.

"That leaves me hamstrung," Alfred says aloud as he continues reading.

"Well, it is *my* business." I look at Ray.

"But I've been brought in as chief financial officer to run it," Alfred corrects me.

"I mean—" I take a deep breath and lower my voice—"that it's my business in the sense that I create the product we sell—and you rely on me to deliver that product. Otherwise, I'm happy to share everything."

"Okay." Alfred looks at me.

I realize that he's only being agreeable because he's been on the job for all of ten minutes. "So here's my budget." I reach across the table and give Alfred the current budget with operating expenses. "And here's the list of custom shoes under current contract, with down payments and shipment dates." I place the report on top of that. "And here are my projected business goals—including the manufacturing of the *Bella Rosa*. This file includes all of Bret's research with the Small Business Administration and some information about foreign manufacturers. But the foreign element is incomplete. You can help me figure out that piece."

"Wow." Alfred seems slightly impressed. Then he says, "I'll read over this."

"Take your time." I stand up. "Ray, thank you for setting this up for us." I extend my hand to him. "I'll probably be calling on you from time to time."

Ray shakes my hand. "My pleasure."

"My goal in life is to sell enough shoes so I might purchase you a proper briefcase."

"Old habits die hard, I'm afraid." Ray pats his old satchel.

"And sometimes they need to," I tell him.

Gram left her bedroom suite behind. The heavy, dark stained oak furniture with its four-post finials and deep carvings on the headboard says 1940 like Rosie the Riveter or garter hose with seams. The bed is made with the same pale green satin spread that's covered it since I was a child.

Gram suggested I move into her room, because it's larger. I've been living in the smaller guest room all these years. My mother's bedroom, across the hall, is a shrine to the 1950s. The wallpaper has a pattern of bunches of violets tied with gold ribbons that gives the effect of a year-round garden. I like the vintage paper but I don't want to move in there either. I'm going to stay put. Gram will be back to visit, I hope, and when she returns, I want her to find some of the old familiar things she loves in place as she left them. Besides, I've grown to love the guest room across from the bath, with the stairs outside my door that lead to the roof. It's home to me now.

My mother's room is filled with stacks of storage boxes that Gram didn't have time to sort through before she left. We packed up her clothes, and some heirlooms from her mother, to take to her new life in Italy. She and Dominic plan to redo his house in Arezzo, so she wanted to start fresh. She didn't even take her reliable spaghetti pot, which signaled to me that she's determined to start over.

I've promised myself that I will go through a box at a time, whenever I get a chance, and eventually I will have distributed these mementoes to my mother, sisters, and Alfred. There are lots of pictures of my mother, the only child, enough to fill a crate, and at least one wall in the homes of each of her four children. My mother's life is chronicled from her birth in black and white to her marriage, in vivid shades of Kodachrome film. I'm getting to know her all over again.

The photographs are so telling of the moods we were in, and what was happening when the pictures were taken. The pictures taken in the 1980s, when Tess, Jaclyn, Alfred, and I were young, tell the story of a family in crisis, and then, once into the 1990s as we go off to college, you see the mood lift and the joy return.

My mother and father survived a crisis of my dad's own design, when he had an affair and Mom moved us into this building during the summer of 1986. Of course, she never told us the real reason she moved us into the city—she said our house needed rewiring—but it was actually our dad that needed the redo. As the years went on, we got bits and pieces of the story, until our parents felt we were old enough to handle it, and then we were allowed to ask anything about it that we wished. Today, if we discuss the past, their story is told in full, complete with my father's confession, my mother's forgiveness, and my father's return to the fold.

My father's ancient infidelity is now part of the fabric of our family. We don't embroider over it, or pretend it never happened—it's just become one of those things—like a cancer diagnosis, a failed driver's test, surviving the mumps, or the celebration of a deserved promotion with the Parks Department. Dad's indiscretion is dropped into conversation like any date or period of historical significance in the story of our family. So, then too, is The Aftermath, the "better years," Mom calls them, after our parents renewed their vows and we, their four children, stood up for them in church, knowing full well what they, and we, had been through. In a sense, they gave us the gift of forgiveness by forgiving one another. It was a lesson that took with my sisters and me, but not with Alfred. We had to convince him to come to the church. Finally, though, after a lot of pleading, he showed up.

Sometimes I marvel at my family's ability to accept the worst, and to forgive, but that's due to my mother and father's determination that no one, not even a seductress named Mary from Pottsville, Pennsylvania, would come between us. How ironic, then, to think that it isn't an outsider that threatens to tear us apart and destroy us now, thread by thread, but a boll weevil from within. The real enemy of our family unity, as it turns out, is a sharp businessman with a cold heart—my brother.

Of all the things Gram left behind, my favorite memorabilia is the collection of annual calendars that used to hang over the desk in the workshop. They are the true minute book of this corporation, an unofficial ledger of business transactions that date back to my great-grandfather's arrival in the United States.

We have the calendars as far back as 1910, each month illustrated by whatever business or supplier sponsored it. The oldest ones were provided by a company that made Red Goose shoes. There are circled dates and notes made first by my great-grandfather, then my grandfather, and finally Gram. The word *affitto* is written on the last day of the month, until 1918, where it changes from *affitto* to *pagamento d'ipoteca*. I could never throw these out—not with my great-grandfather and grandfather's notes scribbled on them—so I flip through them, placing them carefully back in the box without wrinkling or tearing the pages.

I'm the sole custodian of our family history, and not because anyone asked me to be. The truth is, no one else is interested in the contents of these dusty old boxes, nor do they want to store them. I'm the only Angelini who treasures these old documents and is inspired by them.

My sister Tess has no patience with anything antique. Even her home decor is sleek and modern: Ikea meets Richard Meier. Tess rebelled against Mom's interior decoration, ornate English and French, in our family home in Queens. Jaclyn has a streamlined Swedish look in her condo—Gustavian, with distressed furniture and neutrals. Alfred and Pamela are New Jersey chic, a rambling faux farmhouse filled with highly polished Ethan Allen. I don't think any of them have attics or closets filled with junk.

They prune as they go. Pamela would take one look at these old calendars and recycle them.

I flip through 1912, looking at the styles of the time. In less than a hundred years, the world is completely different. They thought they were mod back then, with advertisements for cars with rumble seats and bathing costumes made of fine wool.

I have a separate box of my great-grandfather's sketches. I often refer to them when I'm drawing, as they are the template for our couture shoes, each named after the heroine of a famous opera. For eighty years, there were six key designs, until Gram added a seventh in 1990. Occasionally I get out his sketch pad, but I did a thorough transfer of the drawings from paper to computer, because I didn't want to add wear and tear to the delicate drawings, done in his hand with charcoal and ink.

As I pick up the last calendar to replace it in the box, a sheet of thick sketch paper falls out of it. A woman's dress shoe is drawn in meticulous detail. It has a slim, stacked heel, and it's made of woven leather, with an ornate flap on the top of the shoe, modified from a Louis XIV style. The toe is rounded, while the vamp is sleek. It is unlike any of the designs in my grandfather's hand. He sketched in an architectural fashion, and his renderings have actual measurements printed carefully next to the components and notes written in Italian, specifying grommets, velvet piping, laces—whatever the requirements of the shoe might be.

This shoe, however, is pure fancy. You could hang the drawing on the wall—it's artful and loose, playful and fun. The shoe rests on a cloud, with a thunderbolt indicating a storm underneath it—a powerful image, almost like an advertisement. In the corner of the drawing, I see the signature of the artist. It says:

Rafael Angelini

I've never heard of a Rafael Angelini. I find this odd, as I know all the names of my cousins in Italy. My grandfather was an only child, like my mother. My great-grandfather, Michel, had sisters. There was Zia Anna, Zia Elena, and Zia Enes. No Rafaels. And, as far as I know, none of their children were named Rafael.

Maybe my grandfather designed under the name Rafael. Maybe under a pseudonym, he let go, created with abandon, designed whimsical shoes, fashionable shoes, courant shoes. Maybe he even had the idea, long before I did, of developing a line of shoes that could serve a mass market. But why wouldn't I know this? Surely this would be part of the family story.

I look closely at the drawing. This was definitely not drawn by my great-grandfather's hand. There's another Angelini. But who is he? I lay the drawing carefully on the bed, so I'll remember to ask Gram about it.

Then, I open one of Gram's prized possessions: a turquoise leather case with a white patent leather top. There's a gold metal handle and a buckle on the side. I snap it open. It's filled with record albums.

I can't believe Gram left her collection of Frank Sinatra records behind. Gram never collected china or silver, or Hummels or Lladro; her only vice was The Chairman of the Board.

The dust jackets of the Sinatra LPs are stored alphabetically in the case. They are uncompromised and untouched by time. I would wager there's not a scratch on the record albums inside the sleeves. There's even a pristine chamois cloth folded neatly in an envelope inside in the lid to dust them before playing them.

I remember when Gram would stack the records on the turntable, and the automatic plastic arm would slip across to hold them in place. Then she'd carefully turn the knob, and like magic, one record would drop, the needle would slip over to the outside groove, and then, suddenly, the house was filled with music.

When we were children, we were pretty much allowed free rein with anything in this house, except the Sinatra albums. We were allowed to play Louis Prima and Keely Smith records, or Boots Randolph instrumentals, or even the Perry Comos, but the Sinatra collection was sacrosanct. Only Gram could load Sinatra on the hi-fi.

These were the songs that played through my grandmother's youth, courtship, and married life. When Sinatra was young, so was Gram. She was a bobby-soxer, only twelve years old when she bought her first record in 1940, with "I'll Never Smile Again" on the A side and "Marcheta" on the flip side. She danced to "For Every Man There's a Woman" at her wedding to my grandfather.

My mother remembers Gram taking her to the Fulton Record Shop and waiting when a new album was to be released. Gram was a diehard fan, but she left the sound track of her life before Dominic Vechiarelli behind, which says everything about her desire to start over. All that's left of her years of stewardship over these albums is the nostalgic scent of the old record shop: high gloss ink and plastic. If I needed proof of my grandmother's ultimate intentions, it is here, in my hands. She's never coming home.

I lift out her prized albums and sort through them. I prop them across the headboard of her bed. The covers are a fest of Frank. Sinatra in a single beam of light in front of a microphone; young, thin, and totally sexy. Sinatra illustrated pulp fiction style in vivid tones of turquoise and magenta, on the runway with a TWA airplane behind him, extending his hand to a woman whose lacquered red nails rest in his hand. Another with a sky blue background with a photograph of Frank wearing a dapper fedora. As I shuffle through the collection, Frank Sinatra gets older, but he never loses his luster. The images of the glamorous past get to me. So, I throw on my parka, grab my glass of wine, and head up to the roof, balancing the glass on the stairs as I unlatch the door.

The winter clouds have rolled away, and all that is left is a night sky of the deepest blue, the same shade as the ink on Gianluca's letter. I go to the edge of the roof and look down across the West Side Highway. The blinking red lights of a police car parked by the pier look like ruby buttons on black suede boots. Even this roof feels different since Gram left. It doesn't feel safe any longer, it feels as though it can't be trusted—as if the clouds opened up and carried her away.

This is the biggest change for me. This roof, with its tomato plants in summer and snow drifts in winter, was our sanctuary. In the fall, we would roast chestnuts on the grill, and sit by the fire, waiting for the nuts to cook through, and pop open with a soft crackle. The scent of the iron skillet on the fire and the sweet chestnuts was always a comfort.

I look over at the grill, covered in an old tarp, and wonder if I'll bother to make the trip over to the Chelsea Market to buy a sack of chestnuts to roast. Will I continue to do the things that Gram did, the rituals that brought us such joy? Will I commit to keeping the treasures of the past alive in the present?

With every crate I unpack, with every box I sort, the list of things I must do grows. There's the business, the building, the family obligations. I think it's time to pull the Roncallis together and dole out the traditions, the recipes, and the assignments; to be as specific about who will do what as my mother has been in labeling her jewelry, each piece marked with a name and stored, to be given out after the moment when, God forbid, she passes on.

As I look over to the Hudson River, the expanse of black water seems to widen in the dark, like a pit of velvet quicksand. But I don't feel consumed by my river, or by this night sky, nor do I feel small, standing downstage of the skyscrapers that loom behind me like black daggers. It's the boxes in my grandmother's bedroom, filled with everything my grandmother was and is, that overwhelm me. Papers, contracts, photographs, articles, sketches, and documents filled with the history of our family and the company that made us. Our history can only be told through the things she saved, and now that Gram is gone, it's left to me to decide what's worth keeping.

5

Polka Dots and Moonbeams

GABRIEL BIONDI WAVES TO ME from our booth in Pastis, where we have a standing breakfast date once a month, because if we didn't keep to this schedule, we'd never see one another. Gabriel works nights at the Carlyle, and I work days in the shop, and rarely do the two schedules intersect. We chose Pastis because it's the closest thing to a French bistro we can get in Greenwich Village. And while we live in New York City happily, once in a while we like to pretend we're in Paris.

The antique mirrors, black-and-white-checked tile floors, and polished oak tables give the restaurant the down-home feeling of a warm, expansive kitchen. I weave through the chatty crowd. A couple of tables are packed with men in suits, but the rest are neighborhood locals who come regularly for the best eggs, bacon, and brioche in the Village.

Gabriel gives me a kiss on the cheek, his jet black hair tucked under a beret. He wears a fitted black cashmere sweater over jeans so tight they show off every hour he spends in advanced spin class at the gym. Gabriel has turned his shape into an upside-down triangle: wide at the shoulders and slim at the hips. "I got the poached eggs for me, and I ordered the French toast for you."

"Of course you did. That's why you have no ass and I do."

"I have an ass. It's just pert and shapely. Like a new peach, I like to say. Or I've been told." He helps me off with my coat. "I want to know everything."

I peel off the rest of my winter layers and pile them next to Gabriel in the booth. "You first. How are you? How's work?"

"They cut my hours. Not good. But I have time to think about my life. Excellent. And I have time to focus on my friends. Even better. Where's the letter?"

I open my purse. I store Gianluca's letter carefully in a second envelope, preserving it like a butterfly saved in a ziplock bag for fifth-grade science class. The onionskin stationery is as delicate as wings, and I don't want anything to smudge the ink or tear the paper. After all, this is a document of intention, and I'd like to honor any coming my way. "Be careful."

"Relax. A love letter from Gianluca Vechiarelli is hardly on par with an original Shakespeare manuscript."

"Yeah, well, Shakespeare never sent me a sonnet. This is all I got."

Gabriel unfolds the letter carefully and reads aloud.

" '*Cara Valentina.*' That's a sexy start. '*Please accept my apologies for tonight at the Inn. I was carried away with emotions that I have been feeling for quite some time.*' Boy, he wants you in a big way. '*You could not know of these feelings, for I had not admitted them to myself.*' Smart man. Mention feelings upfront. Reel her in. '*But when I saw you at the church . . . I was filled with . . . great longing.*' Longing. Huh. Aka: pent-up sexual attraction that can only be released via you, my youngish American. '*I have not had the true love I had hoped for . . .*' Translation: Never had it but now I've found it, and guess what? You're it! You're his true love. You! Cara Valentina. It's right here in navy blue. Might as well be a marriage license, sister. '*Your beautiful face.*' He's a goner. '*Reciprocate the feelings . . .*' Good. '*Longing to kisses.*' Hot damn. Marry *me*, Gianluca. '*Do you feel as I do?*' Wow, that's direct." Gabriel gives me the letter. "He's in love with you."

"Do you think?"

"I *know*. Look, a man doesn't show up at a hotel full of family, especially *your* brood, and find the exact room you're staying in and almost seduce you unless he's *cuh-ray-zee* about you. Tommy Tanner wants you so badly he'd risk running into your father in the bidet just to be with you. Think about *that*."

"I don't want to fall for him." The truth is, I don't have time for any man right now. I've got a business to run and a new one to build. The last thing I need is a distraction. "I can't fall for him."

"Too late for that, sister."

"I live in New York, he lives in Italy," I say.

"There are airplanes."

"Come on, Gabriel. It's an impossible situation."

"That's why you carry the letter around like a Dead Sea scroll. It's so impossible that you have to reread his letter over and over again to remind yourself why you can't possibly fall in love with him. Face it, you already like/love him, and you like/love thinking about him."

"I don't want to like/love. I want to be the kind of person who just has fun and doesn't get all wrapped up in it."

"You mean the opposite of what you had with Roman."

"Exactly," I say.

"Well, that was different. Roman works in a kitchen, and people are always hungry. You really couldn't compete with that. It's primal. Gianluca, on the other hand, is a tanner, and once he cuts a few hides, he can take a break. So you've got a better scheduling situation with him, although there's the geographical problem—two countries, two hearts—but really, do you need him underfoot twenty-four/seven?"

"Not right now."

"So enjoy the attentions of an older man. And read the letters. Handwritten letters are a sex life in and of themselves."

Gabriel is right. I read the letter right before I go to sleep and imagine what Gianluca is doing. I hear the inflection of his voice when I read, and I feel his intent. Then I think about him, and how we happened to get to this place. I remember every detail of my visit to Arezzo when we first met, how he was gruff and didn't seem to like me at all. And then, how he made excuses to be with me during my visit, how attentive he was, and how he would make plans, pick me up, drop me off, check to see if I needed anything. And then when he came to Capri, I was swimming, and he suddenly appeared by the pool, a welcome surprise. I was broken-hearted and pining for Roman, but that did not deter him. He's trying to build something with me. Why can't I at least let him try?

Gabriel continues, "Just enjoy the man. Why does everything have to be an emotional circus? Keep it simple. If you can. If you want to."

"Okay, Doctor Love. I get it. So, how about you? Are you seeing anyone?" I ask.

"No. And it's brutal out there. The competition is beyond fierce. Look at me. No one in his right mind would dare kick sand in my face on Far Rockaway beach, but have you noticed? Every guy that checks the 'Yes, I'm gay' box these days is in perfect physical condition. Our BMIs are probably close to our shoe sizes—and that's a national average. Every single homosexual man in America is buff. When did this happen? And why? Now, all of a sudden, if you're gay, you have to attract a mate with your *personality*. You have to be charming to find a boyfriend. Well read. Fascinating. The bod isn't enough."

"You've got a problem, then."

"I know. It's back to the New York Public Library for me. I might wind up having to read David Foster Wallace's oeuvre just to be in the loop. By the way, I'm out of my apartment May first," he says.

"What happened?"

"Well, I was never officially on the lease. It's a sublet—you know my cousin Joey. It's his place, and now that the rents have plummeted, everybody wants to move back into the city, including Joey. And since they've cut my hours at the Carlyle, I have to make some cuts of my own. I'd like to pay less rent, so this is a good time to move. Chelsea Boy may become Hoboken Hottie."

"You can't leave the city! All the glamour would go—sucked right off of the streets and into the Holland Tunnel, courtesy of your moving van."

"Ain't that the truth? But I have to stay open. Realistic is the new black. From now on, it's beauty on a budget. And that might even mean the other B word: Brooklyn. I know, I know. Italian Americans spent a generation trying to move *out* of Brooklyn, and now we're moving back *in*. It's insane."

"Are you open to any offer?" I ask. "You could come and live with me."

"Are you serious?"

"I have all that space. Three bedrooms! Two empty. I miss Gram. I wander around the roof like an old pigeon looking for crumbs. I traipse from room to room with nothing but my memories to make me smile. Besides, my love life only exists on paper. The mail comes once a day, and Gianluca only has so much ink in his pen. I need you."

"Living together might ruin our friendship."

"Why?"

"I don't know." Gabriel's eyes widen at the possibilities of moving in to Perry Street. I watch him scheme.

"We'd see more of each other," I offer.

"We did live together in college," Gabriel reasons. "And I broke you of your worst habits then: wet towels on the floor . . ."

"I have a drying rack now."

"Good. And how's the coaster situation?"

"I never place a cup of coffee on a bare table. I've grown up. I respect wood grains. Always a coaster."

"Wow. You're playing hardball here. This is very tempting," he says.

The waitress serves us our breakfast. Gabriel sprinkles Tabasco on his eggs. "Tabasco burns calories. I even brush my teeth with it."

"I'll keep that in mind. Another reason for you to move in—with tips like these, I'll look like Kate Moss in six months."

"A year," he amends.

"Look, just think about it. I mean, if Prince Charming comes along and drives you and your personality away in his Bentley, that's one thing. But if he doesn't, why not come and live with me?"

"Soirées on the roof . . . under the stars . . . Jersey in the background. I love a roof."

"You can grow roses up there."

"The thought of a trellis on a rooftop is almost irresistible." Gabriel butters his toast with the smallest smidge while I pour a quart of maple syrup on my French toast.

"Think about it?"

"Can I paint?" he asks. "I'm a man who loves to dimple his own stucco."

"Do it. Paint, stencil, decoupage! Anything you want," I promise him.

"Your ceilings are high, and I'm into wallpaper."

"Wallpaper is great."

He leans in. "How do you feel about a classic toile wallpaper with foil accents? You realize I've never had an entire house and roof garden to decorate."

"Now you do, my friend."

My brother Alfred, now a few days in as my partner, still seems surprised at how complex the business of making shoes can be. He responds to the challenges of the Angelini Shoe Company in the same way he rose to valedictorian of his college class. He sits at the desk with his back to June and me as he combs through ledgers in a concentration so deep, it's as though he's studying for a make-or-break final exam upon which his future depends. Occasionally he types into his laptop.

When he was a boy and wanted to learn something, he'd go to the library and immerse himself in research. He'd carry home stacks of books and plow through them. Never one to get by with general knowledge, Alfred's goal was to burrow *into* a subject and come out the other side an expert. Our mother marveled at his intelligence, and used to say, "I don't know where he came from." Then of course, she'd take full credit and say, "I *am* his mother."

There may be a potential upside to our partnership—he may challenge me to find better ways to do my work. I don't know if I could work any harder at designing and building shoes, but maybe I could work smarter.

"We should call Mike to come in and help us with the shipment," June says as she surveys the shipment for McDonald's bridal boutique in Boston. "Your mother packs shoes like a pro."

"She buys them like a pro, too," Alfred says from his work, without looking up.

"Gee, Alfred. A joke." I nod, impressed.

He turns and faces me. "I'm not the worst person in the world, you know."

"Now, now, let's not have any personal feelings in the workplace," I remind him.

Alfred breaks a slight smile.

"Oh, you two are downright docile. There used to be real battles in this room. And I was the referee. Believe me. Your grandparents would go at it—and Big Mike would get so angry, he'd throw the iron against that wall. One afternoon, it almost hit the cat."

"Buttons," Alfred remembers.

"I never worried about that cat. He could take care of himself. They adopted him from the street, and truthfully he needed to be in the zoo. Feral. Used to sleep in the trashcan. But he definitely got his bad attitude from your grandfather."

"Gram doesn't remember the fights." I hold down the pattern paper while June cuts the leather.

"Widows never do. Grief wipes out all bad memories. After your grandfather died, she wrote to the Vatican to have him canonized."

"No way." Alfred laughs.

"Nah, but she would've. She blamed herself for everything that went wrong between them after he died. I had to remind her that he was human and made mistakes just like the rest of us."

"Like having a girlfriend on the side," I say. "This is a particular weakness in our family."

"Maybe, but that was the least of it to your grandmother. She didn't care about that. She cared about stability. Home was on the second floor, and she never took her work problems up those stairs at night. And this is a rough business. You have to show up every single day and produce. It's not easy. I felt for both of them." June places the pattern paper and the leather in a stack for me to sew.

I place a finished kid leather dress shoe on the brushes. I pump the pedals with my foot as the brushes whirl rhythmically, evenly buffing the leather. Small striae of the palest pink begin to peek through the vamp of the eggshell pump. I concentrate on making the patina even. I stop the pedal when the pink is the exact shade of a new dogwood blossom. As I lift it up to the light, I realize that Alfred stands beside me.

"I remember when Grandpop used to buff the shoes on that machine. You're pretty good at it."

"Surprised?" I'm so used to snapping at my brother in self-defense, I do it even when he pays me a compliment. "I didn't mean that," I tell him. "I meant to say, Thank you."

The phone in the shop rings. June's and my hands are full, so Alfred picks it up.

"Angelini Shoes," he says.

I look at June. I'll bet it's the first time in my brother's professional life that he has picked up the phone like a receptionist.

"It's Mom." Alfred gives me the phone.

"Checking in!" Mom says. "What's going on?"

"June wants to retire."

June chuckles as she sorts straight pins and shakes her head.

"Don't let her," Mom says.

"Too late."

"Valentine, listen to me," Mom says. "June has threatened to quit for years. We give her a good long three-week vacation and she comes back fresh and says, 'I don't know how people lead lives of leisure.' Okay? She's not going anywhere."

"Tell your mother I mean it this time," June says.

"Ma, she means it this time."

"Put her on the phone," Mom says.

I bring the phone to June's ear. I can hear my mother through the receiver. June says, "Uh-huh . . . " And listens. Then June says, "Okay, all right, Mike . . . Uh-huh . . . Okay, then. Good-bye."

I take the phone back from June.

"It's all settled," Mom says to me. "June wants a nice break this summer. So you need to get ahead of the game in the shop. I'm coming in to help out."

"When?"

"As soon as I take care of some things around the house," she says.

Mom is fibbing. She doesn't have any chores in Queens. Her house is in tip-top shape down to the hand-polished brass door-knobs she made my father install when she saw them in a layout of an English manor house in *British House & Garden*. Mom is simply buying time to plan her glamorous working-girl wardrobe. Mike Roncalli does not set foot on the island of Manhattan without planning her outfit down to her underwear. Her highest dream is to be snapped unaware by trendspotting Bill Cunningham, the *New York Times* photographer who takes pictures of chic New Yorkers on the street.

"Look, I was an Angelini before I was a Roncalli, and this is a family business. With your brother there, it's all about unity. We all have to roll up our sleeves to help out."

I hang up the phone. "She's coming to work."

"Mom?" Alfred says. "Really?"

"She needs a project. And guess what? We're it."

Now that I've shored up the staff with a plan to add Mom into the mix (so June can stockpile patterns in advance in order to take her long summer break), it's time to focus on the *Bella Rosa*. A long walk on the river to think things through is just what I needed to face the work ahead. The March sky, the color of driftwood, reminded me that spring is here, and with it, the urgency of meeting deadlines on the annual calendar. The fashion world works a full year in advance, and every moment counts as we plan the new line.

As I hang up my coat, I hear Bret and Alfred inside the shop having a lively discussion about the New York Yankees. It sounds like an argument, but I can never tell—when men talk sports, they show a range of emotions rarely exhibited in other parts of their lives.

My brother and Bret have always gotten along on the surface. When I broke up with Bret years ago, Alfred made it very clear that he thought I was making a huge mistake. But, as in most things, Alfred will usually take the adversarial position when it comes to me. His disapproval wasn't as much about Bret as about my inability to embrace the responsible, expected path—marriage to a nice, respectable breadwinner and all the claptrap that comes with it.

Bret and Alfred share the same working-class background, and both were brilliant in school, top of their classes. They even followed the same personal path: they married, moved to the suburbs, and each had two children. They appear to have a lot in common, but I know them both well, and Bret brings empathy to his aggressive business style, while my brother is ruthless. Our new arrangement, with Bret advising me on raising capital, will require some diplomacy, and the middle child (me) will play the middleman.

June left work a couple hours ago, and I skipped dinner to mentally prepare for our first meeting with Kathleen Sweeney from the Small Business Administration. I interrupt Bret and Alfred's sports talk. "Whose idea was it to have a night meeting? I'm beat."

"Kathleen is really backed up at work. It would take weeks to get a regular appointment—I finagled this because she owes me a favor," Bret says.

"Now, we're not committing to anything in this meeting, are we?" Alfred asks. There's a tone of suspicion to his question.

"Alfred, if we're going to grow, we have to be aggressive. There's not a lot of cash out there, and while I'd prefer not to take a loan, we have to."

"Have you looked at investor funds? Other sources of revenue?" Alfred turns to Bret.

"Absolutely. But you know the climate at the banks."

"Yeah, I do," Alfred says impatiently. "That's what worries me. The banks are gouging people, ramping up interest rates."

"I hear you," Bret says.

"Just so you do," Alfred carps.

I look at Alfred. "Hey, Bret is trying to help here."

"Look, Alfred, there are options here. The SBA is looking to support small business. You'd be foolish not to entertain the idea of a low-interest loan to finance the production of the *Bella Rosa*."

"I'm not a fan of taking on more debt," Alfred grumbles.

"But if it yields results, what's the problem?" Bret says.

Alfred senses he is being cornered, two against one. So I say, "Let's see what she has to offer."

"Fair enough." Alfred leans back on the work stool and folds his arms. The showdown between the traditional banker (Alfred) and the Wall Street wonder (Bret) has been diffused for the moment. I hope this Kathleen is on her game. She'd better be, to deal with Alfred.

The buzzer sounds, and Bret goes to answer the door. I open the business file Gram left for me because I don't want to make eye contact with my brother. He can't seem to let go of his old image of me, and refuses to accept that I might know what I'm doing. I won't let him rock my confidence. I can't. The stakes are way too high right now.

"I'd like you to meet Kathleen Sweeney," Bret announces.

Alfred stands and extends his hand. "Nice to meet you," he says.

Kathleen smiles at Alfred. She's petite, with an athletic build, around thirty, with short, layered red hair. She wears a Max Mara coat. Good sign—she knows quality. Her tiny nose has a few freckles, and she has bright green eyes. She comes straight off a poster for the Aer Lingus Welcome to Ireland campaign.

Bret helps her out of her coat. She wears a classic navy blue wool suit with a peplum jacket and a white blouse underneath. She also wears understated gold jewelry, small hoops and simple cross on a chain around her neck. But the gold is real.

"I'm Valentine." I extend my hand.

"Great to meet you. You submitted the loan proposal. Very thorough work," she says.

"Thanks." I look at my brother. He definitely heard the professional compliment thrown my way.

Bret sits down next to me, Kathleen takes the work stool at the head of the table, and Alfred sits across from her.

Bret looks to me to run the meeting. He gives me an encouraging smile that says, *It's your show.* So I step up.

"Kathleen, first of all, thank you for coming over to the shop. It's important that you see the operation firsthand, so you might understand what we do here, and how the Small Business Administration can help us grow."

"You make custom wedding shoes." Kathleen pulls her laptop out of her shoulder bag.

"Yes, we do. And we've been here, on-site, in Greenwich Village since 1922. Our great-grandfather started the business in Italy in 1903, and moved it here to this building, where we've been ever since. We're a family-run operation, but we've employed five to ten additional workers over the years."

"I see that you were in profit last year. But you have quite a debt load."

"Our grandmother took out various loans and refinanced to keep the shop running after our grandfather died," Alfred explains, cutting me off before I can answer.

"So, like every other business in the United States in 2010, you have no cash, but you have a great product and the vision to grow," Kathleen says wearily. Clearly, she's not moved by my enthusiasm; she gets this same spiel a thousand times a day from people just like me who need loans from people like her.

This is a big lesson to learn, and one I have to take in. I operate in a small custom world, and while the craft of handmade shoes consumes me, in the greater universe, our company is just a blip. I have to make Kathleen understand why Angelini Shoes is a special place with a one-of-a-kind American product. "Kathleen, we're not just any shoe company."

Kathleen looks up from her laptop.

"—we've got something very special here."

Alfred smiles. "That's exactly right. And I would also add, there's a great young designer behind the brand." He indicates me. "I recently came on as CFO after twenty-three years at Merrill Lynch."

"So you shored up the think tank." She looks at me. "That's very smart."

"We think so." I haul out the old Roncalli family solidarity, even though my tender ego would rather not. My mother would be proud.

"So, what have you got to show me?" Kathleen looks around the shop, taking in the contents, the machines, and the workspace with a very different eye than what I'm accustomed to. Kathleen is no dewy-eyed bride-to-be here for a fitting, or a customer who wants a one-of-a-kind creation; she's a tough businesswoman who has to discern the viability of my product in the marketplace against all the other applicants vying for the same pool of funds. However, I've got something none of the other businesses have. The power of the shoe.

"I like to let the shoes do the talking," I tell Kathleen as I open the large cabinet behind the worktable and remove seven boxes that contain the prototypes that make up our line of shoes. Bret and Alfred help me carry them to the table. "My passion is in the contents of these red and white striped boxes."

Bret and Alfred help me lift off the lids. I unwrap the gold standard of this company, the exquisite hand-crafted shoes, stored in their pristine cotton sleeves. I know that Kathleen could travel the five boroughs and beyond and never find shoes as magnificent as the ones we make here. When it comes to my work, I know what I'm talking about, and I know how to sell them.

Kathleen's eyes widen as I give her the samples to examine. But in one glance, I can see I've got her. No woman can refuse the glamour of a couture wedding shoe, the kind of thing that would make her Cinderella for a day. She sighs when she holds the *Lola*, marvels at the leather treatment on the *Ines*, wants to try on the *Mimi* boot, can't take in the embroidery on the *Gilda*, she's so blown away by it, comments on the simplicity of the *Osmina*, and then, when she picks up the *Flora*, she's sold. "I always wanted a ballet slipper in calfskin," she says. "Always."

"What size is your foot?"

"I'm a five."

"How lucky. You're the sample size!"

"I always do well at sales," she admits. Kathleen slips off her boot, and slips on *The Flora*.

Alfred and Bret, in full corporate mode, are visibly relieved.

Gram used to tell me that she could tell exactly what kind of customer she was dealing with by the shoe she chose from our collection. A woman who went for *The Flora* was modern, impetuous, and stubborn. Without saying a word, Kathleen has just told me who she is, and now I have the insight I need to close the deal with her. This is a woman who knows what she wants, and moves in to get it—I have to work fast with her. She makes decisions quickly, and from the gut.

Kathleen models the shoes in the freestanding full-length mirror. I watch how she looks at her leg and ankle and the shoes now on her feet. She doesn't look at her body in the critical way that most women do. There's something different in the look in her eye as she scans her image in the glass. Kathleen, unlike most women who've been in the shop, likes what she sees.

"We know we have something special here," I say with warmth and enthusiasm, remembering salesmanship is as important as a great product. "And we're building upon years of experience and quality craftsmanship. Even the big guns uptown agree." I hand her the press kit that Gabriel helped me put together after we were featured in the Christmas windows at Bergdorf's. "But we know we have to grow the brand and make a product that's accessible to all women. And that's the *Bella Rosa*."

I go to the shelf and pull three samples of the *Bella Rosa*, one in pumpkin suede, one in sailor blue leather, and one in chic violet microfiber.

Maybe because it's nighttime and lower Manhattan is doused

in a fog, or maybe it's that the work lights over the table illumi-
nate the shoes to their best advantage while the rest of the shop
recedes in shadow, but whatever the reason, the vivid tones of the
Bella Rosa explode in the light, like diamonds in a Tiffany
window.

Kathleen grabs the violet *Bella Rosa*. "I would totally buy this
shoe!" she says.

"Good. Because your loan will help us put them into production," I say, knowing my job is done. I shoot my brother a look of
pure triumph.

"Where are you on that?" Kathleen examines the shoe.

Alfred takes my cue and opens his research file. "I've had
some conversations with American manufacturers, but our initial
run isn't large enough for them. There are some interesting alter-
natives in China, and I have sent them patterns and samples to get
some bids going."

"I'd like to keep the manufacturing in the United States," I
pipe up. Alfred has been trying to convince me to go to China for
the manufacturing, but I know how Gram would have felt about
that. We're an American company, and I'd like to keep it here, to
honor our tradition and keep the jobs in Greenwich Village.

"The China bids are often half of what it would cost to make
the same shoe here," Alfred says pointedly, talking more to me
than Kathleen.

"I understand." Kathleen looks at Alfred. "If you can make
your shoes according to existing agreements with foreign countries, and it's profitable and economical, why wouldn't you? But
we're also looking for our piece of the pie." Kathleen turns to me.
"Could you do any of the labor here besides the design? We like
to keep as many jobs stateside as possible."

"I could definitely do packing and labeling here. Maybe some
finishing—bows, piping, embellishments. But we need a real factory for the numbers we're hoping to achieve."

"What are you looking at for your first shipment?"

"Ten thousand pairs."

"That's fairly ambitious. So . . . you're looking for a loan to finance the first ten thousand?"

"Yes."

Kathleen types some numbers into her laptop. I look at Bret, who lets me know that I did a great job. As Kathleen squints at her screen, I pray silently that she will come through.

"We can do that," she says.

I clap my hands together. "That would be great."

"I'm going to need a timeline." Kathleen types into her laptop.

"And we need to review the terms of the loan," Alfred pipes up.

"Of course, of course." Kathleen closes her laptop and gives Alfred her card. "Give me a call—we'll make an appointment for you to come in, and you'll be off to the races." She turns to me. "You are not invited. The highest and best use of you is right here in this shop making these glorious shoes. You let us worry about the rest."

"I don't think I've ever loved anyone so much in my whole life," I exclaim.

"That doesn't say much about us." Bret points to Alfred and then himself.

"Well, you guys are all well and good, but Kathleen has the money. And now, we're going to have the *Bella Rosa*."

I spent about an hour at Kate's Paperie on 13th Street searching for the best stationery upon which to write to Gianluca. Every time I reread his letter, I find something new. It's good to be adored.

When things go well at work, it frees me up to think about

my personal happiness. When there is a problem in the shop, I become consumed by it, and I don't rest until there's a solution. Gabriel says the downfall of women is that no matter what we achieve in our work lives, we don't feel successful unless we have a man at home. I argue with him about this, because I don't believe it. I'm not that kind of woman. For me, fulfillment comes from taking a scrap of leather and cutting it to the specifications of a pattern, carving a stacked heel from wood, and sewing trim on a buttress. There is nothing like the satisfaction I get when I make something with my own hands.

I am my best self, the most alive I can be, when I'm creating in the shop. I would never admit this to a man I was interested in, but it's the truth. Love is not the main course in the banquet of my life. It's dessert. My mother would say that's why I'm still single. And my sisters would say that I'm lying. But I know this to be true, that love is my *treat,* my tiramisu, because I'm living it.

I have not been tempted to scrap my life in Greenwich Village and get on a plane and go to Italy to be with Gianluca, even though I crave the idea of him. I know about women who drop the lives they lead in one place to go and be with a man in another. I'm fascinated by their impulse to choose the possibility of love over the certainty of work. I would never leave my work behind for a man, no matter how scrumptious he might be. I am, however, interested in romance on my own terms, and in my own time. I'm no master craftsman when it comes to love, strictly an apprentice in training.

I dump four different boxes of stationery onto the kitchen table. There's the classic airmail blue onionskin paper, a box of note cards with various sketches of Palladian villas (too Italian), a box of plain white stationery with a black mock grosgrain trim (too Upper East Side), and finally, plain ecru note cards with a simple embossed gold heart. I'm going with the onionskin.

March 5, 2010
Dear Gianluca,

*When I was twelve years old, Sister Theresa Kelly FMA
required me to write the Prayer of Saint Francis of Assisi twenty
times in order to commit it to memory. It worked. I will, when
I see you again, take you through the poetry of God's instrument
of Peace. In the meantime, I first and foremost would like to
thank you for the most beautiful letter any man has ever written
to me. I am humbled by the simple beauty of your words. Your
feelings are real and true. Now, I'd like to tell you about mine.
I was not looking for love, and I'm still not sure if I should be.
I think about you constantly, and even in my mind's eye, you
thrill and excite me. Could this be love? I don't know. Could it
one day be love? I don't know the answer to that either. But
I surely wonder what would have happened that night at the
inn. And here's what's true for me: I dream of the possibilities.*

Love,
Valentine

I cross out the *e* in Valentine and replace it with an *a.*

Gabriel looks out the window on the Saturday commuter train to
Chatham, New Jersey. I balance a paint set for Maeve's birthday
party on my lap, while Gabriel holds the Eloise compilation,
wrapped in pink tissue paper and tied with green yarn.

"You're not over Roman," Gabriel says.

"Why do you say that?"

"Because you won't give it up for Gianluca."

"I thought my letter was funny and tender."

"It was filled with doubt. An *I don't know* here, an *I don't know*
there. What do you know? Certainly not the contents of your
human heart. You didn't know nothin' writing to him. And Saint
Francis? Who mentions a saint in a sex plea?"

"What should I have said?"

"For starters? Not *that*. The letter should have been filled with erotica. You either want the man or you don't. Or maybe this ocean between you is just too big. Maybe you need a local love. What about Roman?"

"What about him?"

"Maybe you should go back with him."

"I'm not going to get back together with Roman just so you can get a seat in his restaurant."

"It's as good a reason as any."

"For *you*. Forget it. I'm not calling him."

"Maybe he's done with Becky Bruschetta . . . ," Gabriel muses.

"You mean Caitlin Granzella."

"He only went with her because she was easy pickings. She's *there*, working for him in the restaurant. That should be a lesson to you. A man eats what's in the cupboard."

"Listen to me, Gabriel. Roman and I are done. I have no strings to pull over there any more, so fall in love with somebody else's osso bucco already. There are a thousand Italian restaurants in New York City—"

"Ca'D'oro is pretty spectacular."

"Furthermore, if you love me, and I think you do, you don't want me to spend my life following my husband around to make sure he's faithful."

"You need to get real. And fast. A man can only be faithful in the beginning. You cannot sustain fidelity beyond a month. Six weeks max even if the sex is otherworldly, electrifying, and explosive. Magical sex. But that's why they call it *magic*—because poof, in an instant, it disappears like Siegfried and Roy's white tiger. No, the truth is, you have to watch your man like a hawk. Any man. I know. I *am* one."

"I don't have trust issues," I assure Gabriel.

"Really," he says.

Before I can argue the point, the train pulls into the station in downtown Chatham. It's blustery and wintry cold in March as we deboard. I pull the directions out of my pocket. Mackenzie and Bret's house is just a couple of blocks away, according to the map he drew.

We make the turn up Fairmont Avenue. Staying on the sidewalk, we pass lovely homes, which, even in barren winter, have manicured lawns and evergreen touches in the landscaping.

At the top of the hill is Bret's home, a stately red brick Georgian with two white pillars anchoring a glossy black door with brass embellishments. It's the best house on the block. The street in front of the house is packed with cars. It's a big party. An enormous bunch of pink balloons tied to the railing sways in the wind.

As we climb the steps, there's a wreath of white baby roses on the door dotted with small gift packages wrapped in gold. Glittering white letters spelling out MAEVE are fixed in the flowers. More handmade touches by the perfect mother; and I know one when I see one, because I grew up with the best.

"I hope the book I brought is enough to cover the plate." Gabriel rings the bell. "This looks fancy."

We hear music and chatter and laughing and kids whooping inside. Gabe takes a deep breath. "I hope there's a bar."

Bret's wife, Mackenzie, opens the door, balancing her toddler, Piper, on her hip. "Valentine, Gabe," she says. "You made it."

"The ride was delightful," Gabe says.

Mackenzie laughs. "Now you know why I never go into the city. Well, there's also the fact that I don't want to leave the city once I'm there."

Mackenzie is willowy, on the sporty side, with blue eyes that match her cashmere sweater. Her blond hair is the color of ginger ale, and her legs are still tawny from their midwinter trip to

Disney World in Florida. She wears a simple beige wool skirt and matching Tod's flats.

Maeve, the birthday girl, is dressed like a fairy, with net wings that light up anchored to her shoulders. She peeks at us and then runs past when she sees it's two grown-ups.

"Bret! Your friends are here!" Mackenzie calls out. "Come on in," she says to us.

Gabriel shoots me a look at the mention of "your friends."

Mackenzie has never really accepted us because we were part of Bret's life before she was. To be fair, I wouldn't want any ex-fiancée hanging around my husband either. Her demeanor with us manages to be warm, yet simultaneously chilly, like the first full day of spring.

According to Bret, Mackenzie made it very clear that she wanted marriage and children from their first date, so their romance progressed at lightning speed a year after our breakup. But those were the years when books like *The Rules* and *Marry the Man of Your Choice* topped the best-seller lists; women felt pressure to issue ultimatums, and men felt like they had to cave in, or at least Bret did.

It's as if Mackenzie caught Bret in a butterfly net in Manhattan, carried him into New Jersey, and let him loose directly into the pages of *House Beautiful*. Even with children running around and a party in full swing, the house is neat and in order. The foyer, with a small toile-covered bench and an enormous silver-framed mirror, sets the stage for the rooms beyond it.

Mackenzie has decorated the house in a polished and under-stated way. The furniture is Georgian, all sleek lines and black polished wood accents. A delicate chintz of mint green and beige covers the sleek sofas. The straight-backed chairs have striped seat cushions, with a bit of navy blue trim thrown in to complement the wood. An oval Berber area rug trimmed in navy gives the large room a cozy feel.

There are plenty of polished silver frames filled with family moments on beaches, at parties, and in high chairs. Over the mantel hangs an oil painting of Mackenzie in an elaborate bridal gown. It's obvious that she, like me, grew up idolizing Princess Diana. The portrait is right out of the Great Hall of Althorp.

Bret comes out of the kitchen and is happy to see us. "You're here!"

"I only come to Jersey for corn . . . and for you." Gabriel gives him a pat on the back.

Mackenzie hands Piper off to Bret. "Make yourselves at home," she says as she goes into the living room to corral the kids.

We've had an awkward past, Mackenzie and I. I wasn't invited to their wedding, but after they had been married for a year, Bret invited me out to dinner with them. In the spirit of lifelong friendship, Mackenzie put aside her apprehensions and I dropped my judgments. We were actually fine with one another and had a lot of fun.

Bret is the kind of man who has to have everyone in his life get along. He can't abide acrimony. He wouldn't even break up with me until I promised that I wouldn't hate him forever. Of course, he couldn't rest until he knew I was happy for him and approved of his choice of wife. The truth is, I think Mackenzie is the best woman for Bret.

Piper reaches for me, and I take her in my arms. She puts her arms around my neck. The tension in my body goes as she holds me close. Her skin has the scent of apricots. She rubs her cheeks on mine. Babies are a balm.

"Where's the bar?" Gabe asks.

"In the den at the back of the house." Gabe disappears through the door. "My folks are dying to see you," Bret says to me. "They're in the kitchen." He points.

The kitchen is filled from counter to table with Fitzpatricks. When they're home in Queens, they gather in the kitchen, and evidently, when they go anywhere else, they gather in the kitchen as well. I have many memories of their family dinners, a table full of cousins, aunts, and uncles. There was always lots of laughter, plenty of beer, and hearty casseroles at their table. Bret comes from a close family like mine.

"Valentine!" Bret's mother throws her arms around me. Mrs. Fitz looks like Mrs. Santa Claus. She has smooth pink skin, not a wrinkle on it, and thick, white hair. She's always been warm and dear, and since the day I met her, she's been on a diet. Her husband is tall and lanky, like Bret, and he's nuts about her. "Look, Bob, it's Val."

"So great to see you." I kiss her on the cheek. "And you look great, both of you." I kiss Mr. Fitz.

"Look at him," Mrs. Fitz mock complains as she turns to her husband. "He eats the same amount of fudge I do, and he's a beanpole."

"You know men. They got us coming and going, especially when it comes to metabolism."

"You look wonderful." Mrs. Fitz nods in approval. "Slim." Mrs. Fitz and I have a brand of banter that's all about our figures and what we eat and how we look. I wonder what she and Mackenzie talk about. "Are you seeing anyone?" she whispers conspiratorially.

"Kind of."

"Is it serious?"

"Could be."

"Oh, good for you." Mrs. Fitz squeezes my hand. In one grip, I fill in what she's thinking: sorry it didn't work out with Bret, but life goes on, so go for it.

"Hey, everybody. The Pirate is here," Mackenzie announces from the doorway of the kitchen. "You don't want to miss him."

The kitchen drains of Fitzpatricks, followed by Gabriel, until Mrs. Fitz, Mackenzie, and I are left alone.

"It's a great party," I assure the hostess. "The invitation was beautiful."

"Mackenzie made them herself," Mrs. Fitz says proudly.

"Thanks. My old career in advertising comes in handy." She smiles. "It's my way of staying creative. You know, making necklaces out of Cheerios is only so fulfilling."

"Oh, don't you worry. It all goes by like a shot—and you'll remember these days and wonder where they went." Mrs. Fitz takes a cookie from the Lazy Susan.

An awkward silence sets in.

This is why I don't come to the suburbs. Mothers have a lot to talk about with one another, but what can I converse about with them? Making shoes? How can I relate to their daily lives? Wives and mothers already know the answers to the big questions that loom before a woman when she's unattached and focused on her career: Will love find me? (It did.) Will that love make a family? (It does.) Their world seems complete, renovated, redecorated, and fully loaded. Everything is *done*.

A stay-at-home mother in the suburbs can plan her life for the next fifteen years. The markers are determined by the children themselves, and the calendar follows: the school year, summer vacation, birthday parties, camp, holiday breaks, and piano lessons. A stay-at-home mother knows weeks, months, and years in advance what life has in store for her. There's an order to family life. In contrast, I have no idea what lies ahead. I don't even know what the next six months will bring, much less the coming year. When it comes to a long-range view for my life, I'm still figuring out which pattern to cut.

"Bret is really optimistic about your company. I haven't seen him this jazzed about a business plan in a long time," Mackenzie says.

"It's an exciting time for us. And it's exhausting. I mean, not as exhausting as children . . ."

"Oh, it's a different thing entirely," she says. "I used to put in twelve-hour days in the office, and still have enough energy to meet Bret for dinner and clubbing. Now, I'm bone tired by six o'clock. Stay single. Keep your freedom. This is all overrated. Bret has all the adventures in the family," she jokes.

But is she kidding? I can't tell. "I'm sorry about the late meetings at the shop." I realize that the statement sounds suspicious, so much so Mrs. Fitz raises an eyebrow. I cover quickly, throwing my brother into the mix to make everything seem innocent, which it *is*. "Bret and Alfred are a real think tank. They're brainstorming with the Small Business Administration, doing the loans, raising the money. I do the heavy lifting by making the shoes."

Even Mrs. Fitz seems relieved that I dug myself out of that one.

"I should make you a pair of shoes to thank you," I tell Mackenzie.

"Size eight," Mackenzie says. "Someday, I'll need them. You know, when I'm back on Madison Avenue trying to impress clients, instead of hiring a pirate for birthday parties."

Pirate Billy Bones stands before the mantel in the living room. He's the handsome actor, David Engel on dry land, dressed up like Captain Hook without the hook. He has a blacked-out tooth and wears striped MC Hammer pants and a pile of gold chains around his neck. A wide-brimmed hat with a plume matches the stuffed parrot on his shoulder. At his feet rests a large plastic treasure chest. The children gather closely around him, while the adults form a semicircle just behind their offspring.

Gabriel sips his drink, takes in the pirate's opening joke, grimaces, and pivots back to the kitchen. Gabriel may not like children, but he enjoys children's theater even less.

Bret puts his arms around Mackenzie as they laugh at the pirate shtick. But Mackenzie tenses and, after an awkward pause, removes his hands from her shoulders. Bret continues to watch the show and places his hands in his pockets instead.

I wonder if she has any idea that Bret was being pursued by his sexy assistant last year. I think not. Mackenzie is *appropriate*, and the truth of that is dramatized in every nook and cranny of this party. She invites all of Bret's family over, including Uncle Rehab, the dry drunk. Her largesse is admirable. She makes sure everyone is comfortable, that the food is delicious, the bar well stocked, and the entertainment fun. She really is a wonderful wife, straight out of a storybook. But does she *want* to be?

Is there a perfect life waiting for any of us? I always believed it until, of course, I took the trip to *out there*. Here in Chatham, sadness has a different hue. Mackenzie doesn't struggle with survival, as I do in the city. She struggles with her unmet potential, or the nagging question, *Is this what my life was supposed to be?* I imagine she doesn't have an answer. If she did, she would embrace her husband, and she certainly wouldn't complain about making necklaces out of cereal. But something is going on out here, and it's not the dark suburbia written about in my mother's magazines. This is about personal fulfillment and the best and highest use of an intelligent woman's time.

This is the dilemma that hangs over this birthday party like the hand-painted mural of clouds and breaking sun on the ceiling in the breakfast room. Mackenzie is not happy.

"When are we leaving?" Gabe whispers in my ear. "I can't eat one more carrot stick dipped in ranch dressing. I even had the cotton candy."

"What do you think of the pirate?"

Gabriel checks him out head to toe. "Cute. But he's straight."

"Well, that's that. We're outta here."

Pirate Billy Bones takes his final bow. The children stand and jump up and down, screaming in gratitude.

We weave our way through the guests to say good-bye to Mackenzie and Bret and their girls.

Maeve gives me a big hug while Piper extends her chubby arms to me and falls out of her mother's embrace into mine.

"I could take them home," I tell Mackenzie.

"Anytime." She laughs.

The foyer is cluttered with pink goody bags.

"Do not take a goody bag," Gabe says.

"It's rude if you don't."

"Do we need a Little Mermaid blow-up beach ball and a SpongeBob tabletop croquet set? Sorry. Pass."

The commuter back to the city arrives right on time at the tiny station just off Chatham's Main Street. I climb up the steps and see that the train is mostly empty, yet I have a hard time deciding which seats to take.

"What's the matter with you?" Gabriel chooses our seats. "There's no first class on a commuter. Just grab anything." He takes the window, and I sit down next to him.

"Something's wrong," I say.

"No kidding. You look ashen. Oh, no. Was it the guacamole?"

"I didn't have any."

Gabriel pounds his chest lightly. "I did."

"What *didn't* you have?"

"A makeout session with Uncle Rehab. But he wanted to—believe me. I know why he drinks."

"You do?"

"Closet. In it. Can't get out." Gabriel shrugs.

As the train careens out of Chatham and rolls through Summit, a strange feeling comes over me again.

I can't describe it, but I'm troubled about something. I'm unsettled by the party. By the conversations. By the atmosphere.

I close my eyes and imagine the party again. And then, I remember when Piper fell into my arms and held me tightly. There was something about that moment that was profound. Something happened when she hugged me and wouldn't let go.

I've held a lot of babies, and done my share of babysitting my nieces and nephews, but this embrace, from this little girl, was entirely different. It had meaning beyond the moment. Dear God. This isn't the cry for motherhood women get, is it?

6

April Played the Fiddle

Cara Valentina,   *1 aprile 2010*

I just returned to my new home. I took the rooftop apartment in the old printing press off the square in Arezzo. It has many aspects of the original architecture but is restored with all the modern conveniences. The floors are gleaming squares of white granite that, when hit by the sun, nearly blinds me. I will be shopping for rugs in Florence.

I had dinner with Teodora and Papa this evening. My father is so happy. He is devoted to Teodora. You are not to worry about her. They fill their days with long walks. They cook together in the kitchen. They go to Mass every morning at the church, and according to my father, after they pray, they return home to make love. What a life!

Tonight, at dinner, the conversation was about you. I hope you understand that your grandmother has great faith in you and holds your talent in high esteem. Also, it is important for you to

know that I have not discussed my feelings for you with them.
And it isn't because of our families. It is out of respect for your
feelings, and the hope that they will grow.

Love is built in a series of small realizations. It begins with
a laugh—yours, the first day I met you in our shop. I heard
your laughter long after you were gone. I still do. Then, your
face, which I remember in detail, even as I write this. How
beautiful was your expression of wonder when you held the
fragile silk façonné at the Prato mill. I carried that image with
me when you returned to America. I still do. And then our
kisses. A kiss (not the stolen kisses in Capri, but the kisses at
the inn, where it was your idea and mine, as it should be) holds
the meaning of love. I dream of yours and of you.

Love,
Gianluca

"What do you think?"

June places Gianluca's letter carefully on the cutting table as though it's a yard of rare duchesse satin.

She removes her reading glasses and leans back on the work stool. "You haven't been with enough men to know about love letters. These babies are rare. I never received a letter like this. And trust me, I would have liked to. The man is into details. And he has vision for your future together. He thinks things through."

"It's almost too much. I can't believe it."

"You take every salesman that walks into this shop at his word—why not Gianluca?"

"It's like when I was a kid and I'd eat too much white chocolate—I knew I'd had enough after one bite, but I wouldn't stop. I'd eat the whole bunny and then have to lie down. I get the same feeling when I read his letters."

"You can't be serious."

"I don't know. But I'm glad that I have the time and the distance to think about it. He's there, I'm here."

"How convenient. There's an ocean between you and him that you can fill with excuses *not* to fall in love. I know an avoidist when I see one. But listen to me, sister. This man is one in a million—make that a billion when you factor in worldwide over-population. And not just because he's tall and handsome and Italian, my favorite food group, but because this guy knows what matters to a woman. Some men go their whole lives long and never get it. This one gets it and writes it down and mails it to your door. You don't know what you have here."

"Oh I think I know what I've got. I just don't have any idea what to do with it. When it comes to men, what do you want, June?"

"I always hoped to be seen. You know, not a spotlight thing, I got enough of that when I was a dancer. I'm talking about something deeper. I want a man to see me for who I am."

"That's the problem with these letters. It's like he's talking about a goddess."

"That's how he *sees* you. He's describing his experience of you. I got news for you—that's what love is. It's how he sees you—not how you see yourself. Be the love object. And for Chrissakes, don't object!"

"All right, all right."

"I mean, you want him, don't you?"

"Of course."

"Part of getting what you want out of life is knowing exactly what to ask for." June points at me and winks like a gunslinger in an old western. "What are you looking for?"

"I was hoping I'd recognize it when it came my way."

"This man is for real."

"You're like Tess and Jaclyn. They believe in 'the one.' You meet a good man, fairly young, and then . . . that's it. Forever."

There was a time in my life when I believed in "the one." That, of course, was back when I had it. I'd known Bret all of my life, and then I was in my twenties and had dated him since high school, and then we got engaged. I thought that's what happened to people—they grew up with a boy, then after years of being together and spending lots of time with each other's families, continued the relationship into marriage. Most of the women I know followed that formula, so of course I figured that I would too. And I did, until I found something in my life that would require more of me than teaching school, which I enjoyed, or working in an office, which I didn't. When I decided to become a shoemaker, I had to sacrifice everything—weekends, a social life, and all the things that a woman must do to make a traditional life. I just couldn't see how I could do both—and Bret, at the time, didn't either.

June places the letter on the table. "A man who can seduce with a turn of phrase will not disappoint in the bedroom." June gets up and pours herself a cup of coffee. "We have all been waiting for this one, honey. And if I were you, I'd hurry up and I wouldn't be late. Gianluca's riding in on the night train, and the last place you want to be is the wrong stop. I'd be waiting with my bags, and by God, I'd get on board. I'd take that ride *for* you if I could. I have moments, even now, when I'd try. But he's for you. You take Gianluca and run with it."

"It sounds like I need to yank the emergency cord on the train."

"The only urgent thing in life is the pursuit of love. You get that one right, and you've solved the mystery."

"And I thought when I could figure out a way to survive in this shop by the labor of my own hands, *that* would be the mystery solved."

"Two different things. Work is survival, and love sustains you. You can have work anytime. But love? Not always."

"Why didn't you ever get married, June?"

"I didn't want to."

"Maybe I don't want to either."

"No, you do," she says quietly.

"How can you tell?"

"Women who take care of old people are the marrying kind," she says.

"Gram took care of herself."

"Yes, but you looked after her. It wasn't a chore, it came naturally. Same with me. Nobody else calls me when I walk home from work in the snow. You always do."

"Dear God. I sound pathetic!"

June laughs. "Not at all. You nurture people—and we need you to. But you don't think about yourself enough. And time is passing—it really is. And when you get old, it passes even more quickly, like a lead foot on the accelerator. I hear old people on TV say they don't have regrets. I have about a thousand."

"Name one."

"I would have asked for more. I would have *had* more."

"But June . . . "

"I know, I know, I feasted my way through fifty years of men, all sizes, shapes, and proclivities. God only knows how many miles I schlepped and continents I crossed in the pursuit of pleasure. And when I look back over all the years, and all the men, I would have liked for just one of those men, to sit down, pen in hand, and tell me what he saw when I walked in a room."

June looks out the windows and off into the middle distance.

"No, I had to *guess*. I had to fill in the blanks." She whistles softly. "But you? He's told you plain, right here on paper, what you mean to him. And if you can't take these words in now, put the letter aside and reread it tomorrow when you've had time to think. Trust me, this Gianluca won't come along again, not in your lifetime." June picks up the letter and hands it back to me. "Unless you know something I don't."

June perches her reading glasses on her nose and reads the work list. I pick up a shoe and measure the welt to attach it to the heel. June opens her box of straight pins on the table, then takes her pinking shears out of their chamois pouch and places them on the table. She pushes the work stool under the table with her knee, she loads a bolt of raw silk on to the roller, and I help her snap the dowel and close the traps.

We are two women with so much more than friendship in common. We work together, and while I'm supposedly her boss, the truth is, she is mine. June knows more about the world than I ever will—and in matters of love, she would never mislead me. Teacher to student, she has never told me anything but the truth. Maybe I don't believe Gianluca's pretty words because he's Italian and they're known for their fleur-de-lis approach to life. Maybe I need hardware and nails when it comes to love, not the gentle curves of filigree. Maybe I don't think the pretty stuff is strong enough to hold.

"I've always maintained that this house could use some drama." Mom sits on one of the red leather bar stools behind the counter that separates the kitchen from the living area in Gram's apartment. "Everywhere." She thumbs through *Interior* magazine, tearing out "looks" that she thinks I might like. "The old homestead needs a total redo."

"We'll ask Gram."

"You don't have to. She turned the building over to you to do whatever you want. Go wild. Reinvent yourself in a new environment. Have some fun!"

My life is now developing a theme. Evidently, I don't have enough fun. June wants me to spice up the bedroom, and my mother, the decor. It dawns on me that Mom has another motive entirely. "Has Dad put the kibosh on your renovations in Queens?"

"That has nothing to do with it. But yes, he has. When it comes to interior design, your father is a joy killer. He'd have the same bicentennial red, white, and blue shag carpet from our den in 1976 if I'd let him. He's like his mother in that way. When you vacuum her rugs, there are permanent grooves in the carpet where the furniture is placed. Actual pits. Your father doesn't get that surroundings matter, and that change keeps you fresh, young, and on your toes. You wouldn't wear the same clothes every day, would you?"

"No," I lie. I look down at my uniform: jeans and work smock.

"Then your home shouldn't either. The same curtains for thirty years? Come on, people. Might as well live in a HoJo's lobby. When your father got the prostate diagnosis, the first thing I did after I overhauled his diet with lycopene was to study color therapy. After intense research, I painted our bedroom soft yellow because yellow is conducive to healing. Now, I don't want to take credit for his stellar remission, but you can't tell me there's not a connection."

"There's a connection."

"If only he'd indulge me once in a while."

"Ma. He does everything you want."

"Eventually."

The laptop screen sounds a small series of bells. Then Gram appears on the screen. "Can you see me?"

I sit down and click the camera icon. "Gram, we're here. I can see you!"

"Hi, hon." Gram waves. "Where's Mike?"

"Right here, Ma." Mom puts down her magazine, fluffs her hair, and presses her lips together to release the micro-beads in her twenty-four-hour lipstick. "I'm camera-ready." Mom squeezes onto the chair with me and sees her image on the screen. "Dear God, the lighting is atrocious."

"You look wonderful, Mike," Gram tells her.

"No, I look over sixty. That's what I look. I've been asking every Blue Cross hotline attendant if they have *any* idea who did Susan Sarandon's face work. We are practically the same age, almost exactly, and she looks like she did in the *Rocky Horror* movie while I look like the Rocky Horror."

"I don't think Susan Sarandon had any work done," I tell them.

"Now I feel worse!" Mom throws her hands up in despair.

"How's it going with Alfred in the shop?" Gram looks at me and ignores my mother. I can't believe Gram can pull *that* off on Skype. She knows if we go down the plastic surgery path with my mother, it will be hours on the line. "Are you two getting along?"

"Not bad," I lie.

Gram gives me a look. "Alfred tells me it's going fine."

"Good. I'm glad you checked with him."

"Now, now. He e-mailed me about some tax files."

"Uh-huh." I know good and well that Gram and Alfred e-mail every day. And I know he reports everything I do back to her. But what he doesn't get is that Gram only wants good news to go with her positive new life. He should skip the budget and tax talk with her. "How's Dominic?"

"I'm having the best time here. And our honeymoon. The Black Sea was a stunner."

"Ma, you won't believe it." Mom leans into the screen. "Every time I pick up a travel magazine, there's something about the Black Sea. I never heard of it before you honeymooned there. You're cutting-edge."

"Magnificent. Russian palaces on the coastline—the best caviar I've ever tasted. It was cold, but the water was calm, like a smooth pane of mercury glass. Almost silver."

"I'm so happy for you," Mom says.

As happy as we all are for Gram's new life, and all the things that go with it that she deserves, like amazing trips and an attentive husband, I can't help but wonder if she ever misses making shoes.

"Gram, you know the sketch I found? The one I scanned and sent to you?" I hold up the shoe design by Rafael Angelini. "Do you have any idea who Rafael is? I Googled the name but I couldn't find him anywhere . . . But I did find a Roberta Angelini in Buenos Aires. Do you think she's any relation?"

"She could be."

"Do you know of other Angelinis?"

"Well, there's an old story—but I have no idea how true it is. But your great-grandfather had a brother. There was some estrangement, long, long ago—I think it may have happened here in Arezzo. But I really don't know any details."

"My great-grandfather had a brother?" I look at my mother.

"Don't look at me. I'm only an expert on my family after they arrived in America. Hoboken and forward . . . that's my area of expertise."

I can't believe this. My mother knows the exact count of the family silver, and how we're missing a ladle that she believes was lifted when she invited the Martinelli cousins over for brunch after the May Day crowning at Queen of the Angels in 1979. My grandmother stored and marked heirloom rosaries for each of her great-grandchildren on the day they were born to be given on their First Communions in the event of her demise. This is a family that knows the contents of every drawer, closet shelf, and jewelry box. Our wills are updated like our dental records (and we are fanatical about teeth!). Can it be possible that we have an entire branch of the family, sawed off the old tree for kindling, and nobody bothered to tell us?

"I didn't know much about the brother," Gram says. "They didn't discuss it. And this is the first thing I'm hearing about Argentina."

I just stare at the screen. I want to shout: Yeah, you don't know much—or you just don't remember to share it with me: just like you never told me this building was in hock or that Grandpop had a mistress until you were already in love with Dominic, who you told me about *ten years* after the fact!

I have a notion that if I opened the wrong box in storage, I'd uncover enough family secrets and vendettas to blow the roof off

166 Perry Street. "Well, *I* think it's important. It would appear that there was another shoemaker in the family."

"Why should that matter now?" my mother pipes up.

I look at Gram and then my mother. "Are you serious?" Don't they get it? I'm attempting to grow the brand. I need to know everything about this company and our history. There may be something of value to use going forward—I shouldn't be in the dark. What I don't say is that between Alfred and Gram, I get the funny feeling that's exactly where they'd like to keep me.

"Your mother is right," Gram says. "Let's look to the future. Besides, that sketch wasn't as good as your grandfather's—or your great-grandfather's." She smiles. "Or yours."

"Could you do me a favor anyway?" I ask. "Go to the church there in Arezzo and see if you can find the baptismal records. If Rafael Angelini really was Grandpop's uncle, he'll be there."

"I'm getting chills," Mom says. "Maybe we should consult a psychic."

"Ma, the last time we did, it was a disaster. We gave Aunt Feen a free session, and the lady promised her that she would win Powerball."

"Right, right. And when Aunt Feen didn't win the lottery she wanted to sue the psychic and the gaming commission."

Gram interrupts us. "How is Feen?"

"I went to see her on Sunday." Mom says. "She's as crabby as ever. She signed up for water aerobics at the Y in Mineola. Better she drink pool water than Johnny Walker Red."

My cell phone rings on the counter. I pick it up while Mom and Gram go down the long, lonesome road of life with Feen.

"Valentine, it's Pamela. When did Alfred leave?"

I check the clock. "Around five. He had a bunch of meetings with the Small Business rep downtown."

"He's supposed to be here for Rocco's parent-teacher conference. I have a sitter and everything."

"He's not answering his cell?" I ask.

"It goes straight to voice mail." She sounds completely frustrated.

"I'll track him down. You go ahead to school, and I'll tell him you'll meet him there."

I hang up with Pamela and call my brother. He picks up the phone after a couple of rings. "Hey, Alfred. Call Pamela. She couldn't reach you and said there's some parent-teacher thing at school."

"Oh, no."

"You forgot?" This is not like Alfred at all. He remembers everything—including the grade he got on his calculus final in eleventh grade. "Well, get on the bus, brother. She's waiting for you."

I snap the phone shut, completely annoyed. Along with a partnership I never wanted, I am officially my brother's keeper. What's next? I spend my Saturday afternoons ironing Alfred's shirts?

My mother scans the keyboard on the computer. "How do you shut this off?"

"Are you done?"

"Yes."

I hit the buttons out of Skype. The screen goes black. My mother claps her hands together. "What a trailblazing invention. I just love the 21st century! It's so William Shatner. So Star Trek."

"Do you ever miss old-fashioned ways?"

"Which ones?"

"Love letters written with a fountain pen?"

"Oh, God no. Your father can't spell. He cannot express himself via words at *all*. He tried to write to me when we were young, but I needed a dramaturg to deconstruct his sentiments. No, no, I like how we communicate now. Dutch tells me how he feels to my face. Press a button and my mother's face pops up from Italy. There's nothing like right now, in the moment."

The Small Business Adminstration office is two doors down from the room we are sent to when serving on jury duty. The waiting area is filled with people, laptops out, cell phones on, doing business. I sign in. Whenever you deal with doctors or government agencies, there's invariably a clipboard and a number 2 pencil dangling from a string.

Kathleen pokes her head out the office door and motions to me. I point to the list—there's at least nine names in front of mine. She waves me in.

"I have your paperwork all set to go," she says as she closes the door behind me.

"Already?" I'm amazed and also slightly guilty about the line I just jumped in the waiting room. Kathleen has really been charmed by the Angelini Shoe Company.

"It was a snap. Alfred looked over it and signed it."

"Great."

"Ray Rinaldi approved them and sent three sets back to me for your signature." Kathleen places the documents in front of me and gives me a pen. I sign the paperwork. She stamps them.

"You should have your loan within six weeks. This gives you time to make a deal with a manufacturer."

"I'm on it."

Kathleen stands. "You've been great to work with."

I open my tote bag and lift out our signature red and white striped shoebox. "These are for you."

Kathleen opens the box. "They're gorgeous!" She lifts out a pair of *Flora* calfskin slippers. "I can't possibly keep them."

"Why not? It's not a bribe. The loan has already been approved." I point to a bouquet of flowers with a thank-you card that sits on Kathleen's desk. "We express our gratitude with shoes instead of flowers. Friend to friend."

"I've had a great time working with you and your family."
Kathleen smiles.

I never noticed how pretty she was, or maybe now I see her as
a beauty because she just promised me enough money to make the
Bella Rosa.

I place my copy of the contract in my tote bag. I feel very
guilty when I pass through the waiting room loaded with people
who, just like me, need a loan to survive, and hopefully grow.

I text Bret:

```
  Me: LOAN APPROVED!
Bret: Congrats!
  Me: Thanks to you.
Bret: Now we find a factory.
  Me: In the U.S.?
Bret: Arguing with your brother about China.
  Me: I knew he'd be a problem.
Bret: That's why I'm here. I fight. You make
      your beautiful shoes.
  Me: What would I do without you? I know: I'd
      be in proper therapy!
Bret: You're my therapy. Nobody makes me laugh
      like you.
  Me: Or you!
Bret: xo
  Me: xo
```

Tess, Jaclyn, and I sit in the rotunda waiting area of Sloan Kettering Hospital. Dad is here for his checkup, and Mom seemed
nervous about coming alone, so we all came to give them our
support. You would think, after the diagnosis and months of
treatment, that we would be used to the grind that comes with a
diagnosis of stage-two prostate cancer, but we're not. We live in

fear, but we don't talk about it. We put on big smiles, joke and laugh to keep our parents' spirits up. But all the while we grip the rosaries in our pockets, holding on to the beads, praying for good news every time Dad has to walk through those doors.

We love the word *remission,* and we throw the word *cure* around as our deepest wish (because it is). But cancer is now an official member of the Roncalli family. We don't like it, we didn't ask for it to be born, but it's here, and we have to accept all of it: its cranky moods and unpredictable behavior, its sudden retreat when the doctors try a new drug and tell us to go home and wait for the results. In the meantime, we cope with the toll it takes on our father, who goes from normal to exhausted to sick as the doctors try to make him better.

But today, I'm feeling unusually lucky. With the loan approval, maybe we're on a roll, and things in general will begin to go well for my family. I'm superstitious, though, because I've seen momentum go in the other direction, so I keep my optimism to myself.

"Do you think Dad will get a good report?" Jaclyn asks.

"He looks good. You know, physically."

"Val, he always looks good. The people in our family can be at death's door and they never look sick. They die in the picture of health. You can't count on visuals," Tess says.

"I hope I age like Dad. He's looked the same since he was forty."

"It's the nose," Jaclyn says. "A nose is important as you get older. It holds everything up. Like a tent pole." Jaclyn scrolls through her BlackBerry. "Look. Gram sent a picture of Dominic and her. Check it out."

Gram and Dominic embrace on the deck of a cruise ship. There are foamy white caps on the Black Sea. They are bundled up like sherpas, in down coats, knit caps, dark sunglasses, and thick gloves.

"Are they on their honeymoon, or did they join the Russian mob?"

"It must have been cold over there," Tess says.

"Freezing. Hey, here's one with Gianluca." Jaclyn hands it to me.

I look down at the picture. He's standing by the hood of his car with a peevish expression on his face. Gram and Dominic must have been late to go somewhere. Annoyed or not, he looks gorgeous in the picture.

"Have you heard from him? I mean, any word since I caught him in the bathroom?"

"Yes, I've heard from him."

My sisters lean in.

"Are you Skyping?" Tess asks, trying not to pry, but desperate to know every detail.

"No. We write letters."

"With stamps?"

"Yes, Tess. With ink, stamps, envelopes. The old post office routine."

"Wow. How romantic." Tess says the word without meaning it. Her idea of romance is cards that play songs when you open them, huge floral arrangements, and a diamond heart suspended on a thick gold chain. A handwritten letter is the poor man's way to a woman's heart, and Tess, like my mother, prefers the glitz. "An old-fashioned letter."

"But why?" Jaclyn, not yet thirty, does not remember life before cell phones and e-mail. "How long does the mail take from Italy? Isn't it years? Mom sent us a postcard from Italy, and she'd been home three weeks when the card arrived. Why would you bother with all that when you can text him?"

"He's not a technical guy," I tell them.

"He's old." Jaclyn shrugs, satisfied that she's cracked the Vechiarelli code.

"Yeah, he's older . . . *ish*, but it's not *that*. He really pays attention to the people around him. It matters to him how he spends his time. I don't know him that well yet, but everything he does, everything he says, has meaning. He thinks things through. I've never met anyone like him."

"Do you think it's serious?"

"Don't buy your bridesmaid dresses."

"But Bendel's is having a sale," Jaclyn whines. "I got my eye on a Rodarte sample."

Tess turns to me. "Don't let her push you. There will always be perfect dresses and weddings to wear them to. You make sure he's right for you. Take your time. Eventually, you'll know for sure if Gianluca is The One."

"I hate to disappoint you, but I don't know if I believe in that anymore."

"Of course you do! Look at us!" Jaclyn says. "One Charlie! One Tom!"

"Well, it's worked out well for you guys. I'm different."

"You always say that, but you're really not that different from us," Tess says.

"Believe me, I wish I was exactly like you. You get an idea in your heads, and you see it through. Some people go for the brass ring, and you went for the diamond version. It worked out for you. But I never fall in love with men who do what I want to do. There's always a conflict."

"Maybe this is it. Maybe Gianluca will compromise," Tess reasons.

"When is he coming over to visit?" Jaclyn asks, hoping that gown she likes will still be on sale when Gianluca convinces me to take the next step.

"He's running the tannery alone now. I don't think he can take time off."

"So you have one of these Jane Austen romances where there are letters but no actual sex." Tess sounds disappointed. "No action. Just words."

"Poetry," I correct her.

"What does he say in the letters?" Tess asks.

"None of your business."

I will not make the mistake of showing my sisters the letters from Gianluca. Gabriel's dissection of Gianluca's letter left me stone cold. June's assessment helped because she put her opinion in the context of her extensive life (and love) experience. The last place I'm going to look for validation is my immediate family. I'm long past the days when I have to run everything I'm feeling by my family.

As the last single person in a family of married people, I have become their final frontier, their *project*. They will not rest until I'm taken. I would prefer they use their energy to help Mom install her dream lily pond on Austin Street instead of meddling in my love life.

Mom pushes through the swinging doors that lead to the interior of the hospital. She is dressed head to toe in yellow. Sunshine gold. Mike Roncalli has brought a splash of color therapy into Manhattan's palace of healing.

"Oh, girls! All clear!" Mom embraces the three of us and begins to cry. "Every time I set foot in here and we get a decent report, I realize how completely out of my mind with worry I am every single day. Ordinary life can drain you."

"Yes, it can," I agree.

"It's not the big things, you know—it's the maintenance. But thank God and Saint Teresa, who never fails me, Dutch is all clear for now."

"I'll text Alfred," Jaclyn says.

"Thanks," Mom says, tightening the belt on her yellow princess coat. Something bothers her still. "You know," she says, "your dad notices that Alfred never comes on these appointments."

"He's back at the shop, Mom," I tell her. "He's researching—"

"Don't make excuses for him. You make the damn shoes, Val, and you find the time to come here and be with your father and me. No, your brother doesn't get it. And you know what? He never will! He will hold a grudge against your father until the day he dies."

"Let's hope not," Tess says diplomatically.

"What is it?" Mom throws her hands up. "Why can't children forgive their parents? We don't set out to disappoint you. We really don't. And when we do, we are the first to know it—and as far as I can tell, your father has made reparations. Not that he would use that word—"

"Or pronounce it." I nod.

"But honestly," Mom continues, "the man has made all matters of restitution to me, to his family, to his God. Furthermore, he has tried time and time again to open up the channels of communication with your brother, on Alfred's terms, and he's been rebuffed. Every single time! Daddy isn't selling himself as some perfect parent. He's well aware of his failings, as I am of mine. But for God help me, it's been *twenty* years. It's almost a nonmemory for me at this point. But, for your brother? It's a fresh gash."

"That's just Alfred," Tess says. "You're not going to change him, Ma, don't let it bug you."

Mom considers this. The sadness and anger leave her face as quickly as if she were wiping them off with one of her premoistened makeup sponges. "You're absolutely right. Alfred will get it when he gets it. But, please, my trio of angels, don't let my peevishness ruin your day. You are the best! Each of you have so much on your plates, with children and work and husbands and . . ." Mom looks at me. "Overseas enchantments. Yet with all you have to do, your father and I must have done something right, because you always show up for us."

"Where are we gonna go, Ma? We're family," Jaclyn says.

We sit and wait for Dad to dress and join us, and I think about my brother, and how *somebody* is always angry with him. That can't be good for Alfred. It's sad that he's missing out on this great moment with us. Relief is an instant balm, but it has to be earned.

Alfred ignores the agony, and then he misses the joy. He doesn't make any emotional investment in us. Maybe he saves it all for Pamela and his sons.

Or maybe they, like us, know the truth: none of us are good enough for Alfred, whether we were born after him, gave birth to him, fathered him, or married him. Alfred's standards are so high no one can reach them. I have to remember to tell Bret to keep this in mind. I can't have Alfred derail my relationships at the Angelini Shoe Company because he has unrealistic standards—or because he doesn't want to see the sister who never measured up succeed despite herself.

"I know this is against your religion . . . ," I say into my cell phone. I stand on the corner of 14th Street and 8th Avenue, with one hand over my ear and the other clutching my phone. " . . . but I had to do the modern thing and call you."

"Valentina?" Gianluca could not be happier to hear from me.

"I have good news. Dad got a great report at the doctors."

"*Va bene!*" Gianluca is thrilled by the news, and just as happy to hear from me.

"I wanted to tell you." A bus pulls up at the stop and decompresses with a loud blast as the steps are lowered closer to the sidewalk. "Sorry about the noise. I'm outside. On my way back to the shop."

"The noise is not a problem," he assures me. "I am happy to hear your voice."

"Gianluca?"

"Yes?"

"Be patient with me."

"Valentina."

The soothing sound of his voice, the way he says my name, blankets me. I want to let him know what he means to me, that I couldn't wait to get home and write it on the onionskin paper.

Suddenly, it felt urgent. It only takes a trip to Sloan Kettering to remind me how short life is, and that there's nothing wrong with a little prioritizing. "I'm not as good at this as you are, at expressing myself. I . . ." I pause and think.

He waits patiently until I speak. He doesn't interrupt me. He lets me find my point, and then gives me the time to share it. "I am trying to say that I love your letters. They are very descriptive and honest . . . and I feel so much when I read them."

"*Grazie,*" he says, then amends. "*Mille grazie.*"

"I guess, what I'd like to tell you is to . . . keep them coming. And if you do, I will read them with as much care as you take when you write them."

"Valentina, I must see you."

"When?" I ask him.

"I wish today."

"Me too," I tell him, and I mean it.

"Now, in the shop here, it is difficult. My father is a new man with a new life. The old life holds very little interest to him now. So, I work twice as long each day."

"The same at my shop."

"We're in, how do you say it?"

"The same boat!"

"Right. Correct. That makes us closer still? No?" he asks.

"Yes," I tell him.

When I return to the shop, Gabriel and June are laughing at the cutting table. There is something so natural about the two of them working side by side.

Gabriel wasn't around as much when he lived in Chelsea, but now that he is about to move in, there isn't any aspect of life on 166 Perry Street that he isn't a part of—and that includes the shoes.

"What's going on?" I hang up my coat and look over at Alfred, whose head is buried in a file.

"June is teaching me how to cut patterns," Gabriel says. "I've decided to make the drapes for the living room myself."

"Do you think you can?"

"You should know better than to ask that question. I can do anything I set my mind to."

"He's very good, this guy. Very quick," June says. "He has a real eye for dimension—which is the one attribute every pattern cutter needs."

"And when I choose to learn something new, I insist I learn from the master," Gabriel says.

"Well, that's me, kiddo." June cackles. "Thirty-plus years with these pinking shears. I'd say that makes me the master."

"You feel like a coffee break?" Gabriel asks her.

"Sure," June says.

"I made blondies with walnuts." Gabriel looks at me and Alfred.

"I'm okay," Alfred says without looking up.

"Me too. Late lunch. You go."

June and Gabriel head up the stairs.

"Dad got an all-clear."

"Great," Alfred says.

"You couldn't be more thrilled."

He puts the file down. "What do you want me to do? Dance a jig?"

"No. I'd like you to show up," I tell him. "You've never been to the hospital—not when Dad had the surgery, or the chemo, or the radiation—you just leave it to us. And it's not fair."

"If you remember, I got him into Sloan, and I paid for the extras. I've done my bit."

"You're his only son."

"Yeah, well, that's its own reward, isn't it?" he snaps. "I don't want to fight with you, Valentine," he says wearily.

"No. You're fighting the whole world, and then I'm forced to live in it."

"What does that mean?"

"You don't get along with people. You take a defensive position. Or you issue an order and expect me to fall in line. You decide we're going to make the *Bella Rosa* in China, and that's how it's going to be. You steamroller me, you make Bret unhappy . . ."

"Oh, now I'm responsible for Bret's happiness?"

"When you're working with him, you are. Because he matters to me, I value his opinions, and he's stepped up for this company."

"He'll get his commission."

"That's not the point. He didn't have to take us on. But he did. And if we succeed, and that's still a big if, Bret will have been a major part of that. So act a little more appreciative and a little less imperious—if you don't mind."

"You got it, boss," he says.

"If only that were true. But I got the deal with the devil here."

Alfred looks at me. "Now I'm the devil."

"You can be cruel. I don't like the way you treat our dad."

"It always comes back to that." He turns away from me and goes to sit down at the desk.

"If you'd only make an effort."

"It's not gonna happen." Alfred sits down and props his face on his hand and opens a file. He actually ignores me and goes back to work. So I haul out the big gun, the torpedo of the Roncalli arsenal: guilt.

"Dad isn't going to be around forever."

"That'll be a relief," he snaps.

"Take that back!" I shout.

A rage wells inside me. My brother's deliberate absences make it so much harder for our family to cope with my father's illness. It's almost as if Alfred gets joy in separating from us, from our problems—because as long as he does so, they are not his own. He is not this way with his in-laws. He's dutiful toward them. He's there when Pamela's family is in crisis. He's most comfortable in the role of family member once removed. But with the Roncallis, he cut the tie long ago, and left us hanging.

"If you don't want to make it right with Dad for your mother, or your sisters, consider your sons. Because I guarantee you, if you don't get past whatever it is you have against Dad, it will visit you and your children."

"My sons are different." Alfred turns back to his work.

Alfred's tone tells me he's done talking about this. If I could throw him out of the shop, I would. I don't know how long I can handle having him around. We try to get along, or rather, *I* try to get along with *him*, but I find myself either tiptoeing around the land mines or stepping on them, then dealing with the aftermath of the explosion. We have spats over nothing, and then I have to bring the mood of the shop back to normal. On top of my real job, I have another—trying to please Alfred. I have been doing this all of my life, and I'm tired of him.

I'm also furious. So I'm going to talk to Bret about a time line. On days like these, when the tension is as deep as the ten layers of leather on the cutting table, I can hardly do my work. And then, exhausted from the dance, I lie in bed at night and dream of what it would be like to own this business outright. I imagine the shop, debt-free, all markers paid in full. I'm the boss and answer to no one. Someday I will buy my brother out, and then I'll be free of him once and for all.

It took two days to move Gabriel Biondi out of his cousin's illegal sublet in Chelsea and into 166 Perry Street. There's *that* much stuff.

The eight floors of the ABC Carpet and Home warehouse store on Broadway have less furniture than Gabriel Biondi. We

could easily fill an additional building (if we had it) with his possessions. Boxed and crated, or wrapped in batting, each item is
revered.

There are gilt Rococo mirrors, Art Deco hat stands, demi
love seats in matching zebra print, a set of six straight-backed
chairs shellacked off-white with rattan seats, turn-of-the-last-
century steamer trunks that made it off of the *Titanic* and into
Gabriel's collection, Tiffany floor lamps with bronze tree-trunk
bases, and lamps composed of mosaics of turquoise and rose glass,
and framed posters of Broadway shows since *On the Twentieth
Century* and *She Loves Me* were running long on the Great White
Way.

Gabriel stands with his hands on his hips. "I know, it looks
like a gay tag sale. But trust me, I plan to weed out a lot."

"Like what?"

"A set of Minton china with soup tureens."

"You should keep that."

"Why?" Gabriel asks nervously.

"Because it goes with the English riding saddle you want to
mount on the wall."

Gabriel looks around at the skyscrapers of brown paper boxes
in my living room and is about to ask, "What saddle?" when he
realizes that I'm joking. "Oh, ha, ha. *You.*"

"Really, you have more stuff than a holding cell at the Met.
Every period in interior decoration is represented here."

"Except early American. I loathe it. I like Abraham Lincoln as
much as the next guy, but I can't abide major furniture that looks
like it was whittled."

"Me neither."

"I know I have a lot of stuff. But I dream of a summer home
in Bucks County. I imagine it—in full. And everything you see
here is a part of the backdrop of that dream. I see a four-story
white clapboard farmhouse with black shutters on a green hill in

Pennsylvania, surrounded by clear acreage. There's a swimming pool, a patio with slate floors, a kitchen with copper pots and a butcher-block island, and sumptuous interiors.

"I imagine parties in my home with guests who fascinate—Doris Kearns Goodwin and Tina Fey in one corner, with the Coen brothers and Lady Gaga in another. Oh, look! It's Tony Kushner arguing theater economics with Joe Mantello. Michael Patrick King zings with bons mots as Mike Nichols intercepts them. Imagine a tan and freckled au naturel Frances McDormand reading aloud pithy scenes from *Arsenic and Old Lace*, while Bartlett Sher looks on and then gives a Juilliard critique. Afterward, we have grappa and cigars by a roaring fire, and after Mary Testa sings a couple of numbers from *The Rose Tattoo*, we discuss the fate of our national theater—that is, of course, if there's one left by the time I buy my dream house.

"Oh, Valentine, I have big, big plans for my enormous life! And when I'm able to afford it all, and yes, that means buying it all for cash, and installing full-grown trees just like Moss Hart did sixty years ago because I, like he, am not one to wait, I will fill that house with things that matter to me. Decor that inspires me. Furniture that moves me. Basically all the stuff you see right here."

"So what do we do with it in the meantime?"

"We can use it here."

"Okay, how about this. How about you redecorate the living room with your things—these prized possessions . . ."

"They are prizes, believe me."

"I agree. But whatever doesn't fit, or you don't think works, you put in storage."

"Fair enough. I definitely can afford storage because you gave me such a break on the rent."

"I'll offer Gram's stuff to my family. Except the farm table. The table has to stay." I run my hand across the edge of the table that has been the center of our family gatherings since before I was born. I can't imagine this apartment without it. "That's the only rule. This table, in this very spot."

"No problem. I like the table," Gabriel agrees. "But I may want to refinish it."

"Permission granted."

"And we'll keep the chandelier. I've always loved that touch of Venice."

Gabriel and I immediately fall back into our old college room-mate dynamic. It's an easy give-and-take—I let him do whatever he wants, and he rides roughshod over me like a cowboy on horseback galloping through a dry creek bed in the Great Plains during a cattle crossing.

"Is this a record player?"

"RCA Victor. Truthfully, though, I use it for an end table."

"Does it work?"

"I don't know. I never turned it on. We've got all of Gram's old Sinatra albums upstairs."

"Brilliant! I can redecorate to Old Blue Eyes. Francis Albert will be my muse."

"I'm going to go down and lock up the shop," I tell him. "June and Alfred went home hours ago."

"How's the shipment coming?"

"Our twelve-hour days are paying off. Harlene Levin at the Picardy Shoe Parlor in Milwaukee is going to get her order on time."

"Need me?"

"Nope." I go to the top of the stairs, think better of it, and poke my head back into the apartment. "What's for dinner?"

"Chicken Florentine, a fresh tossed dandelion salad with steamed artichokes, and a crème brûlée for dessert."

I place my hand on my heart. "I love you."

"Why wouldn't you?" he says.

I go down the stairs and push the door of the shop open. June left the work lights on over the iron. I move across the room to turn them off, grabbing the keys to lock the window gates as I go. Then I notice that June has already rolled them across the glass and locked them.

I go to flip off the work light. But then I stop, sensing I am not alone.

Someone is in the far shadows of the shop, where we organize the shipping. I freeze. I can't believe the security alarm didn't go off. My thoughts whirl, we're being robbed, who is it, what do they want, what do I do? But the burglars don't move. They don't try to flee. I realize they don't know I'm here.

I squint to see who it might be.

I gasp, letting go of the breath I held in fear. Kathleen Sweeney, who was here for a meeting, is in the arms of my brother. They are kissing passionately, and don't hear me or see me until I step back toward the entrance door to escape and accidentally drop the keys. In the quiet they sound like steel hitting iron.

Kathleen scurries into the bathroom, while Alfred turns away.

"Alfred. What are you doing?" I barely get the words out.

He doesn't answer me.

"What is going on here?" I put my hand to my head, knowing full well what I have seen, yet not wanting to believe it.

Alfred doesn't answer.

I put the keys on the table and go out the shop door, closing it behind me. I climb the stairs—my legs are weak beneath me, but I take them two at a time, wanting to put what I've seen, and now know, behind me.

7

Love Lies

GABRIEL OPENS THE OVEN AND pulls out a rack of fresh scones. The apartment fills with the sweet scent of butter, eggs, and vanilla, which makes me ravenous, and also reminds me of Gram, and the delicious cakes she would make from scratch whenever we had down time in the shop.

Gabriel and I don't chat much in the morning, but we have fallen into a comfortable routine. I put on the coffee, while he retrieves the *Times* from the entry downstairs. He comes upstairs, hands me the paper, and goes into the kitchen. Gabriel is from the Land of the Proper Breakfast. There has to be something hot served, or it's considered cheating. For example, Gabriel doesn't eat a bagel out of the sack or pour himself a bowl of cereal. Breakfast is bigger than that.

A bagel must be *oven* toasted, then served on a platter with a dollop of cream cheese, a fan of smoked salmon, chives, and capers, with a side of fresh-squeezed orange juice. Eggs are on the menu three times a week, either poached or scrambled or whipped into a healthy scrapple of fresh onions, peppers, spinach, and egg whites in a skillet.

I believe my new roommate is adding years to my life span with his healthy eating habits (if I skip the desserts!). I never drank pomegranate juice until he moved in, and now every Sunday morning I have a glass.

Despite all Gabriel's positive influences in the health department, I've been having trouble sleeping. The apartment, usually neat and tidy, is in disarray while Gabriel sorts through his boxes and figures out what to keep and what to store. Down in the shop, June and I do our best to keep the mood light, but it's nearly impossible, since Alfred, who used to invoke my wrath, now drains the same well of emotion leaching my pity. Who would have thought after years of avoiding him, now I'd be *worried* about him.

I can't mention Kathleen and The Kiss to him, and he certainly isn't volunteering an explanation. We never communicated well, and now it's worse. The jabs are gone, replaced with self-loathing silence. I long for the days when I could ignore him, and just do my work. But now he's made that impossible. He has changed. Imperious Alfred has been replaced with a sullen version, practically depressed, and terribly sad.

We need to talk, but I don't know how to broach the subject. It's too painful, or maybe I just don't know what to say. And once we get past the awkward acknowledgment that I know and he knows, what's to be done? Even if we do talk about *her*, I hold no sway with Alfred, so any advice I might give him would be ignored. I have to do something, though, because it's affecting our day-to-day lives in the shop. When we're working, it's obvious his mind wanders and is clearly not on the job at hand, while mine returns to the same subject over and over again: *How could you do this to your family, Alfred? How could you?*

Gabriel sets the table for breakfast while I open my e-mail on the laptop.

The first message that grabs my eye is from Roberta Angelini. The subject line reads:

I Believe We Are Family

I open the e-mail. Roberta Angelini of Buenos Aires knows of Michel Angelini. She writes that she has information that would be "of interest" to me.

What an odd phrase to use, as though she's daring me to open doors that have been closed for generations. But I have more than a passing interest in understanding why there was a schism in my family a hundred years ago, and why the rupture has been buried for so long.

Going through Gram's boxes, I have learned that our family history has been recorded in ledgers, legal contracts, and sentimental letters marking important passages and dates. They do not, however, tell the whole story. There is no record of the reasons behind the decisions made in the documents. There are gaps, and omissions. My great-grandfather wrote his own brother right out of the family story. But why?

You would think that estrangements that occurred a hundred years ago are irrelevant, until I walk into my own shop. I still can't get along with my own brother, and there are times, when I fight with Alfred, that the wound seems ancient. Maybe the answer lies in the past.

After all, history is the energy that flows through our work in the shop. Everything I create is based on the designs my great-grandfather left behind; wouldn't it also stand true that we also carry certain behaviors forward when dealing with one another?

I IM Roberta. "What do you do?" I click send.

A few moments pass. I wonder if she'll give me the brush-off. Then, an instant message pops up from Roberta.

"I operate and own the family business," she writes.

"What business?

"We manufacture men's shoes. We're the Caminito Shoe Company."

Roberta types in the name of her company, just as I do my own. A chill goes through me. "Gabe, you won't believe it. Roberta makes shoes."

Gabriel sits down next to me and reads the e-mail exchange. "This is crazy."

I type: "Would love to discuss everything with you. May I call, or do you prefer e-mail?"

Roberta types: "Send me your questions, and then we'll talk. I have a new baby, and my hours are difficult."

I exit out of e-mail and click into Google. I type in: "Shoe Manufacturing in Buenos Aires." I type in "Caminito Shoe Company." A series of articles about Argentinian shoe manufacturers pops up. My hands shake as I type.

"I can't believe it. I have a cousin who makes shoes, too!"

"Everybody has a twin, you know. Maybe she's yours. Northern hemisphere, southern hemisphere—separated by the equator. I wish we'd found your twin in Rio, though—I always wanted to go to Carnival."

"Sorry, I wouldn't care if she had a mill on the moon."

Gabriel places a cup of coffee with a small scone next to the computer.

"For me?" I place the pressed linen napkin on my lap.

"If you're going to dig up family secrets, you need to eat."

"You're better than a husband."

"Or a wife. Deciding to keep the Minton china made me feel British. I just had to whip up some scones." Gabriel places the jam in front of my plate.

I nibble the buttery fresh biscuit. "You should open a bakery."

"I've thought about it." Gabriel pours me a cup of coffee and then one for himself.

"Can we talk?"

Gabriel sits. "I'll talk about anything—including NASCAR, which I know nothing about—I just don't want to talk about Alfred."

"I'm sorry. I'm obsessed. But it's because I don't know what to do."

"Do *nothing*. You can't be sure you saw what you saw."

"Oh, I *saw* it."

"Okay, for the thousandth time, let's say it was what you thought. That they were kissing. What if it was the first time they kissed?"

"What difference would that make?"

"A lot. Nothing puts the brakes on a budding affair like getting caught in an illicit lip-lock. Put yourself in Alfred's shoes. The only thing worse than your *sister* catching you fooling around is your *wife*. I can't imagine that the Redhead and your brother didn't talk later and say, 'This was God telling us to stop.' "

"You watch too many Lifetime movies."

"I know," he says.

"The tension with Pamela makes sense now. She calls the shop all the time. She can never find him. He forgets to show up for stuff at the school. He's late. And he hides behind the job here. He uses me and the shoes as an excuse."

"So what?" Gabriel shrugs.

"I don't like it."

"Oh, I think you like it a lot. You finally have something on that brother of yours who never did right by you."

"That's not true. I didn't want to find out that my brother was this kind of a guy. I'm very sad about it. And mostly sad about it because he tortured my father emotionally all these years for doing the exact same thing!"

"That's their business."

"Yeah, but the rest of us were dragged into it. "

"Okay, look, I've known your brother almost as long as I've known you. I've always thought he was a little stiff, and I never liked the way he treated you—but I never pegged him as a bad guy. A superior guy? Yes. He was always a snob. And he never failed at anything. Well, he didn't until he left his job at the Bank of All Money."

"He was let go." I correct Gabriel.

"Got it. The only difference between a vice president and a receptionist is that when a vice president gets fired, he gets to spin it and say he left first—they do not extend the same courtesy to the working class. We are, simply put, shit-canned and shown the door."

"Got it."

"What you don't get is that at the age of forty—this is the first time your brother has been shown the door. He has had an enchanted life up until now. And that's worse than taking your lumps all the way through, like the rest of us. We are used to disappointment. We know failure. We not only expect the other shoe to drop, we're there to catch it when it does. We know what it takes to come back from a blow. Alfred really hasn't been tested. And guess what? Now, he's been tested. And he's scrambling."

"I know. And I actually feel sorry for him."

"You know what? I do too. The man is in a pickle. He looks at his life with the wife and the kids and the house in Jersey that costs a fortune—that he's always been able to pay for, and now he can't. Now everything will change. He's looking at cleaning the pool himself, and mowing the lawn himself, and asking Skinny Minnie to go out and get a job to help out, which he never had to do before, and the guy feels like he's been asked to put his balls in a shoe bag. Okay? Your brother is falling apart as he's trying to hold it all together."

"As smart as he is, he didn't see it coming. The collapse. The banking disaster."

"Oh, they all saw it, they just didn't believe it. They didn't want to believe it. And why would they? Who would want to believe that the money would ever stop! And you know, it killed him to have to come here and work with you."

"I know, I know."

"And I will guarantee you that Gram told him in the beginning, Just look out for Valentine, okay? She never proposed a partnership. Gram probably didn't want to bother him, she probably said, Check in on Val at the shop once in a while, help out with the financials—and he said, Gram, it's over at the bank. I need a job. You can't just have me check the books—I need a stake in the thing, because I have no other options right now. I'm telling you as I'm standing here, I swear on my mother, father, and our standard poodle Brutus—all dead by the way—that your brother groveled for this gig."

"You could be right about that. I mean, Gram never mentioned a partnership until we were all in Italy together for the wedding."

"A little late to sit you two down, don't you think?"

"Absolutely."

"So almost on cue, when Alfred is feeling the most vulnerable on all fronts, and like a loser in general, then Missie the Redhead makes the scene."

"Kathleen."

"Yeah, her. Alfred couldn't feel worse about himself; he's watching June cut patterns and you making art, and he's lived a life pushing around a bunch of fake numbers. He's the lowest he's ever been because he realizes that he's spent his life not making anything. Missie the Redhead works for the government in a crap office downtown, and she's ten years younger, therefore ten years dumber, and she looks up to your brother—who probably spun some tale to her like he's gone back to his roots by choice to run this shoe company, and she looked at your brother, with his big life, and all his experience, and his full head of hair, and said, I want me some of that. And that's what she's having down there by the powder room. Some of *that*."

"Dear God."

"And everybody wins—at least in the short term. Your brother is nicer to his wife, the mistress has something to look forward to other than people like you filing loan applications—and Alfred gets his groove on. After the biggest disappointment of his life, he feels smart, scintillating, and desirable again, and then hot sex ensues. And the world goes round. Got it?"

"Oh, I got it." I put my head in my hands.

Gram used to say if you are lucky enough to live a long life, you see everything come and go at least twice. If I had to predict the things in life that I would have seen twice, it would have included a lot of trends: the return of thick eyebrows, the resurgence of curly hair, and the reinvention of skorts. But I never thought I would have lived through Dad's indiscretion twice, and I surely didn't think it would be my own brother Alfred, so wounded by it so many years ago, who would repeat the mistake.

Gram's absence, her move and new life, have never had such impact as they do right now. She was the calm center of our family, the glue. She would know what to say, and what to do— she'd knock some sense into Alfred, as she did my own father so many years ago. But family problems in a long lens aren't nearly as potent as they are when they're percolating in the next room. The distance between our shop on Perry Street and Dominic's kitchen in Arezzo is so far, it might as well be a galaxy away.

No, we will have to sort this one out on our own. And whether I confront my brother or stay silent and stew, as he has done all these years in the shadow of my father's mistake, will be *my* choice. I just wish my brother had made a better one.

I've dragged the last of the garden supplies onto the roof to plant the tomatoes. The potting soil, sticks, and planters are good to go. All I need are the plants, which my dad has promised to pick up in Queens, where they are sturdier and cheaper than the ones I would buy here in town.

I considered not planting them at all this year, but figured it had to be bad luck not to. I don't want to be the first person in my family to cancel the family garden after decades of relying upon it for the August harvest. Even though Gram is gone, the tomatoes must go on.

I pull out my cell phone and sit down on the chaise. I dial Gram.

"Have any luck finding out about Rafael?" I ask.

"You were right. Michel and Rafael were brothers. I scanned the baptismal certificate and sent it to you. And they were about a year apart in age. Michel was the older of the two."

"Unbelievable." I can't imagine what horrible transgression could possibly sever the relationship of two brothers forever. I know there is nothing that could come between my sisters and me. Alfred is different. And maybe part of the reason I want to understand the past in our family is to help me cope with my brother in the present. "What do you think happened between them?"

"I don't know." Gram is puzzled. "I was very close to my father-in-law—I can't imagine why he wouldn't have told me about this."

"It must be something pretty awful."

"Or maybe it's just money," Gram says. "My father-in-law watched every penny. And if anyone ever tried to take advantage of him, he cut them out."

"Well, I'm about to find out what happened. I'm going down there."

"You are?"

"I can't tell enough about Roberta from e-mails. And I want to see her factory. Wouldn't it be something if we could work to-gether?"

"You're doing so much more with the business than I ever could," Gram says wistfully. This is the first time since her wed-ding that she sounds like she misses the Angelini Shoe Company.

"In the end, Gram, we're still making shoes. It's all about the shoes."

She laughs. "I guess you're right about that."

"Gabriel moved in. I hope you don't mind."

"I think it's great."

"I do too. Now, here's the big question. He wants to redecorate. Now, if you don't want him to, I won't let him."

"How do you feel about it?" Gram asks.

My eyes sting with tears. "I guess I'm okay." But I'm not. I'd do anything if Gram would say, "Don't change a teacup. I'm on my way home." But that's never going to happen. Sometimes I think her move to Italy is God's way of preparing me for our final parting, which I do not like to think about—ever.

"Valentine, I was apprehensive about moving over here. I was afraid to start all over again at my age. Yes, I had Dominic here to help me, but it's still an enormous change. But I swear, once I got past the fear and threw myself into life in Arezzo, I feel twenty years younger. Just waking up to different walls—never mind a new husband, a new village—has given me a whole new perspective. I've got a new pep about me. Don't be afraid of change."

"Okay, okay," I say.

"And don't be afraid of color. I always meant to put more color into the rooms."

"Gram, Gabriel is choosing the paint chips—I don't think that's going to be a problem."

The Bus Stop Cafe is empty. The groggy waitress pours us the first cups of coffee from the pot; we're her first patrons at the start of another long day. Greenwich Village is waking slowly, an occasional cab passes by on 8th Avenue, but the streets are empty, and the new morning sun throws very little light on my neighborhood.

Bret pours the cream into my coffee, extra light, no sugar, just like I like it. We used to hang out at the Bus Stop Cafe when we were teenagers, and felt so grown up. Everything has changed in the world, except this diner. The fry cook, the owner, and the waitress are still here twenty years on.

"We're old," he says.

"What makes you say that?"

"The staff."

"Maybe they're old, and we're still young."

"Keep dreaming. You don't have children yet. Now, *that* reminds you the clock is ticking."

"What's it like?"

"Kids? They're the best. They're always happy to see me. They're uncomplicated except when they want something, and then it's hard ball. Mostly, though, they just want to play. What could be better than that?"

Bret hands me a file across the table. "Chan Inc. is the best manufacturer of shoes in Beijing. They build Kate Spade, Macy's private line, and get this: Nike's. They do all styles and materials, and the minimum order is only five thousand pairs."

"Sounds promising."

"Alfred contacted the reps. They need patterns when you can send them."

"I'll scan them and send them right away. I'm surprised he's doing his job at all. His mind is elsewhere."

"Well, you just stay focused. This is all going to work for you."

"You know, good deal or not, I almost don't want to give Alfred the satisfaction of going to China. You know he's been pushing for it. But now I feel sorry for him, so I'm ready to sign on for whatever he wants to do."

"Don't worry about Alfred. If it's a good business deal for you, it's a good deal *period*. No matter where you do production."

"What do you think of Buenos Aires?"

"I've heard it's gorgeous."

"Well, I have another option to present to you. It turns out that I have a cousin down there. Roberta Angelini. And she runs a factory that makes men's shoes. I'm thinking about asking her to expand into women's wear."

"Argentina is known for its superior leather goods."

"That's what I was thinking. And you know I love the family business model. So then I was thinking, we could brand the *Bella Rosa*—you know, made by the Angelini family. We could do the cutting and assembly down there and the finishing here."

"Now you're thinking like a marketing person."

"There's something compelling about a family brand in tough times. It says something. You know, quality, attention to detail, tradition, that sort of thing."

"So, how do we proceed? Do you want me to talk to Roberta?"

"Her e-mail is in the folder. She just had a baby, so she's overwhelmed, but I told her about you—that you were putting together the financing package for us, and that you helped us secure the loan with the SBA, so that she understands that the money will be available once we've found the right factory. When I found out my great-grandfather had a brother, I Googled around and found Roberta. She told me she'd give me the whole story—Rafael's side—when I get there."

"Lot of intrigue in the Angelini family."

"And even more now that my brother is running around," I add.

"It's hard to believe. Alfred is so pious." Bret shakes his head.

"Those are the ones to watch," I say.

"No, you have to keep an eye out on all men. We're all vulnerable. You saved me from a big mistake last year.

"You knocked some sense into me. You reminded me of everything I'd lose if I had an affair with Chase. I was really tempted. She was cute and young, and a lot of fun. Available. And

I was close to messing up my whole life for nothing. I see the guys at work who fool around—and eventually, it catches up with them. The wife doesn't necessarily find out, but you see that they can't handle the guilt. And then all sorts of bad stuff starts happening: drinking too much for one. No, you showed up at the right moment. As you always do."

"I will always tell you the truth—just as you are always honest with me."

"You know, at the time, I actually believed that Chase was attracted to *me*. I really did—and what I realized, thanks to the expression on your face when you saw us together . . . "

"What'd I do?"

"You gave me the old Sister Bernadette scowl from Holy Agony on the roof of the Gramercy that night. The old 'I know what you're thinking, buddy.' Well, it made me think beyond what I wanted in that moment. We have a long history, Val, and you know me. I might see myself as a twenty-five-year-old—but I'm not—I'm careening towards forty, and I'm not complaining about it. Chase treated me like a peer, though, like I still had it.

"But she wasn't interested in me, she was enamored of my power at the office and my position."

"What happened?"

"When the fund downsized, her opinion of me downsized almost instantly. You could say the biggest recession since the 1980s helped me stay faithful in my marriage."

"Funny how that works."

"Anyhow, I've never thanked you. You saved my marriage."

"Why were you tempted? Mackenzie is a beauty—and she's so pulled together. Why would you even look at another woman?"

Bret looks away and out the window. When we used to go together, I remember that look. He really thinks about things, in a way that I can appreciate and understand. We were like-minded then, and we still are. "Things change when the babies come.

And Mac and I didn't have a lot of time together before we had the girls. It all happened very fast."

"What changes when you have children?"

"Well, a woman's attention goes elsewhere. As it should—she's taking care of a whole family. But things become routine. You long for things to be easy again. Uncomplicated. But they're not. It all seems so life-and-death with babies—you run to the doctor, you check for fevers, you're up all night. Mac got impatient with me, and I felt helpless. Pretty soon, you start arguing about little things, and on top of the big things, you realize you're fighting all the time."

"How are things now?"

"With Mac? Better. But they're not kidding when they say marriage is a lot of work."

"Why is it *work*?" The unmarried one wants to know. I don't understand the concept of that; why should love be hard when life is already impossible? Shouldn't marriage be the easy part—after a long day, you look across the kitchen table and feel understood and safe and welcome? "Marriage sounds awful."

Bret laughs, even though I'm not trying to be funny. "Let me explain it like this: Mac has an idea of what life should be, and I have an idea, and sometimes we're in sync, and other times we're not. This is the work part. I married a girl who always had everything she wanted, and she expects the same from me. The way you and I grew up in Queens was different. We *appreciate* the house and the car and the nice restaurant meals. Mackenzie *expects* them. It doesn't make her a bad person—it is what it is. She doesn't know any differently."

"How is she dealing with the changes in your work?"

"She's scared. You know, I'm lucky, because I've always worked to establish new companies and businesses. But when Mac goes to the park, or to the girls' play dates, and she talks to the wives whose husbands went from getting million-dollar bonuses to being unemployed overnight, she hears how tough things are out there. And I think that helps her appreciate what she has. It was a long road to gratitude, I guess."

I take a sip of the coffee and look out the window; the corner of Hudson Street that curls into Bleecker is now bathed in full morning sunlight. The pedestrians move quickly on their way to their jobs, the bus stop is already crowded with folks waiting for the M10. A woman checks her watch, steps out onto Hudson Street, and squints to see the bus approach in the distance.

I come from a family of women who work. My stay-at-home mother occasionally threatened to get a job, but only out of her desire to be relevant in the outside world, not because of financial necessity. My parents lived within their means, in a house they could afford, in a neighborhood of like-minded working-class people, like the Fitzpatricks, who lived just down the block.

My parents took care of everything they had. A car was never purchased new, but used and in good condition. I don't remember a painter or a plumber visiting our home; my father repaired everything himself. My mother even helped my father pour a concrete walkway in the backyard when it was her dream to have one.

My mother aspired, and still does, to possess the finer things of life, but even those markers—a marble foyer, a Jacuzzi in the bathroom, a state-of-the-art kitchen, all the features of fine living and upward mobility—were provided by my father through the labor of his own hands. He did the work wealthy people hire other people to do. My mother didn't sit around while he made things, she became his eager assistant. It may seem that Mom has airs, but she never lived in a rarefied atmosphere.

I remember my parents working together on projects around our house. They made my mother's obsession for a beautiful home a family project. I remember paint chips, and swatches, and Saturday afternoons at the lumberyard, where they'd scheme a new room, or improve an old one. Their marriage is one of true minds—they're a team, and they like figuring things out together. My mother never had a career, but she always had an agenda. And my father dutifully went along with it. So my mother got her dream life, and my father, a purpose.

"There's a real art to a good marriage, isn't there?"

"I think so," Bret says. "Making someone happy is a full-time job."

"Mackenzie's lucky," I say. "But she's also smart. She picked a good guy who gave her everything she ever wanted."

"I hope so." Bret smiles. "Thanks for noticing."

But it's me who is grateful to him—no matter what, Bret Fitzpatrick believes in me—and maybe it's old loyalty carried into adulthood, but whatever it is, I can always count on him. We come from the same place.

The Fitzpatricks and the Roncallis are people who gather in kitchens around a tray of homemade manicotti, not in fancy living rooms where silver trays of canapés are passed. Where we come from, champagne is for toasting, good china is for holidays, and silver place settings are heirlooms while love is given freely, not something exchanged in hopes of material gain or social status. There is something to be treasured about people who know instinctively when enough is enough.

Across the way, the Bleecker Park playground, nestled under old elm trees, comes to life with toddlers on their early-morning play dates. A mother guides a stroller with one hand while pushing the wrought iron gate open with the other. A father, his hair wet from the shower, wears a business suit and holds his son's hand as they walk quickly toward P.S. 41 in time for the bell.

The swings in the park, filled with children, begin to sway, and I watch a little girl, her legs pushing higher and higher as she leans back into the swing. Soon, it seems she might take flight.

Cara Valentina,   *18 aprile 2010*

    I made a delivery of kidskin to the Prato mill and thought of you. I thought about your pink dress and how you looked very much like a peony the day I brought you here a year and a half ago. Signora inquired about you at the mill. I sent your regards. Prada is doing a boot made of velvet and leather for Spring 2011, and Signora cannot get enough Vechiarelli leather.

    I have reread your last letter over and over again, knowing that you are very busy and cannot write as often as I do. Your words stay with me, as does the sound of your laughter. How I long to hear it again. I will call you. The sound of your voice must do, but please say you will come to Arezzo in the summer. The lavender will bloom in your honor—I promise.

                        Love,

                        Gianluca

The workshop is in pre-shipping mode, which means that every surface is covered with open red and white striped shoe boxes. It's like falling into Aunt Feen's pressed glass candy dish, which was filled year-round with peppermint wheels except at Christmastime, when she replaced the old Brach standbys and sprang for the chocolate and hazelnut Baci in the blue-and-silver foil wrappers.

I survey the box count against the shipping lists, propped on the table with instructions. I put down my coffee and flip on the work lights. The gates on the windows have been rolled back. Alfred is already at his desk. It's six o'clock in the morning, and he usually arrives at nine.

"Hey," I say softly so as not to startle him. "There's coffee up in the kitchen."

"I stopped at the deli."

I make space for my coffee on the table. I open the finishing closet, filled with layers of pumps, by size, separated by thin sheets of muslin. The pale pumps, soft calfskin dyed in shell pink, mint green, buttercup yellow, and beige, are stacked by size. The scent of sweet wax and leather fills the air.

"I think we should talk," Alfred says.

"Sure." I sit down on the work stool. I have been dreading this moment, when Alfred actually admits he's having an affair with Kathleen Sweeney and swears me to confidentiality. I'd really like to pretend that I didn't see Alfred and Kathleen together, and life could go on as it has before. It was so much easier when I disliked my brother for the way he treated me. Now I have to dislike him for the way he treats his wife.

Alfred takes a deep breath and says, "I think I should go to Buenos Aires with you."

The look on my face must be one of total surprise. Alfred agreed that I should go when we discussed this weeks ago.

He quickly adds, "I'd like to see the operation there."

"I don't know if Roberta even wants to bid on manufacturing the *Bella Rosa*. And since we may have to send you to China eventually, I think we should keep costs down and just one of us should go. And I think it should be me, because I need to figure out how to put the shoe in production on-site."

"This isn't about your ability. You absolutely know what you're doing," he says.

What's going on here? Alfred has never been supportive of me. Something is up. His tone throws me off guard. "Okay, where's the hammer?"

He looks at me, confused.

"Lower the hammer. You know, this is the moment when you say, 'Just kidding. If I, Alfred, walked out of here, you'd fold in a week.' So go on. Say it."

"But that's not true."

"Alfred, now is not the moment for *earnest*. I need honest."

"You work hard, and you produce. You've kept up production on the custom shoes while developing the new line. You're committed. You're careful about costs. You even took in a roommate who pays rent—and all that helps in running the building and bringing down the debt. I can't be critical of you."

"Well." I think for a moment. "Thank you," I say.

I'm a classic middle child. If someone is nice to me, I'm nice right back. If they're mean, then I can be too. But when behavior crosses over into cruelty, I retreat entirely. So in light of Alfred's lovely observations about my work ethic and product, I feel I should return the compliment. "Alfred, you've come up with good ideas—and I think we're producing at a level we never did before because you're doing our budget and the financials. I mean, I've never done a shipment this size, knowing exactly what it costs, and what we'll make. We never thought about the profit margin. You've introduced real business standards to our company."

"It's nothing special."

"It is to me. I'm grateful to you for all you've done."

"But we still fight," he says.

"We do, and I don't like it. But it's getting better. And I'm completely confident leaving you here to run the shop while I'm gone."

He looks up at me, and the expression on his face is heartbreaking.

"Listen, Valentine. I know you don't really need me in Argentina. I just need to get away."

My brother is suffering. I've never seen him like this. No matter how I felt about him all of these years, and how he perceived me, he's in pain, and he needs to talk.

"Alfred, what is going on in your life?"

My brother gets tears in his eyes. The last time I saw him get misty was at our grandfather's funeral. They were a lot alike, and Alfred felt he was losing the most important man in his life when Grandpop died. Nothing we could say or do would cheer him up. He seems as sad in this moment as he was that day.

"I'm a jerk," he says. "I never intended for anything like that to happen."

"Are we talking about Kathleen?" I ask.

He nods. "I thought I'd go my whole life living in a way that I believed in."

"So . . . it *did* happen." Clearly, I didn't catch a first kiss. I caught a hot in-the-middle-of-an-affair kiss that was about to become more. "What are you going to do?"

"I don't know."

His answer shocks me, because my brother *always* knows *exactly* what to do.

"What do you mean, you don't know?" I say gently. "You have Pamela and the boys. Does she know?"

He shakes his head no. "I haven't let her know *anything* lately. It took me two weeks to tell her when I was let go from the bank. I got dressed every morning and got on the train as usual. I'd come into the city and sit in Central Park and think. And then at five, I'd get back on the train and go home, having rehearsed a way to tell her what happened—and then I'd get home and I couldn't tell her I'd . . . *failed*."

The thought of my brother wandering around the city in a suit with no place to go brings tears to my eyes. He could have come here, to the shop. We could have had coffee at Gram's table. He could have gone to the roof to be alone and think. But Alfred couldn't admit defeat—not even to his own sister.

"Alfred, listen to me. The wolf has been at the door so many times over the years that we invite him in for manicotti. At least we have this business to hang on to, and this little shop might save all of us. Our great-grandfather built something for us, and long after his death, he continues to take care of our family—through these shoes. It's a beautiful thing—not a failure—to work here. We own it. It's *ours*."

"I'm ashamed of myself," he says quietly. "I judged our grandparents all these years. You know, I thought they were simple, and that was a lesser thing—to be simple—to work, plain and hard, till you were so tired your back ached so deeply, you couldn't stand up. Grandpop would put in such long days, working so hard, he had to soak his fingers in ice water at night."

"I remember. The calluses on his fingers never went away."

"And now I'm here. Just like he was—they were. I went to a fancy school and got a big degree, and now I'm back here."

"Is it so terrible?"

"No," Alfred says softly.

"So why are you sad?"

"Because . . . it's not enough."

"Oh, boy." I take a sip of my coffee. "So that's why Kathleen."

Alfred doesn't answer.

We sit in silence until he says, "I'm sorry you walked in on us. I'm a hypocrite. Maybe you even like that I'm one."

"Come on, Alfred."

He looks up at me. "At least let me be ashamed of myself."

"Too late. Self-flagellation is not going to help you now."

"It's over. With Kathleen, I mean."

"That's a start."

"What else can I do? I can't even face myself. I have to tell Pamela."

"Oh God, no! You can't tell her. This is one secret you need to keep until you're dead."

"But I've broken my vows! I have to ask forgiveness."

"What good would it do? Pam's already terrified about the future. She's not a girl who can heavy-lift. She's a good woman and a fine mother, and I'm sure a pretty wonderful wife, but she's not one to stare into the fire and find the meaning. Keep this to yourself. Forever."

"But how can I move forward if I don't tell her?"

"You got dressed and went to an imaginary job for two weeks and never told her! You've proven that you can keep a secret.

You'd only hurt her, and the truth of the matter is you'd end up feeling better and she'd end up feeling worse. As the guilty party, you have to bear the burden here, not Pamela. Love builds in a series of small realizations." I quote Gianluca's letter to my brother. As soon as it's out of my mouth, I'm surprised I retained it, and even more surprised that I believe it. But in an instant, I see exactly what Gianluca meant.

"And then once it's built?" Alfred asks. "Then what?"

"You hold on, I guess." I take a deep breath.

Alfred nods. "That makes sense."

"Try and remember why you chose Pamela in the first place. Go back to the beginning. Think of the things you couldn't live without—and the things you couldn't wait to live with—and then marry her all over again."

"All right, Sis." Alfred turns and goes back to his work.

I wipe my eyes on my sleeve. My brother hasn't called me "Sis" since we were kids. He needs me, and in all my life, I never thought he would.

On top of everything else I've had to learn, I have to learn how to be a sister to my brother again. I imagined battling my brother in our version of the Hundred Years' War for the rest of our lives. For what? For validation. And here it is, the moment when he needs mine.

Talk about shame. I have it. I thought if I ever had the chance to one-up Alfred, I would make him pay, and enjoy every second of his misery. But he's my brother, and his unhappiness and broken heart are as real as my own.

I Skype Gram. Her face comes up on the computer screen.

"Take me through your *pizelle* recipe. I have a little competition going with Gabriel."

"Got a pencil?"

I nod that I do.

"Okay, melt down a pound of butter and set it off to the side. Then take one dozen eggs, three cups of sugar. Beat those together. Then drop in two tablespoons of peach schnapps. Throw in four tablespoons of vanilla. Then take seven cups of flour and eight teaspoons of baking powder—add the dry to the wet. Then, preheat my press—it's in the kitchen . . ."

"I got it."

". . . and take my shot glass—you know, the one with the Empire State Building on it?"

"Yeah."

"That's the one. You dip it into the bowl of batter. I don't know why the shot is the exact amount of batter you need, but it is. Pour batter onto the hot griddle—but in the back, not in the center. And it will spread—and when it bubbles up, lower the top half of the iron down—and then it's seconds before it bakes through."

"Thanks, Gram."

"How's Alfred?"

"He's all right." I smile. "You might even say we've hit a new level of understanding. It turns out that Alfred Michael Roncalli is a human being."

"You didn't know?" She laughs.

"You're the one who made him a saint."

"I think your mother had something to do with that."

"A little. But you're the one who encouraged her."

"True. What did he do that made him human?" Gram asks.

"He failed."

"Even bankers make mistakes." Gram shakes her head. "Was it a doozy?"

"It was. And he was sorry."

"I'm happy you could forgive him."

"I did better than that, Gram, I helped him figure out how to forgive himself."

"I'm proud of you," Gram says, then adds breezily, "Gianluca stopped in this afternoon." Gram's nonchalance is completely transparent. She leans into the screen and whispers, "Am I not supposed to know anything?"

"He writes me letters, Gram."

"That's lovely."

"They are."

"He asks me a lot of questions about you." Gram lowers her voice.

"Really? And do you present me in a fabulous light?"

"Always." Gram laughs. "I may have married a Vechiarelli, but I'll always be an Angelini."

The Angelini Shoe Company resembles Santa's Workshop in the North Pole on Christmas Eve, except it's May and we're on a deadline of a different sort. Boxes lie open everywhere, ribbons with the gold seal are spooled out on the table, and the sounds of packing tape ripping, tissue paper rustling, and our laughter thread through shipping day like music.

I run a tally on the computer as I count the finished shoe boxes and load them into the shipping boxes like I'm stacking precious gold bricks. Gram taught me that shipping is like presentation on the plate when preparing food. You want the recipient to open the box and gasp at the beauty of the contents before they even open a box of shoes. So we use bubble wrap around the edges to hold the boxes, and then over the top, we secure the boxes with a square of red velvet with an embroidered *A* in the center. Harlene Levin at the Piccardy shoe parlor makes throw pillows out of our packing materials—that's how luscious the boxes look when she opens them.

Jaclyn and Tess are wrapping the pumps in tissue paper, placing felt shoe bags over the paper, and closing the lids. My mother affixes the gold medallion dead center on the red and white striped boxes. She is never a millimeter off—she's been doing this since she was a girl.

My father does the heavy lifting. He checks my math, counts the boxes, and then weighs, seals, and closes them. Alfred then places the shipping label on the outside of the boxes and stacks them in the entry, ready for pickup by Overnight Trucks, who we hire to cart our shipment cross-country.

"Dad! Make her stop!" Tess hollers from the back of the shop. "Jaclyn's rumpling the tissue paper."

"Jaclyn, cut it out. You are *not* my favorite angel," Dad chides her.

We laugh. My dad hasn't used that line from the television show *Charlie's Angels* since Jaclyn was a girl.

"What self-respecting Italian Americans name one of their children after the pretty one on *Charlie's Angels*?" June says.

"They were *all* pretty on that show," Mom corrects her. "I will always love Farrah the most. May she rest in peace. She was in my group." Mom considers any movie or television star within five years under or over her age one of "her group"—never mind that she's never met them, she considers them her cultural equal. "We let the children name the baby."

"We almost named you Wonder Woman," Tess says.

"Yeah. That was our other favorite show," I tell her.

"Don't let us interrupt." Pamela stands in the doorway with Rocco and Alfred Jr.

"Hey, buddies!" The boys run to their father.

"I need some help over here, boys," Dad teases them.

"Can I help?" Pam asks.

I look at my sisters. Usually, we never take Pamela up on her offers to help, whether it's yard work or the dishes. But now that Alfred works here, Angelini Shoes belongs to all of us. It may be time to treat her like one of the family and not an in-law.

"What do you like to do?" I ask Pamela.

"Anything."

"I think you're a medallion sort of girl. Right, Ma?"

"Come over here, Pamela, and I'll teach you the fine craft of affixing the company logo to the company shoe box. This way, if I'm ever hit by a bus, God forbid, somebody will know exactly where the logo belongs."

"Great." Pamela smiles and puts down her purse. She goes to my mother, who shows her what to do.

Rocco and Alfred Jr. are being carried through the shop by Alfred, who laughs as he hauls them like sacks of flour slung over his shoulders. He catches my eye. My brother smiles at me with the same relief my father had on his face when he got the last "all-clear" report from the doctors at Sloan Kettering. They are more alike than they know.

"June, when are you taking vacation?" Mom asks.

"Right after we finish the shipment. I'm going to take off when Valentine goes to Buenos Aires."

"Who's going to Buenos Aires?" Tess asks.

"I am."

"I've always wanted to go there!"

"Well, maybe next time. Although, if we're going to be fair, it will be Alfred and Pamela on the next trip. My partner gets first dibs on international travel."

"And we'll take it!" Pamela smiles.

"Who would have thought it? Valentine and Alfred are true partners," Mom says. My mother has replaced Saint Jude, the patron saint of impossible cases, with her son and daughter, the improbable partners.

"It's a miracle," Dad says. "You act like grown-ups. Well, you are, I guess. And I'm proud of youse guys."

"Break time." Gabriel enters the shop carrying a large tray of freshly baked chocolate-chip cookies. He places them on the desk. He checks the coffeepot. "Stone cold. How can we have cookies without coffee?"

Gabriel takes the pot back to the sink to wash it.

"This is like the old days," Mom says.

"Yep, somebody always bitching about something," Dad says.

"Now, Dutch," Gabriel says. "Watch your language in front of the boys. And I mean . . . me."

June spoons coffee grounds into the maker. "Let me make myself useful. I can't teach my apprentice when the table is being used for shipping."

"What apprentice?" Mom asks.

"Me," Gabriel says. "That's right, you Los Angelinis—you better look out. I've moved in, and I'm taking over. I started with the living room, and now, like a good Italian mold on veiny cheese, I'm seeping down into the workroom and into the shoe business. Soon you'll all be wearing the Biondi."

"He's got a gift." June breaks a cookie in half and tastes it. "And our lunches during the training sessions are to die for!"

The buzzer rings in the entrance. "It's probably the truck." I holler over the din of my family as they gather around the cookies, "Let them in, Dad."

Dad goes to answer the door. He comes back into the shop, followed by Kathleen Sweeney. She wears a red trench coat. She stands out like a cardinal who lands on the roof in snow.

"Val, Alfred. Somebody here to see you."

I look at Alfred. The color drains from his face. He doesn't move. Luckily Pamela has her head down, concentrating on the medallions.

I spring into action. "Hi, Kathleen! Come on in. Everybody say hello to the patron saint of Angelini Shoes—Kathleen Sweeney, from the Small Business Administration."

Kathleen stands next to the cutting table. She looks so small there, among the stacks of shipping boxes. She ignores the packing hoopla and focuses on the people, taking in my mother and father, sisters, Pamela, and the boys as if she's parachuted into enemy territory and has to gather as much information as she can as quickly as she can before the searchlights come on and she is discovered. This can't be easy for her. But as it is for all mistresses, exposure to the family of the lover is a learning opportunity, and

she is taking it all in to better understand Alfred, or even to help
her make a deeper connection to him.

Gabriel stares at Kathleen with a sense of wonder. No Italian
comare that he has ever heard of would have the nerve to show up
at the family place of business. But Kathleen is part of the Angelini Shoe Company—not directly, but she has helped us secure a
loan we might not have gotten without her assistance. Whatever
guilt I have about this, I'll have to sort out down the line. I have
enough to worry about when it comes to the welfare of the people
in this room.

Without taking his eyes off Kathleen, Gabriel grabs a cookie
off the platter, bites it, and chews. It's as if the cast of *General Hospital* is doing a live scene in the shop. He's riveted.

Rocco runs up to Kathleen. "You have hair like Raggedy Ann."

"I know." Kathleen smiles. "Who are you?" Kathleen kneels
down to talk to Rocco. Gabriel shoots me a look. The melodra-
matic kneeling makes this scene something out of *Jezebel*.

"I'm Rocco."

Alfred Jr. pushes Rocco to the side. "I'm Alfred Junior."

"You are?" Kathleen acts impressed.

"Yeah. That's my name."

"That's a cool name," she says. Kathleen takes in Alfred's children. She looks at them carefully, as though she wants to wed the
conversations she had with my brother about his family to the
reality. She might even be wondering what her children with
Alfred might look like. "I've heard a lot about you."

Suddenly Pamela looks up from her work. My mother and
sisters look at one another.

I jump in to cover for Kathleen. Doesn't she know all Italian
mothers and sisters are on high alert for interlopers? Tess alone
could blow this affair wide open with a couple of pointed questions. "Oh, I bore everybody on the planet with stories about my
nephews and my nieces. I make them look at pictures. I'm a very
pushy auntie." I go in for the save.

Gabriel shoots me a look that says, Stop it. You're overcompensating. If he could, he'd take the ruler and rap my hand and say, "Bad actress! Bad actress!"

"This is my wife . . . Pamela." Alfred introduces her to Kathleen.

"Nice to meet you." Pamela extends her hand.

From the look on Kathleen's face, I don't think she counted on The Wife being so attractive. Pamela's long champagne blond hair hangs loose, with chalk-colored highlights around her face, and her cigarette-leg jeans show off her lean shape after two babies. Kathleen cannot blame the affair on Pamela with the old "the wife let herself go" excuse. Kathleen will have to invent some other reason for Alfred's fall.

"Why don't we go upstairs?" I offer. I turn to my family. "Back to work, people. Alfred and I have some business to attend to. I want this table cleared by the time I get back."

Kathleen, Alfred, and I go up the stairs to the apartment. I show her to the table, offering her a seat. She sits and opens her briefcase. "I make it a habit to visit the establishments that we give our loans to. I'm sorry I interrupted family time downstairs."

"No problem. I just put everybody to work on shipping days."

Kathleen looks down at the paperwork. She shuffles through it. She pulls out a document and gives it to Alfred. "Here is the loan repayment plan." She avoids eye contact.

"Thank you," he says.

"And here's the check." Kathleen hands me an envelope containing enough money to produce and launch the *Bella Rosa*, the first design in our *Angel Shoes* line.

"Thank you. This is really going to help us."

"I'm happy to have been a part of this venture."

Kathleen Sweeney has tears in her eyes. I feel bad for her, even though I know she's been involved with my married brother, and I believe that's wrong down to my bones. But I'm afraid she may actually be in love with my brother. She looks at Alfred with sadness. "I'd also like to say . . ." Kathleen looks at me. "I'm sorry."

I look over at my brother, whose eyes fill with tears.

"Everything is going to be all right," I say—for the life of me, I can't think of anything else that would be apt. If you'd asked me a month ago, I would have imagined yelling, "Get out of my house, you tramp!" at her. But the truth is, she isn't a tramp, and I would never have the temerity to judge another woman anyway.

I stand to go. I don't offer my hand in gratitude, nor do I embrace her. I am, after all, part of the family that her actions could have destroyed. I have to stick with my team, even when I understand the weakness of the opposition.

Kathleen stands up. I can tell that she would like a moment with my brother, alone. But this is my house, and it's my shop, and my sister-in-law is down the stairs, innocent of their nonsense, so I say, "I'll see you out."

I show her to the stairs. Alfred stands by the table, not knowing what to do. Instead of following Kathleen and me, he stays behind. When I look back before leaving him, his expression is one of pure loss.

I follow her out into the street and pull the door shut behind me.

"That was rough," Kathleen says. She holds her shoulder bag tight to her body with one arm and runs her hand through her hair with the other. "I'm sorry," she says with frustration. "I have to think about myself right now. I didn't set out to cause any harm," she goes on. "I wasn't looking for . . . I wasn't planning on a relationship . . . it just happened."

It's so hard for me to imagine a love affair *just happening*, unfolding like a strip of fine leather under the roller. Wouldn't it be nice to be one of those people who wanders the world and runs into love like it's a corner bodega? Kathleen is one of those people who is surprised when love arrives, as if it is made of whim and fancy, and not of choice. But that's never been true for me. I have to choose. I've always had to look for trouble to find it, and the same goes for love.

"I have to go," Kathleen says, looking up at the street sign, looking for the quickest route out of here.

"Kathleen, before you go, you need to understand something. Thank you for putting your feelings aside, for letting go of my brother—for whatever reason. You've saved us all a lot of heartache. But . . . I'm with them. My family. They come first. If you need to discuss business with me, I'll come to your office day or night. I'm very grateful for all you've done for me. But I don't expect to see you on Perry Street again. Understood?"

As she walks away, perhaps she is thinking about how she could have saved her own heart from breaking. But it's too late for that now.

I watch as Kathleen crosses Perry Street, avoiding the pits and grooves of the cobblestone street. I wish my brother would have navigated his path as carefully.

Alfred should have known better, after all we had been through with Dad. Alfred always knew best until it came to his own life. Now he'll have to figure out a new philosophy, because the one he chose walks away with every step she takes.

I fold my arms as Kathleen makes the turn onto Washington and disappears out of my view, and, I hope, out of my brother's life, and the story of our family—for good.

My suitcases are lined up next to the door, and my outfit is laid out for the flight to Buenos Aires. My mind races. I think of a thousand things that I will need to do, should ask, and hope to accomplish in Argentina.

Roberta has been cagey about providing any family information. She wants to share it all in person, which is fine, but I hate to travel a few thousand miles to get upsetting news. On the other hand, I'm excited about seeing her factory, and about the potential business opportunity for her and the *Bella Rosa*.

I am grateful for the timing of this trip. Alfred and Kathleen's secret affair took a toll on me, as did the shipment to Milwaukee. Gabriel has begun to implement his renovation and redecoration of the apartment, and it will be helpful for him to have the space to himself to get the job done. Alfred will take over the shop in my absence, June's vacation is planned, and Gabriel will be on hand to help out when he's needed. It would seem that all is in order. Until I open the most recent letter from Gianluca.

> *Cara Valentina,*   *18 maggio 2010*
> *Enclosed is the leather sample you asked me to send. It's a basket weave of suede and leather, which gives the look of double-sided satin. I think you will agree that it is exquisite. Thank you for your letter. All is well here. I know you are busy, so I will close.*
>
> *Love,*
> *Gianluca*

I let his letter fall onto the floor next to my bed. Gianluca's first dud, written and sent without poetry or passion, and on the eve of my big adventure. I would have liked a sexy opus to read over and over again on the plane, but I guess I'll have to turn to the new Jackie Collins novel for *that*. Gianluca knows I'm nervous about this trip, and I've shared my reservations with him. You would think, wise old man that he is, that he'd come up with the exact right thing to say to make me feel more confident.

I hear a fire alarm in the distance, somewhere in Chelsea. I can't sleep. I get a special brand of insomnia before I fly. I imagine turbulence, a horrible flight, the plane is struck by lightning, a belly landing because the wings have snapped off, and once I'm on the ground, having slid down the emergency chute, Roberta meets me and hates me on sight. I develop a rash over my entire body and cannot walk. I'm put in a bad local hospital where they pump me up with drugs and change my name. I develop amnesia and have to be airlifted out on a gurney to a small hospital on the

Galapagos Islands where a voodoo doctor can cure the rash but cannot restore my memory. I join a nunnery because the rash has so disfigured me I can only live in a colony where they wear veils. But wait! I know what's keeping me up this time. This letter was never intended as an endearing send-off. It's a *blow-off*. He's breaking up our imaginary relationship! We're only together on paper, bound by good stationery and his Italian-to-English dictionary. We're doomed. It's over. God help me, but if the plane goes down, the last words I will have read from Gianluca will be about a leather sample. Well, it was literary and luscious while it lasted. I actually believed his words, and hoped he really saw the woman he described in letters to be just like me. But she's gone. His pen ran out of ink. The compliments, the insights, the idolatry—they've dried up like an old inkwell.

Face it, Valentine, I say to myself. He's probably found someone new. Probably some shoe designer from Russia with long legs, high cheekbones, and bangs that lie flat. Or maybe she's Ukrainian. She's a brunette with rosebud lips and real pearls in piles around her neck. Or French. Busty and makes a good pastry. Gianluca would be a catch anywhere in the European Union. And to think, for a while, he wanted *me*.

I turn over and fluff my pillow into a comfortable position. Even though it's spring in New York City, it's autumn in Buenos Aires. Fall is my favorite time of year. I blossom in the autumn. So I'm going to put the letter out of my mind (Gianluca will be lucky if he gets a postcard from Argentina) and focus on the *Bella Rosa*. At least I know what I'm doing when it comes to shoes. Love will have to wait.

8

Be Careful, It's My Heart

AS THE PLANE DESCENDS INTO Buenos Aires, it dawns on me that my mother should be living my life. When she was thirty-five years old, she had four children, a husband, and a teaching degree that lay dormant like hyacinths in winter. The closest she would ever come to leading the life of an international jet-setter was listening to the rhythmic rumble of the airplanes over the old neighborhood in Queens as they made the turn to land at La-Guardia.

Mom was practically giddy at the airport as she helped me check my luggage. Whereas most normal travelers loathe the paperwork and lines, my mother revels in the boarding process. She counts on the helpful redcaps. She waits patiently as she takes her place at check-in where they hand you your seat assignment. She makes pre-boarding relationships, cultivating "new friends" on her way to "new experiences." My mother holds a boarding pass the way most people cradle a winning lottery ticket.

I peer out the window. Nightfall over Buenos Aires is a swirl of purples; the clouds dimpled with blue hold up a moon that looks like a silver pocket watch.

I planned an evening arrival in order to get a full night's sleep before hitting the ground running in the morning. The hotel arranged a car service to pick me up at the airport. The Four Seasons Buenos Aires is deluxe—and I would *never* have the means to stay there, except that Gabriel tapped into his Carlyle hotel contacts to arrange the deal of a lifetime (though I'm told bargains are the norm in Buenos Aires). I put on fresh lipstick, because you never know who you might meet. My mother once ran into Dr. Christiaan Barnard in 1975 and still moans that she "didn't have her face on."

I wonder what this trip will bring. Fourteen days to fill with possibilities. Will I meet anyone like Costanzo Ruocco—the great Caprese shoemaker—or the likes of the Neapolitan D'Amico sisters who make our shoe embellishments in Naples?

This time, unlike on my trips to Tuscany and Capri, I won't be distracted by a boyfriend who cancels at the last minute or a hot Italian who wants to step into the void. I won't be worried about Gram's welfare. I won't be concerned about my father's health or my mother's hope that I marry before she needs a face-lift. I'm on my own.

When I'm working in the shop on Perry Street, I have to steal time to sketch new ideas, because building custom shoes takes up most of the day. There are also appointments with vendors and fitting sessions with customers. I lead a very structured life in order to meet my deadlines, but all of that changes when I travel. Time becomes my own.

If I want to sketch all morning, it's my choice. If I want to play with patterns on paper long into the night, I can. I have uninterrupted spools of hours on end to look at the world in a new way. Fresh color combinations ignite, classic notions are scrapped, and new techniques are introduced as my imagination goes wild with possibilities. I can think freely when I'm away from home because I'm not worried about the boiler, the water bill, or the mortgage.

Maybe Gram is right—maybe the best thing an artist can do is to leave her comfort zone. Maybe creativity is all about the guts to try something new, somewhere new. I close my eyes and reboot my imagination as the car careens through the streets of Buenos Aires. When I open them, the city, completely new to me, is a blur of deep blue split by seams of light. I'm glad I landed in the dark; there is nothing to distract me as I remember my purpose. I have a job to do, and I won't rest until it's done.

The porter at the Four Seasons greets the car, opening my door with a flourish, as though I'm a party guest and not a hotel patron. At first glance, the La Recoleta district in Buenos Aires looks like the Upper East Side of Manhattan. Sleek glass towers loom among the frill of old world architecture like pavé diamonds set in stainless steel.

The entrance to the hotel is as grand as the neighborhood. Flowing fountains set amid classic statuary create the feeling of a piazza. I follow the porter under the awning and through the polished brass doors. The lobby is regal, with black-and-white marble floors and high arched ceilings. The sleek furniture is covered in navy damask-and-gold velvet stripes. I feel as if I've landed in a Dorothy Draper candy dish.

There is barely a wait at the front desk. When I am handed my key, the night manager says, "It's our pleasure. We have upgraded you to a suite."

"Upgraded is my second favorite word," I tell him.

"And what's the first?" He smiles.

"Complimentary."

He laughs as he shows me to the glass doors that lead through the outdoor gardens to La Mansion, a French inspired villa, the original hotel building behind the modern tower. As he opens the doors, soft teal beams of light shoot up from the ground onto the stone façade, etched in scrollwork. Romantic balconies jut out over the garden, spilling over with greenery and lush white blossoms. The effect is pure Marie Antoinette, Rococo details and neoclassical design in the heart of Buenos Aires.

I follow the porter outside and through the gardens to the entrance. I tiptoe, looking over the hedges to the oval swimming pool, anchored by waterfalls. The pool is the color of lapis, a blue so deep it's practically indigo. The surface shimmers in the light as though it's been sprinkled in gold dust.

The porter opens the door to my room, which isn't a room at all but an opulent suite, with a large living room decorated in moss green and honeysuckle yellow, in French toile and deep rose velvet. "It's too much," I say aloud.

The porter nods. I'm sure he's heard *that* before.

He loads my luggage into a closet as big as my bedroom in New York. I tip him, and he goes, leaving me to wander through the beautifully appointed rooms. I open the louvred doors that lead out onto the balcony. The breeze blows through and billows the silk draperies like regal capes.

The balcony has a view of La Recoleta. The endless sky over the city's many neighborhoods is not obstructed by buildings or mountains. The city below seems carved into the earth like an intricate mosaic of colored tiles. The stars poke through the night sky like silver straight pins.

I kick off my shoes and lie back on the king-size bed. I've fallen into a vat of feathers, and the pristine white sheets carry the scent of a clean summer day. Paper crackles under my back. I must be lying on the breakfast order form. I reach under and pull out the paper. But it's not a menu. It's an envelope addressed to me, in a familiar script, handwritten with a fountain pen, in cobalt ink.

A total surprise. A letter from Gianluca. I open the envelope slowly, so as not to tear it. I pull out the letter inside, unfolding the sheer paper carefully. Okay, signor. Redeem yourself.

> *14 maggio 2010*
> *Cara Valentina,*
>
>   *I hope you had a restful flight, and that your room, with its balcony, pleases you. I know you like to sit outside at night, under the moon.*
>
>   *I'm in the tower on the eleventh floor, looking out over the city. I am taking a swim at the pool by the mansion. Perhaps you would like to join me.*

I put the letter down. Dear God. My heart is pounding. I think I'm having a stroke. I could use Aunt Feen's blood pressure cuff right about now. He is *here*. In Buenos Aires. *Now!* Right *now!* In the next building! I inhale deeply and continue to read his words.

> *. . . then, if it pleases you, I thought we would have dinner. If you are tired, of course I understand, and will see you in the morning. And only . . . if that also pleases you.*
>
>   *Love,*
>   *Gianluca*

I spring off the bed like I'm tinsel that's been shot out of a New Year's party horn. *Please me?* Oh, he has *no i*dea.

I go to my suitcase in the closet and zip it open. I shuffle through the ziplock bags lined up like selections in the frozen food bin of a grocery store, searching for my bathing suit. Did I pack one? No. Now what do I do? The gift shop! I wonder if the gift shop is open.

As I turn to go to the hotel manual by the phone to call the front desk, I see a box on the closet shelf, tied with purple ribbon. My name, in Gianluca's familiar script, is written on the tag.

I open the box. It's a bathing suit. A tasteful yet sexy black one-piece maillot, with a plunging V in the front and sheer black mesh panels on the sides. It's a classic suit. And it's retail; this is no Chuck Cohen knockoff from the Loehmann's sale bin.

I take off my clothes and slip into the suit. Even the mirrors in this hotel are flattering. Then I remember it's chilly outside. I plow through my suitcase again and find a black velour hoodie and pants. (My mother insisted I bring it; "It's casual chic for breakfast in the hotel," she said. Yes, yes, Mama is always right.) I pull it on over the suit. I slip into a pair of black *Bella Rosa* flats, and grab the keys.

I almost skip through the mansion foyer and out the door to the gardens. Then, like an eighteenth-century duchess in a maze looking for her lover, I zig-zag until I figure out a direct path, and run through the hedges, toward the pool, to him.

I slow down as I approach the deep blue water, lit from within.

The pool reminds me of the lakes inside the Blue Grotto in Capri. The surface ripples in the breeze. I look around. I'm alone. No Gianluca. Was it a dream? Did I imagine the invitation? No, I couldn't have—who dreams up a new bathing suit? But I read the letter so fast—maybe I missed the instructions. Did he say to call first? I'm about to turn to go back to the room to call him when I hear, softly, from behind:

"Ciao."

I turn to face Gianluca. In this light, he's actually more handsome than he was at Gram's wedding. How is this possible?

"How was your trip?" he asks.

"Who cares?" I throw my arms around his neck. He laughs. The strong tilt of his nose and his firm jawline are as sleek and fine as the carved river stones that form the waterfall behind him.

"How do you like the room?" he asks.

"Did you upgrade me?"

"I cannot upgrade you. You cannot upgrade the very best."

"Do you always say the right thing?"

His expression, his eyes, the color of the deepest night sky, so clear, say more than his letters ever could about how he feels about me.

Gianluca takes my hands in his. The rush of feelings that goes through me is familiar, yet completely new. I reach up to embrace him, I kiss his cheeks, his nose, and then he pulls me so close, my face rests in his neck like a velvet collar. His lips find mine, and this time, I'm ready.

"Did you come alone?" he whispers in my ear.

"Yes."

"No nieces?"

"No."

"No nephews?"

"Uh-uh."

"No Aunt Feen?" He kisses my ear.

"No, none of the above."

"Just you? Alone?"

"I swear."

He kisses me tenderly. I'm lost in the moment—I forget the country, the hemisphere, the place. As we kiss, I could be anywhere—we *are* anywhere, the corner of Hudson Street, or the platform of the train station in Forest Hills, or high on the cliffs of Anacapri when the moon is out—it doesn't matter. There is no world outside this kiss. Everything is a blur, forgotten, gone. The wind rustles the satin leaves of the eucalyptus trees, filling the air with the scent of clean mint.

"Do you really want to swim?" I ask.

"Do you?"

"Well, the suit fits." I unzip my hoodie.

Gianluca laughs. "Then we swim."

I dive into the pool; the water is as warm as a bath.

Gianluca dives in and finds me in the water. His arms wrap around me like silk ropes. I kiss his neck. "Your last letter was terrible."

He laughs. "Too short?"

"It read like instructions for assembling a washing machine."

"My apologies."

"If you're going to seduce me . . ."

"Tell me how."

"As if *you* need instructions."

"Tell me what you need."

"I don't know. I like when you compared me to a peony. That was good. And when you write how you feel. That's always good. Here's the deal, Gianluca. Have I mentioned that I like to say your name? It has the entire history of Italian civilization in its delivery. At least I think so."

"Thank you."

"As a general rule, you should never write love letters filled with imagery and then send a swatch of shoe leather. The sentiments in letters should delight and build until the woman is so enthralled she cannot imagine the world without you."

"Ah."

I let go of him and swim off into the deep end, into the blue water.

The night air on my face is cold compared to the warmth of the water below. But the contrast is lovely; it's waking me up in every way, from the long flight, from my anxieties about meeting Roberta, and from my ambivalence about getting involved with a man who might take me away from my work, when my career needs my undivided attention.

Gianluca meets me at the deep end. "Are you hungry?"

"Not really. Are you?"

"No."

"So, what should we do?"

He smiles, and that's his answer.

Good answer.

∽

Room service has left a good-night tray with a silver service espresso pot, cream and sugar, and a plate of fresh fruit: mango slices, strawberries, and kiwis, artfully arranged like a sunburst. There's a polished sterling silver bowl filled with chunks of fragrant dark chocolate. There is also a fine bone china platter of tiny almond cookies sprinkled with candied orange bits. A small gold card with a handwritten note from the porter is propped on the tray. It says: "Complimentary."

"Why are you laughing?" Gianluca wants to know.

"The way this night is going, I'm getting everything I want."

"That is how it should be."

"And what do *you* want, Gianluca?"

"Do you have to ask?" he says.

"Yes, I do. I don't like questions answered with questions. Have you ever heard of . . . show, don't tell?"

He thinks for a moment. "No."

"Well, it means that I prefer to express my feelings with action, not words." I climb onto his lap, and this time, unlike on Gram's wedding night in Arezzo, I don't withhold my feelings.

"I like both. Action and words." He kisses my neck.

"But I'm not a poet, I'm a shoemaker."

"A good shoemaker *is* a poet," he says.

"Right." I kiss him.

"Do you think you can find the words tonight?" he whispers. "To tell me how do you feel about me?"

I take his face in my hands. "I think I can't describe it."

"Try."

"Okay, I never imagined you before I met you. You're the kind of man who ends up with women who wear high heels and aprons."

He laughs.

"I didn't see myself with a man who had children, or was older, or who had a big life before he met me. And by big life, I mean a long marriage. "

"I understand."

"But, and here's what I pray for, I pray to stay open to the possibilities of everything in life. I also hope to never limit my choices by my own prejudice—or the limitations of my upbringing. But, here's where I need your help. I was surprised by my feelings for you, too."

"Why?"

"When I met Orsola—and she's as fine a woman as any I've ever met, and you raised her—I could see that you are a wonderful father. Most women have to wait to find out if a man will be a good father. If they ever do. But with you, I knew right away."

"Orsola is the best part of my life."

"That's very obvious. You've been a good father. As a daughter myself, I don't think there is anything more important than that. It says more than anything else I know about you, who you *really* are. But here's the problem . . ."

Gianluca waits as I find the words to explain my feelings. At Gram's wedding, when I was helping corral my nieces and nephews, it dawned on me that I might like my own children to chase and coddle, to correct and defend—that it wasn't enough to be an aunt with an extra pair of hands. And then, later, when I held Bret's daughter Piper in my arms, I felt the yearning that can only be instigated by the embrace of a child holding so tight, she almost became a part of me.

I have walked past Bleecker Park, filled with children, hundreds of times and never looked inside the fence to see what was going on. I tuned out their laughter and loud yells, their games and their joy. But lately, on my coffee run, I stop and observe them. I find myself standing at the fence, wondering if this exotic zoo is a place I will visit, or will I actually live inside someday? Will I ever be one of those mothers chasing her four-year-old down the ramp on the beat-up public scooter that the neighborhood kids share? After a while I check my watch and realize a mound of work waits for me back at the shop. On the way back, I consider what a child would mean to me in my life. I usually dismiss the notion once I'm back at the cutting table and tackling my to-do list. I put motherhood out of my mind until the next time I find myself outside the gates of Bleecker Park.

There's a moment for every woman who loves her family and embraces their good qualities while attempting to negotiate the mania, when she decides that she might want a family of her own to love and shape. It's only natural. I'm in my mid-thirties, and time tells me I must think about these things, or make the decision to brush past them and build a life without a family of my own.

I shape my question to Gianluca carefully because, depending upon his answer, I only want to ask it once.

"Why would a man who already has everything I hope to have someday be interested in retracing those steps and starting over, building a new life? Last year in Italy, you said you weren't interested in having another child. Have your feelings changed?"

Gianluca inhales deeply. My heart races; I realize I'm afraid of his answer. He pulls me close. He says, "That would depend upon you."

"It's all up to me?"

"I think so. A baby is the woman's choice," he says. "I don't know how else to say it. Why do you speak of children tonight?"

"I went to a friend's house recently. A birthday party. And there was a baby there who reached for me, and when she fell into my arms, I felt something I had never felt before—a connection, I guess. A possibility of some sort. Maybe it's my age. Or maybe it was just that particular little girl. I don't know."

"Or maybe you are thinking about life in a different way now," he says gently. He kisses me. The kiss is like the soft wax seal on the envelope of a letter. There is something final about it—for him. Then he says, "Maybe you are ready for more."

The concept of *more* for a woman who has to stretch to reach for *enough* is almost unthinkable. I have no idea what I deserve, because I never know what to ask for. Gianluca has already had the life that I think I want. He already knows how the story ends. Gianluca begins a second life tonight, a new act, a new phase, as I move into my first one. I have no idea what to expect.

I try to let go of the old habits and prejudices I have about love in order to make room for the mystery. I don't have any control over what will happen. I'd like to know where this is going because I don't want to get hurt again, but I don't have any control over that either. I have to accept that I don't know where this leads—I have to be bold about it and move toward happiness and trust that everything will work out the way it is supposed to.

"Do you want to be with me?" he asks.

The truth is, he already has my answer; he had it in Arezzo in February. He knows that I want him, but do I want all that goes with my desire for him?

Love builds in a series of small realizations, he wrote.

Maybe tonight will be one of them.

Gianluca moves toward me and takes my hands. The same shivers I had on the balcony in Capri, at the church in Arezzo, from the accidental way his hand brushed mine when we reached for the same panel of fabric at the mill in Prato, ripple through my body.

His beautiful hands have the strong and sure grip of an artist, one who walks in the world first through feeling, and then through touch. Gianluca is a craftsman who makes something lasting from nothing, who knows when to be gentle, and when to be certain, and when to be direct, and when to step back and observe. He is an artist who considers the angle, the placement, and the frame of the object he desires, so as best to appreciate it. Tonight, he is the lover who makes me beautiful; in his hands, I am the best I can be.

How succinct Gianluca's purpose was in winning me. How clear his vision as he removed every obstacle one by one, until he had me alone. Gianluca knows exactly how to treat me, because he took his time to observe me with an eye no other man ever has. As he kisses me, I feel something I can't name—it's as if we've already written our history, and this love affair resumes from long, long ago, when in fact, it is just beginning.

As his lips travel down my neck, I see moments in my mind's eye, of times we were together, in Capri floating on the turquoise waves of the Mediterranean Sea, and in Greenwich Village, on the roof with a blue afternoon sky behind him, when I disappointed him and let him go, and now in Buenos Aires where the sky is saturated indigo, where the stars make lavender pools of light in the dark and I finally see clearly enough to choose him.

With each picture I see, I remember him and how he looked at me and took me in. He appreciates me for exactly who I am, and he understands me as I wish to be understood.

Gianluca and I embody that old Italian word: *simpatico.* We are like-minded souls who say and do things that please one another, because it comes from a place of recognition.

We lie down in a field of feathers, sinking deep into the covers, finding one another as we move through; we're tumbling through clouds, weightless, nothing but an endless sky over us, and the world below, beneath us, so far away, its details blur so as not to matter.

In Gianluca's arms, I stay.

We sail, we fly, and we sail and we fly deep into the night, long into the blue, with no destination in mind, just now, just this very moment.

9

The Street of Dreams

GIANLUCA SLEEPS DEEPLY IN OUR bed. Even breakfast, rolled into the living room on a silver trolley filled with delicate croissants, raspberry horns, and a pot of rich, black coffee, did not disturb him. I pull the silk draperies closed against the early morning sun so as not to wake him.

I'm showered, dressed, and ready to meet my cousin Roberta. I went through my morning ritual with such urgency, I kept dropping things in the bathroom. There is a lot more riding on this trip than I want to admit.

I text Gabriel.

```
  Me: Gianluca is here.
Gabe: In BA?
  Me: In my room.
Gabe: OMG. Ding! Ding! Ding!
  Me: I know.
Gabe: You realize that you had to actually
      leave the airspace over the continental
      United States to get laid?
```

```
  Me: Enough!
Gabe: How's the food?
  Me: Trays of fruit and chocolate and
      cookies.
Gabe: Sex and cookies. My favorite marriage.
      Go and get busy with John-lucky.
```

"Where are you going?" Gianluca rolls over in bed and looks up at me. His eyes are a clear china blue in this yellow room.

"I was just leaving you a note. I'm going to the factory."

"I'll go with you."

I sit next to him on the bed. "No, no, you stay and rest."

"Because I'm old and I need it?" he teases.

"Yes."

He reaches for my hand as I turn to go. I look down at him.

"You look beautiful," he says.

"Thank you." I lean down and kiss him.

"Don't worry," he says. "She will like you."

I close the door to the suite and walk to the elevator. It's slow to arrive, and the empty moments send me into a slight panic. I have a few free minutes to think about all the things that could go wrong. Roberta will think I'm an idiot, so we'll be forced to make the shoes in China. Then I up my anxiety. It's rude to abandon Gianluca after the night we shared. Are we now in a *relationship*? Will it last? Ridiculous, improbable, disjointed thoughts tumble over one another until the elevator doors open. I check my tote for the files I brought to share with Roberta. My sketches of the *Bella Rosa* are printed in color and include a grid of specifications. I've done my homework. I remind myself that I am completely pre-pared. I can't help it, I'm afraid. I can only hope these jitters are about my first-day-of-school nerves, and not the work itself. I am walking into a completely new and therefore uncertain situation.

The cab speeds through the streets of Buenos Aires, through the barrios El Centro, San Telmo, and Palermo, whose moods

change from residential, to arty, to high-tech and whose architectural styles flip from French Colonial to Spanish to Italian with
every turn of the wheel.

Last night, Buenos Aires was washed in every shade of blue,
and this morning, in bright daylight, it's as though this city was
built out of candy.

The stucco on the Mediterranean houses is the color of orange
circus peanuts; the doors are painted in shades of bubble-gum
cigars: bright yellow, soft lilac, and hot pink. Garden walls are
washed in vivid tones of bright white, magenta, and periwinkle,
trimmed in licorice black, resembling a dish of Good & Plenty.
Tall wooden fences are drenched in bright Kool-Aid blue. Even
the textures of the landscaping burst forth like showers of candy
from a piñata: low mounds of nasturtium stuffed with buds that
resemble Red Hot Dollars, and the pecan trees seem to be loaded
with Root Beer Barrels.

The cab pulls up in front of 400 North Caminito, a large,
rustic pumpkin-colored factory building with rows of Catholic-
school-style windows propped open. A weathered sign says:

Caminito Shoes Inc.
Since 1925

I pull out my phone and take a picture of the sign, noting that
the factory is named after the street, and not the family.

There are two metal entrance doors. One reads "Oficina,"
and the other says "Fábrica."

I enter the office, which has the familiar scent of rich leather
and beeswax. The scent soothes me, and reminds me of home and
also why I made this trip in the first place—to find a way to grow
the Angelini brand while keeping it all in the family.

I approach a woman who sits at a desk behind the entrance
window.

"I'm Valentine Roncalli from New York."

She smiles. "*Si, si,*" she says, coming out from behind the window. "We are expecting you. I am Veronica Mastrandrea."

"Just like Perry Street," I say as I take in the office. The steady hum of the machines in the factory beyond the front office creates a rhythmic buzz that stops and starts.

The industrial flap windows, propped open on metal bars, create a nice breeze and also let in lots of bright light. The furniture is plain and functional, built from heavy oak, stained dark.

The desktops are cluttered with papers, ink pads, and stamps. Shoe boxes lie open on the desk, used as filing boxes for stubs and bills (I do the same at home).

Thick, leather-bound ledgers are propped open, with figures written in the margins in pencil. On the far wall, a shelf is filled with a series of hand-carved wooden lasts, the forms upon which shoes are sized. The lasts are lined up neatly by size. Computer screens are lodged amid the old-world equipment, sticking out obtrusively like pay phones in the jungle.

There are a few dusty framed certificates on the walls, written in Spanish, some garnished with gold seals. A spiral-bound calendar for 2010 hangs on the back of the door, just like the ones I found in storage after Gram left, flipped open to the month of May.

"I am Roberta Angelini."

I turn to face my cousin for the first time. She extends her hand.

"I'm Valentine." As I look into her eyes and take in her face, I lose my ability to speak. "You're . . . Roberta?"

A tight smile breaks across her face slowly.

Roberta Angelini is beautiful, and to my surprise, she is black.

As she takes me in, I can tell that I am, on the other hand, *exactly* what she was expecting.

"You're shocked," she says, placing her hands in her apron pockets.

"I am." I did a poor job of hiding my surprise. "I didn't know you were black."

"And yet I knew for sure that you would be white."

As we look at one another, obvious family traits become apparent. Roberta's nose is like my sister Jaclyn's: small, with a short bridge that comes to a very exact point. Her café-au-lait skin is smooth and flawless, like my mother's. She wears her hair pulled off her face ballerina style, in a high ponytail looped into a delicate bun, like Tess. Her eyes tilt upward, but the lids are languid. She is trim and small.

I long to call Gram and tell her the news, if this can even be called news.

"Before we talk business," Roberta says, "I will show you the factory."

As I follow her, I picture the members of my family in a group shot—I line up the cream-colored people like wooden pins in a bocce set, face by face, build by build, baby by baby. We have Italian (Angelini, Roncalli, Cavalline, Fazzani) and Irish (McAdoo) under an American tarp, and the lone Japanese cousin who married my dad's nephew, but that's as much diversity as we got—until now.

"This is production," Roberta says, opening the door. I follow her into the main room, an enormous airplane hangar of a room, with distressed wooden floors that buckle under the weight of rows of machines.

The noise that was a low and steady hum in the office now blares at full force inside the factory. The machines grind, pulse, and whir in rhythmic bars of sound. Roberta shows me the first section of machines, which resemble large sewing machines. The base of the machines has heft, curves of iron with a silver wheel, which the operator spins to and fro to control the speed.

The operators sit behind their machines on small rolling work stools. They assemble the separate leather pieces cut from a pattern, and then sew the shoe's upper together, tongue to vamp, with deft movements that come from years of rote practice.

The operators move the pieces under the thick needles as they pulse up and down, the speed of the needle controlled by a pumping action made with operator's knee to the pad affixed under the worktable. A foot pedal on the floor serves as a brake. When a seam is complete, the operator pulls the shoe, snips the thick thread, and sends it down the row to the next operation.

A wooden last, or shoe model, is inserted into the partially assembled shoe. Operators toss the shoe and last into a bin, which is wheeled to the next section of operations.

A row of more compact versions of the sewing machine is used to sew the welt to the shoe. The shoes then move to the next fleet of machines, where the heels are attached by a press, using sleek nails and cement. A trimming machine, which employs small and speedy blades, trims away excess binding and leather, cutting the shoe to size. The toe caps are stamped on a set of machines that look like upright hammers that pulse back and forth.

A large rolling machine works the leather and makes it pliable. I am envious of the machine, which uniformly stretches and presses the leather simultaneously. I roll the leather by hand, and it takes me hours to get it loose enough to work with, and to sew. Hand-rolling is a painstaking process that takes hours; here, it takes mere minutes, and the results are just as beautiful.

The roller, with its shimmering, smooth wheels and flexible mount, is the machine that put the custom shoe business in the museum.

Workers operate small drills with fine points that perforate the oxford with holes for laces. A small hand-held press snaps the metal grommets into place. Then a piping machine attaches trim, while a buttonholer creates finished seams around the grommets. Once these tasks are completed, and the shoe has been passed down the line, the operator tosses the shoe into another set of deep cloth bins with wheels.

I follow Roberta into finishing. The physical space fans out to accommodate machines that serve several functions to complete work on the shoe. Here, some of the operators stand to do their work, and like the rest of the workers in the factory, they move quickly. There are wooden lasts affixed on poles at eye level, where a worker takes the shoe, places it on the last, and works the pliable leather by hand to remove any creases and to check the accuracy of the size and measurements.

In our shop, I use a small brush machine, operated by foot pedals, to buff the leather. Here, the same idea is expanded to accommodate hundreds of shoes. A long conveyor belt with brushes attached on either side runs through the center of the finishing department. The finished shoe is fed onto the belt, held in place by the movement of the brushes.

The completed leather shoe, minus the laces, is anchored by the thick sable brushes and polished to a high gloss by the time it reaches the far end of the belt. It would take me an hour to achieve the same level of shine manually.

At the far end, the freshly machine-polished shoe drops into a bin, where it is checked by hand and sorted into separate cubbyholes in a large, freestanding wooden grid, shaped like an open egg crate. Workers are positioned on either side, one loading from the conveyor and one on the other side retrieving the finished shoes, to inspect them before boxing them to be shipped.

"Is this similar to your shop?" Roberta shouts over the noise.

I shake my head that it's not. I hold up my hands to indicate something much smaller. "This is my factory."

"Many years ago, we were the same. But we have expanded several times, and now we employ over two hundred people."

"I can see that. Where do you do the cutting?"

She motions for me to follow her. We pass through the finishing department and climb a small flight of stairs to the second floor.

The cutting room resembles an oversize operating room in a

hospital. Bright honeycomb-shaped work lights hang over one long table that extends down the center of the room.

Over the table, an oval track extends the full length of the table. A large circular saw for cutting leather is attached to the track. The serrated blade peeks out from a metal sleeve, which is strapped to a rig that has a full range of mobility in the hands of the cutter.

Assistants layer the leather, in flat sheets, methodically on the table. The leather is about five layers deep, separated by layers of sheer pattern paper. The assistants step back, while the presser comes forward to smooth the pattern paper against the leather with a flat board.

The head pattern cutter pulls a pencil from behind her ear and marks the periphery of the paper.

From my point of view, the pattern paper looks like an elaborate map, with complex blue veins and small gray markings that will guide her movements and the path of the blade as she cuts the leather.

Roberta motions to the cutter who oversees the process.

"This is Sandra Forlenza." Roberta introduces a tall woman with jet black hair. She has regal Inca bone structure and is all business. "Her people are from Ecuador. She is the best cutter and forelady in the business."

Sandra shakes my hand. "You come at the most interesting time."

The workers speak about process to one another in Spanish. How I wish I had paid more attention in Wade Miller's Spanish class at Holy Agony. I could really use it now.

"What kind of shoes are you making?" I ask Roberta.

"Dress shoes. Men's. These are oxblood leather for Ermenegildo Zegna."

Roberta motions for me to stand back.

Sandra grips the handle on the overhead saw and guides it to the layers of leather on the table. Then, with one calibrated movement, she drops the blade onto the paper. The motor shrieks as the blade bores into the blue veins.

Sandra guides the machine with her hands, anticipating every nuance and movement of the blade as she goes. She uses the strength of her entire body as she carves. Her shoulders separate as she lifts the blade and guides it to and fro over the pattern.

I cut from June's pattern by hand; my margin of error is great. Sandra, however, must maintain complete control; she has to hit the mark every time she drops the blade. One slip, and the layers of expensive leather will be ruined.

Roberta motions for me to follow her back through the factory to the office. Roberta walked a few steps ahead of me throughout the tour. She doesn't do chummy, and while she is polite, her manner is brusque. I can see that there's warmth beneath the frosty veneer, but she's not letting out much sunshine on my behalf. I hope she likes me, but I really can't tell yet.

"I appreciate the tour," I tell her. "Your operation is very impressive."

"Not what you were expecting?" she asks.

"I didn't know what to expect."

Roberta looks off. Her expression reminds me of my grandfather, a man who never worried about pleasing people, but rather, took his time when deciding about someone. Like him, Roberta is emotionally detached. I'm not offended by her cool demeanor; I find her attitude familiar, so I understand it. Roberta Angelini is first and foremost a professional.

I noticed when we went through the factory that she did not speak directly to any of the operators, and yet she connected to the work they were doing. Sometimes she would nod, or touch a shoulder here and there, or pick up a last and check the workmanship. It was apparent that she has the respect of the workers. I imagine with this size of an operation, she would have to be a tough taskmaster. The leadership role seems to come naturally to

Roberta. My new cousin is a straight shooter, and I will have to be the same when it comes to dealing with her.

"Roberta, look, let me say this up front. I'm here to see your operation because I need a manufacturer for my shoes. And I would like to keep the contract for the *Bella Rosa* in the family."

"We are family," she says. "But a fractured family."

"Maybe we can repair the damage. Whatever it is. I know that we just met and this is all so new—for both of us. In fact, I didn't know my great-grandfather had a brother at all—"

"Ah," she says. "And we knew all about Michel."

I find this odd. I am very curious to find out why there was a big secret—and why one brother, Rafael, kept the reason alive, while my great-grandfather did not.

"It sounds like there was a very big problem," I say.

She nods.

"Roberta, I'm here to explore the possibility of going into business together. It would benefit you—and it would benefit me."

"Of course. And maybe then, we can come to a place of peace."

Her use of the word *peace* tells me that there must have been one hell of a war between the brothers. Roberta does not separate her family life from the world of her work; in that way, she mirrors our tradition on Perry Street. Family loyalty is the backbone of her operation, and she protects it as she does the level of workmanship in her factory.

"I would like to try," I tell her.

"But to be honest, I don't know if that is possible," she says.

Roberta is tough. This isn't going to be easy. It's as if she knows what I'm thinking, and gives a little.

"My mother knows the story best." Her expression softens.

"May I have the honor of meeting your mother?" I ask.

"She takes care of my son at home. Today is not good."

"Tomorrow, then?"

"I will ask her," Roberta says.

"Thank you. Would you mind if I spent the afternoon observing in the factory? I know you're busy, and I don't want to take you away from your work."

"Of course you may stay. I can place you with the foreman."

"I would like that."

Roberta goes into her office to make some calls. I pull out my cell phone to call Gianluca at the hotel. The phone in the room rings and rings. The call reverts to the front desk. The operator asks if I want to leave a message. I leave my cell phone number for Gianluca, and the message that I will spend the rest of the afternoon observing production at the factory. I'll be home in time for dinner.

I ask the receptionist to call me a cab.

Once outside the factory, I feel as though I can breathe again. The urgency of the work inside the factory, the noise and the intensity of the operation, have exhausted me. It's so different from our shop on Perry Street. There, it is peaceful in contrast. We work long hours, but we take our time. Here, it's a mad rush to the finishing department.

I spent the afternoon observing the assembly of the shoes. The more pieces to the pattern, the more difficult it is for the operator to assemble the shoe. I sketched as I observed, trying to figure out how to get the *Bella Rosa* down to four pieces instead of eight on my master pattern. If I can consolidate the operations on my design, it will speed the process in production, and as a result we will be able to make the shoe more cheaply without sacrificing quality. I want to use microfiber fabric, and it appears that the use of fabric will also speed up the process, compared to cutting leather or suede.

The cab drives up and stops in front of the factory.

"Valentine?" Roberta comes to the doorway as I'm about to jump into the cab. "How was your day?"

"I learned a lot. Thank you."

"Will I see you in the morning?"

"First thing." I thank her and get into the cab. I give the driver my destination, and then I slump down in the back seat, exhausted.

I didn't see Roberta all afternoon; she left me on my own. The foreman in production was helpful, but I didn't want to bother him with silly questions, so I just watched carefully and stayed alert through the process and shift changes. I learned a lot watching the mechanics of the operation.

I call my mother. Dutiful daughter that I am, I know she wants daily reassurance that I've not been kidnapped by roving Argentinian gangs looking for prototype sample shoes.

"Ma, I have news."

"Roberta can make the shoes?" Before I answer, I hear her calling out to my father. "Dutch? Dutch—Valentine is fine. She got there, landed, and went to the factory." She comes back to me. "Oh, Val, this is wonderful. What is Roberta like? Is she like our people? I mean, after all, she *is* our people."

"She's very pretty. Devoted to her work—she runs a big factory, and they do it all—cutting, production, finishing. It's really amazing."

"How are your clothes working out? Your wardrobe?"

"You were right. The black linen suit is a classic, and it goes anywhere. Mother knows best."

"Toldja," Mom says smugly.

"Ma, I was a little surprised when I met Roberta."

"Why? Was it déjà vu? Did you get chills? Was it spiritual? Does she look like us?"

"Um, yeah, a lot. She has Jaclyn's nose."

"Isn't that just uncanny? The Angelini onward and upward tilt! It's a great nose. Wish I had gotten it without the help of Dr. Mavrakakis."

"Yeah, and she has thick, shiny hair like Tess."

"I *knew* she'd be a brunette."

"And one more thing. Um . . . she's black."

There is a pause on my mother's end.

"Oh, honey, you know depression runs in my father's family."

"Ma, I don't mean black *moods*. I mean black skin."

"We're *black*?" My mother is mystified. "Huh," she says deliberately. "I didn't know there were black Italians."

"Well, evidently there are."

"You learn something new every day." My mother takes a bath in a bucket of cliché whenever she is perplexed.

"Ma, you okay?"

"I have to call my mother—and after I tell her the story, I'll call your sisters and Alfred. It's a shock." She goes on, "But it's also . . . courant. I mean, look at our president. I thought our cousins in B.A. would look along the lines of Julio Iglesias—you know, more Spanish than Italian, but Italianate nonetheless. The last thing I expected you to find in Argentina was a family of black cousins. But here it is."

"It's here, Mom." I really don't want to sit and listen to my mother as she shares every single thought that she has in her head.

She goes on, "I don't know what your father is going to say. I don't think they have any black people on his side."

"Probably not. But Ma, it doesn't matter. Roberta has so much going on. She is forty-four and she just had a baby."

"Then, you see, there's an inspiration for you. A late-in-life baby in a wing of our very own family. But hold on. Fertility can only be tracked through your maternal line, so Roberta's particular apparatus is irrelevant."

"That's what I'm thinking."

"Well, give them . . . give them our best." The ole lilt returns to my mother's voice.

⌒

I enter the hotel room, throw down my purse and tote in the entrance, and slip out of my shoes. "Gianluca? I'm sorry, hon. I'm home."

He doesn't answer. I go into the living room. The lamps have been dimmed. The golden light is romantic, and a far cry from the blazing work lights in Roberta's factory. I look beyond to the bedroom. The French doors to the balcony are wide open. "Hello?" I call out.

I go out onto the balcony. Gianluca stands by the railing. A lovely candlelit table, set for dinner, twinkles in the dark. He takes me in his arms.

"I'm sorry I'm late."

"I didn't know when you were coming home. So please don't apologize."

"I called—did you get my message?"

"No, but it's not a problem—"

"But I called!"

"It doesn't matter. So tell me, how was it?"

"It was a factory. Noisy. Big. Dusty. Exhausting."

He kisses me. The tension of the day leaves me, the hum of the machines that I couldn't shake until I walked in the door. He runs his thumb across my nose. "Did you help grease the gears?"

"No, but I got pretty close. Oh, and did I mention, the factory is also dirty?"

"I see."

Gianluca takes me by the hand and walks me through the bedroom to the bath, where the deep eggshell tub is filled with bubbles. "I'll be right back," he says. I take off all my clothes and sink down into the hot water.

The tub is so deep and wide. I let the water surround me like a satin coverlet. I close my eyes.

Gianluca returns with two glasses of wine. He pulls up the

vanity chair and sits down next to me. He gives me a glass of wine and toasts me before taking a sip. Then he leans over the edge of the tub and kisses me.

"What did you do all day?" I ask.

"I went to the Palermo barrio. I walked through it, had lunch, went to the galleries there."

"Anything interesting?"

"The paintings. You would enjoy them. Primitive, bright, and very Sicilian."

"I hope I get some time to be a tourist."

"I hope so too," he says.

"I'm sorry. I wish I didn't have to work. I wish I could just be with you." I did miss Gianluca, but it was a productive day. When I think of time at the factory, I wish I had more. I'm energized by what I saw, and what I hope to learn. But I don't need to share that with him. He's been waiting for me. He deserves all my attention.

"Tell me about Roberta."

"Let's start with the basics. She is very nice, accommodating—not American at all. She is quiet, contemplative—a thinker. And she carries the family grudge."

"What is it?"

"She didn't tell me. Oh, and I'm leaving out the shocker. She's black."

Gianluca's expression is interest, not surprise. "There are black Italians."

"Evidently. Although my mother didn't think so. Until now. I called her on the way back."

"Your mother has a very deep disinterest in history."

I laugh. "Except for the history of fashion. In that department, she's an expert. Oh and beauty products. She can describe the evolution of face cream from Helena Rubinstein through Estée Lauder. Those are her areas of expertise."

"Did you tell your mother I was here?"

"Now why would I do that? How do you say 'ruin a good thing' in Italian?"

"You say 'ruin a good thing.'"

"Besides, our romance is not front burner for Mike Roncalli. No, in the *New York Times* of my mother, you and I are strictly Metro section. The Black Angelinis carry the front page."

Gianluca leans down and kisses me. As he kisses me, I reach up and unfasten the buttons on his shirt. His chest and shoulders are broad; years of lifting and pressing leather have given his muscles strength and definition. It's a working man's body, not one that can be fashioned in a gym. I pull him toward me. "Do you notice that we never get to dinner?"

"Are you hungry?" he teases.

"Of a stripe. Yes." I push his shirt off his shoulders, take his hands in mine, and kiss them. I look up at him. "At some point, though, I'm going to have to eat the local cuisine—if only to describe it when I get home."

Gianluca sinks into the water next to me, and his long legs wrap around mine. The furthest thing from my mind is food. I may never eat again. Wine, bubbles, and his kisses are all I need to live—maybe ever.

10

Here's that Rainy Day

THIS MORNING GIANLUCA WOKE UP early with me. We've fallen into a Buenos Aires routine. I get up early and leave for the factory, while he sleeps. This morning we changed all that. We dressed and had breakfast together. I promised to keep the day at the factory short and be home in time for lunch. He wants to take me down to the river walk this afternoon, knowing how much I love my river at home.

I spent the morning in the cutting room. I photographed the steps of pattern making to show June, and also to compare to other manufacturers. I believe the cutting is what makes Roberta's work special. Her team has an understanding of the leather, and they cut to the grain, which makes for the most pliable material. If they can achieve the same with fabric, in her hands, the *Bella Rosa* could become the best affordable flat in the marketplace.

Roberta seems to have warmed up today—or maybe she's just getting used to seeing me around. I'm slowly becoming part of the scenery, like the old lasts on the shelf—familiar, and therefore a part of things.

"I'm going home for lunch. Would you like to come?" Roberta asks.

"Well, I was going to go back to the hotel . . ." I tell her. No, the truth is, I *need to* go back to the hotel. Gianluca is waiting for me. But didn't I make this trip to spend as much time as possible with Roberta? So, I quickly say, "You know what? I'd love to. Thank you." I can't squander any opportunity to be with Roberta, and I've been waiting to meet her mother. Gianluca will understand that.

"Let me call my mother to let her know."

Roberta goes into her office to place the call. I take out my cell to call the hotel. The hotel room phone rings and rings. I imagine Gianluca went out exploring. The phone rings through to the operator. I leave a message that my plans have changed—I'll be home for an early supper instead. Then I instruct the operator to leave a hard copy of the message under the door. I don't want to take the chance that Gianluca will miss the message.

"Let's go," Roberta says. "Do you mind walking?"

"Not at all."

"We live very close."

As we walk to Roberta's home, she tells me about her neighborhood. La Boca is known as the Greenwich Village of Buenos Aires. There are many similarities; there's a meatpacking district, a series of small antique shops nestled among clubs and restaurants, and a thriving subculture of businesses that make handcrafted items—like Angelini Shoes. But the detail that gets to me, that says *home* to me in a way nothing else can or ever will, is the cobblestone streets of La Boca. I stop and take a picture on my cell. I send it to Gabriel's phone. Just like Jane and Perry and Charles, Avalos and Olavarría and Suárez streets are paved with old, glorious, and bumpy cobblestones.

Roberta unlocks the gate, which opens into a complex of Mediterranean-style homes that face a common park. This is another small village within the village, off the busy Caminito Street.

The homes are surrounded by a privacy wall covered with waxy green vines. There is an old fountain in the center of the complex, its marble grooves worn smooth from weather and time. At the far end, in the midst of all this antiquity, is a plastic jungle gym for kids.

Roberta points to her home, a town house with a clay roof. The stucco is painted white, and the small entry porch is covered in multicolored tiles. Roberta opens the door and invites me in.

The furniture is cozy, childproof white-muslin-covered sofas and chairs, comfortable and washable. Antique chests made of hammered silver are tucked in corners. The walls are filled with paintings in an amalgam of styles, floating impressionism set amid realistic sketches done in charcoal and still-life renderings in watercolor.

Over the mantel is a whimsical oil painting of a theater tableau, a woman singing, surrounded by a chorus of peasants. I go to the mantel and look up to get a closer view. The signature in the corner is Rafael Angelini, the same man who drew the sketch that I found at home.

"My great-grandfather's painting," she says.

"He was very good."

"I love it because he painted it," she says.

An older woman brings the baby to Roberta and places him in her arms. "This is Enzo. My son. And this is my mother, Lupe."

Lupe is around my mother's age, small in build like Roberta, with black eyes and a deeper hue to her complexion. She embraces me.

"I am so happy to meet you," I tell her.

"Thank you for agreeing to meet me," Lupe says.

Lupe shows me to the veranda beyond the kitchen. The words my cousins choose are very telling. *Agreeing to meet, peace,* these little phrases must add up to something. It's almost as if their words are preemptive, either to avoid an argument or to start one.

Lupe has set a beautiful table under a shady elm tree. The navy blue ceramic dishes pop against an apple green tablecloth. The center of the table has a lazy Susan, with a clay pot in the center, surrounded by strips of thin bread, called fainá, long, slim wedges of yellow and red peppers, a bowl of olives, and fronds of fresh green lettuce.

Lupe invites us to sit, while Roberta pours our glasses full of fresh lemonade made with honey. Lupe takes the baby from Roberta's arms. "Time for Enzo's nap." She takes the baby in her arms and goes.

Roberta takes the lid off the clay pot. She picks up my dish, ladles a fragrant stew of meat and vegetables called *estofado* on the center of the plate, surrounds it with the fresh vegetables and the bread. She follows suit with her mother's plate and then her own. Roberta sits and shows me how to eat the stew, scooping up the meat with the vegetables.

"I'm in awe of your factory," I tell her. "The workforce . . ."

"Most of them have been there for many years."

"I could tell. So quick, so professional. And the machines, the cutting room. What an operation."

"I just took over for my father after he died and I do exactly what he would do. That's all."

"It's impressive."

"It's a lot now, with the baby," she admits.

"Do you have other children?"

She smiles. "A daughter. Ines is eighteen, and in university. I'm forty-four. Enzo was a surprise."

I can't imagine how Roberta runs a factory and takes care of a newborn baby. Of course, she has Lupe, and that's a big help. My mother made it clear before my sisters and brother had children that she wanted to spend lots of time with the kids, but we were not to consider her a nanny. Lupe lives here with Roberta's family, but even with the workload, she seems very happy.

I'm so tired at the end of a day, I can't imagine having to take care of a husband and children. Tess and Charlie have figured out a schedule with the girls and Jaclyn, who works in an insurance office, runs to day care at lunchtime to see the baby with Tom. Mackenzie, who doesn't have a job outside her home, keeps plenty busy chronicling the life she creates for Bret and their family with invitations, scrapbooks, and homespun projects like taking classes in organic gardening. Roberta's life seems more like my own, or at least how my life would be if I had a family.

"What does your husband do?"

"My husband is an artist. I brought him home twenty-two years ago. And Mama said, 'No artist!' Because we come from a family of them, all dreamers. But finally, my mother said okay."

"And now, a whole new chapter with a new baby. Enzo has lots of cousins to play with in New York." I decide to broach the topic we've both been avoiding. "The whole family would love to meet you. Whatever happened in the past, Roberta, is the past. We should move forward from here—I hope we can."

Roberta's expression softens, so I continue. "Can you tell me what happened with Rafael and Michel?"

"I suppose I will have to tell you if we are to move forward," Roberta says. "What do you know about Rafael?"

"All I know is I found a sketch in an old calendar. And then, what you've told me. If you don't mind, let's start at the beginning. Why did Rafael come to Buenos Aires?"

"He had to."

"Was it about money?"

"No, no. Not at first. My great-grandfather's goal was to stay in New York and work there, side by side with his brother. But then Rafael fell in love with my great-grandmother, Lucretzia."

Roberta looks down at her hands. Her tapered fingers are lovely, but they are working hands with short nails and a thin gold wedding band. She wears no ornamentation beyond the ring.

"She was black. Michel did not support the union."

"Because of her color?" I ask.

She nods.

I try to imagine New York City through the eyes of Rafael and Michel. Boundaries were clearly drawn. Italians did not venture above 14th Street except to make deliveries or to do building and maintenance work for hire. Immigrants laid claim to particular blocks and tenements, careful to carve out a place in the city where they could speak in their native language. But the barriers of race trumped religion and nationality. An Italian immigrant and a black woman would have a nearly impossible journey.

"But they married anyway?"

"Eventually. Here in Buenos Aires. They were banished, in a sense, by Michel, in every way. Lucretzia and Rafael planned to return to Italy together, but she had family here, so, they came to Argentina instead. They had one son, my grandfather. His name was Xavier Angelini, and he married Daria, a local Argentinian woman of Italian descent. My father, also named Xavier, was their only child."

"My mother is an only child also," I say.

"My father would have loved to know her. He used to complain that he had no cousins—he longed for a big family."

"My mother would have liked that very much, too." My sisters and I always say that my mother had a big family because she was an only child. I imagine the same to be true for her first cousin. Everyone, it seems, tries to create what they don't have, or what they believe they've missed, hoping it will fill them up.

"Did your mother take over the shoe shop?" Roberta asks.

"No, not at all. My mother raised a family—I'm one of four."

"So how did you come to work in the shop?"

"My grandmother and grandfather took the shop over from Michel after he died. When my grandfather died, Gram operated the business alone until I became her apprentice six years ago. She got married again this year and moved to Italy."

"Are you the only shoemaker?"

"I was, and now my brother Alfred has come into the business."

"Do you like to work with your brother?"

"At first I wasn't sure. For so long, it was just my grandmother and me, and our pattern cutter in the shop. Her name is June, and she's the best. It took some adjusting when Alfred joined the team. But now we accommodate one another."

"Sometimes a company needs to change. My father loved the art of making shoes by hand, but he also wanted to make money. It wasn't enough to make a quota each year of custom shoes. My father saw that there was no way to make a profit when the number of shoes you could build a year was so limited. So he convinced my grandfather to go into machine production. Together, they ran the mill I operate now." She smiles. "We do well at the factory, but even better in La Boca real estate. This complex is owned by our family. We rent out all the houses you see here."

Even our fundamental family investment strategies are the same—we anchor the business with real estate: we own the building on Perry Street, and here, the Angelinis own the housing complex in La Boca.

Lupe joins us at the table. She refills our glasses before she pours her own.

"Mama, tell Valentine what you know about Rafael before he came to Buenos Aires."

"There are many stories. These come from my father-in-law who heard them from his own father." She sits down. "Rafael had a brother named Michel. I was told that Michel had a hard life. He was widowed young and had a child."

"That was my grandfather."

"The story goes that Michel could not bear to stay in the village where his wife had lived in Italy—"

"Arezzo."

"That's right. So Michel begged Rafael to go with him to

America, to begin again. The plan was to open a shoe shop together, and raise your grandfather."

"This part of the story is exactly as I know it, except I did not know about Rafael," I say.

"It is understandable," Lupe says. "Because there was an argument and then an estrangement, which left Rafael to leave New York for Argentina."

"I told Valentine all about Lucretzia," Roberta says.

"When Rafael decided to marry Lucretzia and leave for good, he asked Michel for his money. You see," Lupe continues, "the brothers sold their building in Italy, split the money, and then moved to the United States to start over. They were partners."

"Michel paid Rafael part of the money, but there was a balance on what Michel owed. Your great-grandfather sent money to his brother for a few years after he moved here with his wife, until the debt was paid off," Roberta explains.

"But it didn't heal the rift between the brothers, once the debt was paid?" I ask.

"It might have, but Michel did not accept Lucretzia. So Rafael never reconciled with Michel. He was forced to choose his wife over his brother." Roberta shrugs. "And for both families, it was as if the other side never existed."

The three of us sit in silence for a moment. We contemplate the loss we've shared, the years we've missed, and the opportunities to have the big, close family that my mother and her first cousin dreamed about. I hope it's not too late to try and salvage what's left, but Roberta would have to meet me halfway. "I'm here in the hopes that we can do business together."

"I understand your goal," Roberta says. "But I have only made men's shoes in the factory."

"Well, maybe it's time to expand and make women's shoes also. I couldn't help but notice that your operators are very adaptable. In the two days I've been observing, they have assembled three different styles. Now, one of those styles was incredibly complex—"

"The *Ermenegildo*—"

"That one. I won't saddle you with a difficult shoe. In fact, watching your operators inspired me to simplify my design. If you would look at my samples—"

"Did you bring them with you?" Roberta asks.

"Yes. I have three prototypes to show you." I open my bag and give her the shoes.

Roberta looks at them, examining them like the seasoned shoemaker she is. She looks at the lay of the leather, the strength of the seams, she feels the interior of the shoe, then bends the flat to see how the leather responds to movement. Then she pulls the sides from the vamp, to check for gaps and elasticity. She hands the samples to Lupe, who does the same.

"This is a beautiful shoe. Very simple," Roberta says.

"Thank you. The design can take many materials—in fact, you could suggest materials you think would work. I like microfiber."

"I have a fiber material, a stand-in for suede—it's brand-new. It was developed here in the city by a textile designer who wanted to come up with a replacement for suede that mimics animal hide. It has give and is also supple. Very durable—especially for a flat shoe. And I'm working with color—it takes dye beautifully."

"I would love to see it," I tell her.

"What is a practical first run for you? What can you afford?"

"We can finance an initial run of ten thousand shoes," I tell her. "But my brother has been soliciting from China."

"I've lost a great deal of business to the Chinese," Roberta says.

"This isn't a competition. The costs need to be close—I won't lie to you. I can't give you this contract for more than the Chinese bid. But this is where my heart is. This is historically a family company, and if I can, I'd like to keep it in our family."

"You want to make amends for Michel."

I sit back in my chair. "I don't think that would be possible.

It's also unfair to expect me to make a situation right that I did not have a hand in."

"Fair enough," she says. "I don't hold you responsible for what happened. But you must understand, in your family's view, we disappeared. It's difficult to embrace a family that abandoned us so long ago."

"Roberta, to be fair, you could have contacted *us*," I say. "But that's behind us. I'm here *now*, Roberta, as Michel's heir, and I'm ready to move forward with you—if you want. Think about it. We could start fresh. A new beginning. Maybe the legacy of Rafael and Michel works better with a couple of generations in between for cushion."

Roberta laughs. "That could be."

"I'm almost an expert in dealing with family now. I had to make huge adjustments quickly when Alfred joined the company."

"What is he like?"

"Well, that's a long story and requires several cocktails, and as delicious as this lemonade is, it won't ease the pain of the details."

She laughs again. "I see. He's a difficult one."

"Exactly. But he's also very smart and forward-thinking. He's in charge of the bids and the financials. Alfred has a breakdown of the costs and the comparables, and also, we could sweeten the deal by doing the finishing in New York."

"Why?"

"To lessen the work on your end."

"But we have an excellent finishing department. My girls are perfectionists. They have experience with grosgrain and patent leather finishing on my formal men's shoes. I believe they would do an excellent job on your design."

"Okay, then, I'm officially open to finishing the shoes here."

"Good."

"So you'll consider this?"

"I like you." She leans back in her chair.

"My daughter rarely likes anyone," Lupe says.

"I'll be right back." Roberta gets up and goes into the house.

I reach over and take Lupe's hand. "Thank you for this delicious lunch. I hope someday you'll both visit us in New York City, and I can return the hospitality."

"I've never been to New York."

"Well, when you do, you stay with me."

"Thank you."

Roberta comes out of the house carrying a small bundle of envelopes. She gives them to me. "When my father died, he gave me these letters. They were handed down from Rafael to his son Xavier to my father. They were tied with this string, never opened, and never answered. My father always said that even though Rafael held a grudge against his brother to his death, he must have loved Michel, because he saved these letters. Maybe you would like to have them. I believe they belong to your family."

I look down at the bundle, kept in pristine condition. There must be a dozen envelopes. The black fountain pen ink has faded to charcoal gray. The U.S. postage stamps are dated from 1922 to 1924. At the bottom of the stack is a series of empty envelopes, addressed to Rafael and opened with a letter opener.

"Those were the envelopes with the checks. My great-grandfather opened them and deposited the money. But he did not open the letters. He did, however, leave a note that said, 'Marker paid in full.' I think that's important," she says.

Roberta and I appear to be very different. She's a mass-production shoemaker and not a custom cobbler—but she is every bit as particular as I am when it comes to her product. Roberta's keen artistic eye follows all the same principles that I follow when constructing a pair of high-quality shoes: it's about design, line, shape, and execution. It's about seeking the finest of materials from around the world—leather, suede, and silk—procuring them, and insisting upon the best techniques to build the shoe, so when it goes to be sold, the craftsmanship will showcase the value.

I saw firsthand how Roberta demands the same quality in the production of her machine-made shoes that I do in my custom line. As I grow the brand, I will need the best manufacturer I can find to build the *Bella Rosa*. I believe I have found her, here in Buenos Aires. And the best news: she's family. So, three generations later, we meet again, this time on Rafael's terms, and with the hopes of Michel that went unrealized because two brothers could not find a way to forgive one another, and accept one another's choices. Maybe we can be better; maybe we can even *do* better.

After lunch, Roberta took me to the textile mill where the new microfiber fabric has been created from cotton and hemp. It's thick and luxurious, and a strong possibility for construction of the *Bella Rosa*. As I head back to the hotel, I'm far later than I thought I would be, but the trip to the mill was informative and important. I feel guilty that I leave Gianluca on his own day after day, but he doesn't seem to mind. And after all, I'm here to work, I remind myself.

I check my BlackBerry. My heart sinks when I see that I've missed three calls from Gianluca. I hope he received my message and spent the day by the pool. I'm looking forward to his strong arms around me. I call the hotel to let him know I'm on my way. The phone rings through, but he doesn't answer. The operator comes on and asks if I'd like to leave a message. I don't leave one.

I'm in the habit of getting business done whenever I can, even in the car between the hotel and the factory. I don't want to lose a minute of play time with Gianluca, so I have to hustle when I have a spare moment. So I text Bret:

```
    Me: Amazing factory in BA. Cousin wants to
        sign on. Details pending.
  Bret: Great news.
    Me: If not for you, for the loan, for
        everything, this would not have
        happened. How can I thank you?
  Bret: Close the deal!
    Me: XOXO
  Bret: XOXO
```

I text Alfred.

```
     Me: Looks good with Roberta. Go ahead and
         connect. I will send numbers.
 Alfred: How did it go?
     Me: I think you can carve out a deal! The
         factory is first-class.
 Alfred: Unbelievable.
     Me: How are you?
 Alfred: Better.
     Me: Hang tough, brother.
 Alfred: I will!
```

I cut and paste Roberta's numbers into the phone and send to Alfred. I quickly return e-mails to Tricia Halfacre, my button salesman, who found some oversize patent leather medallions she thought would be "fetching" on the *Bella Rosa*. There are messages from Gabriel, who misses me, and Tess, who wants to know, oddly enough, about Argentinian food. I swear sometimes my family doesn't understand that I have a real job. Somehow, they still see me as a ten-year-old girl sewing a pair of felt boots in the shop for my teddy bear. If only they could see me now.

When I push the hotel room door open, there are no lights on. How strange. I move to go into the living room. "Gianluca?"

I call out. I look in the bedroom, and then the bath; no sign of him. When I return to the living room, I trip over his suitcase. Then I see that the French doors to the balcony are open.

Gianluca sits on the balcony with his back to the doors. I put my arms around him from behind. He pulls away.

"What's the matter?" I ask, knowing full well what's the matter. I'm hours late when I promised to be home early.

"It's ten o'clock at night," he says.

"Did you get my message?"

"I received a message that said you wouldn't be back for lunch, but that you would be home for an early supper. I called you three times. I've been waiting here for hours, and I did not hear from you."

"I would have called you back right away, but Roberta took me to the textile mill, and I didn't hear my phone. I didn't realize that you had called." My gut fills with guilt. I could've called him, many times. And when I was in the car and didn't get him on the phone, I should have sent the porter. Instead, I answered e-mails and texts—and even communicated with my button sales-man. As a girlfriend, I am about as low as you can get.

"I was worried about you," he says tensely. "I don't know this cousin of yours, or the barrio the factory is in—you left me here with no information, no other way to reach you."

"I'm sorry."

"You've apologized a great deal on this trip. You say 'I'm sorry' often."

"That's because I *am* sorry."

He is really angry. And he's not buying my contrition for a second. I know I've crossed the line. He knows I could have con-nected with him—he knows I put the shoes first. And he's abso-lutely right. I have really screwed up here. Gianluca sits in silence.

"I can't help it," I whine. "Roberta had been frosty, and today she thawed—and invited me to her home for lunch with her mother. I got the whole story about my family. And then I had to see where they make the microfiber."

Gianluca looks off, uninterested.

"You couldn't care less," I say, more a revelation than an accusation.

"I didn't come this far to be treated poorly," he says.

"You knew I had business here. This isn't a vacation for me—it's work. I'm sorry . . ." I stop. I am apologizing all the time to him. He's right on that count. What am I sorry for exactly? Putting him out? "No, I'm not sorry, Gianluca. You surprised me here, and I'm not going to apologize for doing the work I came here to do. I thought you, of all people, would understand that."

"You have your priorities in place. I am not one of them."

"How can you say that? I thought we were at the start of a good thing here."

"I'm not interested in 'a good thing,' as you call it. I want more from you than that. Valentina, I want more *for* you than that. But what I want does not seem to matter to you."

"I don't think you should assume what matters to me—or what doesn't."

"That's correct. I have no idea what matters to you. For all I know, there's someone else."

"There is no one else!"

"Then why do you treat me this way?"

"Am I treating you badly?" I place my hands on my chest. I can feel my heart beating.

"I don't spend enough time with you to know."

"I'm doing the best I can. Give me a break here. I'm working all day and coming home to you at night. But that's not the issue, is it? I think our real problem is that I'm not the girl in the pool in Capri."

"What do you mean by that?" he asks.

"You fell for a sad sack who'd been abandoned by her boyfriend. You swept in and made it all better. Well, this go-round,

I'm on a different track. I have a purpose here—and it's not love first and foremost. But you were changing my mind about that."

"Was I? Then why do you leave me here? Why don't you ask me along, to be with you? You hide me in the hotel like a gigolo."

"Are you serious?"

"Even your response insults me. I am not your tanner. I was your lover."

"Was?"

"This is not going to work, Valentina."

"Hold on a second. Don't tell me what works and what doesn't. If you would live in the 21st century, we might have a chance! I could text you and tell you that I'm going to be late, but you refuse to text—you don't even have a cell phone that works, you have one of those cheesy international models for emergencies. Well, guess what, it's an emergency to me when I can't get hold of you. I've got news for you, Gianluca. There aren't any carrier pigeons with heart-shaped vials carrying handwritten notes through the air that say, 'Hang on honey, I'm gonna be late for dinner.' "

"It has nothing to do with phones." Gianluca raises his voice.

"Then what is it?"

"You don't trust me."

"What are you talking about?"

"You say you love me, but it isn't possible to make love and mean it unless you trust."

"I don't understand!" I shout, but it's unconvincing. Even I can hear the uncertainty in my voice.

"If you trusted me, you would honor me. You would put me first. You would tell Roberta that I was here, waiting. Did you tell Roberta about me?"

I shake my head that I didn't. And now I'm forced to ask myself why I didn't. I'm not ashamed of him. I'm not hiding him. But I am just beginning to sort out what he means to me—do I

have to announce that I'm falling in love with Gianluca to everyone I see? Am I required to call my mother and ask her? I begin
to explain my logic, but he cuts me off.

"You see, you aren't really in love with me. The sex is good,
and you like coming back to the hotel and having a good time, but
you don't want more than that. You say you do, but you don't."

"You're the one who said you didn't want any children!" I
blurt. Now, why would I bring *that* up? This man is forcing me to
look at things I would rather not confront. I feel myself getting
angrier.

"I said it was up to you," he says quietly.

"What kind of a commitment is that?" I yell.

"I told you, it's up to you. But even *that*, even the decision to
have a baby, you want me to make for you. You don't want to
decide anything for yourself, Valentina. I don't like this wait-and-
see-what-happens attitude that you have. I find it cowardly. "

"You don't make me feel very secure." I don't know where
this is coming from either. I'm not the woman that needs a man to
make her feel confident. I am confident!

"How can I? You're insecure within yourself. You tell me you
cried when you caught your chef with another woman, but you
were in fact relieved."

"Do not bring up Roman!"

"He is part of this! He did to you what you expected—he
chose someone else over you, because in your mind that's what all
men eventually do. They leave. So why not show them the door
first? Why not mistreat them until they are forced to go? Why not
honor your word and show up when you're supposed to? You
can't. Because you don't want to!"

"I didn't mean to mistreat you. I'm trying to be here for
you—and get my work done. I don't have the luxury of taking
time off to fall in love and cruise around town with you!"

"And I do? I will go home to Arezzo and a backlog of work
that will take me weeks to complete."

"Oh, now you have to sacrifice for me—"

"What do you think a relationship is, Valentina?"

"Evidently, I have no idea!"

"Finally the truth! You've treated me poorly. Maybe you expected me to take it, but I've had far too good a life to spend what's left of it waiting around for you to grow up."

"You are wrong! I am a grown-up!" I sound about thirteen years old.

"No, I am exactly right about this. You are a child. You have not grown up—you have not made your life your own."

"Yes, I have!"

"How?"

"I took over the business. I . . ." I can't think of any other grown-up things that I've done.

"You took over the business because you had to, not because you chose it. Don't you see that you *never* choose?"

"I left teaching to become a shoemaker. I chose that."

"And now, that's your excuse for everything. Work. Work is always the excuse. I hoped that you were the kind of woman who wanted love as much as work. You don't. You cannot be a real artist if you turn away from love. Without love in your life, you will be a journeyman, never a master."

"Now you're the expert on me?"

"No, I'm not. Far from it. I have no idea who you really are, because you won't show yourself to me. You don't trust me, Valentina. And I cannot be with a woman who doesn't."

"I don't think you'll cheat on me," I say quietly.

"This is not about infidelity. It's about trusting me with your heart. You don't. I see you act upon it in small ways—you don't believe me, for example, when I say it's cold outside, you go to the balcony and check for yourself. When you ask if there are any messages when you come in the door after work, and I tell you there are not, you call the front desk and check anyway. When I ask you to meet me and you agree to, when you don't show up, it tells me that you don't really want to be with me."

"I don't know what to say." And I don't, because he's right. I'm so used to being on my own that I don't know how to let him in—or if I even want to.

"You say you love your father and you forgave him for how he treated your mother—but you haven't forgiven men in general for being human. You have high expectations, and then when we aren't perfect, you say, See, there it is, you disappoint me. You make love to me, but you won't make love a part of your life."

Gianluca makes his way to the door.

"So that's it. You invent me in your romantic letters, and then when I'm a human being and make a mistake, or a few of them, you leave. Now who isn't being real?"

He picks up his suitcase. "I'm going back to Italy. Is that real enough for you?"

"Now you're being cruel."

"I believe it's cruel to dismiss someone that you have feelings for."

"But I didn't do it deliberately! Okay, I've made about a million mistakes with you. But, you can't just bail on me at the first sign of trouble. It might be Italian, but it's not American. We fight for what we want."

"I don't believe you want me."

"Oh, come on. I never said I was perfect, Gianluca. You made me that way in your letters. *I'd* fall in love with me the way you described me! But I'm more than a rendering of your imagination. I'm a mess."

"I see you as a woman who has everything. Why would I pretend otherwise when I wrote to you?"

"Because I *don't* have everything. Not even close! I know I can be horrible and selfish and single-minded and judgmental. I'm just hacking my way through this forest trying to get to daylight.

I don't know everything—but I was learning a lot from you. And if you do decide to leave me, you should know that."

"I do know that," he says quietly.

"I don't know why I didn't jump in the cab and come back here when I couldn't reach you. And I don't know why I didn't bring you to the factory. And I don't know why I didn't check my phone! I'm so used to separating my work and my love life—because I've always had to. And maybe I saw, when I was a kid, that my grandparents' marriage suffered because they worked together, and then they went up the stairs every night and lived together—it was just too much."

"Or maybe they were happy."

"Maybe they were." I throw up my hands. *That* possibility is not one I ever contemplate.

"You cannot love me in the shadow of what you come from. You have to love me in cold, hard light. You have to trust me," he says insistently.

"You have to meet me in the middle. You have to look at how different we are, or this will never work. You feel a great longing for a time that's passed. But I'm not from another time. I am right *now*. I'm *of* the moment, and I have to stay *in* the moment. And it's not just about being hip, or young—it's *survival*. It's the big stuff, and then the little things too. Like . . . it matters if I pick purple or green for the color of the fall collection in 2011. I have to invent what comes next, or my company will fold. I will fold. I can't live in 1812 in my love life *or* my work life. I know I'm asking you for a lot. I know I am a conflicting combination of the traditional and the modern—but do not mistake my honor of tradition as an excuse for me to look to a man to take care of me. I can take care of myself."

"Then what is my role in your life?"

I put my hands on my face to think. I haven't thought about this. I simply try to take Gianluca a day at a time and hope that our time together is building toward something. I've looked for-

ward to seeing him each night when I return home. But I don't
know what his role is. I haven't defined it, in a relationship where
it is a requirement of his to know where he fits in the big picture.
And I don't know yet. But I can't say that to him; he will think it's
just another excuse for me to avoid falling in love and committing
myself to him. So I say what I'm feeling.

"I love you," I tell him. And then I think for a moment before
I say, "And you love me. Equal. Reciprocal. Back and forth. Give
and take. Not one of us idolizes the other, and then the other fails
to live up to some standard that doesn't even exist. I'm made of
sturdy stuff. I promise you."

My eyes sting with tears. I have never knowingly hurt anyone
in my life, but I know I've hurt Gianluca. I *have* been hiding him
away—I don't talk about him to my sisters, I didn't even tell my
mother he was here. But I find the time to call her, don't I? If
Gram brings Gianluca up on the phone, I'm the ultimate in casual
disregard. I share very little about him with Gabriel. It's almost as
if I'm planning the breakup before I commit to the relationship.

Dear God, I'd go into therapy and figure this out if only I had
the time!

But I have to sort this out with *him*, because he's right, and I
know he's right. I don't believe he'll stay when he sees who I
really am. I will invent some way to undermine it. I'll blame my
work, I'll blame my family, I'll even blame the *weather*. I pretend
to want love because I don't want to end up old and bitter like
Aunt Feen. But that's the path I've been on all along—in refusing
to grow up and own my life. I know exactly what will happen to
me if I stay on course, if I choose to never trust anyone. I'll wind
up all alone in assisted living wearing a muumuu and bunion
pads, nursing a highball with nothing but my bitter thoughts to
keep me company.

Real love requires surrender—and I've been faking it.

Gianluca puts down his suitcase. He puts his arms around me
and gives me a warm hug, one you would give your mechanic

when he fixes your transmission for free. I step back and look at him. I almost can't believe it. It's a final embrace.

"I'm going home," he says. "Take care of yourself." He picks up his suitcase and goes.

I stand in the spot where he held me for a very long time. I think of the words he wrote in the first letter he sent to me: *Love builds in a series of small realizations.* Well, he was right about that. And now, I have one for Gianluca. Love also *ends* in a series of small realizations.

The full moon over La Recoleta shimmers like a pale pink sequin. I close the robe tightly around me and pull the sash. I love a balcony. I like to be high above the ground, up and away from people, from noise, from clutter. I can think so much more clearly with an endless sky overhead. And I've done a lot of thinking tonight. And a lot of weeping.

I've cried on and off for hours. Ending a love affair in a foreign country is worse than breaking up at home. A woman needs familiar things around her when her heart has been broken. This hotel room is beautiful, but there's no comfort for me in the opulent bed and the bath. I see Gianluca everywhere, and when I do, I just feel worse. Only Gabriel made me laugh; when I called him, he said that his mother always warned her children "to never get involved with anyone from the other side." I guess there's a history of Italian Americans dropped by Italians from across the ocean. Well, tonight, add me to the list.

The colors of Buenos Aires are saturated like hand-dyed silk, especially after midnight, when the candy colors fall into shadow and striae of ink tones emerge, deepest violets, berry blues, ruby reds, and burnished gold. The green foliage seems to be cut from velvet, framing the autumnal buds that sparkle like beads in tiny bursts of indelible color.

My particular lover's dream has ended badly in one of the

most beautiful places in all the world. And while I'm tempted to stay another day, another week, or another month in hopes that this sadness will fade amid such beauty, that's just a fantasy. It's time for me to go home too. Whatever I will become will be decided under a different night sky, somewhere else in the world. I imagine anything is possible, except a future with Gianluca Vechiarelli, and even if that was a possibility, I know I would need the stars and so much more to find my way back to him.

I'm organized in my seat on the plane back to New York when I call Roberta one last time before I leave Buenos Aires. "I just want to thank you for everything. And Lupe, too. Please give her my love."

"I will. I am so happy we met. Your brother and I are talking. I find him charming."

"Good for you."

She laughs. "He's family."

"Right, right," I agree. I can't believe how far Roberta and I have come on this trip. I feel as though I am just getting to know her, but the future is promising. That's all that matters. "Before I let you go, Roberta, there's just one thing I failed to ask you. Why did your great-grandfather name the company Caminito? Why didn't he name it after himself?"

"Simple. There was already an Angelini Shoe Company," she says.

Long airplane flights are truly the last bastion of electronic disconnection in the modern age. No phones allowed, so planes become bubbles transporting unknowing passengers from Point A to Point B in a general fog. It's great—I needed an eight-hour blackout to think things through before landing in New York. I have my sketch pad out, my pencil at the ready, and the stack of letters that Michel wrote to his brother Rafael for reading material.

If my love life has been a disaster here, my work made up for it. I have sketched an addition to the *Bella Rosa* line, a flat called *La Boca*, made of deep blue suede, with gold knots scattered on the vamp—very simple, but inspired by this new place that I've come to love.

I bought Tess a local cookbook. Let's see if she can re-create some of Lupe's dishes. Argentinean food, created from a Mediterranean base but kicked up with Spanish spices—cumin and chili pepper and saffron—has changed my palate. I've eaten soft buds of yellow rice flecked with fresh hot pepper, an alternative to our sweet, creamy risotto. There are apricot glazes and guava nectar drizzled on moist cake instead of a powdered sugar finish.

And after dinner, they serve the blackest coffee and the darkest chocolate. The wines are smoky and hearty, with an intensity to them that you don't find in Italian varieties.

Buenos Aires takes the best of European and African culture and reinvents it in the heat. The breads, soft, spongy bagels and honey-soaked cake, from the Jewish section; the pastas tossed with herbs and butter from the Italians; the tender filets of beef rubbed with spices and slow-cooked Spanish style; and the fresh syrups reduced from mangos and coconuts, pure African. The mélange of all these cultures somehow works together, proving that if it can be done with food, surely people can follow suit.

The greatest lesson I have learned in Buenos Aires is that tradition and the moment can live side by side in complete harmony. One does not have to pull against the other.

This trip has given me a worldview. I realize now that I didn't have one before. I was content to become a master shoemaker, perfecting designs as old as my family itself, with my head down at the worktable hours a day, years on end, concentrating on technique and detail: making a straight seam, and sewing leather together in stitches so small, they are practically invisible. That was my goal—to mimic what had come before me, and work at the same excellent level my grandfather and grandmother had achieved.

But that was their level—not mine. I want more.

I wonder. Did *they* ever imagine more? A hundred years came and went, with the company working off Michel's original sketches, the tried-and-true styles—classic, yes, but did we challenge ourselves? Did we keep dreaming? Did we even acknowledge the present, and all it has to offer?

Looking back, our company was fearful of change. To be fair, my great-grandfather and my grandparents had to make a living—and survive immigration, the Great Depression, and then a postwar economy that favored industrial manufacturing. Challenge after challenge, the Angelini Shoe Company prevailed. But did we commit to growth? I must build the brand to save the company in this economy. It's not really that different from what Rafael Angelini had to do so many years ago; he had to leave everything he knew in order to reinvent his life and his craft.

I unwrap the letters he received from his brother Michel carefully from the stack.

I unfold the first letter, and in my sketchbook, clear a page to translate Michel's letter to Rafael.

August 5, 1922
Dear Rafael,

My brother, I do not receive a response to my two letters, and now wonder if you are alive. I pray this is true. I do not forget your kindness to me when my Jojo died. I do not forget your kindness to my son, who is without his mother. My son Michel asks for you. He went to the Feast of Our Lady of Mount Carmel and paid an indulgence for your return. Brother, we must make amends. We must make peace, for our sakes and

*for my son, who only has you and me in the world. I fear that I
am raising a cold son, one who cannot know love because he has
been so bitterly disappointed.*

   *Please help me help my son. Come home and be with your
brother and nephew. I wish the coin we tossed had been in your
favor. It was a mistake to ask you to go. Come back and we will
be partners again. The shop is thriving, I am very busy. The
Dutch who come to work here, no good. Kind people, but not
good with leather. Only the Italians can work the leather. I
think of you, brother. Please write to me and let me know that
you are well.*

Your brother,
Michel

I put down my pencil and pick up the letter. I close my eyes,
all the while holding the delicate paper in my hands. It took guts
for Michel to write letters to his brother especially when he didn't
receive a reply.

I'm ashamed that I thought Gianluca's old-fashioned letters,
written on similar onionskin paper, were somehow less relevant
than a text message, which can be delivered instantly.

A handwritten letter carries a lot of risk. It's a one-sided conversation that reveals the truth of the writer. Furthermore, the
writer is not there to see the reaction of the person he writes to, so
there's a great unknown to the process that requires a leap of faith.
The writer has to choose the right words to express his sentiments, and then, once he has sealed the envelope, he has to place
those thoughts in the hands of someone else, trusting that the
feelings will be delivered, and that the recipient will understand
the writer's intent. How childish to think that could be easy.

It wasn't easy for my great-grandfather or for Gianluca.

I used to believe that people don't change, that it's impossible,
that we just become more of who we are as life goes on. But that's
not true. When we're loved, we're presented with options to

change. We can hold on, we can forgive, we can sever ties completely. We can disappoint one another, or celebrate the best of ourselves—but what we can't do is turn away. The truth is right here on paper.

How ironic that the love letters I received from Gianluca, and doubted, or even dismissed, now seem to have been written in a whole different light. He fell in love with me when he chose to describe his feelings on paper. And then, he came to Buenos Aires to convince me that I was worth loving. And what did I do? I didn't believe him, and I didn't trust him, because what are words? Facts? But when I read this letter written brother to brother, the truth becomes apparent. And the truth, when it's all over, is the only thing that remains.

II

It Isn't a Dream Anymore

"WHEN I TELL YOU TO look, open your eyes," Gabriel says.

I take my hands away from my face and drink in Gabriel's handiwork, the newly decorated living room and kitchen at 166 Perry Street. "Oh, my God—or should I say, Oh, my William Haines."

"I *knew* you'd get it. I knew you'd see old Hollywood in the new decor!"

"I saw it immediately!" My mother beams from the kitchen. "Like bang! Bang! Bang!" She shoots an imaginary gun around the room at the window treatments, the paint, the re-covered, and sometimes replaced, furniture.

"Very elegant," Tess comments.

"I'm gonna have you do my house," Jaclyn promises. "I love the blue."

"I'm so happy the Sisters Roncalli concur."

"You've got a flair, Gabriel," my mother practically purrs.

"Yes, I do. And I have the taste to back up the pizzazz. The blue, Jaclyn, is because this level is just a floor away from the sky itself. The sky was my inspiration. I want you to feel uplifted when you enter."

The living room is wallpapered in cream with a black-striped border. Gabriel has positioned his zebra-print love seats in front of the windows. He created draperies that mimic stage curtains, opulent turquoise silk drapes with black silk braid tiebacks. He used Gram's simple black onyx-based lamps to anchor the love seats. He took the old wooden coffee table and painted it with high-gloss black enamel. There's a crystal vase filled with white roses placed artfully on the table.

He kept the farm table—but refinished the top, which now, instead of stained flat walnut brown, is rubbed through to show the natural woodgrain finish. He re-covered the seats on the twelve dining chairs with a calm but fun flowered chintz in sea green, sky blue, and beige.

The marble kitchen counter, which used to fade into the chrome stove behind it, pops against the new wallpaper. He re-covered the red stools at the kitchen bar in black patent leather, using the same bronze studs from the old rendition.

Gabriel repeated the wallpaper in the kitchen area. He mounted the oil portrait of my grandfather making shoes in the shop (which previously hung in Gram's bedroom) on the wall behind the table.

"I hope you like Gramps." He points to the portrait.

"My father resembles Vincent Price in that painting. In real life, his features were not nearly as pointy," Mom says critically. "But the gold-leaf frame is to die for!"

"Thank you, ladies. I know you've lived with the same old, same old for all these years, but I couldn't take another minute of it."

I take in the beauty of Gabriel's work while I remember the way things used to be.

"What's that look?" he says to me. "That wistful thing happening on your face. What's that all about?"

"Was I wistful?"

"Terribly."

"Well, I was just remembering what it was. And I guess I had a moment of sadness."

"Then we'll put it back," Gabriel says, not meaning it.

"No. I love it. I am embracing change and all that comes with it," I tell him. "I think it's magnificent, and I can't thank you enough for doing all this work."

Gabriel exhales, relieved. "I was so nervous."

"Why?"

"Well, it's your house."

"It's *our* house. You generously pay rent."

"Better you get it than cousin Joey. He blows it at OTB on the horses. Besides, I've redone every rental I've ever lived in on this island, and why should this be any different?"

I roll back the gates on the windows in the shop, letting in the morning light. I'm about to sip my morning coffee when Bret sweeps into the shop. "I've got good news."

Bret throws his valise on the worktable and opens it. "Or should I say: a great opportunity for you."

"But we got the loan—I've already put the check in the bank. What could be better than cold hard cash?"

"I was in a development meeting with a group of investors that has come together to buy up companies on the cheap. This is the only good news in a recession—it's a buyer's market. Anyhow, I told them about you, and they're interested in selling the *Bella Rosa* in their chain."

"Who are they?"

"They're a group that sells to major department store chains—like Neiman's, Saks, and Bloomingdales."

"I've heard of them," I joke.

"They usually go for household name designers, but you're an up-and-coming brand, at least, that's how I pitched you. I showed them the samples and the portfolio, and they were very impressed. They wanted to know how far along you were in production."

"Alfred and Roberta have been talking—they're saying fall is a safe bet. We could have the order complete by then."

"I want you to meet with them."

"Absolutely."

Bret sits down on the work stool and looks at me. "What happened to you?"

"What do you mean?"

"You're different."

"Me? Really?"

"Something changed," he says.

"I had a love affair."

"Who is the lucky guy?"

"Gianluca Vechiarelli. You met him."

"But he's in Italy."

"He surprised me in Buenos Aires. And we had a great time—and then he surprised me again, when he broke up with me."

Gabriel comes into the shop. "I know, I know. I'm up at the crack. Why? Because I'm on fire. Now that I've got the living room done, I'm doing the master bedroom. I have appointments at the D&D building—Scalamandre silk, by the bolt, on sale for a song. The only good thing about this economy are the deals."

"What's your vision for the master bedroom?" I ask.

"It's gonna be an homage to Lady Mendl."

"Whoever that is." Bret smiles.

"I don't have time to teach you." Gabriel checks his pockets for his wallet and keys. He does this whenever he leaves the house. I know about Gabriel's habits more than I would a husband, if I had one. "I'm tired of being the arbiter of taste for all those who know me." He looks at me, then at Bret. "What's wrong? I know why *she's* sad"—he points to me—"but you?"

"I was about to tell Val when you walked in." Bret sighs.

"You know it. You can always count on me." Gabriel sits down on a work stool and props his face on his hand. "So?"

"Mackenzie and I are going through a tough time."

"What's the matter?" I ask.

"She's not happy."

"Buy her a bracelet," Gabriel suggests. "Those suburban housewives love a diamond tennis bracelet."

"She has one already," Bret says.

"Make it sapphires. Very hot gemstone right now."

I glare at him. "Bret is serious."

"I don't know what to do. I thought all marriages went through these periods—and you know, you work through it and come out the other side. But she's not content to ride it out."

"Is she leaving you?" Gabriel asks bluntly.

"No. But she wants us to go through counseling."

"That's the kiss of death."

"Gabriel!" I could kill him.

"Well, it *is*. If you're going to unload in front of a third party, you probably have hit the rocks."

"Ignore him. Counseling will help," I assure Bret.

"How do you know?"

"It saved my parents' marriage," I remind Gabriel.

"Mac's parents weren't so lucky. They went to counseling. Then they divorced." Bret's eyes fill with tears.

I reach out and place my hand on his. "Now, come on. This will all work out. She's not going anywhere."

"I really love her. And I love my girls. I can't imagine having them grow up with divorced parents. I can't fathom that."

"Then you work it out," Gabriel says. "People hit snags every day . . ." He looks at me.

"And they bounce back," I reassure Bret.

"Thanks guys," Bret says. "I just didn't see my life going this way. I thought we were better than this."

"Trouble doesn't know a stranger," Gabriel says. "My grandmother used to say that in Italian, but I can't remember how it went—but that was the gist. Bad times visit all of us. Just as sure as they come, they will go."

"Thanks, Gabe." Bret turns to me. "I'll call you later." Bret snaps his valise shut and goes.

We sit in the early morning quiet of the shop for a long while. Gabriel reaches across the worktable and takes a sip of my coffee. "You realize that out of everybody we know, *we* have the only marriage that's working."

"That's because I give you free rein with the decorating."

"Uh-huh," Gabriel agrees.

"And I'm grateful for your cooking."

"That's true." Gabriel looks off, out into the early morning light, and thinks. "And you know why we'll last a lifetime and beyond?"

"I have no idea."

"Because we have never ever had sex, and we never ever will. Our relationship is the most satisfying of all because we will never disappoint each other."

I stand back from the mirror as June models the gift I bought her in the Palermo barrio in Buenos Aires. The box I sent from the hotel finally arrived. In the age of texting, old-fashioned mail seems to take a lifetime to reach its destination. "What do you think? Handmade."

"I am loving this!" June buckles the low-slung belt of braided leather with a hammered silver belt buckle low over her tunic. She turns to see the view from the back in the mirror. "Is this sexy or what?"

"Very sexy on you."

"You know, I've never been to South America. All my travels, and I never went there. I did Mexico. And a soft-spoken Mexican named Gordo."

"So many countries, so little time."

"And now I'm old. That bus is parked permanently. The battery is dead. And I can't remember where I put the jumper cables."

"I doubt that, June." I pour a cup of coffee for June, and then one for me. "How do you think Alfred is doing?"

"I believe the affair has ended," June says.

"Good."

I have been playing catch-up in the shop for most of July and August. I haven't had an in-depth conversation with my brother. We have so much to sort out about the business that Kathleen's name has barely come up. "I think my brother realized what he had at home."

"Maybe he did. You know, I've had a married man here and there. And there's laws of the jungle where they're concerned. Now, I say this as a free, single woman who was once upon a time involved with a married man—or *twice* upon a time, back in the day, and I'm not particularly proud of that. But in the case of a fella named Bob DuPont—not those DuPonts, I'm never *that* lucky—I learned from him that a married man doesn't want to see himself as someone who is out there looking *just* for sex, even though the point of having an affair is sex, it's *exactly* what you're looking for. But we're intellectual animals, and we like to think that there's something more involved than the dovetailing of two libidos. But when the sex wanes—and it always wanes, honey, trust me—you have to justify the time spent. So you have a few dinners to wind down, some without dessert and some with 'dessert,' if you know what I mean. You have to shed tears of 'poor us, had we only met in another time,' but this conversation only happens after you know the affair is kaput. Then you feel cleansed. You are able to say good-bye and move forward. That's what Kathleen and Alfred have done, I'd bet on it."

"I hope so."

"You know, I feel for your brother. It's no secret that I've always thought he was a prig. He's sanctimonious, and those are the first ones to fall. And when they do, they hit the ground hard, like a lead pipe. The pious types are tortured by their own weakness."

"I've learned a lot about Alfred since he came to work here. For the first time in his life, my brother is making mistakes. It's been painful to watch, but at least he's learning from them."

"Do you think his wife knows?" June asks.

"I told him not to tell Pamela anything about it—ever. No good would come of that."

"You're right. I am not one for true confessions—not ever. I think they're cruel. Besides that, time is the only thing that can soften the impact of a hard fall. Always has and always will." She sips her coffee. "So, what about you?"

"I'm trying to get over Gianluca."

"Still? Have you written to him?"

I shake my head that I haven't.

"Why don't you try?"

"I don't know what to say."

"Sure you do."

"No, June, I really don't."

"Why don't you start by writing how you feel about him?"

"I don't think he'd believe me." During our fight, I flailed around, unable to express my true feelings. He stood firm while I grappled. This is the difference between an impulsive woman and a wise man. He knew what I was going to say before I said it.

"Of course he would. He'd believe you," June assures me. "He's in love with you."

"He *was* in love with me. He was so furious with me that he got on a plane and went back to Italy. He crossed *continents* to get away from me."

"You're under his skin."

"In a bad way."

"That is yet to be determined," June says. "You know, when you went with the chef, I was worried. Roman wasn't as smart as you. Nice guy. Roving eye—I don't blame him, he can't help that, it's *in* a man, or it's not. But this Gianluca is different. He really understands you. I don't think you should walk away from that so quickly. Why don't you call him?"

"I'd just cry."

"Then write to him."

June goes to the desk and pulls typing paper off the printer. She grabs a pen from the cup. "Here." She hands me the paper and pen, clears the corner of the cutting table, and kicks the rolling stool toward me. I sit.

August 28, 2010

When I write the date I realize the entire summer has passed without a word between Gianluca and me.

> *Dear Gianluca,*
>
> *I don't know if you remember me, but we were together in Buenos Aires in June and I made you so angry you got on a plane and went home. I think about you every day and feel terrible, then there's the night, when I feel worse. I'm writing this letter to apologize for being such a fool. I never meant to mislead you or to hurt you, but I managed to do so many things wrong that I lost you. I hope that you've found happiness with a normal woman who treats you well. But if you haven't, I know a real nut here in New York City who would give everything she has to see you again. I'm writing this on thick paper from the printer, because it's an impulse letter and I'm not stopping to run up the stairs for pretty stationery. (At least I'm not writing to you on the back of a button order form or a water bill.) I*

*remember how it felt when you held me the whole night through,
and how I wished I could reach up and push the sun back over
the horizon just to buy a few more hours of that bliss. But I can't
control everything—and maybe I control nothing. I only know
that my heart is broken without you—and maybe sometime, if
you can forgive me, you might think about coming home.*

Love,
Valentina

This has been the summer of broken hearts (mine) and paint fumes (Gabriel's). When Gabriel was done with the Re-Fabulous (as he calls it) of the second floor, he turned his attention to the roof. He allowed me to keep the tomato plants (mainly because we eat them), but everything else needed and received a facelift. Those items that could not be refurbished were banished.

He sanded the old wrought iron table and chairs and repainted them deep lilac. He made new seat cushions for the seats (Cecil Beaton–inspired, bold black-and-white stripes).

Saint Francis of Assisi got power-washed and painted eggshell white. He fixed the hose in the fountain—which my mother swears has been broken since 1958—and now free-flowing with sacred water once more, it is affixed with tiny pin lights (for night drama), and scattered with blossoms in the clamshell.

He even painted the old black charcoal grill a deep lilac to go with the furniture. "It looks like a spaceship for my people," Gabriel said when he stood back and viewed his handiwork. "Italians?" I said. "No, the gays," he corrected me. Our grill now resembles a giant L'Eggs egg, the container for fine women's hosiery formerly found at D'Agostino's on a spin rack.

The final and most dramatic touch looms overhead. Gabriel made (by himself!) an awning out of lavender duck cloth. He trimmed the Greek key edges in white, and stretched it across four brass poles, anchored into the roof. This canopy creates an al fresco living room. My mother is overjoyed—finally, she has access to a glamorous outdoor space worthy of the ritziest guests at the Carlyle Hotel.

I press the flesh of ruby red tomatoes. Gram would be so pleased. It has been a great summer for tomatoes. I sent her pictures of the harvest over e-mail, and she returned the favor by sending me a picture of Dominic standing at the base of a twelve-foot sunflower that he grew in their backyard in Arezzo. We have a healthy competition between our transcontinental gardens.

I pluck the ripe tomatoes and place them carefully in a basket. I've lined up four bushel baskets: one for Mom, one for Tess, one for Jaclyn, and one for Alfred.

The newly painted screen door snaps open.

"Hi." Mackenzie looks around the roof. "Gabriel said I'd find you here."

"Here I am. This is a nice surprise," I tell her.

"Wow, what a burst of color up here. Lots of purple." She comes out onto the roof, shielding her eyes from the sun that has begun its late afternoon descent over New Jersey. Mackenzie is dressed in black linen pants and a cropped white jacket with bell sleeves. Her tennis bracelet dazzles against her tanned summer skin in the late afternoon sun.

"Isn't it great? Gabriel has redone the building. Except the workshop, of course." I dig my trowel at the base of the tomato plants. The rich, dark earth turns easily. "Bret said you had a dinner date."

"We're going to Valbella on 13th Street."

"It's very romantic. Just the two of you?" I ask.

"Yeah." She looks around the roof as though she's searching for something she has lost.

"A little pre-back-to-school/end of summer celebration?"

She just looks at me without answering. This friendly visit is not so friendly. "Valentine, I know about you and Bret."

"Excuse me?"

"Oh, come on," she says impatiently. "I know he still has feelings for you."

"Feelings?" Is she kidding? I hold up my hands in floral garden gloves with spores of plastic grips on the backside. "You could not be more mistaken. We're old friends. And that's it."

"I've read the e-mails."

"What e-mails?"

"Let me quote. 'You're the best, what would I do without you?' You sign love—and x's and o's. I've seen them. I'm not stupid—those mean hugs and kisses."

"But that's the way I sign off—I do that with everybody. Customers even. I just sent a big round of XO's to Craig Fissé at Donald Pliner. You can't be serious."

"Okay, fine, whatever. But you're doing it with my husband, and I don't like it. "

"I won't sign my e-mails to Bret in that fashion anymore."

"Whatever." She looks away.

Her dismissive attitude annoys me. So I say, "Mackenzie, it's impossible for me to be involved with your husband."

"Impossible?"

"I'm in love with someone else," I blurt. I have no idea where that came from. I've come to a place of acceptance about blowing my relationship with Gianluca. It's almost as if the sadness of losing Gianluca for good walks with me through the ordinary business of my life, like an old faithful dog. I won't tell Mackenzie that the love I profess is unrequited, and that I wait by the mailbox hoping Gianluca will write to me, or that I reread his old letters as though they're still true.

"Oh." She looks down at her bracelet, and spins it around her wrist by flicking the diamonds one by one.

Her nonchalance is a strange reaction, given the fact that she hiked all the way up to the roof to confront me about my internet x's and o's. "Mackenzie, you know good and well that I'm not involved with your husband. You know that he loves you and your daughters. What's really going on here?"

"What do you mean?" she says.

"This phony thing you're doing."

The word phony catches her off guard. "Phony?"

"Trumped up. You know Bret is not interested in me. Besides, you don't have the indignation of a woman scorned."

"Look, I read the e-mails, and I've had my suspicions all along," she argues.

"If there is a man to be trusted on the planet, it's your husband. But you know that, because you've actually *read* the e-mails. Deep down, you know the truth. You know that they are entirely innocent. You want to tell me what you're really doing here?"

"I don't know what you're asking me."

"You're looking for evidence against your husband. Why?"

Mackenzie does not answer me.

"If my e-mails are the most suspicious communication you've found, you got nothing," I tell her.

I'm tempted to tell her how many women throw themselves at Bret, but I'm not going to engage this nonsense.

I continue, "You are very lucky to have married a good man who loves you."

"I'm sick of hearing about how great he is. He's not perfect. Nowhere close."

"I didn't say he was perfect."

"We're having problems, okay? But I'm sure you knew all about that, given how much time he spends here."

"I don't know anything," I lie. "He only tells me how much he loves you and how proud he is of you and the girls."

"Okay. Well, look, I'm sorry. I'm sorry I accused you of something that you aren't guilty of. It's just that you two have a history, and I guess I just assumed that it was more."

I can't believe her tone of voice. She is actually *disappointed* that I'm not having an affair with her husband. She came up here looking for weapons of mass destruction, and all she found were tomatoes. Mackenzie turns to go. I stop her.

"I don't know what's going on here, and it's really none of my business. But what you have—you know, a good man and two beautiful, healthy girls—it's not just a given in life, it's an actual gift. And sometimes we mistake a malaise for something worse. You shouldn't do that. You earn your future happiness when you fight for it. He's worth it. You're worth it."

"You're not married. I don't think you understand."

I hold up my trowel. "Fair enough. I'm not a marriage expert. But I have been friends with your husband since we were kids. And out of all the women in the world, he chose you."

"I don't know if that's true."

"What do you mean?"

"I chose *him*. I was twenty-eight. I wanted to be married by thirty. And I wanted a baby right away, so we had the baby. And then Bret really pushed for the second baby, and I went along with it. And now I'm a full-time mom."

"But isn't that what you want?"

"I miss the city." Mackenzie goes to the edge of the roof and looks out over the Hudson River with the same sense of complete awe and peace that I do. If she could drink the river in, she would. She turns to me. "I miss conversations with grown-ups. I have them, but you know, I always feel like I'm cheating on my life. I'm torn every single day."

"You're tired. Chasing kids is the hardest work in the world."

"I mean, I'm grateful for all I have. I am," she says. "But the life I have . . . is not enough."

"Does Bret expect you to stay home?"

"I don't know. It's how it's worked out. We didn't really talk about it."

"Maybe you should."

"I need a purpose. You know, something that I create. That's all mine. Bret has a life. He goes off every morning to work, full of ideas. I remember having an idea! He's challenged. I love a challenge. My husband goes to work, and he uses his mind. Since I quit working, I don't use my mind. Where is my creativity?"

"You make things by hand, like those beautiful birthday party invitations. You're a wonderful hostess. Your home is a show-place."

"That's the trick of it. I thought it mattered that I made the best cupcakes and knew the difference between Berber and sisal carpet. I thought it mattered that I run every morning and stay in shape— you know, to keep my energy up for this big life I'm leading."

"But you are leading a big life."

"It doesn't feel like it. My life gets smaller every single day. I worked until a month before I had Maeve. I was supposed to go back to work after six months, and I just never did."

"But you were taking care of a baby."

"I'm not saying one is more important than the other. Of course the needs of a child are more important than any career. But just try and live it day after day. And see how you feel."

"The definition of happiness is very personal. What might make me happy—"

"I'm not happy," she cuts me off. "And maybe there are a million reasons why, but the truth is, I only need one to justify changing my life."

"I'm sorry," I say.

Mackenzie looks at me. "Besides, it's too late. It's just too late."

"Why do you say that?"

She holds the screen door open. She shifts from one foot to the other, looking to escape. This conversation has gone too far, and she knows it. She did not plan to go down this road. "I've already seen a lawyer."

"Does Bret know?"

She shakes her head.

"He'll be devastated," I promise her.

"These things happen."

"They happen because you let them happen," I tell her.

She looks at me. "I need to go." The screen door snaps shut.

I go to the edge of the roof to catch my breath.

"What the hell was that?" Gabriel says. "She clomped down those steps like a show pony."

"She's dissatisfied with her marriage. With Bret."

"Oh, please. We hardly know the woman. You recall we were shunned from the wedding. How dare she come up the stairs and dump all over you?"

"She accused me of having an affair with Bret."

"I've always said you and Bret aren't over."

"Gabriel."

"Sorry. I know nothing is going on between you two . . . is it?"

"No."

"Just checking. After all, Bret is *here*, and it's over with Gianluca. I don't know what you do when I go off to work at the Carlyle at night. This place could be a love den, for all I know."

"I get up early, work all day, go to bed early, and start over again."

"No secret life?"

"There is one thing."

"I knew it!"

"I wait for the mailman every day."

"You love Mr. Vinnie?"

"No, I'm just hoping that one of these days, he'll have something in his sack for me marked Italia."

Gabriel thinks about this for a moment. "You know what it's like living with you? It's like watching a Bette Davis weepie."

"Better than being *in* it, my friend," I tell him.

Gabriel goes back inside. I till the earth around the tomato plants with the trowel. I pour some water from the can into the planter.

Marriages break up, and the excuse, at the heart of it, is "growing apart." I pull back the leaves on the tomato plants, pulling off dead ones and making room for new foliage.

I can't help but notice that the small buds of the new plants, created from the seeds of the older ones, are fresh and green, and grow hardy in the shade of the parent. If Mackenzie were a gardener, she would know that it's the rare shoot that survives outside the nurturing of the parent plant—that it takes the strength of the whole to give way to a full harvest.

I Skype Roberta in Buenos Aires. The first face I see is baby Enzo's, who sits on his mother's lap. Roberta shifts her screen.

"He's getting so big!"

"I can't believe it." Roberta smiles. "I spoke with Alfred. You know I had my doubts about taking on new product. We've been making men's shoes all of these years. Why would we change? But I was walking around the mill yesterday, and I was thinking, the last time we grew the business, and tried something new was when my father started manufacturing. It was that long ago. And then, when you came to visit, and you had so many sketches, so many ideas—I thought, I've lost touch with the art of my work. So I went to my staff. And Sandra in cutting has always wanted to cut women's shoes, and also to work with new fibers. She likes change. And then I went through and looked at each department. We can handle the work—and if we can't, and if you decide that you don't want to use us, we will still consider expanding our physical plant, and pursuing new business."

"Good for you."

"Thank you for giving me a push."

"You're welcome."

"And no matter what happens, if you choose Caminito Shoes or not, we will always be friends."

"And family."

"And family." She smiles.

The early morning sun fills the workroom with light. The work table is covered in small stacks of deep blue suede, a sea of pattern pieces pinned with sheer paper, and measurements marked by June.

I open the ledger on the desk and view Alfred's report chronicling the comparables between Chinese manufacturers and Roberta's factory. He has done his homework.

Our squabbling days are, hopefully, over. Maybe it's distance from the end of the affair with Kathleen, or his efforts to get along, or mine, but whatever the reason, we are on the right track. June has been helpful—she doesn't play referee, but she is the Common Sense Cop when we need her. Bret and Alfred have found a way to communicate. Alfred is no longer threatened by Bret's ideas, and Bret has come to a place where he sees that Alfred, when he puts the company first, makes sound decisions.

This has been difficult for Alfred. I'm sure he wanted to focus on the big picture for the future of the shoe company, but I needed him to run the business on a daily basis. Bret is out in the world, and he knows how to raise money and find it in places Alfred would never have access to. A common goal will do that. It took all of us, becoming better listeners and considering one another's ideas, to bring us to this morning, when we will finally choose the factory that will make the *Bella Rosa*.

Alfred pushes through the entrance, carrying two coffees from the deli. He's learned the basic laws of life in our shop— whoever ventures inside from the outside is responsible for the coffee run. We've been so busy of late, the old pot on the cart in the back of the shop has been empty, and we rely on the neighborhood Greeks for our caffeine hit.

"Sorry for the early morning," I tell him.

"The train was empty—it's actually an easier commute."

Alfred sorts through the paperwork sent by our cousin Roberta while I pull the box filled with Roberta's samples of the *Bella Rosa* off the shelf to show Alfred.

Roberta made two dozen pairs of flats from the patterns we sent to her. I also bring down the box filled with the Chinese samples—Roberta's competition. We asked Sung Ma Inc. to run the same pattern and assembly and price it out for us.

"The Chinese samples are solid," I tell my brother.

"Are you leaning toward going with them now?"

"They do good work," I concede. I have learned how to negotiate with my brother. If I came on strong and insisted we go with Roberta, he'd fight me. So I let him think that I have an open mind. I lift Roberta's samples out of the box and hand them to Alfred. "But, I really like Roberta's work," I say.

"There is a delicacy to her stitchwork. The Chinese are bolder," Alfred says.

"I'm sure we could have the Chinese mimic Roberta's stitchwork, if we go that way. I would still like to do the finishing here—because I have more control—but Roberta's finishing is fine."

"Not great?"

"There's a finesse to our finishing here—you know, the buckles are given an extra buff, I re-press bows when they don't lie perfectly flat—but the general construction is excellent."

"Maybe you could design embellishments that don't require handwork to set them," Alfred offers.

"Like a fabric buckle?"

"Yeah, something that can be stitched on. Simple."

"That's a good idea," I say.

"Roberta's company assembles some of the big names. She is used to high standards. You can tell her what you want—she's used to the demands." Alfred picks up a sample. "In the end, her overall technique really is the best." He studies the seam along the heel.

"Well, you old pro." I take the shoe from him. "I agree."

"I've gone from a banker to a cobbler's assistant in nine months. I think it's apparent I'm a prodigy," he jokes.

"Just ask our mother."

"So it's your call," Alfred says. And this is the biggest change in him over the past few months. He actually defers to me. "Shall we go with Roberta?"

"Let's do it," I say.

"I'll get the paperwork to Ray." Alfred stacks the files for our attorney.

"How long will that take?"

"Quick turnaround. I made copies of these and sent them over three weeks ago when you were leaning towards going with Roberta," Alfred says.

"Efficient. I like it." I smile at my brother.

"I think this line is going to take off, Val." If anyone had told me last February that Alfred and I would reach this point, this moment in our partnership where he could admit that we could make a go of this, I would have never believed it.

"Wouldn't that be great? For us?"

"Absolutely." My brother beams.

I hand the rest of the business files over to my brother.

"How are things at home?" I ask.

"We had a good break on the Jersey shore with Pam's family. I really needed it—and she needed it. Things are much better. I owe a lot of that to you—for screwing my head on straight when I needed it the most."

"Alfred, don't give me any credit. You love your wife, and you got through it."

"I couldn't have done it without you."

"And you won't have to," I tell him. "Nobody is more surprised than me that our situation here is working. And I owe you an apology. I didn't think we'd make good partners, but you've been very generous with me. You let me do what I do best. I don't know if I could have done it all by myself. You deserve whatever success we have as much as I do."

"Fingers crossed," he says. "I'd like nothing more than to fight with you over profit margins."

"You're on," I tell him.

Gabriel enters the shop. "The apprentice has risen and is shining."

"That's what you call yourself now?"

"No, my master and mentor June Lawton calls me her apprentice."

"Oh, please. She doesn't care about your skills as a junior pattern cutter, she just likes to hear about your love life."

"That too. I like to call it a combination of high brow artistry—pattern making—and down-and-dirty details of my life as a single man looking for love. There's only so much excitement in cutting leather."

"Can you count me out?" Alfred jokes, turning away from Gabriel and back to his work.

"No one ever counts you in, Alfred. Relax."

June whistles as she pushes open the entrance door.

"Full staff meeting without me?" June asks.

"No staff meeting. Just paperwork. We're going with Roberta."

"Oh, you made your mind up when you were in Argentina." June waves her hand at me. "No-brainer."

"The Chinese were more expensive in the end—that really made the decision for me."

"You see we finished cutting the rest of the samples yesterday," June says.

"They look great."

"Who are these for?"

"Bret needs them for the funding meetings—he wants as many prototypes on display as possible." I turn to Alfred. "Did you send Bret the paperwork?"

"When I sent it to Ray, I sent Bret his own set."

"I love synergy!"

"As a very wise person once noted, a fish rots from the head—having said that, it also thrives from the head. You're a damn good boss, Valentine," June says as she passes a stack of patterns to Gabriel, who sorts them.

"Don't be so quick to give her all the credit. I like to give due to feng shui. That's right—the upper levels of this building have been transformed. First we ditched the crap, and then I schemed the dream—the apartment has gone from deadly dull to dazzling, and ever since then, we've gotten lucky around here. Or am I the only one who has noticed?"

"It's you, Gabe. All you," I tell him. "And the ancient art of feng shui."

I pick up the phone and dial Roberta. "Roberta? We've made our decision." I look around the workroom at my co-workers, June, Gabriel, and Alfred. Then I say, "You got the job. It's Angelini and Caminito from now on."

"Thank you! We are very pleased!"

"Great. Alfred will be in touch shortly with all the details."

"Thank you, Cousin."

I hang up the phone.

"Congratulations," Alfred says. "You did it."

June and Gabe break out a bottle of champagne from the mini-fridge while Alfred goes on a hunt for plastic cups. I feel a sadness in my gut because this is a moment I have dreamed of, and worked toward, and I have no one to share it with. My eyes fill with tears of regret. How I wish I could go back to Buenos Aires and make everything right with Gianluca. I miss him. But he has not called or written to me, and while I may not be the wisest woman around, I'm astute enough to know when a man has moved on. My letter, filled with humor and hope, was not well received. If it had been, I would have heard from him by now. Silence is the most direct answer of all.

I check the clock. My Skype appointment with Gram is on. I turn on the computer and dial through. After a few moments, Gram's face appears on the screen.

"Hi, hon! All's well here in Arezzo. I'm going to miss Thanksgiving turkey, though."

"You and Dominic can jump on a plane."

"Why don't you come and see us?" Gram asks.

"I can't leave the shop right now. But if the *Bella Rosa* takes off, or the economy improves in the next couple of months—"

"Valentine, don't put too much pressure on yourself."

"Did you get the *Bella Rosa* sample that I sent? Roberta built the prototype."

"It's handsome. How do you like working with her?"

"On my end, it's very easy. She's built my shoe according to specifications. She beat the Chinese. But Alfred says she drives a hard bargain in the cost department."

"That's an Angelini trait," she says.

"I need your stuffing recipe. Gabriel is cooking this year."

"No problem."

"Yeah, we're having the whole family over—kids, parents, chestnuts on the roof—every dish and everybody but you and Dominic."

"We'll be there for Christmas."

"I know. It's just not the same. You know, Thanksgiving is your holiday—nobody will roast the chestnuts like you. Even Aunt Feen is coming over. I'll hide the liquor."

"I just called her."

"How is she?"

"The same." Gram sighs. "How about we have a mod holiday—we'll Skype!" Gram says.

"Okay. Great."

"Shall I e-mail the recipe?"

"Sure, sure. You can send it right to Gabriel."

"How's the roommate situation working out?"

"I love it. Gram, you won't believe the changes he's made. The house is beautiful."

"He's got the energy to do it. I never did."

Before Gram met Dominic, especially in the years after my grandfather died, I noticed that it was all she could do to put in a workday downstairs and then go up the stairs for dinner. Toward the end, I took over most of the chores; I would do the shopping and the cleaning. But beyond a coat of fresh paint, in the same colors that had always been on the walls, we never did much to upgrade our living space. Now I understand why she kept the same sofa for thirty-five years. There wasn't the time or energy to look for a new one. Making shoes takes stamina; the business takes its toll on our time and resources, and whatever is left goes to the essentials.

"You will love the new look," I promise her.

"I'm sure I will."

"So have you seen Gianluca?" I ask.

"Not a lot. He's been traveling to Florence quite a bit."

My stomach turns. I imagine Gianluca in his Mercedes with a willowy redhead draped across the front seat, one of those Italian girls who speaks four languages, gives a great neck massage, and makes a killer dish of linguine alle vongole.

Gram continues, "The tannery is busy. Gianluca's always working, it seems."

"Yeah. Me too." I couldn't sound less enthusiastic. "Has he asked about me?" It's out of my mouth before I can take it back.

"Gianluca?" Gram leans in. "No, he hasn't, honey."

"Well, do me a favor. Don't tell him I asked you if he asked about me."

Gram looks confused. And she should. Gianluca accused me of being a child, and I sound like one. At least he didn't burden Gram with the whole Buenos Aires saga—although part of me wishes he had.

"Okay," she agrees. After a slight pause she continues, "I'll get that stuffing recipe right out to you."

"Thanks."

The screen goes black like my mood. Gianluca has totally moved on. No agonizing and regret for him! How adult! Maybe he's even checking in on Carlotta from time to time—after all, nothing like reigniting an old fire and basking in that familiar glow. This is going to be a lovely holiday season around here. Thanksgiving and then Christmas, with a fresh pine tree, and me—single, lonely me . . . pining.

I wake up to the scent of fresh sage, pumpkin, and bread baking on Thanksgiving morning. I'm about to roll over and go to sleep, when I hear:

"Val, time to get up! I need a pair of hands down here."

I sit up in bed and look out the window. The treetops along the Hudson River Park have only flecks of gold left on their mostly bare branches. The gray river looks like a shard of hammered silver where the sun hits the surface. "Coming!" I holler.

Gabriel is in the kitchen, running the mixer. He wears a black-and-white bandana around his head. He turns the mixer off. "Do the table for me. I spent half the night glittering the place cards."

Gabriel dipped miniature fresh pumpkins in orange glitter, then stuck a small green flag, on which he had written the guest's name in calligraphy, next to the stem.

"My, we are fancy."

"Is there any other way?" Gabriel goes back to fluffing his pumpkin mousse.

June made a tablecloth out of orange cotton, and trimmed it in white fringe. I center it on the table. Then I take the tray of pumpkins and place them one by one down the center of the table on either side. I set the table with Gram's china, which Gabriel set out and counted.

"No kiddie table?"

"I don't believe in them. Sitting at the kiddie table scarred me for life. I won't visit that agony on your nieces and nephews."

"Hey, it's your party."

"And yours," he reminds me.

I unpack a large solid chocolate turkey from Li-Lac's on Hudson Street and place it on a gold serving dish. I open a bag of orange, green, and silver foil kisses and surround the turkey. The details of the table design were decided on a legal pad a week ago. I follow Gabriel's plan down to the placement of the last foil kiss.

"What time are we expecting the family?" I ask.

"Noon. They're going to the parade till eleven. Then they'll catch Santa in Macy's Square, hop the subway to Christopher, up to the roof for hot apple cider and chestnuts, and downstairs for carving of the bird. We'll eat promptly at one thirty."

"You play serious ball, my friend."

"Have to. I'm doing soufflés for dessert. Can't have those sitting around like Barney, the Macy's balloon, when he hit the streetlight on Broadway and deflated. Not a good idea."

"I love you for many reasons, Gabriel. Your soufflés might be number one."

"Thank you. I love being loved by you. And I hope none of your love affairs work out—ever."

"Well, Gabriel. You don't have to worry about that. I am destined to be alone. You know what gay men and I have in common?"

"I'm dying to know."

"We were not raised for happily ever after. That's another reason why you and I have the perfect marriage. You understand that. I'm going up to the roof to start the grill," I tell him.

"That's a good wife," he says as I go.

I grab the large cast-iron skillet and head up to the roof.

Gabriel winter-proofed the garden, and instead of putting old feed sacks on the plants, he took muslin from the shop and draped it over them, tying the material at the base of the containers with enormous red ribbons. Everything that man touches turns into art.

I load the charcoals onto the grill. I take a long matchstick and light it, throwing some lighter fluid on the coals. They ignite into orange flames, the exact color of the stubborn leaves that remain on the top branches of the maple trees across the highway.

I lean over the roof ledge and look down the Hudson to where the river opens up into the Atlantic Ocean. Gianluca is just an ocean away, I'm thinking, as I watch the white caps roll out to sea. "Stop it," I say out loud. Stop thinking about that man! He does not want you anymore.

"Valentine."

My mother hauls a sack of chestnuts across the roof. "Yoo-hoo." Mom wears a pumpkin-colored suit with matching high heels. A brooch in the shape of a turkey, made with chocolate pavé stones, shines in the sun. "I didn't want to scare you. What are you doing? You're looking off to sea like a besmirched scullery maid in a Philippa Gregory novel."

"Actually, I *am* pining. I'm going to be alone for my entire life, Ma."

"I promise you that will not be the case."

"How do you know?"

"A mother *knows*," she says definitively. "In the meantime, you and Gabriel have put together quite the holiday. The table looks gorgeous. We picked up Aunt Feen on the way in. She's down in the kitchen grousing about the traffic. June is here, and she's helping."

"I'd better get down there."

"Alfred called from his cell. He's bringing the boys. Pamela is coming in from Jersey on the train."

"Pamela didn't go to the parade?"

"No. You know she hates crowds. She's such a tiny little thing. She'd have been tossed to and fro."

"Oh, yeah. Right." Any deviation from Alfred and Pamela's routine gives me a jolt of worry. Alfred assures me that everything is fine, but is it?

"What's the matter?" Mom asks.

"I can't shake him, Ma. The Italian."

"I'm sorry." Mom puts her arms around me. "Maybe you can go to Italy when you get the *Bella Rosa* launched. Maybe if you go there, Gianluca will listen to reason."

"I don't want to make a trip just to be rejected again."

"Good point. Why don't you invite him here for Christmas?"

"Because he'll say no."

"You don't know until you ask." My mother uses the same strategy she employed when I was sixteen and needed a prom date. She'd haul out the yearbook and paw through it, making a list of names just as she would from the phone book when the drain clogged and she needed a plumber. "Tell Gianluca that we'll put on the dog for him. He hasn't lived until he's had the Roncalli Feast of the Seven Fishes on Christmas Eve."

"What a lure," I groan. "Hmm. Gianluca . . . please choose . . . me, a comely thirty-five-year-old or . . . a fish fry. Come one! Come all!"

"Hey, it's the best I got," Mom shrugs. "But Val . . . first we have to get through Thanksgiving. We could be in for a little tension at dinner."

"Why?"

My mother lets go of me and pushes her Jackie O. sunglasses up the bridge of her small nose. "Tess and Charlie have been having a little ongoing argument about our family down in Argentina. And, well, it's the race issue. Charlie feels that Tess shouldn't tell the girls about the Argentinian side of the family."

"Are you kidding?"

"Charlie feels it's complicated."

"You mean he's prejudiced."

"No, no, I don't think that at all. It's just new information. He doesn't know how to tell his daughters."

"You just say, we have family in Argentina and they're black."

"That's what you would do, but the Fazzanis—you know how they are. Those people have airs. His mother wanted finger bowls at their wedding reception."

"I remember."

"They're awfully proper for a bunch of carpenters from Long Island—but proper nonetheless. And small-minded. I cannot deal with pea brains, but in this instance, we *have* to."

"Mom, I'm not going to hide my cousins."

"I'm not asking you to hide them. I just would rather you don't Skype Roberta in when Charlie's around."

"That's crazy."

"It is what it is." My mother purses her lips together. "Give the man time to accept our new family."

"I'm going to talk to Charlie."

"No, don't bother. Let it go."

"I thought it was weird. Charlie's been keeping his distance. I've hardly seen him—now I know why."

"He doesn't judge you. And he doesn't blame you for going down there. Not entirely anyway. He doesn't understand why you have to get into business with them."

"I really don't care what he thinks. Charlie can judge me all he wants. But I'm not putting up with this—and my sister knows better."

"That's her husband." My mother throws her hands up. "We marry who we marry, and then we have to cope."

"Then she better enlighten him."

Mom shakes her head and goes back down the stairs. Something tells me this Thanksgiving won't be a peaceful meeting like the one between the Pilgrims and the Native Americans. I have a feeling this one could be war.

12

Autumn in New York

GABRIEL CHANGES INTO A SUIT for Thanksgiving dinner, or the Feast of the Cassoulets, as we referred to it during the preplanning stages. I throw on a skirt and heels, because wherever there are glittery pumpkins, dressy clothes are required.

Tess whistles when I enter the kitchen. "Put on the apron," she says. "Cashmere is a bitch to clean."

I throw it on. She gives me a pastry gun filled with cannoli filling.

"I made the shells myself," Jaclyn says.

"They look divine." I fill a delicate pastry horn with creamy filling. I take a bite.

"Excellent!" I tell them.

"Roll the ends in chocolate," Jaclyn instructs. "I learned that from Giada De Laurentiis. She eats everything she makes on TV. How does she stay so thin?"

"I have no idea." I shove the rest of the cannoli into my mouth and chew.

Tess places a bowl of dark chocolate curls on the counter. I pick up the horns and fill them, then roll the tip ends in the chocolate.

"Italians are the only people in the world who prepare dessert while they serve the main meal," June says as she ladles mashed potatoes into a server.

"We like our sugar," Jaclyn explains.

Aunt Feen is parked at the head of the table nursing a cup of weak tea, because that's all my mother offered her. The new elephant in the living room of the Angelini family is Aunt Feen's drinking problem. Our solution is to hide the hard stuff and hope she doesn't notice. Alfred fills the crystal tumblers at each place setting with ice water.

Charisma, Rocco, and Alfred Jr. watch the recap of the Macy's parade on TV in the living room, while Tom feeds baby Teodora a bottle. Charlie uncorks the wine. Dad carves the turkey on a cutting board on the counter. As he slices, my mother stabs the pieces and places them artfully on a tray festooned with spinach leaves.

"Chiara, call everyone to dinner." My niece sits on a stool, playing with a handheld computer game.

She doesn't look up at me. "Do you have a bell? Grandma Fazzani has a crystal bell with a little silver dinger."

I look at her. "Yeah, I got a bell." I take the computer game away from her and give my niece the egg timer shaped like a hen. "Crank it and ring it."

"Nice attitude," Gabriel whispers as he grabs the matches to light the candles down the center of the table. "Makes me happy my family is dead."

"That's not funny."

"Well, they are dead. Can't bring 'em back."

"No, you can't," Aunt Feen bellows. "And you're better off. I got a few relatives taking up space in the bowels of hell."

It's always fascinating that Aunt Feen pretends to be deaf when you want to send her a message, but when something is whispered, she gets it in total.

Chiara lets loose with the egg timer close to baby Teodora's ear. The baby wails.

"Chiara!" Tess shouts. "You'll make the baby go deaf."

"Sorry," she says, but the look on her face is anything but contrite.

"That's the little devil who interrupted your coitus, isn't it?" Gabriel says confidentially in my ear.

"The very one. That kid was on a mission."

Dad takes his place at the head of the table, while Mom places the platter of turkey before her place setting, as she will serve it.

"I took a nibble of the stuffing, Gabriel—and it's just like Teodora's. You nailed it, seasonings and all," Mom brags. "Savory. And light in texture."

"Thank you," Gabriel says proudly.

One by one, the family finds their seats as they check for their names at the place setting.

"Where's Pam?" I ask Alfred.

"She's upstairs. She has a migraine," Alfred says, tapping his forehead.

"I told her to lie down in my room." Gabriel places baskets of fresh rolls down the center of the table. "The serene green walls will cure whatever's ailing her."

"This year, we're gonna join hands . . . ," my father begins.

"I am *not* holding hands," Aunt Feen complains. "The Catholic Church went in the toilet when they started that—I don't like it in church, and I don't like it at dinner."

"Okay, then we won't hold hands," Dad says.

"Wait a second, Dad," I interrupt. "Aunt Feen, if Dad wants us to hold hands, we're going to hold hands. He's the head of this family. You're our beloved great-aunt, but what he says goes."

A silence settles over the table.

I bow my head. I close my eyes, and instead of picturing Jesus on his heavenly throne surrounded by a choir of saints, I see Gianluca. Our relationship may be as dead as the autumn leaves in the centerpiece, but the things I learned from him are very much alive. He would be proud that I defended my father and his role. Gianluca taught me that tradition isn't something we *do*, it's the way we *are*. And now that 166 Perry Street is my home and this is officially the first holiday where this is my table—and Gabriel's—it's my call. I make the rules in this house.

"Hold hands," I say firmly.

"Aw, what the hell." Feen grabs the hands of Gabriel to her right and Charlie to her left.

"Dear God, we want to thank you. It's been a year of trans-missions—"

"*Transitions*," Mom corrects him.

"—transitions. We got my mother-in-law in the old country with a new husband. We got the grandkids growing healthy and strong, we got Aunt Feen on the mend from the bruising she took in Arezzo, we got an all-clear on my prostrate—"

"*Prostate*." My mother sighs.

"And we got Gabriel handy with the paint can and the sponge, turning 166 Perry Street into a Phoenecian palace."

My mother is about to change *Phoenecian* to the correct *Vene-tian*. I squeeze her hand so she won't. Egypt and Venice are close enough. Mom takes the tip and leaves Dad's vocabulary alone.

"What I'm saying, dear Lord, is that we are grateful. June, you're a good Irishman, and we love to have you anytime—"

"You got it, Dutch," June says, her head bowed.

"And we thank you for this bee-you-tee-full food and table, the Vegas pumpkins, the wine from your grapes, I got my eye on you, Aunt Feen, no fair guzzling. The last place we wanna celebrate this Thanksgiving is the emergency room at Saint Vincent's—"

"I don't want to be no trouble," Feen grouses.

"So, dear Lord," Dad continues, "we got another year under our belts. And we thank you for that. In the name of the Father, Son, and Holy Ghost . . . Amen."

"I'm going to check on Pamela," Alfred says, as my sisters pass the platters. He goes up the stairs as we help the kids load their plates.

I fill my plate with turkey, stuffing, whipped potatoes, and green beans. I place my napkin on my lap. I listen while my brothers-in-law and father talk college football, and as always, the chatter loops around to Notre Dame, and will the Fighting Irish place in the polls this year. The number of the year may change, the children may grow older, and we may add in a new baby or spouse here and there, but every autumn, and every Thanksgiving, the talk turns to Notre Dame football and will they or won't they.

Alfred returns to the table with a look of concern on his face.

"Is Pamela okay?"

He nods that she is.

But I notice that my brother isn't eating. I'm not hungry either. Something is going on, something under the surface, looming in the depths. I can see the shadows. I can't name the beast, but it's there, lurking. I can feel it. And when I look at my brother, I know that he can too.

"Oh, Val, tell Feen about Buenos Aires. She hasn't heard any details," June says.

My mother kicks me under the table.

"It was really nice," I say.

"That's *all*?" Feen says critically. "I get on the bus and go gambling in Atlantic City—now that's nice. But Argentina? That should be something more. Am I right?" Feen waves her fork around.

"Tell about the river walk, and the cobblestones," June persists.

"They were lovely."

Silence settles over the table. "But you have people there, right?"

"Yes, Aunt Feen."

"I never saw any pictures."

"I have them. I can show you later."

"Okay. Nothing like waiting months on end to see your relatives who I never met and probably never will. I'll be dead, and then maybe you'll get off your duff and think, Sheesh, should've shown Aunt Feen the pictures. You'd think you'd have made a video or something. I'm never gonna get on a plane again. I'd like to see your long-lost cousins before I die."

"You will, Aunt Feen," I assure her.

The kids giggle as they poke the glitter pumpkins with their forks. "Don't destroy the table," my mother says to them nicely.

"You know, when you get to be my age, it's a bad idea to withhold anything. That includes mail. I could win the lottery, and if I died, right before I found out, let's say. You know, none of youse could collect the money? That'll show you. You know, I could go in a heartbeat. Boom. One minute here, the next, I'm code blue. So, if you wouldn't mind, get the pictures."

"Later, Aunt Feen," Tess pipes up.

My brother-in-law Charlie shifts uncomfortably in his seat.

"Who wants to go to the park?" my brother-in-law Tom says.

Chiara, Rocco, Alfred, and Charisma leap out of their seats. "The baby is fussy. She needs air." He kisses Jaclyn on the cheek. The truth is, Tom needs air. These family dinners don't sustain him—they literally *choke* him.

Tess helps the girls into their coats. Alfred zips up the boys' parkas. "You want me to go with?" Alfred asks Tom.

"Nope. We'll be fine," he says as he drops baby Teodora into the snuggly. "The big girls and boys will help."

"We will!" Chiara promises, but that devilish look returns to her face as she narrows her eyes. She probably plans to hail a cab, throw the baby in, and send her on a joyride through the five boroughs.

"And when you guys get back, we'll go up on the roof for chestnuts and marshmallows, okay?"

The kids shout in delight as they race down the stairs.

"Kids, they are balls of energy," June laughs.

"That's why I never had any." Feen takes the napkin from her lap and tucks it into her collar and spreads it across her chest. "They destroy everything they touch."

I drain my wineglass. I look down at my food, which I still haven't tasted. But I'm on my third glass of wine. Not good.

"So get the pictures," Aunt Feen insists.

"Later." I force a smile.

"Val's not done eating, Aunt Feen," Mom says hurriedly.

"She can eat, and I can look at pictures."

"We are not looking at pictures!" Charlie bellows.

"Why the hell not?" Feen demands.

"Not while my children are here."

"Technically, they're at the park," Mom offers helpfully.

"What difference does *that* make?" Aunt Feen looks around, confused. Her eyeballs bounce around in her head like slot machine lemons.

"I don't want them to walk in and see the pictures," Charlie says firmly.

"Are they pornos or something?" Feen throws up her hands.

"They are not . . . pornos." My mother squeezes the word out, not wanting to allude to pornography at a family meal (or any other time, for that matter).

"Tell your aunt what the problem is, Ma," Charlie says.

"There isn't a *problem*," I correct him. "At least not to thinking people."

"What are you saying?" Charlie looks at me.

"Stop squabbling and get the pictures," Aunt Feen says. "When Tessie and I die, you people are all that's left. Our blood line will collapse like a tapped vein. So you found some relations on your side and I want to see them. What's the big deal?"

"Not *now*," Mom says.

"But I don't understand why . . . ," Aunt Feen persists.

"Because they are black," Charlie blurts. "That's right. African American."

Aunt Feen is confused.

"They can't be African American—because they are not *American*. They are Argentinian," I correct him. "But even that isn't exactly right—they are a mix of many cultures, Ecuadorian, African, and Italian."

"No matter how you mix it, there's still one predominant color—and that would be black," Charlie corrects me.

"No, it's a *mix*."

"A mix." Feen is surprised. I guess Gram didn't paint the fine details about our long-lost relatives. Aunt Feen thinks. Then she says, "Well, what did you expect? They're south of Mexico."

"That doesn't have anything to do with it," Mom interjects.

"Huh. Look at a map." Feen shrugs.

"Okay, look. Before this careens headlong into a stone wall, let me just say that I met our family, I like them, they're good people, and Alfred and I are in business with them. Yes, they are black, and they are also Italian."

"Blah blah blah," Feen mumbles.

"That's right. They are *both*. And they're beautiful people." I sound like an idiot. But I realize, in the center of this ridiculous argument, I react like one.

"Of course you'd say that." Charlie taps his fork on the table.

"What the hell is that supposed to mean?" I turn to Charlie.

"You accept anything. You're a liberal."

"What does that have to do with our family in Argentina?"

"You're happy to have black people in the family. Sure, sure, let everybody in." He waves his arms around. "What's the difference to you?"

"There is none. Who cares what color they are?"

"I do. I don't want my girls coming home with black guys. Okay? I'm all for equal rights, and everybody's one and the same in God's rainbow. I just don't want them to marry it."

"Charlie!" June pushes her chair away from the table. "Are you serious?"

"He's serious." Tess shakes her head sadly. Clearly, they've been fighting about this for months.

Charlie looks around the table for support. "Dad, back me up on this."

"Hey, since I got the cancer, nothing bothers me." Dad holds up his hands. "I love the world and everybody in it."

"Thanks," Charlie sneers.

"It's not my husband's fault that we have blacks in the family," Mom says.

"It's not anybody's *fault*, Ma," I say.

"I didn't mean that like it sounded." Mom shakes out her hands as she does whenever she's nervous. "It's just that whenever we start talking about race relations, I never say the right thing."

"You're fine," I reassure her. "There's nothing wrong with having black relatives."

"Not to you," Charlie says.

I turn to him. "It's not like I discovered our cousins are running a drug cartel."

"How do we know they're not?"

"Oh, Charlie—you're really sick." I can't help it. I haven't eaten, and I'm losing all perspective. I could bite the ass of a wild bear right now.

Mom defends me. "Look, Charlie. Valentine did not go to Argentina to unearth some family secret—"

"Oh, yes, she did—she found that goddamned drawing, Tess told me, and then she went on a hunt to find Ralph—"

"Rafael," I correct him.

"Rafael—whatever—and then she gets on a plane and goes down there and gets in business with these people. Come on. What are we doing here?"

I find myself standing, leaning across the table. "Charlie, how dare you! Nobody has asked you for anything—ever. You rolled into this family, and we've been damn good to you. When you and Tess needed help buying a house, we all pitched in—"

"Oh, now you throw that up in my face—"

"It's true. But you're not grateful. Well, the black side of me loaned you the money, okay?" I yell.

Tess stands up. "Everybody calm down."

Gabriel hands me a bread stick. He lives with me. He knows a low blood sugar dive when he sees one. "He needs help!" I point to my brother-in-law. I realize that I'm tipsy. I hold the table.

Charlie gets up from the table. "Sit down, Charlie," my father yells. "Nobody leaves the room."

Charlie sits down.

"I will not have this." My father pounds the table. "I will not have a rift. Nobody leaves until we settle this."

"Well, good luck on that front, nephew." Aunt Feen picks her teeth with her name-tag flag from the pumpkin.

We sit in silence for a moment, not knowing what to say or do.

"I'm leaving," Pamela announces from the doorway behind us.

We turn to face Pamela, who stands in the entrance to the hallway. She has on her coat.

"Oh, Pam, you're up, how's that migraine? Come and eat. The stuffing is as good as my mother's," Mom says.

"Don't condescend to me."

"I wasn't condescending." Mom looks around the table at all of us. "Was I?"

Tess and Jaclyn shake their heads that Mom was not.

"Go ahead. Stick together." Pamela looks at my sisters.

"Are you all right, Pamela?" June asks. "Am I missing something?"

"This. This is what you're missing. And what I've been missing." Pamela hurls a piece of paper on the table. I pick it up and smooth it out. From the looks of it, Pamela has had it balled up in her angry fist for hours. It's a printout of an e-mail.

"Read it," she barks at me. "I printed it out at home and memorized it on the train. Go on. Read it."

"Read what?" my father asks. "What's on the paper, Val?"

Alfred puts his face in his hands. "It's me. It's my fault."

"What is your fault?" My mom asks softly.

"Everything. It's my fault."

My mother strokes her turkey brooch and thinks. Then she says, "Did you . . . did you break the law? Did you steal, Alfred?"

He looks at her like she's insane.

Mom leans back in her chair, relieved. "He did spend twenty-three years on Wall Street. Every day you pick up the paper and some other muckety-muck is on his way to the slammer for things he was unaware he was doing. The financial world is so complex."

"Then what in God's name did you do?" Feen barks at Alfred.

"He had an affair!" Pamela shouts. "An affair. He cheated on me. Happy Holiday, everybody!"

"Pam . . . ," my sister Tess says quietly.

"Don't Pam me. I'm Clackety-Cluck—remember?"

"Clickety-Click," Jaclyn corrects her.

"Whatever. Feel free to call me anything you want because I'm outta here! You made me feel like the outsider all these years, and guess what? It was true. I was different. I was normal—and you, you're all crazy! I knew you were a pack of loonies before I married him, but it's only gotten worse. And I only put up with you quirky bastards because I loved your son. But your son has decided he doesn't love me anymore. He went out whoring around—"

Alfred leaps to his feet. "That's not true, Pam. I love you."

"Words! Words! That's all you got for me? They got a million of those in the dictionary!"

Dad nods. "True, true."

Pamela runs her hands down the sides of her body, from her bust to her waist and down to her hips. "Alfred. Look at *me*," she commands.

Alfred looks down at the table; his head hangs in shame.

Pam lowers her voice to a growl. "I said. Look. At. Me. "

Alfred looks up at Pamela, his eyes filled with tears.

"I kept the deal. I am the girl you married. I didn't change. I didn't gain fifteen pounds, then lose five and gain back twenty on that Jenny Craig seesaw your mother's been on all of her married life."

My mother gasps.

"That's right!" Pam shouts. "Lose the damn weight already!"

My mother, horrified, pulls her tummy in and sits up straight.

" Look at me. Size two December 1994 and size two November 2010. How many women can say *that* at forty-one years of age when they've given birth to babies with heads the size of bowling balls?"

"Sweet Jesus," my father mutters.

"I got you all pegged. Each and every one of you. He cheats, but you all cheat! You *all* lie! You spread stories, you gossip—"

"We discuss things, yes, but—" my mother tries to defend herself.

"Ma, you're the worst!" Pamela charges the table. "Everybody knows you tuck tags into dresses you've bought and wear them once and return them for a full refund!"

"Only once! I did that once!"

"It's cheating, okay? It's against the law!"

"It was a chartreuse gown, and it didn't do a thing for me. But my back was against the wall, and I had to wear it."

"And you." Pamela points to me. "You're a thief. Your neighbor, Mr. Matera, was dead for two years and you took his newspaper and read it every morning."

"It was a glitch. I reported it to USA Today eventually." My face burns hot with embarrassment.

"And you—" Pamela points to Tess. "Telling the ticket guy at Great Adventure that both of your children were under six, when they were seven and nine at the time. You made your own children crawl into the park on their *knees* to get in for free."

"They wouldn't honor my coupon," Tess says in her own defense.

"It's still cheating!" Pamela screeches.

"And you—" She points to Jaclyn. "You re-gift! That's right. I gave you the Estée Lauder makeup kit for your birthday, and it wound up under the Christmas tree for Tess . . . from . . . *you!*"

"It was more her palette, not mine," Jaclyn stutters. "I'm a winter, and she's a summer . . . "

"It doesn't matter. It's still cheating!"

"I was with you till the re-gift," June says generously. "That's just a skin tone thing."

"Her point would be that we're all sinners here," Dad explains to June.

"Yeah, Dad, that's my point. And chew on this. I can't believe I got mixed up with this bunch when I knew better. I saw all the signs, but I loved you so much, Alfred, I sucked it up and joined this lot of losers! Out of all the families in Queens, out of the millions of families, I marry into this one!"

"I take umbrage—" My mother raises her voice.

"Take the umbrage. Take it all. I'm done with you people." Pamela paces back and forth behind the table like a prosecutor on *Law & Order.* "And you know what? Charlie and Tom feel the same way. That's right, when you're whispering about us, you got it: we're talking about *you!* That's right, the in-laws carp about you! Why do you think Tom is always going out for walks? Nobody likes fresh air that much! He can't take you people! And Charlie? Tell 'em, Charlie. Tell them how you make up phony excuses about work so that you're only forced to attend two major holidays a year!"

Tess turns to her husband. "Is that true?"

Charlie shrugs that it is.

"Well, then—" Tess explodes. "Guess what? Our next vaca-

tion destination is Buenos Aires! That's right! We're camping out
with the South American side of the family!"

Charlie, embarrassed to be outed, reaches to put his arm
around Tess. She lurches away from him.

"I've listened to you people complain for eighteen years, and
I'm over it! If it wasn't politics, it was religion. If it wasn't RC In-
corporated, it was your almighty gravy." Pamela holds her hands
tightly in fists and shouts. "I don't care if you use garlic powder or
real cloves in your gravy! It's just sauce! Tomatoes and water! Eat
it and shut up already! Stop complaining!"

"Who complains? I don't hear any complaints," Feen says.

Pamela ignores her and continues. "Thank God I didn't let
myself go! I wanted to—believe me. I wanted to wear Uggs and
eat potato chips and watch *The Real Housewives of South Bend*, but
I didn't! I kept it all together! I hung on! It's a damn good thing I
kept my figure, because now I'm gonna be on my own—and this
body is gonna be my revenge!" Pamela holds her hands high in
the air in victory. "It's my ticket out! You watch me."

Gabriel is draped over the kitchen counter with his face
propped in his hands as though he's riveted to Night 3 of *The
Thorn Birds* on TCM. Without taking his eyes off the theatrics, he
dips a spoon into the bowl of cannoli filling and eats it. Aunt Feen
cackles with glee under her breath as our family crumbles like
blue cheese on greens before her eyes. My mother weeps into her
napkin.

I read the crumpled e-mail silently to myself.

Dearest Alfred,

    Our time was not now, our days were not
our own, but our feelings were real. Never
forget how much I love you. Happy
Thanksgiving, dear Fredo, I will always be
grateful for the time we had together. My
love always, Kathleen

The laptop computer, open on the kitchen counter, rings once. Then again. Then a third time.

"It's Gram on Skype," I say.

"Close the lid!" my mother shouts, turning to Gabriel. "Close it!"

Gabriel turns as Gram's face comes up on the screen. He snaps the screen shut, then takes the moppeen from his shoulder and wipes his brow.

"Let her hear! Let Gram hear it *all*! I got nothing to hide! I don't care if the whole country of Italy knows I've been be-smirched!" Pamela shouts.

"It's not you." Alfred tries to calm his wife down.

"I know it's not me! It's you. You're one of them, even when you tried not to be. You're just like them. *You* turned on me too."

"Pamela . . . ," he says gently.

"She calls you Fredo." Pamela pushes against Alfred's chest as he holds her close. "I call you Fredo. *I* call you that." She weeps as Alfred puts his arms around her. "Let me go. I want my boys. Where are they?"

"At the park," Tess and Jaclyn say in unison.

Pamela breaks free of Alfred's grip and turns to go.

"Pam, please sit down. Please don't go." My mother stands. "Maybe we can help."

"You? What are you gonna do? Tell me I didn't read the e-mail? Tell me it's not true? You don't see Alfred denying any-thing." Pamela places her hands in the prayer position. Through her tears, she says, "Thank God I watch *Oprah*."

My father moans.

"That's right, Dad." She glowers. "Oprah *helps* me. She did a show on money management, and I watched it because, you know . . ." And then Pamela does the strangest thing. She puts her hands on her hips like Susan Boyle when she was flirting with Simon Cowell and Piers Morgan on *Britain's Got Talent*. She shimmies her hips from side to side as she says, "My husband was fired from the bank . . ."

"I thought you resigned," Feen pipes up, gleeful at all the misery. "Some resignation. Turns out it was Das Boot!"

My mother glares at her.

"Oprah was giving women tips about how to save money during tough times. I followed her advice, because why? Because I'm a good wife and I want to ease my husband's burden! Fat chance of that! He was easing it on some government employee!"

"Thank you Pope-rah!" Aunt Feen licks her lips, hopeful for more gory details.

Pam continues, "They brought on a therapist who said that men were very vulnerable right now—that women should be sensitive to their . . ." And then she does it again, she wiggles her hips and says, "*huzz-bands*, because of the economic downturn. Now, I didn't think too much of it, because Alfred seemed so happy here with the elves making the shoes. And our life at home was fine. That's right, even our sex life!"

My father puts his face in his hands. This diatribe might kill him.

Pamela screeches, "But the expert on Oprah said, 'Check the man's e-mails.'" She lowers her voice and growls like Linda Blair after the head spin. "And so I did. That's how I found Kathleen Sweeney." Tears roll down Pamela's face.

"Wait, Pam." Alfred reaches for her. She won't let him touch her.

"You told me you'd never cheat on me. You said you never would because your father cheated on your mother."

"Now, just a minute . . ." My mother stands.

Pamela looks at my mother. "Well, he did. And you put up with it. But I think a little more of myself than you ever did of yourself." She looks at Alfred. "You stay here. With your crazy sisters and your cheating father and your vain mother and your drunk great-aunt—"

Aunt Feen throws her head back and laughs. "That's me!"

"Because . . ." Pamela tightens the belt on her size 2 coat. "I'm getting my boys and going home. Do you remember where that is? Home. The place where I made a life for you."

Pam goes down the stairs. Her stilettos go clickety-click, clickety-click all the way down. Alfred follows her out.

The entrance door downstairs snaps shut.

"Anyone for dessert?" Gabriel says from behind the counter. "I could use a digestivo. Fernet Branca? Bitters, anyone?"

"Gimme a slab of tiramisu," June says. "This is the goddamn-est Thanksgiving I have ever spent."

"I'm sorry, June." Mom dries her tears. "I'm sorry you had to hear that."

"This family needs to grow up." June pushes her plate aside.

Aunt Feen applauds. "The wheels are off the bus. Off the bus! Off the bus!"

"Shut up, Feen." June turns to my great-aunt. "You're a mean old broad. You got a camel's hump of misery on your back."

"That hump is from osteo. Bone deterioration. I had a difficult menopause," Feen explains.

"I don't care where you got it. You're the only old lady I know that gets dumber as the years roll on. And all these people dance around you in fear. I'm not afraid of you."

"You attack a lonely widow on Thanksgiving. Nice," Feen says quietly, milking any pity her blood relatives may still have for her.

"Poor Feen." June turns and faces her. "It's never enough for you. Is it? Your sister kowtowed, your niece, everybody's afraid of you. Everybody fears your temper. Not me. I see who you are. You're just an ungrateful old nag. You never got your portion. Never got a fair shake. And when you did, it was never enough. Nobody could fill the empty sock of your awful child-hood. So you never got what you wanted. Boo hoo. Most people don't. But the difference between you and other people is that they move on. They don't calcify. They don't blame everybody else for their troubles, and call the lawyer to sue the city every time they take a spill on the sidewalk. Put down the wineglass and pick up the magnifying glass and look in the mirror. Face yourself."

Aunt Feen's spine straightens in self defense. "Why you—"

"I'm not done." June levels her gaze at Charlie, who looks away.

"Shame on you, Chuck. Open your eyes. The world isn't black and white anymore—it isn't even brown—it's shades of something completely new. And not a minute too soon. Time for God to liven up the paint box. So your sister-in-law gets on a plane and finds out you have black people in the family—hardworking people who make their own way, and speak Spanish and grow olives—what's it to you? Really, how does that affect *your* life? Do you really want to spend the precious moments of your life hating people you've never met from two continents away? If that's your idea of living, then that's your business, Chuck, but don't bring the rest of us down to your idiot level. You're embarrassing yourself with your ignorance."

"June," Tess warns.

"Shut up, Tess. I've known you since you were a baby. I'm talking to your husband." June turns back to Charlie. "Let me tell you this about black people—and I know, because I've loved 'em all, black, white, Filipino—or at least I think he was—maybe, come to think of it, he was Hawaiian. It doesn't matter. I have tasted God's smorgasbord from Boston to Buhl, and I'm better for my experience. Does that offend you?"

"This is some Thanksgiving." My father sighs.

June looks at Charlie. "Well, does it?"

Charlie shakes his head.

"Didn't think so," June continues. "You should be proud to tell your daughters they have family in another country and that those folks have a little different patina from you. But let's cut to it here, Charlie. You're Sicilian, your people are a mere paddle in a canoe from North Africa. And you *know* it, and yet you have the temerity to act as though Sicily is the land of pilgrims and Wonder Bread. I got news for you—you're already family—you *are* African. It's just pigment, Charlie. Pigment. So knock it off. I'm annoyed with you already."

Gabriel places June's tiramisu in front of her.

"I'm sorry," my brother-in-law says meekly.

"Let me tell you who your daughters will marry. They will marry men exactly like you, Charlie. So if you want them to bring home a couple of small-minded bigots with a size twenty-two and a half collar, well, then, you'll get your wish."

Gabriel pours June a cup of coffee. He places the cream and sugar in front of her. June dumps cream into her coffee and stirs. "It's a café au lait world, people." She sips. "Get used to it."

I help Aunt Feen into the back seat of a town car. She grips the Macy's bag full of Thanksgiving leftovers on her lap like they're gold bricks hot off a Brinks truck. I ask the driver to see Aunt Feen to her apartment door, and he agrees. She waves me off.

I push the entrance door open and see a light on in the workshop. I kick off my shoes; the heels are killing my feet. My toes throb like my head, everything hurts after the worst holiday I've ever spent, anywhere, anytime.

I poke my head into the workshop. Alfred sits at the desk, his head down. My father sits at the worktable, watching him.

"Hey guys," I say, pushing the door open. "Alfred, are you okay?"

He doesn't answer. I look at my father. Dad looks at me and shakes his head.

"Alfred?" Dad says softly.

Alfred doesn't respond.

"Son?" Dad gets off the worktable and goes to Alfred, placing his hands on Alfred's shoulders. Alfred begins to weep. "It's going to be all right, Al," Dad says.

Alfred turns around and stands. He puts his arms around my father and buries his face in his shoulder. He is now heaving with tears. My dad looks at me as he pulls Alfred close to him.

"I've ruined everything, Dad. Everything."

"It's a dumb mistake, but you didn't ruin anything."

"She's leaving me."

"She'll forgive you, son."

"Why would she?" Alfred asks.

"Come here." Dad helps Alfred sit down. Then he pulls up a work stool next to him. He takes my brother's hands in his own. "You're a good son. A fine man. I've been proud of you every day of your life. Even when you weren't proud of me. I've done things that weren't right in my life, and the goddamn thing still haunts me. And now I've visited it on you."

"And I judged you, Dad. I judged you, and then I did the same thing."

"That's okay that you judged me. It meant that you knew I did wrong."

"I'm a hypocrite." Alfred hangs his head.

"Hey. Listen to me. I left my marriage for a while, and I'm not proud of it. I was in a dark place when I had that affair. I didn't know it at the time, but looking back, I wasn't thinking straight. I felt like my life was over—I wasn't where I was supposed to be. And I blamed your mother that I wasn't a big cheese. I don't know, I grew up in a household where my mother pushed my father. I guess I thought that's what a wife should do. I'd missed out on a promotion in the Parks Department, and I went home to your mother and she said, 'Dutch, don't worry. It'll come around. Try harder.' I should have appreciated her even more, but it just made me feel bad about myself, and I couldn't shake it. I needed to feel good about myself again. So, I went looking for trouble because that made me feel alive, back on my game. But it was a temporary fix. And when I went with the other woman . . . my heart . . ."

My father wipes away a tear, but he recovers, and focuses on my brother.

"My heart was breaking because I turned away from the people who loved me, for someone who was looking for the love I already had. Now, this seems like a . . . like a . . . contradiction . . ."

I exhale softly as my father at long last finds the exact right word.

". . . but it wasn't. The best thing about me was that I had a good wife and four children. That was my calling card in the world. That's what made me a cut above. But I had to throw it all away to find that out. I had built, with your mother, a bee-you-tee-full family. But at that time, I thought I needed more, attention, appreciation. Whatever the hell you want to call it."

"I don't want to lose her," Alfred says.

"You won't, Alfred. You won't. But you gotta persist. And when she's ready to forgive you, you'll get a chance to start over. You'll have to build your life with her again."

"I don't know if I can do that. If she'll let me."

"It's not easy. The hardest thing I ever had to do was win your mother over a second time. And every man is different. But you're made of far better stuff than me. You're smarter, you're more loyal, and you're stubborn. You can turn it around. And I'm here to help you however I can. If you'll let me."

"I'm sorry, Dad."

"You owe me nothing, son. Not an apology. Nothing."

"I hurt you, too."

"Because I hurt you. That only makes us even."

Dad holds Alfred close.

I watch them for a long time. I never thought this day would come.

"I suffer, too," I say aloud. I didn't intend to speak, but the words just come out of me. I place my hand over my mouth.

My father looks up at me.

"Dad, I know you love us, but there's a reason I'm not married. There's a reason I can't . . ." I feel tears coming, but I stop them. "I can't trust any man. It's really hard for me. I forgave you, but I never beat my own fear. I'm still afraid of loving someone and being disappointed."

"I'm sorry, Valentina," my father says.

Only two men in my life ever call me Valentina, my father and Gianluca. Instead of making me sad, it makes me smile for a moment.

Gianluca did everything he could to help get through my fear, and I turned him away because I couldn't face myself. I wouldn't show him who I really was, so at the end, he had to go because he didn't recognize me anymore. I didn't even fight for him. I didn't chase him when he left our room at the Four Seasons, I just stood there, frozen, inside and out, unable to move. I guess I thought if I went after him, I wouldn't know what to say when he stopped, I wouldn't have known what to *do*. So instead, I let him go. I let a good man, rare as an emerald, go because I couldn't think of one reason to make him stay.

"Alfred?"

My brother and father look at me.

"At least you know what happens when you break a promise. I can't even make one."

I leave Alfred and Dad in the shop. I pick up my shoes and climb the stairs. I think about the pithy letter I wrote to Gianluca to woo him back. I was being funny after I broke the man's heart. Now, that's inappropriate. No wonder he didn't write back. He sat there in Italy and thought, "She still doesn't get it." Maybe someday he'll forgive me for my ignorance. I wish, on this Thanksgiving night, that there was some way to reach out to him. But this isn't one of Gabriel's soufflés that fell on the way to the table from the oven. This is Gianluca's happiness I destroyed. What I couldn't know then was that I destroyed my own as well.

"Feen is on her way out of Manhattan," I announce to my sisters and mother who sit around the farm table after an endless meal that was long on courses and family drama.

"Where's your father?"

"He and Alfred are talking in the shop."

"Oh, good," my mother says, ever the optimist.

I pull up a seat at the table. I place the wooden nut bowl in front of me, and commence cracking walnuts. My sisters and mother have small piles of shells where their plates once rested.

"June and Gabe are on the roof. They said they were roasting chestnuts, but I think they're smoking pot," Tess says. "That, or they've charred the chestnuts."

"Good for them," I say. "Either way."

"I agree," Tess says. Then she looks around the table. "What are we going to do?"

"Well, clearly, I'm going to go on a serious diet after the holidays," Mom says.

"Oh, God, Ma, Pam was just taking potshots," Jaclyn says.

"I only did Jenny Craig twice. I never saw myself as a yo-yo dieter." Mom hacks the meat out of a walnut with a small, silver pick. She chews. "Do you?"

"No, Ma," we say in unison.

"You know what? I like her," Jaclyn says.

"Who? Pam?"

"Yeah. She's got moxie. I had no idea she was that tough. I thought she was weak, and look at her, she stood up for herself."

"If you look hard enough, you can find something to like about anybody," Mom says diplomatically.

"She's got good taste," I add. "She has very dramatic sense of color when it comes to her clothing."

"Always well dressed," Tess says, cracking a pecan in half. "You can't say she let herself go. She was right about that. "

"She was," I agree. "So why didn't we like her?"

"I don't think we ever liked her because we're all scared of Alfred." Tess smooths her nutshells into a pile like she's racking the balls for a game of pool.

"You're right. We've danced around him all our lives. Trying to please him, or stay out of his way—it's him. It's not her," I realize. "It was never her."

"I disagree. I'm not afraid of my own son."

"Mom, when we were kids, you'd have a pot of sauce on the stove for rigatoni for dinner. When Alfred came in from the library and he didn't want marinara, you'd turn off the sauce, put the pot back in the fridge, and start pounding cutlets. You were afraid of him too."

My mother picks up a nutcracker and decimates a pecan with one squeeze. "Do you kids analyze everything your father and I ever did or didn't do?"

"Yes," we answer in unison.

"I don't think that's healthy." Mom frowns.

The last of the relatives have left with the last of the leftovers. June grabbed a cab after a parting whiskey shot. She has another party tonight in the East Village.

I finish the last of the dishes. I go to the table and blow out the candles, which have burned down to flat orange puddles in the holders.

I grab the last two cannoli and climb the steps to the roof. The scent of roasted chestnuts fills the air.

Gabriel has his feet up on the chaise, looking at the moon. I sit on the empty one beside him.

"Nobody ate the chestnuts," Gabriel says.

"A lot of drama today. They forgot." I hand him a cannoli.

"I can't. I got no room."

I put the cannoli aside and lean back on my chaise. The full moon is lit like a diner sign on the off-ramp of the Jersey Turnpike, so close I could reach up and write Open 24 Hours on the face of it.

"You prepared a beautiful meal," I say.

"It didn't matter. It went down like gruel."

"How about that Kathleen sending an e-mail?"

"I never liked that redheaded hussy," Gabriel says. "Not for a second. "

"I was surprised she'd send an e-mail like that."

"Then you need a wake-up call. She *wanted* Pamela to find it. Holidays suck for mistresses. They're sitting home scheming! There they are: all alone in the dark with their black thoughts and a Morton's pot pie. And instead of going out and finding an available man, they want to wreck the holidays for the married ones. In the old days, they did drive-bys. My mother called the police one Christmas when my father's mistress cruised by for the fiftieth time before the manicotti. Now, all these home wreckers have to do is e-mail. Saves on gas, I guess."

"Your father cheated too?"

"Of course."

"Is it inevitable?"

"There's a study. Around sixty percent of all people in long-term relationships stray. Except, I don't go by those statistics. They say five percent of all people are gay, but that number can't be right—if you count up the hairdressers alone, you got at least fifteen percent of the general population right there. I think men have a hard time being men. Straight men at least."

"Why?" I ask.

"Women give men a place to go. A man is a useless piece of equipment whose purpose is lost if it were not for women."

"What are you talking about?"

He nods, warming to his subject. "It's like this. A man might go out and get a job, but only for someplace to go during the day. And he's only working that job to give the money to his wife. And then, if he does really well . . . to buy her good jewelry. And only because she asks for it. Diamonds aren't a man's idea. The first woman sent the first man into a hole in the ground, and when he emerged with the first diamond she looked at it and said, 'It's too small. Dig farther.' Men are not ambitious outside of their desire to impress women. A woman, in return, gives a man's life shape. A context. A place to go. It's very simple."

"You mean that every man is motivated not by ambition or power or wealth, but because he wants to please a woman?"

"Absolutely. Think about it. A straight man doesn't care about surroundings, or good food—unless we're talking Mario Batali or Tom Colicchio, but they're an anomaly. No, women are the inspiration behind anything that has ever been invented, made, or built by men. Women, in fact, rule the world because of that power, and I've always thought it a waste that they don't see that."

If Gabriel is right, and I think he could be, I might still have a chance with Gianluca. If he lives to love and please a woman, why not me?

Gabriel continues, "If there were more of us, gay men would rule the world, because we have it all. We know how to create a place to go, and we like being in it. We're homebodies with flair. We are. But we're outnumbered by the straights. No, this life . . . is all about women. When you girls say it's a man's world—well, if only that were true! I'd be loving it. You ladies should own your power. You need to pick up the ball and run with it. I only use that analogy because of all the football talk at dinner."

"Sorry about that. The men in my family mistook your lovely table for a tailgater."

"If only straight men could take that passion they have for a ball flying through the air, and apply it to making the world better, they could fix global warming, ocean dumping, and mountaintop removal in the time it takes me to stuff a turkey."

"Or make twenty individual soufflés."

"I am handy, aren't I?"

"Beyond." I reach over and take Gabriel's hand. We look up at the midnight blue sky.

"What's to become of us, Valentine?"

"What do you mean?"

"We're thirty-five years old."

"That's not old," I say.

"It's not young either. Do you ever think about the future?"

"I try not to."

"You live in a bubble."

"I like my bubble. It's blue and shiny. And you should know, you did the interior decorating."

"So stay there." Gabriel smiles. "It's a gorgeous Tiepolo blue, and it works well with your skin tone."

"Thanks." I don't have the heart to ruin Gabriel's holiday by admitting that I spend a lot of time worrying about the future. Time is passing, and I feel I have nothing to show for it. Sometimes I flip through my sketchbook and remember places and times, the color of the afternoon sun on old bricks or the exact shade of red on a cardinal that landed on the bench in Hudson River Park while I was drawing, but in general, I'm amazed at how quickly the days fade in my memory. What will I remember about these days ten years from now? Will I agonize that I didn't do enough to build a life with a man that loves me? Will I be like June, who knows how to party but likes to go home alone? "Gabe, I have an idea. I don't want to get the number elevens between my eyes. Why don't you worry about the future for both of us?"

"Not a problem. Once this economy turns, I'm going to start to save money, and I'm going to get rich. I'm going to plan for my retirement. I'm going to need a lot of cash. A gay man living on social security on a fixed income? I don't think so. The only fixed item I want in my life is that North Star up there." Gabriel points up to the sky, where small specks of silver peek through the blue. "No, I'm going to need cash that *flows.* I need a big budget—just for decorative lamps. I've got a plan. How about you? What are you going to do with the second half of your life?"

I think for a moment. When I'm on this roof, I feel anything is possible and I have since I was a child. I search the sky as far as I can see beyond the point where the Hudson River meets the Atlantic Ocean. The answer lies somewhere between here and there, the home I love and know, and the greater world beyond, which I'm not so sure of.

Finally I say, "I want to love a man who can be true."

"Aim low, wouldja?"

I laugh. "That's *all* I want. And one other thing. Don't ever leave me."

"Where am I gonna go?" Gabriel asks.

"I don't know. Away. Somewhere. My family is crazy."

"I've seen worse," Gabriel assures me.

The autumn moon slips behind tufts of low, gray clouds. "A storm is rolling in," I say. And while I can't be sure about the weather, somehow, when I say it aloud, it sounds like a promise.

13

A Little Learnin' Is a Dangerous Thing

GABRIEL AND I CARRIED OUR first Christmas tree home from Jane Street and decorated it last night—two full weeks before Christmas. We like a blue spruce scent for as long as we can have it.

I carry my morning coffee over to the sofa and put my feet up. There's nothing like the twinkle of sky blue, soft gold, ruby red, and bright green lights glowing deep in the branches first thing in the morning. Watching the lights reflect in the old glass ornaments is the closest I will get to inner peace. This has been some year. Gabriel and I couldn't decorate the tree fast enough. We figure, with the way our family holidays have been going, celebrate early and celebrate often, because you never know.

"Val, Alfred and Bret are downstairs." Gabriel stands at the top of the stairs.

"Is June in?"

"Any minute."

"I'm on my way."

I follow Gabriel down the stairs and into the shop.

Bret gives us each a report. "So here's what's happening. In about an hour, Shelley Chambers DaSilva is going to come into the shop and observe. She wants to see what inspires your designs, how June and Gabriel cut patterns, and Alfred's role as your brother and business partner. She's a consultant, and she reps the major department stores. They send her out to see how you create your product. She's on the lookout for a solid operation with good business practices. She's looking at you, Val, to understand your approach and sensibility and how Angelini shoes fit in their over-all selling plan."

"You should show her your new sketches. Like the *La Boca*," Alfred says. "That's a real calling card."

"Thanks." I look at my brother, who has been here since dawn. His methodical style, left over from years as an executive in the banking industry, comes in handy on mornings like these, when we have to present our wares to a wider world. The folders are neatly labeled on the cutting table; there's a cup of number 2 pencils, a pot of coffee brewing, and a small box containing bat-teries and cords in case Ms. DaSilva's laptop needs a boost. Alfred considers every scenario always. I've come to rely on his sense of detail in business. "Have you told the rep about our production deal in Buenos Aires?"

"She knows all about it. In fact, she has contacts in Argentina, and they've already gone over and checked out Roberta's factory. They were impressed with the quality of the manufacturing. Roberta met every standard. So now all we have to do is sell them the initial order," Bret says.

"Our hope is that they take the full order for ten thousand pairs of shoes. It would make our lives so much easier if we didn't have to find another vendor to stock the remains," Alfred adds.

"Do we have to do anything special for this Shelley person?" Gabriel asks. "I would love to demonstrate my pattern-cutting technique."

"No need to grandstand." Bret smiles.

"Who, *me*?"

"Just be yourself," Bret assures him.

The phone in the shop rings. "Angelini Shoes," Alfred says. He looks at me. "She's right here." Alfred hands the phone to me.

"Valentine, we met a few years ago at June's place. This is her neighbor, Irv Raible."

"The club owner?" I remember Irv had a piano bar that June used to frequent with Gram. One night, I joined them.

"Yeah, that's me. Well, June called me this morning, really early. She wasn't feeling well, and so I went over. And I was going to take her to Saint Vincent's—over to the emergency room. But she had her breakfast and seemed better. And now . . . well, I think you should come over right away."

"To June's?"

"Yes. Please. And hurry."

I hang up the phone. "I'm sorry, guys, I've got to go. Something is wrong with June."

"I'll go with you," Gabriel says.

"No, no, you stay and do the meeting. I don't know how long I will be." I grab my coat and purse and run for the door. Snow begins to fall, steady and white, onto the cobblestone street.

I run to the corner of Washington and hail a cab. As the cab whisks me from the West Village to the East, my heart begins to pound. I jump out on East 5th Street and find June's brownstone apartment building. I ring Irv's bell and then June's. He pokes his head out of the second-story window of June's apartment. He throws me the keys.

I race up the stairs.

Irv, a muscular but small man of sixty with a shaved head and a gold hoop earring, stops me in the door. "I'm sorry, Valentine. She's gone."

"*Gone?*"

I push past Irv and into the bedroom. The Weather Channel

is on the television set. I shut it off and turn to the bed. June lies still on top of her Indian madras bedspread; the bed is made underneath her. She is dressed for work. Her bright red pigtails sport ribbons. I touch her face. Her skin is cool to the touch. She hadn't yet put on her lipstick. She smiles peacefully; her face has the countenance of a child's.

"I think it was a heart attack. Very fast," Irv says from behind me.

"I can't believe it."

"I know. I know. The picture of health."

I go to the window and close it.

"Have you ever found somebody . . . somebody who just died?"

I shake my head that I haven't.

"It's the strangest thing. They don't leave right away. You know she's still here."

"What do you mean?"

"Her spirit is in the room. I'll go down and wait for EMS. You take your time."

Irv goes, closing the door behind him. And for a moment, I want to follow him out. I've only been to wakes and funerals, where the dead lie in fancy caskets, dressed in their Sunday best, in full makeup and surrounded by bouquets of flowers. This is new and strange to me. I kneel next to the bed.

I take June's hand in mine.

I bow my head, not to pray, but to picture her coming in the shop with coffee every morning, and on Fridays with a doughnut for each of us. And I think about all the things she taught me that no woman in my family could ever say for fear of compromising their moral code. But for June, it wasn't a compromise at all. June believed in love and making love and making better love. She lived in her body without apology. There was so much more for me to learn from her.

And now, all there will be is mourning. June tried to prepare me, but I wouldn't listen. So now I have to hold on to everything she said, like directions given in a storm; her words will lead me to safety. I cry when I realize I won't be able to talk with her ever again.

"Are you here, June?" I look at her peaceful face. "Whatever you're seeing, must be pretty amazing."

I look out the window.

"It's snowing, June. You would've been bitching this morning." I smile and remember how she hated the snow. "Thank you, friend. Thank you for being Gram's best friend, and then, when she moved away, you became mine. You never treated me like anything but a peer. You always made me feel that I earned my seat at the cutting table. You taught me so much. I don't know what I'll ever do without you." I hold on to June's hand. And it's the strangest thing, the longer I hold on, the more it feels like she's leading me somewhere. I don't release my grip for a long time.

It's a blur when the police come with EMS and Irv explains what happened. I hear them when they declare her dead, then lift her carefully onto a gurney and carry her out.

I stand alone in her very neat, spare apartment, with its low-slung leather chairs, futon sofa, and long bamboo coffee table, a stack of books from the public library in the center. June had checked out *Mrs. Astor Regrets* by Meryl Gordon, a biography of Wallis Simpson Windsor called *Mrs. Simpson* by Charles Higham, and a large book of Louise Dahl-Wolfe photographs.

The walls, painted bright white, are covered with posters, one of the ABT ballet season in 1967 and another of a bluegrass music festival in West Virginia in 1975. Nothing crafty lies around—no hobby equipment, no knitting needles or sketchpads, only a yoga mat, rolled up neatly in the corner. And there's an upright piano. I had no idea she played.

I go into the kitchen, mindlessly really. I look in the sink. Spotless. Her cereal bowl is washed, single spoon, mug for tea. All clean, as though she knew she was leaving. I open the fridge. It's nearly empty. I remember that she leaves work early on Mondays to go grocery shopping. That's why the cupboard is bare.

"You all right?" Irv says, leaning against the wall that connects the kitchen to the living room.

"Not really." I close the refrigerator door.

"She talked about you all the time. You and your family. She loved the Angels. That's what she called you guys. Not the Angelinis, but the Angels. You know, you were the only number she had on her emergency call list."

"You mean my grandmother."

"No, *you*. Valentine."

"Really." This makes me smile.

"She loved young people. Had friends of all ages."

"Yes, she did."

"I got her stash out," he says matter-of-factly.

"Excuse me?"

"You know. Her *stash*. Her marijuana."

"Oh, my God." I rub my eyes with my hands.

"No worries. I think quickly on my feet. Especially right after I call the cops." He smiles. "Do you want it?"

"The pot? No thanks, Irv."

"Well, here's her key. You can clean out the apartment whenever you wish. She told me the contents were yours. I'm sure there's a will here somewhere."

"Are you the landlord?" I ask.

"Yep. Been her neighbor and landlord for twenty-seven years. When I was a kid like you, I rented in this building, and then I saved and saved, and one day, I saved enough to buy it *before* the boom, thank you Jesus. The first thing I did was move June in. She chose this apartment for the light."

"I remember when she lived on the Upper West Side."

"You've known her a long time."

"All my life."

"When she moved down here, she found her bliss. You know,

you can still be yourself in this part of town. Did you ever see her dance?"

"No, I never did."

"She was a wonder. Long lean body, legs that went on for days. When she was young, she had no peer. Red hair to her waist, flying behind her when she'd do these amazing jumps. She started out with Paul Taylor. So did I. That's how we first met. I'll never forget her dancing. That's for sure."

I stand on East 5th Street in the Village in the snow. Through the flurries, I can see strands of Christmas-tree lights across the street at the neighborhood stand where they sell trees. Red, green, and blue Roma lights sway in the wind, punching color into the gray morning.

"Oh, June," I say out loud. "You left me at Christmas." Tears and snow sting my face, but I don't move. I can't. June is gone.

The first thing I do after I tell Gabe, Bret, and Alfred about June is go up to the roof. The snow has stopped, leaving a dusting on the roof. I take in big gulps of air, hoping it will help me stop crying. But I can't.

I asked Alfred to call Mom and my sisters. I told him that I would tell Gram. I pull out my phone and scroll down to Gram's number. I look down at it, and think better of it for a moment and scroll back up to the previous number: Gianluca Vechiarelli.

I don't want to call him, and yet, he's the only person in the world I want to talk to. He will comfort me. He knows how. I press the send button. The phone clicks into the international line, and I hear faint buzzing and then a series of beeps.

"Pronto." I hear Gianluca's voice, bold and strong on the other end. I begin to cry. "Pronto?" he says again.

"Gianluca, it's Valentine. In New York."

"What's wrong?" he says softly.

"June died."

"Oh, Valentina."

"I need to call Gram, but I thought you could be with her when I called, in case she gets upset." My cries turn to weeping.

"Of course, of course," he says. "I'm so sorry, Valentina."

"I don't know what I'm going to do," I wail. "I was waiting for her to come to work this morning. And now I'll never see her again."

"Where's Gabriel?" he asks.

"Down in the shop. He's a mess too. June taught him how to cut patterns. I mean, she trained him, you know? She taught him everything she knew."

"She was a wonderful woman."

"And she was all alone," I wail.

"No, no, *carissima*. She was surrounded by love."

"No, I went over there and she was all alone. I couldn't bear it."

"That was her choice. June wanted her privacy at the end. That's different from not being loved. She was loved. You took good care of her."

His words soothe me. June was Gianluca's greatest champion. She only met him a few times last fall, but she read all of his letters and loved every single word he wrote. I blurt, "I'm sorry about everything, Gianluca. I never meant to hurt you. I didn't follow you when you left the hotel. I was too proud. And I'm sorry about that stupid letter I sent. I'm always joking around, as if humor is what is required in every situation. It's not. There's nothing funny about your feelings . . . or mine. I never meant to diminish you in any way with my dumb, cavalier attitude." My face stings where my tears meet the cold.

"I understand," he says softly.

"Thank you."

"I go to Papa's now. You call there, okay?"

"Okay."

I flip the phone shut and hold it close to me. A cold winter wind kicks up and blows the snow off the roof west toward the Hudson River like a sheet stretched across a summer clothesline. The snow clouds hang low over my river in a veil of gray fog. I can't see anything. Everything, it seems, is gone.

Gram and Dominic changed their airline tickets to come to New York sooner than they planned for June's funeral. June's friends have planned a funeral/life celebration, a hybrid Catholic/ Buddhist ceremony at Integral Yoga on 13th Street.

June took yoga classes there for years. Of late, she had started Pilates, but yoga was a passion with her. She'd often grab a class during lunch when she worked in the shop. A few blocks from the Angelini Shoe Company, she'd throw her rolled-up mat in its case on her back like a sack of arrows for her bow. She'd return an hour later, centered, calm, and ready for an afternoon of hard work.

Gabriel taps on my bedroom door. He peeks in. "You ready?" Gabriel adjusts his black tie which he wears with a black shirt, and a black suit.

"Not really." I straighten the zipper on my skirt. "Do you think I'm overdressed?"

"Have you ever been to Integral Yoga? You're *way* over-dressed. And so am I. People meditate in their underwear over there."

"It's not the grocery store, is it?"

"The natural foods section is downstairs. We're going upstairs to the yoga studios. What did you think? We'd put June to rest in the raw nuts section?"

"I have no expectations."

"You're better off," Gabriel says. "I shop there from time to time. And those vegans are the least healthy-looking people I've ever seen. Their skin tone is puce. They need to eat a burger. But I'm not getting involved in that movement. Believe me."

Gram and Dominic are dressed and waiting for us in the living room. Gram looks beautiful in a navy suit that June liked. Dominic wears a black suit with a navy-blue-and-white-striped tie.

"Gabriel, what you've done with the house is marvelous."

"Gram, I was a nervous wreck before you got here," he tells her. "I really changed it up, you know."

"I approve. I love what you did in Mike's room upstairs. You kept the wallpaper and painted the furniture."

"Are you comfortable in there?"

"Very much." Dominic smiles.

"We'd better go," I tell them.

Even though Integral Yoga is only a few blocks from our building, with the snow and ice, I didn't want to take any chances of Gram or Dominic falling, so we ordered a town car. As we drive across Perry Street, we bounce on the cobblestones. June would have gotten a kick out of the town car going such a short distance. She didn't like anything on wheels, except her work stool. She'd take the bus, but only in a pinch. She walked everywhere in this city, regardless of the weather.

When we arrive at Integral Yoga, there's a hand-printed sign on the door that says

JUNE LAWTON

with an arrow pointing up. Gabriel holds the door open. Gram and I go up the stairs, followed by Gabriel and Dominic.

When we arrive at Studio C, the room is filled with a few rows of folding chairs, and on the floor, a series of small yoga mats laid neatly in front of them—for anyone who wants to sit pretzel style during the service, I imagine. It's a fairly large room with polished blond wood. The long wall opposite the door is covered with floor-to-ceiling mirrors. The mourners hang their umbrellas and snow gear on the barre. A large window overlooks the back garden. A lonely old tree, with gray gnarled branches, is glazed with ice.

My family takes up two rows of folding chairs. We are dressed like a pack of devout Catholics, while June's friends, ages nineteen to ninety, mill around in jeans, spandex skirts with leggings, and for one gentleman, in a bright blue kimono. My family looks completely out of place, like Capodimonte lamps at a Conran's yard sale. June would love the contrast.

Mom is already weeping. She wears a black pillbox hat with a whimsy that cascades over her eyes. When she sees Gram, she gets up and goes to her.

My sisters and their husbands anchor the second row, having saved seats for Gabriel and me on the end. They draped my mother's black pashmina scarf over the chairs to reserve them.

Alfred stands in the back in a proper suit. He nods to me as Gabriel and I take our seats. Bret waves to us from the corner.

The makeshift altar is simple and beautiful. A statue of Buddha, carved out of ruby marble, rests on a pedestal directly in front of the seats. Three small candles are lit at the base.

On a small table next to the icon is a framed photograph of June. It's black and white in a black lacquer frame. She is dancing, jumping high through the air. June is also *nude*. My father stares into the eyeballs of the Buddha to avoid looking at young, naked June.

"From my collection," Irv whispers, tapping me on the shoulder and pointing to the photograph.

"*Bellissima*," I say to him.

The photograph is pure June, caught in the vigor of youth. Her body was a work of art; her thigh muscles, down through the extension of her long and graceful calves, appear chiseled in granite. Her slim ankles and pointed toes complement the bold arc of her hand, which practically touches her toes as she does a flying backbend in midair. Her hair flies behind her like a silk cape.

A Catholic priest, wearing black slacks and a Roman collar

under a sweater, enters, carrying a small leather book. I recognize him from the express Mass at the chapel at Saint Vincent's Hospital. He is followed by a bald Buddhist monk in red robes.

My father turns and looks at me, raising both eyebrows with an expression that says, *This oughta be rich.*

"Good afternoon, friends," the priest begins. "I'm Father Bob Bond, and this is my friend, Buddhist monk Bing Lao." The monk bows deeply from the waist. "We both knew June, and we thought we'd talk a bit about her, and then you, her loved ones, can get up and speak if you wish."

"Where's the body?" I hear my father ask my mother. She puts her finger to her lips so he won't ask any further questions. The Church of Unorthodox/Integral Yoga is not my father's thing. When it comes to death, my father needs familiar rituals he can count on to get him through. This isn't it.

The door to the yoga studio pushes open. Pamela, in a dress coat and matching hat, looks around for our familiar faces. My sisters and I wave to her. We have turned into the sweetest, most solicitous sisters-in-law in history since Alfred and Pamela hit the rocks. We could not be more supportive. We give her space and free babysitting services whenever she needs them. When Pamela's eyes meet Alfred's, she weaves her way through the crowd to the back of the room to stand with him.

My father takes my mother's hand and squeezes it.

Father Bond begins, "June was born and baptized Roman Catholic. She was born in Brooklyn, attended what used to be called Saint Joseph's Academy on Long Island. She went to college for two years at Marymount, when she was chosen to tour internationally with the Paul Taylor Dance Company. June went all over the world—Ireland, Poland, Germany, Italy.

"June cherished her years as a professional dancer. She became a devoted yoga practitioner, and often taught class here at Integral."

"Did you know that?" Gabriel whispers.

"I had no idea she taught classes."

"June attended Mass at the Dorothy Day Center in the East Village."

"I didn't know *that* either," I whisper to Gabriel.

"I thought she was a collapsed Catholic. Like me," he whispers back.

"June would say, 'Father, remember to pray for me, because I pray for you.' This was the essence of this good woman, now in God's hands. She looked out for those she cared about, and she walked in the world with a big heart. She will be missed."

The priest steps back as the monk steps forward. "June expressed herself through the physical, in a way that most of us cannot."

"She sure is expressing herself in that picture," my father whispers to my mother.

The monk continues, "June danced, and when she did, she became a work of art. She shared her talents, and understood the core of Buddhism, which is renewal and, ultimately, renaissance. She understood that one must change in order to grow. That one must move through life, not stand still, but move with it . . . "

"I just wish she had done it in a leotard," my father mumbles.

"June believed that about happiness, and also pain. Her death reminds us that if we stay present, we can die on an ordinary morning, without fanfare or drama—but in a state of peace and contentment. I take this lesson from June's life—and her death: Let go and let be."

We sit in silence for a moment. The priest then says, "We offer the floor to anyone who would like to speak."

My mother clears her throat, stands, moves before the altar, and stands between the priest and the monk. She goes into her purse and pulls out her eulogy.

Mom unfolds the paper. I can see she printed it out in extra large letters so she wouldn't have to wear her reading glasses in front of strangers.

"Thank you all for coming to June Lawton's memorial service. My name is Mike Angelini Roncalli. Though I've never met most of you, I'm sure you all loved June as I did, as my family did." Mom inhales deeply, so as not to cry. "I was young when I met June . . ."

"She was thirty-six," Tess whispers and rolls her eyes.

"I already had a family and responsibilities. June was a Greenwich Village bohemian—you don't see too many of those around anymore—and she was also a best friend to my mother, who is here today.

"Nearly thirty years ago, June was looking to do a job that was creative but challenging. She became the best pattern cutter my parents ever had at the Angelini Shoe Company. But she was so much more to us. She was a confidante and a friend. One of us, even though she was a glorious Irish redhead with eyes as blue as the waves of the North Sea on a summer day.

"I have many fond memories of our dear June, but I'd like to leave you with this little story. I was going through some problems in my life, and June knew it. She took me out for a long walk, and in that very honest way she had, she told me I was full of baloney, and I needed to buck up and stop being a ninny."

The underdressed mourners nod in approval.

"June didn't suffer fools. And while . . ." My mother goes off script. She folds her speech in half and puts her hands behind her back.

Jaclyn and Tess lean toward me. This could go south quickly.

"And while I can be a fool, I thank God June could spot one. She set me straight that day. And I think that's the most loving thing a good friend can do, to be honest when you need it, and even when you fail, she stands by you."

Mom looks up to heaven.

"Thank you, June." Mom takes a step to go back to her seat.

Irv Raible stands and hits a portable CD player. Miles Davis plays Ravel as we sit and listen. When the music concludes, the priest says, "Thank you for coming and honoring our friend today. I know she would be grateful."

My mother pops up and announces, "Oh, and everyone, please come to 166 Perry Street after the service for lunch. Father . . ." The priest nods. "And Mr. Monk Lao . . ." The Buddhist priest nods that he will attend. Then Mom looks out over the mourners. "There'll be plenty of food"—she looks around—"tabbouleh for you veggie Buddhist people . . ."

"Your mother always knows the exact right thing to say," Gabriel says softly.

The Buddhist monk smiles at my mother, and bows deeply to her from the waist.

"Thank you," he says.

And then, my mother, the nice Catholic girl from Perry Street, bows to the Buddhist monk on the day we say good-bye to our June.

After we put Gram and Dom back in the car and sent the rest of the family back to Perry Street, Gabriel and I settled up with the folks at Integral Yoga before walking back to join June's funeral luncheon. Two popular yoga classes had to be canceled to accommodate June's ceremony, and we felt it was only right to compensate the venue.

"You okay?" I ask Gabe.

"I'm sick of it."

"Of what?'

"Death. Funerals. I'm over it."

"That's the point of a funeral, to begin to heal and move through it. You heard the monk."

"Yeah. I guess. You know, I think June had a plan."

"Really?" I never saw June as a woman who made plans in advance; she seemed always to be of the moment. I never asked her to dinner a week in advance—she would never remember the date. But if you grabbed her after work for a pasta run to Piccolo Angolo, she was up for it.

"June wanted to leave things neat," Gabriel says. "June taught me to clear the cutting table every night. She never cut a new pattern at the end of a working day. She said you should only ever show up to a clean work space."

I think about June's apartment. Everything was clean, pristine, and in place. She was dressed. She was ready to walk out the door.

"Do you think she knew?"

"That she was gonna die? No, I don't. Irv's been clearing her answering machine and calling people. And there was a message from June's dealer. I think if she knew she was dying, she would have canceled the order."

As we cross 8th Avenue at Horatio Street, I see that our Village has changed. The Greenwich Village of June's heyday is gone. Now our neighbors are polished and in many ways predictable. Bohemians of the new order wear Theory suits and boots from Jeffrey's. They talk on cell phones and rush around just like uptowners.

I look ahead, down Jane Street, where June made her way to the Angelini Shoe Company on foot every morning. And I swear for a moment I see her, walking at a clip, her dancer's neck leading her forward, her legs extended in long, graceful strides, her bright blue coat unbuttoned in the cold flapping over her work smock, as she juggles two coffees from the deli. She makes the turn onto Perry Street, with a yoga mat slung across her back, her red braids flying behind her in the wind as she goes.

14

Don't Ever Be Afraid to Go Home

WE ORDERED SANDWICH PLATTERS, LOADED with wraps, cru-dité trays, and fresh fruit plates for delivery from Whole Foods for June's farewell. Never say "free lunch" in Greenwich Village to former dancers—you are assured a full and hungry house.

Toward the end of the lunch, Irv comes into the kitchen, where I'm helping Gabriel fix the last shaker of martinis for the Corps de Ballet Mourners.

"This was lovely. Valentine, I'd like you to have this."

Irv gives me the framed nude photograph of June that graced her memorial service.

"Are you sure?" I say to him.

He shrugs. "I want you to have it. I've enjoyed it all these years . . ."

My father eavesdrops as he pulls the creamer from the fridge. "Who wouldn't?" He chuckles.

"Irv, did you meet my dad, Dutch Roncalli?"

Irv and Dad shake hands.

"I have some photographs of me from the same show."

"Irv was a dancer too, Dad."

"Were you wearing pants in your picture?" my father wants to know.

"Excuse me?" Irv raises his eyebrows.

"You know, *pants*." My father grabs the thigh of his suit pants and grips it.

"No, I was nude, too," Irv admits. "The photographs were similar."

"Why break up the set?" my father wonders aloud.

"I've got to get going," Bret says, placing his plastic cup in the recycling. "I'm taking the girls to the Chatham gazebo to meet Santa."

"Sounds like fun," I tell him. "Thank you for coming."

"Of course. I loved June, too."

"And she knew it."

Finally the last of the guests go, and just our family remains. Pamela has been antsy all afternoon. I noticed she got into a long conversation with the yoga instructors from Integral. Maybe she will find inner peace on 13th Street. She pulls her coat on to go.

"The boys are at karate. I have to pick them up," she says.

"Isn't your mom meeting them?" Alfred asks.

"Yeah, but I like to be home when they get home."

"If you wait, I can go with you."

"No, no, you stay. I can get the train."

"But Gram would like to visit with you."

Tess is hosting Christmas Eve with the dinner of the Seven Fishes at her house, and when she called to invite Pam, Pam was very nice, but said she hadn't made up her mind about her holiday plans yet.

"I spoke with Gram," Pamela tells him.

"Okay." Alfred gives in. He kisses Pamela on the cheek. She turns to go.

"Pam?" My mother stops her.

She turns to my mother.

"I need to talk to you," Mom says.

"Not today, Mom," I say firmly.

"It's okay," Mom says, as she sips her second martini.

"No," I say firmly. "It's not a good time."

I implore my sisters to help me.

Pamela throws her purse down on the chair. Then she sits down on the zebra love seat.

"All right, Ma. I'm all ears. I have no secrets in this group. Have at me. But if this is about Christmas, I haven't made up my mind yet."

"I know. And there's no pressure," my mother says.

Pamela looks at me in disbelief.

My mother stands and holds on to the top rung of her chair. "Thank you for coming today."

"You're welcome."

"Pam, I was so happy when you came in the door over at Internal Yoga."

"*Integral*," I correct her.

"All right already. Integral." Mom waves her hand.

"Of course I would be there. I thought the world of June," Pamela says. "She was one of the last honest people on earth." Pam looks down at her manicure.

"Where's my mother?" Mom looks around.

"She and Dominic are down in the shop."

"Good."

Mom looks around the room. Only my father, my sisters, and their spouses remain. The rest of the mourners have gone.

"I'm very proud of my family." Mom cries.

Tess hands her a tissue.

"God knows we are a flawed group. But you know it isn't *chance* that brought us together. We were meant to be a family. And Pam, you are like my fourth daughter. I relate to you. I've lived through your pain. I understand it. Just because I like my shoes to match my bag, that doesn't mean I'm an idiot. I have a mind."

"Is that in dispute?" My father bites into a brownie from the dessert tray.

Mom shoots him a look. "You've been an excellent daughter-in-law, Pamela. You're a wonderful mother—and I know you've been a good wife. This situation is not in any way your fault."

"Thanks, Ma." Pamela stands, so my mother can quit while she's ahead. But my mother doesn't.

Mom continues, "Marriage is like working in a coal mine. You hack away in the dark, day after day, busting rock, and you think you're not getting anywhere, and then all of a sudden, this little sliver of sunlight appears and you say to yourself, Oh, that's what I've been waiting for—just a little light, just a little bit of hope—a sign, maybe, that will get me through. And Pamela—it does. You cannot throw away sixteen years of love and life with someone over a stupid mistake. You just can't."

"Ma, Pamela needs time to think," Alfred says.

Pamela speaks directly to my mother. "I respectfully ask you all to butt out. We're too close—or rather, you're too close. I'm not comfortable discussing my life with you. I have my friends to talk to—"

"Just a word of caution about friends, Pamela. I looked like a fool to a lot of my friends when I took Dutch back in 1987. They thought I had a head full of church teachings, or I was afraid to lose his pension—or the house—or that it happened on the cusp of college for our kids, and that maybe because of all that, I stayed out of fear. Well, I think you know me pretty well, and there aren't too many dragons I won't slay—I'm pretty tough. And so are you. I stayed because I knew I could love him again. At the time I didn't love him—sorry, Dutch, but it's true."

"I knew it to be true," Dad agrees. He leans back in the chair and closes his eyes.

"I wanted nothing more to do with him. But I stayed, hanging on to the idea that if I loved him once, maybe I could love him again. You owe it to yourself—because I promise you, many, many months down the road, you will be grateful that you stuck it out. And my friends? Now that I'm—now that I'm of a certain age . . ."

My sisters and I look at one another. We try not to smile.

"Now that I'm older and wiser, the very friends that advised me to kick Dutch out are remarried—and in some cases, unhappy in second marriages themselves—and we talk about staying versus going; and they admire that I listened to my own voice, and not theirs. And now I have this—the satisfaction of a life with a man that tested his love for me, and found out that he loved me all along. That's my prayer for you. That you keep your *own* counsel. And whatever you decide, you will always be my daughter."

"Thanks, Mom." Pamela turns to go. She digs into her coat pocket and finds a clean tissue. She dabs her eyes. "I've really got to get home."

"We can finish up in the morning," I tell Alfred.

"Okay, great." He grabs his coat and pulls it on. "Pam?"

She turns to Alfred.

"I'd like to ride home with you."

Pam looks at him. Then she fixes the lapel on his coat.

"Okay," she says.

They go down the stairs. My mother calls after them, "See you at Tess's!"

My sisters and I glare at her.

"Where you gonna hang Nudie?" Dad asks Gabriel.

"Over the sofa."

"You better put some swatches over the private areas. We got kids around here."

ভ

The roof is lit from the apartment across the way, in the Richard Meier Towers. It seems someone finally moved into the fourth-floor apartment. But we wouldn't know. Gabriel put up a trellis, high enough to obscure the direct view. All that comes through the lattice is the light, throwing squares of bright light on the roof.

I'm wrapped up in a down coat, hat, and mittens.

I look up at the night sky, and there's no moon, no stars, just gray clouds in odd shapes. June filled the sky with pattern pieces tonight, just for me. I think about our conversations in the last several months of her life. I search her words and reactions for clues that might have portended her death. But I don't think June knew. I don't think she had any idea she was going to die. And more to the point, I don't think she cared. My friend June was all about life—the living, and the moment.

I remember when she tried to quit work, and I wouldn't let her. She could have retired, it was her right to insist upon it, but she didn't. She saw the fear in my eyes when she suggested leaving me alone with Alfred in the shop. She knew I needed an ally in the transition. She was one for me, and so much more.

Then, crafty planner that June was, she trained Gabriel to take her job, even though Gabriel still keeps a night shift at the Carlyle. She made pattern cutting, one of the most serious operations in our shop, sheer fun for Gabe—he almost didn't notice that she was teaching him a new skill that required concentration, technique, and focus. She trained Gabriel, knowing that if she succeeded in passing along all she knew, he'd be ready in the event that she could no longer work. And now that day has come, and Gabriel is ready to take over.

I picture the faces of the people that came to her memorial, such a disparate bunch of people—old artists, young dancers, gays and straights, village diehards, and of course my family. June lived in a world of her own design. How many people can say that? She chose the people in her life carefully, and then she took care of them, nurtured them, and encouraged them.

She didn't have to *become* a mother; she *was* a mother.

"Would you like some company?" Gram says through the screen door.

"Sure, sure." I jump up and run to the door to help Gram across the icy roof. She grips my arm as I guide her to the chaise next to mine.

I explain the seating arrangement. "Gabriel and I come up here and look at the sky."

"It looks lovely up here. Besides you and my family, this roof is what I miss the most about my old life in New York."

"Do you like the new look?" I ask her.

"It's a real roof garden now."

"When Gabriel finished the interiors, he came up here and painted and planted. And down in the shop—June trained him, and he works really hard."

"I can tell. I looked at his pattern work. Not bad."

"Do you think he can ever be as good as June?"

"Give him thirty years."

I shrug. "Where am I going? I got thirty years."

"I wish I did." Gram smiles.

"You have a lot of time, Gram."

"June was younger than me." Gram turns to me. "Did she really just go fast like that?"

"Her neighbor Irv called me. I jumped in a cab, and when I got there, she was gone."

"Isn't that marvelous?"

"Well, I guess. For June."

"Think about it. You get up, eat your breakfast, get dressed. Then you lie down, and cross over. I think it's just about the best exit I've ever heard of," Gram says.

At Gram's age of course she thinks about dying and how and when it will happen. I don't give it much thought but I probably will from now on. June's death has rattled me. I always felt so young. But now I see the future as finite, not an endless bolt of silk that unfurls perfectly across the cutting table.

"I feel so guilty, Gram. June wanted to retire, but I wouldn't let her."

"Don't you feel bad for one second. June always did exactly what she wanted to do. If she didn't want to work, believe me, she wouldn't have been here. I had to force her to take vacation. She never asked for time off because it's a family-owned business, and she knew if she wasn't there, I'd have to do her work. And she knew, once I left, when she took off, *you'd* have to do her work. Please don't worry about that."

"But, she gave up a lot to work here."

"Why do you say that?" Gram asks.

"I don't know. She didn't have a husband or a family."

"She didn't want either of those things."

"She didn't?"

"No, she did not. She had a very difficult childhood. She got over it, but it left her a committed free spirit. Her goal in life was to be self-sufficient and live alone, and do exactly as she pleased. I know she was afraid about getting older, and only because she was always fearful of having a stroke and going into a home. That's nothing new. I have the same fears. But she didn't have a family to make decisions for her."

"I was her emergency contact."

"She made a good choice." Gram pats my hand. "You know, she called me in Italy quite a bit. She kept me in the loop. She was so proud of you. June marveled at your determination to make the business more profitable. I worked here over fifty years, and I never even changed the way we record in the ledger. And look at you. I'm barely gone a year, and you're launching a new line of affordable shoes. Your grandfather is dancing in heaven."

I imagine my grandfather looking down at me dressed in a dapper tuxedo like Fred Astaire, leaping over the clouds to music.

I never saw my grandfather in a formal suit, only in work clothes and a cobbler's apron.

"Do you ever think about Grandpop?"

"Sure. I talk about him with Dominic. And he talks about his first wife too. When you fall in love later in life, you marry the history of the person. And I think you know how I feel about my memories. They're my treasure. And Dominic's are his, too."

"You know, those letters Roberta gave me helped me understand Grandpop. No wonder he was so sad sometimes—and so prickly. He had a rough childhood, losing his mother, and then his uncle."

Gram nods. "He did."

"But you were a good wife to him."

"Not good enough. I couldn't help him beat his sadness. You know, Valentine, this is the thing. You can fall in love with someone, and believe in that person, but it doesn't mean that you can build a life together. I never got in there with your grandfather. I don't know how else to say it. Dominic understands me—and it's not complicated. It was so complicated with Michael. So complex."

"It should be easy," I say. "You know, I think I've found the perfect husband."

"Really?" Gram turns to me, surprised.

"Gabriel Biondi. Gabe and I are like those gears on a Swiss movement watch. We spin in tandem like two interlocking gizmos without a glitch. We never fight. We don't fuss. We work together beautifully in the shop. It's just easy."

The clouds move overhead, rippling like pattern paper. The edges of the horizon over New Jersey, beyond the river, flutter like ruffles. June, high in the heavens, places the moon in the sky like a silver button on a blue-velvet boot. "June will never leave you," Gram says.

"I'm counting on it."

Gram and Dominic went out for dinner at Da Silvano's, where the stars go. Gram used to eat there back in the 1970s when it first opened, and she wants to share the cuisine with Dominic, and hopefully find some native Italians for him to talk to.

Gabriel is at the Carlyle. Tonight, he is going to give the big boss a month's notice. He has decided to focus on pattern cutting at the Angelini Shoe Shop as his new career, and I couldn't be more thrilled.

Christmas is ten days away, and I'm trying to keep my spirits up. I sit here on the sofa, all the lights out except the ones that twinkle in the tree. I inhale the fresh scent of the blue spruce. I imagine the old familiar holiday rituals will comfort me this year. 2010 has been a year of loss and change.

I pull out my sketch pad and flip it open to a new, clean page. I have an idea for a new shoe for yoga practitioners. Of course, I'll call it the *June Lawton*. I poise my pencil over the bare page. But, instead of beginning with the clean lines of the vamp, I write,

December 13, 2010
Dear Gianluca,

   I hope this letter finds you well. Your health and happiness are never far from my mind.

   Dominic and Gram are out to dinner, Gabriel is at the Carlyle, and I'm here alone for the first time since June died. I have had a lot of time to think about her and the things she taught me. I also have been thinking about how she lived. June was truly independent. She made a life for herself on her own terms. She had a way of knowing what was right for her. This is the big lesson that I've taken away from her death. I have been thinking about what's right for me and how I should live going forward.

   I ruined everything with you. By now, I'm sure you've found a good woman who loves you and wants everything in life that you do. I know it is too late for us, but now I

understand all the things you said to me, and the meaning behind your words. I resisted those words because I wasn't ready to hear what you had to say. I said I heard you, but I did not. I was too busy talking and finding ways to push you away because I believed you'd wake up one morning and see who I really was . . . and run.

I have pushed so hard against what I come from, and at the same time, I'm compelled to re-create it. I have never looked at my life as my own, but rather, part of a whole, which includes my family. But this year, I have seen that the boundaries in the Roncalli family were never drawn, that we rely on one another, which is good, but we also blame one another when we fail (not so good). There must be a way to invent a life that is all my own and I hope I'm learning how to do that. The first step is writing you this letter. I don't want you to think of me as the petulant girl I was in Buenos Aires. I'm trying to grow up, and I think losing June has forced me to look at myself.

I don't want to get to the end of my life without having loved. I've played at love and pretended to love, but I've never given myself over to my life in a way that made it my own. I was waiting for someone to come along and show me the way. Now, I realize that everyone has shown me the way. My parents, in their crazy way, see things through, even when they'd rather not. My brother, in failing, showed me it's okay, the world doesn't end when you screw up, and maybe letting someone you love forgive you makes you both a little stronger. Gram has shown me that you can live with your history but still experience a new life inside the old one. Well, I could go on and on. And then, of course, there's you.

It's hard for me to admit that I pushed you away. I like to think that you left me when you saw that I didn't have any idea what I was doing with you. I hid behind my work, hoping that a higher purpose (Art!) would fill me up more than love. I can count on art, right? It won't let me down because it comes from *me, I create it: from my whims and fancy. But you were right. There is no art without love. Only love can open someone up to the possibilities of living and creating art. And I thought it was paint—and pencils and this sketch book and my ideas that inspired me to make art. But it's not any of those things. It's love. And you. It was always you.*

I'm going to send this letter Federal Express International. I'm going to imagine the white truck as it motors up the hills of Tuscany in the rain. I'm going to imagine the deliveryman knocking on your shop door, and you inside, in your apron, cutting a yard of expensive kid leather with precision. And how you'll scowl because the knock at the door interrupted your process. And then, I'm going to imagine you sitting on the work bench and opening this envelope and reading these words. And I hope when you're done, when you get to The End, that you will know that I truly understand all that I've lost. I can only wish for that—and for you to have a Merry Christmas, a Buon Natale as you say in your beautiful hills.

Valentina

Gabriel and I sit across from one another at the table. We have signed up to make dessert for the Feast of the Seven Fishes, our Christmas Eve tradition. Tess and Charlie are hosting the whole family at their home this year. Gabriel wants to go all out, which means thorough planning and a shopping trip to Little Italy for supplies.

Gabriel snaps his fingers. "Hello?" He looks at me. "Could we focus here? I have a week to get this dessert for a cast of thousands together. I need your help."

"I'm here," I tell him. But I'm not. I'd like to skip Christmas entirely this year, and just sit home alone and weep under the tree.

"June would not like this. She would be peeved that you're still a mess."

"I know." Tears fill my eyes. "It isn't just June."

"You didn't hear from Gianluca yet?"

I shake my head sadly.

"You can't trust FedEx in Italy any more than you can trust the fact that the olive oil they send over here is first cold pressed. Maybe he didn't receive it."

"He got it. The next morning. I tracked it." I put down my pencil and push away from the table.

"Well, you don't want to hear this from me, but I don't think writing a letter is enough."

"I poured my heart out!"

"You need to call him."

"What would I say?"

"If you called him, you could hash this out once and for all. Find out if he still loves you. Then you can let this go. I always say, never mourn a man longer than you dated him."

"That makes sense," I admit. "But I need a reason to call."

"Think of one."

I had hoped that Gianluca would receive my letter and call *me*. The man I knew was direct. He was always clear about his feelings. Gianluca did not write to me after he received my letter. Whatever I wrote did not compel him to contact me. I wrote the letter to find out if he still cared. If he did, I wanted to invite him for Christmas. "I'd like to invite him for Christmas."

"Here." Gabriel hands me the phone. "Do it."

I flip open my cell and scroll down to Gianluca. Before I press send, I imagine Christmas without him. I will be the good auntie, playing games with the kids, dressing new dolls, assembling toys. I'll do the dishes and help the old folks move from table to couch and back again. I'll serve wine, cut the timbale, light the candles. I'll be useful. The thought of another holiday spent taking care of everyone else forces me to press the button. I hit send. The machine picks up in the shop. I cover the receiver. "I got the machine."

"Leave a message!" Gabe whispers.

"Hi. *Pronto*. Gianluca? It's Valentina. Um, I'm calling to see how you are—and if you have any plans for Christmas. I'd like to invite you here. Um. If you would like to come, please call me back. You have my number. Thank you."

I hang up. "What do you think?"

"Charming," Gabriel says dryly and goes back to his list.

I'm in the middle of a deep, delicious sleep when my cell vibrates on the nightstand. I reach for it, groggy and half asleep, and open it.

"Valentina? Is it too late?"

I sit bolt upright in bed.

"Gianluca?"

"Yes," he confirms. "Is it too late?" he asks again.

"For us?" I blurt.

He laughs. "No, I meant late at night."

I could die. I look over at the clock. "Oh, it's about three o'clock in the morning. But, I'm awake."

"I received your letter a few days ago," he says.

"Oh." This is all I can say, because I feel the boom is about to be lowered. Carlotta is rolling over in bed next to him, having forced him to call me and break this silly thing off so she can move in with her mink.

"I would like very much to come for Christmas. Thank you for the invitation," he says. "I didn't want to call until I had my tickets. You know, it's not easy to travel at Christmastime."

"I know."

"Valentina, I need to tell you something." He continues, "It's something you said in your letter. You assumed I found someone else. The truth is, there is no one else."

Tears fill my eyes. I wasn't expecting this. I was hoping, yes. But I didn't think, in a million years, that he still cared. "Are you sure?"

"Yes," he says plainly. "There can't be anyone else, Valentina."

"Why?" I wipe my tears on my pajama sleeve.

"Because there's only you."

"I'm so happy you called."

"I'm sure about my feelings, Valentina. Are you?"

"Nothing will ever keep us apart again, Gianluca. I want your happiness more than my own. If you called and said that you had moved on, I would have been happy for you. That's the truth."

When I close the phone, I lie back on the pillows and look up at the ceiling. A small beam of light from the streetlight on Perry cuts across the ceiling, singular and clear. I stare at it for a long time. This isn't a dream. After so long, Gianluca is on his way, and with him, the best Christmas of my life.

The passengers from Alitalia Flight 125 pour through the exit doors from Customs into the pickup lobby at JFK. I scan the crowd for Gianluca.

My BlackBerry vibrates in my pocket. I fish it out of my purse. A text pops up.

"Ciao."

I look down at the word, then to the address that the message came from. GV@roma.net.

Me: Gianluca?
GV: It is me.
Me: Where are you?
GV: I live in 21 century. Look up now.

I throw my BlackBerry into my purse and look up.

Gianluca spots me as he comes through the doors. He holds his BlackBerry high in the air, triumphantly, like a trophy. He looks gorgeous—his hair is longer, and he wears a magnificent cashmere coat, long and black with slim lapels. I never knew him in winter, so it's the first time I've seen him in a proper coat. He wears jeans and a navy turtleneck sweater underneath.

I am in love.

He takes me in his arms and kisses me. All of my sadness falls away, my grief about June, my depression about Alfred and Pamela, my empathy for Bret and Mackenzie—all of it goes. It's just him and me, and these kisses, and the scent of his skin, his neck, citrus and leather. The sounds of the airport fade around me. I don't hear the clanging carts, the shouts of the passengers, and the cop's whistles outside baggage; I float in his arms.

"I love you," I tell him. I waited until he was in my arms and I could say these words in person. I hold his face in my hands.

His blue eyes narrow. "Are you sure?" he teases.

"Oh, I am *sure*."

"I love you, Valentina." We hold each other in the crowd. I feel like I've been found for the first time in my life. I've been wandering through the world looking for something, for someone, and here he is, the love of my life, the love *in* my life.

I don't even know how long the ride from JFK to Manhattan takes—the driver keeps complaining about the traffic, but I don't notice. We kiss from baggage to Barrow Street, and barely let go of one another as he checks into the Soho Grand and we make it to the room.

The coat, the luggage, my dress, the purse, the shoes, the stockings, the hat, the gloves, all fall away like cherry blossoms when the wind kicks up on the last day of spring and there's a snow shower of petals, and the air fills with pink blossoms and all that's left behind are the bare branches where they once bloomed.

We make love, and it's urgent, passionate, direct—I'm making love for every woman who has ever been in love, including June, who winks through the quarter moon, and encourages me to love this good man who loves me like no one else can or ever has. "Sex is life," June used to say. She felt sorry for people who didn't understand that, didn't get it, and didn't go for it. Sex is what tells us we're alive, and we're connecting, and roots us in the present.

I am learning what Gianluca wants from me.

It seems such a small thing to learn what a man wants, but for me, it's an enormous lesson. I assumed Gianluca would tell me what he needed without having to ask him. I've learned to ask the questions, listen to the answers, and move with it.

Gianluca's needs are simple, but if he is denied them, life becomes complicated—or maybe he becomes complex, or maybe they are one and the same. Gianluca craves time, open hours without plans, endless walks without destination, slowly prepared food, long meals, and conversation that ends in sleep, and resumes upon waking. He also needs me to be honest. I will happily tell him the truth, because now, in his arms, I'm living it.

Gianluca's lips travel down my neck, and I breathe from so deeply within my body, he stops to hold me. This is what it *really* means to be in love—this is the thing I've been waiting for, wondering about. I've been waiting to *mean* this much to someone.

Oh, this is a merry, merry, merry Christmas. No package, no present, no surprise of any kind could *ever* be this wonderful. And this night, this one, this particular moment, is for Gianluca, and for me—but it's also for June Marie Lawton, who knew how to live.

I spritz Terre d'Hermès perfume on my neck.

I'm dressed for Christmas Eve, the Feast of the Seven Fishes at Tess's house. I went with the silver lamé sheath I wore to Gram and Dominic's wedding, this time, without the clutter of pearls. I'm tempted to throw them on. After all, Dad will read *A Christmas Carol* by Charles Dickens after supper, and I could be the sound effect when Marley's chains rattle.

Gram and Dominic have been at Tess's all day, preparing the scungilli, shrimp, octopus, lobster, white flounder, clams, and mussels for our feast.

Gianluca has gone out to run a final Christmas errand. Gabriel stands in my doorway.

"I want to give you your Christmas present."

"Gabriel, you shouldn't have."

"Liar. Nobody likes a gift more than you. Come on. Grab a coat," he instructs me.

I pull Gianluca's dress coat from behind the door and throw it on. I pull the cashmere closely around me. It has the scent of him, so I pull it closer still.

"Follow me," Gabriel says.

I follow Gabriel up the stairs to the roof.

"Okay, now stand over there," he tells me. "By the wall. Then turn around."

I shiver in the cold.

"This will only take a second."

Gabriel goes to the wall in the roof's alcove. As he returns from the corner, the roof fills with sound. With Frank Sinatra.

I put my hands to my face.

"That's what I'm talkin' about. Rooftop Ambience. The Chairman of the Board, ladies and gentlemen," Gabriel announces.

"I thought the roof was finished!"

"It wasn't done till the installation of surround sound."

"I love it! Thank you!"

Frank Sinatra's voice pours out into the sky over Greenwich Village on this blue Christmas Eve. I look down onto Perry Street, with its pools of golden light from the street lamps, as last-minute shoppers make their way home, underscored by Sinatra, who sings them home to their destinations.

"I took all of Gram's old albums and copied them on to CD's, and then I made a program. Six hours of Sinatra on a loop. Hear that? It's 'Shake Down the Stars.' Big hit for Frank in 1940. Real roof and sky music!"

"Gram is going to go crazy for this," I say. "We only ever had an AM radio up here." I run over to Gabriel and give him a big hug. "How can I thank you?"

"No matter what happens, you'll always have Sinatra . . . Valentina."

This is the first time Gabriel ever called me "Valentina." And I'm going to pretend that I don't know what he means, because then maybe what he is about to tell me won't be true.

He takes a deep breath and looks at me. "We're Tiffany candlesticks, you and me. The best of the best. But now it's time to break up the pair. One of us has fallen in love. There's only room for one man in this house."

I close my eyes. It has to be twenty degrees on the roof, but I don't notice the cold. I'm filled with the possibilities of the life that lies ahead for Gianluca and me.

"It had to happen someday," Gabriel says softly. "And here it is. It couldn't happen to a nicer girl. I'm happy for you." Gabriel hugs me tightly.

"But you're the best husband I ever had."

"Well, maybe it's time for me to go out there and find my own." Gabriel sighs. "Now, come on. I hate rubbery scungilli—and it's a long train haul to Jersey."

The apartment buzzer rings on the roof.

"Is that what I think it is?"

He nods. "Yep. That's the second part of my gift. I put a buzzer up here—for when you're on the roof and you get company. No more running down two flights of stairs and just missing UPS."

"You're a genius! Gianluca must've forgotten his keys," I say. I hit the buzzer to let him in.

"Works like a charm," Gabriel says proudly.

"What am I going to do without you?"

"You'll see me in the shop every day. I just won't live here anymore. It's time for me to go on Craigslist and find a deal. Somewhere close."

"Please." I hug him again. "Around the corner."

"I'll try. Now, I'm going to go and pack up the timbale. I will miss the kitchen. I love a workspace with a marble counter. Oh, well. New Year on the horizon and new beginnings. I'll send Gianluca up." Gabriel opens the screen door. "Kiss him to Sinatra. If you do, he'll never leave."

I turn up the sound system and wait. After a few moments, I hear him ascend the stairs.

The sound of footsteps on the stairs fills me with anticipation.

Then Bret appears in the doorway.

"Bret?"

Bret pushes through the door and comes to me. He is deeply upset. His face is red from the cold. It looks as though he's been crying. "What's the matter?"

"Mac and the girls are at her parents for Christmas Eve . . . ," he begins.

"Uptown?" I straighten the collar on his coat. He's disheveled. A mess. He never has a hair out of place.

"81st Street." He rubs his hands together. They are chapped from the cold. He must've been out walking for a long time.

"Why aren't you there?" I ask.

"I couldn't stay." His eyes fill with tears.

"Why?" I ask. I take his freezing cold hands in mine to warm them.

"I pressed her, I guess. I had a gift for her. A sapphire bracelet . . . But she wouldn't take it. She said that it's over. Our marriage is over." Tears begin to stream down his face. He looks like a boy, just like the boy I remember from Austin Street.

"Oh, Bret, it's just the pressure of the holidays," I tell him.

"No, it's not the holidays. She's in love with someone else." He puts his hands on the wall and hangs his head. I throw my arms around his shoulders as he heaves and cries.

I'm stunned. Even though Bret confided that there were problems, I never thought they would lead to *this*. I thought they
would work things through, that Mac would choose her ordered
life over the chaos of starting over.

I think back to the summer, when Mackenzie stopped by, and
right here on this very roof accused me of an affair with her husband. Now I realize that she already had made her mind up long
before she climbed these stairs. She knew she was leaving him; she
just needed an excuse to let go. Mackenzie wanted *me* to be the
excuse. She already had someone new, and she wanted Bret to
have someone too, so she could leave him without guilt.

"Oh, Bret. I'm so sorry."

"I don't know what to do. For the first time in my life, I don't
know what to *do*." I pull him close to me and hold him as tightly
as I can.

"There's nothing you can do right now. It's Christmas, and
you've got the girls. You have to think of your girls," I tell him.

After a few moments, Bret pulls away from me. "I'm going to
go. I don't know why I came here."

"You can always come here. I'm here for you," I promise
him.

He looks around. Clearly, the man I knew, unflappable and
strong, is breaking before my eyes. There's a desperation to him
now. Of course there is. The life he built is over.

"You have plans," he says. "You have your family."

I've known Bret since I was a girl, and I've never seen him
like this. "You can't go. Come with us. We're going to Tess and
Charlie's."

"I can't. I should go home." When he says the word *home*, a
look of complete devastation fills his eyes.

I take Bret in my arms. I hold him close, his face against my
neck as he begins to cry. I take the coat and pull him inside, to
warm him. "It's okay," I whisper. "It's okay."

I feel his lips against my neck, and then softly on my cheek.

The ease we have, the comfort we feel with one another, all the history, wraps around me like fine cashmere. I want to comfort Bret. I want to hold him. I want to be here for him. His warm tears turn cold against my cheek. I feel his lips against mine. He pulls away at the exact same moment I do.

"I'm sorry," he says.

"No, *I'm* sorry." I can't believe what just happened. What did I do? I wanted to comfort him, not kiss him.

I hear the snap of the screen door behind me. I turn. I look for Gabriel, but it isn't him.

It's Gianluca.

I have a feeling of doom in my gut, but I can't leave Bret alone. I look to Gianluca, and extend my hand, and I'm about to explain the kiss, but he has already pushed through the screen door and is gone.

"Val, I don't know why I kissed you. I shouldn't have," Bret says. "Forgive me." He lets go of me and goes to the door. I implore him to stay, but he's down the steps before I can stop him again.

I turn to follow Bret, pulling the coat close to me. I have to find Gianluca and explain what happened. He'll understand when I tell him that Bret's wife left him on Christmas Eve. I was only trying to help. The kiss was a total accident. I bury my hands in the pockets of Gianluca's coat.

Deep inside, there's a box in the pocket. I feel its size, and its velvet texture.

My heart begins to race. Instead of going down the stairs, instead of following my instinct to do the right thing and go to Gianluca and explain, I stay.

I move to the trellis, where the roses were, by the light. I reach down into the pocket and pull out the box. I know I shouldn't, but I open it. It's an emerald-cut diamond, in a polished platinum setting. Dramatic and brilliant, its facets grab the blue light and it glistens in the dark.

I snap the box shut and shove it into Gianluca's coat pocket.

A wave of sheer panic peels through me. Marriage. A husband. A life. Am I ready for this? And then, I'm deeply ashamed for having looked . . . for ruining *everything.*

Couldn't I tell that Gianluca's intention from the very beginning was to marry me and to take care of everything? Gianluca did not change when he fell in love with me; he remains who he always was: a traditional man. And I am his great love. He has made this as clear as the white-hot diamond that hides in his coat pocket.

I look up into the sky and search it as if a sign will appear to guide me forward, something, *anything,* to help me understand what I'm supposed to do, what I'm supposed to say.

I look for the moon. But it is nowhere to be seen. I look for light, from anywhere, from the stars, but there are none. Not even a cloud passes over to remind me that the sky is always in motion— changing. Instead, it is bleak and completely still. Not a clue as far as my eye can see. Where are the puzzle pieces that June made for me in the night sky? They too are gone.

I race down the stairs. Gianluca is in the kitchen with Gabriel, packing up the desserts.

"Bret said to tell you he was going home," Gabriel says.

"Thanks." I take off Gianluca's coat and place it on the back of one of the dining room chairs.

"Okay, we're all set," Gabriel says. "Let's go, kids."

I go to the closet for my coat. I pull it on. "What do you want me to carry?"

"The Tupperware," Gabriel says. "In the shopping bag."

I'm afraid to, but I look over at Gianluca, who takes a seat on one of the stools at the counter. He snaps the lid shut on the cooler that rests on the counter and locks it.

"Gianluca, if you don't mind, take the carryall, please?" Gabriel says.

"I'm sorry, Gabriel. I'm not going," Gianluca says quietly.

"Why not? You don't feel well?"

"No," he says.

"Well, then, the last place you need to be is a fish fry. Is it your stomach? There's Brioschi in the cabinet. Throw a capful in a glass of water and chug. You'll feel better in no time."

I can't look at Gianluca, but I feel his gaze on me.

"Gabe, I can't go either," I say.

"What's *your* problem?" Gabriel looks at Gianluca and then at me. "Okay, okay, I get it. Little Christmas Eve private time going on here. A little whoo-hoo-hoo by Ye Olde Tannenbaum."

"Yes, that's it," I say.

"So, what do I tell the family? That you've been hit by a bus?"

Gianluca doesn't answer. So I say, "Yeah, that's fine."

"They're gonna be pissed. Especially Tess. She ordered steamers. You know that requires a head count."

"She'll be all right," I tell him. "Will you be okay getting to the train?"

"Screw the train. I'm taking a cab."

"To Tess's?"

"That's right, sister. A yellow cab all the way to Jersey. Merry Christmas to me," he says, gathering up the bags and carryall. "Have fun you two," he says. "Don't wait up for me," he calls as he goes down the stairs. The entrance door in the foyer snaps shut behind him.

Gianluca stands and turns to face me. He folds his arms and leans against the marble counter. I stand behind the chair and run my hand over his cashmere coat.

I remember this same standoff from the Spolti Inn, when I didn't have any idea what Gianluca wanted from me. Now I know, and I'm still standing behind a chair for protection.

"Let's go up to your roof," he says. "I need air."

I follow him up the stairs with dread. He called it *my* roof.

That's a bad sign. The last time he was in New York, when Gram fell, he came up to this same roof and asked me to choose him, and I couldn't. He didn't like my river then, and now he probably detests it. I've ruined everything all over again.

Gianluca pushes through the screen door and walks out onto the roof. He goes to the wall that overlooks the Hudson and leans against it. I stand next to him. It's a clear Christmas Eve. The city is quiet, just a car or two on the West Side Highway. Gianluca looks out over our corner of the Village. Finally, he asks, "Did you kiss him or did he kiss you?"

"I don't know."

"It's important."

"His wife left him. She has fallen in love with someone else. She told him tonight."

"And you comforted him?"

"No. He couldn't be comforted."

"Then why did you kiss him?"

"I went with Bret for almost ten years. From the time I was a teenager to my late twenties. He was my first love," I explain.

I'm thirty-five years old and I've read all the books that advise women to stay mum about their romantic past with their current lover. But my romantic history is a simple one, and he's met both Bret and Roman Falconi already. Besides, the eighteen-year age difference means that Gianluca has a certain wisdom about love and life. And after the past couple of nights we've shared at the Soho Hotel, honesty is the only choice on the room service menu.

"Do you want to go back to him?" Gianluca looks at me.

Tears well in my eyes. "No."

"Then why did you kiss him?"

"I don't know, Gianluca. But as soon as it happened, I knew it was wrong. I don't love him in that way. I feel sorry for him—he's losing everything."

"Pity is always a woman's downfall when it comes to men," he says. Then he walks away from me.

"Please try and understand." I follow him.

"*Va bene*," he says with resignation. He goes to the far side of the roof and looks out over the West Side Highway. We stand in silence for a very long time.

"I wish you'd yell at me," I say.

"You were being kind. That's something to admire."

"I don't feel very admirable right now." The kiss was bad enough, but I feel worse about the ring in his coat pocket. The Christmas I dreamed of is slipping away.

"It was a mistake," he says.

"A big one. I don't love Bret. I don't love any man as much as I love you. I want to spend my life with you. Every day of it."

Gianluca takes my hand. "You're cold," he says.

"Please. Just yell at me. Let it out. Get it over with. I did something wrong. I hurt you."

He kisses my hand. "I forgive you," he says simply.

"Why?" I can't believe he's calm. If the situation were reversed, I would be throwing ceramic pots off the roof in a blind and jealous rage. "How can you forgive me?"

He takes my face in his hands. "Because I love you."

And then he kisses me. He pulls me close, and whispers in my ear, "And I trust you."

And there it is. Trust—the elusive goal, the foundation of true love and Gianluca's gift to me on this Christmas Eve, given freely and without reservation. He believes me. He knows what I say is true. Trust was the secret of my parents' reconciliation, the balm that will heal Alfred and Pam going forward, and for me? Trust means I can be secure in the knowledge that no harm will come to my heart. Trust means we will figure out a life plan that includes his dreams and mine. Trust means I have someone who loves me and is on my side even when I fail, come up short, or do something rash. Gianluca proved that tonight. I can trust him because he *knows* to trust me.

"Oh, Gianluca, let's go." I hold him close. "They're waiting for us in Jersey."

"I don't like the Feast of the Seven Fishes."

"You don't?"

"I want my Christmas Eve with you. And only you."

"I don't deserve you," I tell him.

He holds me. "There is only one way to fix this."

"How? I'll do anything. I'll even paint your house."

"That's not necessary." He laughs.

"What can I do?" I ask him.

"Marry me," he says.

I take a deep breath. "You know, I read an article once . . ."

Gianluca rolls his eyes.

I continue, "A man never asks a woman to marry him unless he's certain she is going to say yes."

"I like that article." He smiles and takes my face in his hands. "But I would rather have the answer from you." Gianluca pulls me close. He already knows the answer, but the gentleman that he is, the man that I love and know him to be waits patiently and trusts that my answer will be the right one.

"Yes," I tell him. "I will marry you."

He kisses me, as Greenwich Village spins indigo and green and Christmas red around us.

At last the midnight blue sky opens up, and the moon, a milky pearl, pushes through. Silver light dances on the water of the Hudson River in a shower of sapphires.

"What do you think of my river now?" I ask him.

He looks over the wall, past the highway, and down the Hudson. "I like your river," he says. "I like it very much."

Acknowledgments

I dedicate this novel to my sister Lucia Anna "Pia" Trigiani whom I have idolized since the day I was born. Pia is gifted, but down to earth. She is wise, but never condescends. Pia throws great parties; she's an elegant hostess, but she is also an attorney, which means she knows how to clean up a mess. Wherever Pia works or plays, she brings people together and makes a family. I have always counted on her for the big stuff and the little things, too—in all matters, Pia has never let me down. As life goes on, I realize what a rare thing this is, and so, because I could never possibly thank her enough—Pia, this one's for you!

At HarperCollins, I am published by a stellar group of people led by the discerning Jonathan Burnham. (Nobody fights harder to get every detail exactly right.)

Lee Boudreaux, my editor of enormous strength and taste, is the writer's gift that keeps on giving, sentence by sentence, book by book. Lee's right arm, Abigail Holstein, is talented *and* kind, a rare combo. Leslie Cohen designs beautiful tours and gets the word out with style and grace. Christine Boyd dreams up marketing schemes and we all follow happily. Virginia Stanley keeps me front and center with my beloved librarians and it's a good thing because my mother was one! The jacket art, perhaps more important than good teeth, is designed by the brilliant Archie Ferguson and the dazzling Christine Van Bree.

Also at Harper's, my evermore gratitude to the hardworking and diligent: Brian Murray, Kathy Schneider (she moves heaven and earth and crates of books), Michael Morrison (the champion), Angie Lee, James Tyler, Kyle Hansen, Tina Andreadis (you want a Greek girl running your press), Katherine Beitner, Jocelyn Kalmus, Cindy Achar, Lydia Weaver, Miranda Ottewell, Michael Siebert, Emily Bryant, Doug Jones, Carla Clifford, Kathryn Pereira, Alexis Lunsford, Jeanette Zwart, Andrea Rosen (special market queen), Josh Marwell, Brian Grogan, Kate Blum, Carl Lennertz, Carrie Kania (tops in trade paper and accessories), Jennifer Hart (delight with an Internet bullhorn), Stephanie Selah, Alberto Rojas (clone him), and Meredith Rusu. Allison Saltzman of Ecco provides advice and guidance—always appreciated! Sandi Mendelson and Cathy Gruhn at Hilsinger Mendelson are dynamic, fun, and work harder than ten men.

At William Morris Endeavor, where the work ethic rivals those of Italian stone masons, Suzanne Gluck represents me with smarts, panache, and understanding. The tireless Nancy Josephson has been my agent and friend since I was young, and she gets the 3:00 a.m. call, because she's amazing and because she's the only friend I have who is still up and on her BlackBerry at that hour. My thanks also to Global Graham Taylor, beautiful Michelle Bohan, Sarah Ceglarski, Caroline Donofrio; Cara Stein (perfection), Alicia Gordon (her mother should be proud), Natalie Hayden, Philip Grenz (his mother should be proud), Erin Malone, Tracy Fisher, Elizabeth Reed, Eugenie Furniss (my UK angel), Claudia Webb, Cathryn Summerhayes, Becky Thomas, and Raffaella de Angelis (who will get you published in countries you've never heard of and then you want to visit).

In Movieland, thank you Diane Nabatoff, Larry Sanitsky, Claude Chung, the Sanitsky Company, Lou Pitt, Julie Durk, Rita McClenny, Richard Thompson, Susan Cartsonis, and Roz Weisberg.

Thank you, Michael Patrick King, for your wise counsel as we keep the faith.

Everybody needs a brass section: thank you, Elena Nachmanoff and Dianne Festa, for all you do, and all you are!

The world of Buenos Aires, Argentina, unfolded in Technicolor through the eyes of Osvaldo Cima, Irwin B. Katz, Diane Smith Rigaux, and Dr. Armand Rigaux. Thank you for your guidance and valuable input.

My everlasting gratitude to my teachers of the Wise County public school system, and beloved librarians, Mrs. Ernestine Roller, Mr. James Varner (the bookmobile!), and Ms. Billie Jean Scott, who recommended books I treasure and reread to this day. Ms. Faith Cox, a great educator, has always been a wise mentor, and good friend.

Thank you, Costanzo and Antonio Ruocco of da Costanzo, Capri, Italy, for your craftsmanship and knowledge in the art of shoemaking. The Italian translations were provided by Dorina Cereghino-Hewitt, and further Italian pizzazz from Gina Casella. My grandfather, shoemaker Carlo Bonicelli, was the inspiration for this series of books.

Thank you to the world's best assistant, Kelly Meehan, the fabulous Molly McGuire, and our diligent intern, Allison Van Groesbeck. Jean Morrissey is a crack copy editor and without her, I'd be lost. Jake Morrissey offers endless and free advice, and I hope I'm always smart enough to take it. My love to all my Saint Mary's sisters around the world with whom I share memories and a lot of laughs.

Ann Godoff, thank you for opening the door to my literary career. Thank you in the UK to the dazzling Amanda Ross of Cactus TV for the Richard and Judy Book Club.

Bravo and *grazie mille*: Dolores and Dr. Emil Pascarelli, Kate Benton Doughan, Sharon Hall, Adina and Michael Pitt, Cate Magennis Wyatt, Steven Wyatt, Laura Bermudez, Ian Chapman, Suzanne Baboneau, Nigel Stoneman, Mary Ellen Gallagher

Gavin, Nelle Fortenberry, Jasmine Guy, Rosalie Posellius, Joe O'Brien, Greg D'Alessandro, Wendy Luck, Ruth Pomerance, Rosanne Cash, Liz Welch Tirrell, Rachel Cohen Desario, Gail Berman, Debra McGuire, Donna Gigliotti, Nancy Bolmeier Fisher, Constance Marks, Catherine Brennan, Antonia Trigiani, Craig Fisse, Todd Doughty, John Searles, Jill Gillet, Kim Hovey, Libby McGuire, Jane Von Mehren, Laura Ford, Debbie Aroff, Meryl Poster, Gayle Perkins Atkins, Christine Krauss and her Sonny, Joanna Patton, Bill Persky, Mario Cantone, Jerry Dixon, Tom Dyja, Carmen Elena Carrion, Cynthia Rutledge Olson, Susan Fales Hill, Wendy Luck, Doug Leibacher, Mary Testa, Sharon Watroba Burns, Barbara and Tom Sullivan, Jim and Mary Hampton, Amanda D'Acierno, Dee Emmerson, Joanne Curley Kerner, Jack Hodgins, Elaine Martinelli, Sally Davies, Sister Karol Jackowski, Sharon Ewing, Beth Hagan, Jane Cline Higgins, Alex Marvar, Brownie and Connie Polly, Veronica Kilcullen, Rosalie Signorello Ciardullo, the fabulous Vechiarelli family (led by Beth Vechiarelli Cooper), Max and Robyn Westler.

Thank you, Tim and Lucia, for making our home the most peaceful place on earth, and when it isn't—even better.

And now a word about the chapters—the titles are all Frank Sinatra songs recorded when my grandparents were young, and my father younger still. Now that they are gone, I find their music a comfort, and even insightful. I remember stories told about places they went, dreams that came true, and some that didn't. Whenever my family gathered when I was small, I remember the music, and those great Italian boys who delivered it with gusto, whether it was Perry Como, Louis Prima, Tony Bennett, Dean Martin, Jerry Vale, Al Martino, or the Chairman of the Board himself. Sometimes I wish I could go back and stand next to the record player with the gold mesh sides and the brown leather top as they sang . . . and swang, but alas, those moments are gone. So this is my way of remembering.

About the Author

A DRIANA T RIGIANI is an award-winning playwright, television writer, and documentary filmmaker. The author of the bestselling Big Stone Gap series and the bestselling novels *Very Valentine*, *Lucia, Lucia*, *The Queen of the Big Time*, and *Rococo*, she has also written and will direct the big-screen version of her first novel, *Big Stone Gap*. *Viola in Reel Life*, a young adult series for Harper Teen, debuted in September 2009. She lives in New York City with her husband and daughter.